THE SPECTRE OF ST GILES LEPER HOSPITAL

An Anne Edwards thriller

Copyright © Barrie Jaimeson 2025

All rights reserved.

No part of this publication may be reproduced, stored in a retrieval system or transmitted, in any form or by any means without the prior permission of the author, nor be circulated in any form of binding or cover other than that in which it is published.

This is a work of fiction and all the characters in this book are fictitious and any resemblance to actual persons living or dead is purely coincidental. Also, this is not a history book and any historical inaccuracies are for the purpose of the story.

Cover art by Rhys Timson.

There is an ancient legend in Maldon concerning a pile of old rocks and stones in a field at the side of Spital Road, one of the main thoroughfares into the town centre. The site is known as St Giles Leper Hospital, although none of the hospital itself can be seen. The stones that are left are the ruinous remains of a twelfth century building, including parts of the chancel and transepts of a chapel where services were held for the poor and infirm of Medieval Maldon which still reveal a beautiful early 13th Century lancet window. The hospital was founded by Henry II for the relief of the inhabitants of Maldon suffering from leprosy and later granted to Beeleigh Abbey who held responsibility until the dissolution of the monasteries under Henry VIII.

In the grounds are paths made up of cobblestones converging to a small circle just to the right of the chancel, presumably where the font once stood. There is no glass in the surviving window, just three stone arches in the one remaining wall. The fragments of the transept basically consist of two walls, each with a wooden-framed doorway. No roof. The stones that make up these walls date from earlier than the chapel. Roman rubble intermixed with the Medieval rocks reveal a previous form of recycling.

Behind the chancel, one can see through the window an ancient oak tree, its huge girth supporting long overhanging branches, providing a dappling light over the rear of the building. Beneath the tree, some of the grass seems to have been cultivated at one time, hoary plants still poking their heads above the ground.

The foundations of the rest of the original hospital, which covered ninety acres, are said to be buried beneath the earth, modern houses now residing on the land reclaimed for building. The site of the remains is protected by a metal railing alongside the road and a high hedge runs along a path to the left side. The site is owned by Maldon District Council.

But what of the legend? It is said that on a misty evening, a strange figure can be seen floating above the ground, through the gloom. The figure is dressed in a long flowing garment with a hood. Closer inspection will reveal a long knife or dagger in the spectre's hand and it is said that anyone viewing too closely will not see the light of the next day.

'It is said' is a cliched platitude, but even though few will admit to having ever seen the hooded monk, the belief in his existence still holds sway in many a pub's conversation to this day, it is said. 'It is said' is a phrase that occurs regularly in any observation of St Giles Leper Hospital.

PROLOGUE

'It hurts, Mummy.'

Elizabeth Hall had been whinging for days. Her mother, Catherine, was at her wit's end. Elizabeth was thirteen and Catherine put her child's behaviour down to growing pains and changing hormones. Her eating habits had altered, inasmuch as she hardly ate anything Catherine put before her. The girl was worried she was putting on weight, she'd said, her mother exasperatingly explaining that it was just puppy fat and would go away once she started to grow a bit. Elizabeth refused to believe her and was eating like a sparrow. The fact that she was now complaining about stomach pains did not surprise Catherine in the least.

'If you don't eat properly, Elizabeth, your stomach will hurt. Get yourself some toast or something, Mummy's busy.'

Catherine *was* busy. She was desperately trying to save a business that had been run into the ground by the recent pandemic. The country had been in lockdown, which meant very few people were earning the sort of money they needed to afford Catherine's designer handbags. She'd started the business barely three years ago and for the first twelve months it had gone from strength to strength. She'd taken premises close to her home in East London and employed a couple of staff to help with the demand. She'd been proud of her work which ranged from bags made from recycled clothes – denim jeans and printed material – to brightly coloured leather satchels. Now, she was still paying for premises she no longer needed and the help from the Government had been less than adequate as her business had not been operating for long enough to qualify for any of the grants that had been doled out to big companies that frankly, in her opinion, were not in need. She'd had to let her staff go, which had upset her – and them – and was now trying to work from her kitchen table, satisfying the few online orders that came in. Elizabeth was refusing to go to school, as she was supposedly ill, which meant she was around all the time, moaning and wailing like a two-year-old.

'I want to see a doctor,' whined Elizabeth.

'You're joking, aren't you? Have you any idea how long you have to wait to get an appointment these days?' Catherine looked at Elizabeth. This was a step forward, she had to admit, actually wanting to get a medical confirmation of what her mother had been telling her for weeks. However, she also knew that unless it was an emergency she'd never get to see a doctor. They were still tied up with the backlog caused by COVID.

'It hurts, Mummy,' moaned Elizabeth again.

Catherine sighed, put down the pair of jeans she was metamorphosing into a backpack, and turned to the girl.

'Where does it hurt, Elizabeth?'

The girl pointed to her stomach. Catherine put her hand there and gently caressed in a circular motion.

'Is that better?'

Elizabeth shook her head, tears were streaming down her cheeks now as she doubled up, pushing her mother's hand hard into her abdomen. Catherine was starting to worry. Maybe the girl really was ill. As she pulled away to fetch her phone to call an ambulance, an earth-shattering scream emanated from Elizabeth's lips. Blood and mucus trickled down her legs. Catherine stopped and turned back.

Elizabeth was on the floor now, writhing. She tore at her underwear as more gore gushed out of her. Catherine knelt beside her. Elizabeth grabbed hold of her hair in her fist, screaming and screaming. Catherine didn't know what to do. She hadn't reached her phone and couldn't leave the girl. Suddenly in the midst of the mush she spotted what had caused Elizabeth's problem. A small barely formed foetus.

She looked up at her daughter, tearing her hand from her hair.

'What have you done, Elizabeth? Who did this to you?'

'I haven't done anything,' she blubbed through her tears.

'You were pregnant, you've just had a miscarriage,' yelled her mother. 'Who were you sleeping with? For God's sake, girl, you're only thirteen!'

Elizabeth's face turned even paler than it already was, apart from her eyes, wet with weeping, being two red holes, her pupils wide and scared.

'Who, Elizabeth? Who was it?'

'I can't say,' she muttered.

Irrespective of her daughter's distress, she took her by the shoulders and shook her. 'Who?' she screeched. 'Who was it?'

'Daddy's…'

Catherine let go of the girl, who fell back to the floor. What was she saying? Was she accusing her husband of fifteen years? Her faithful, supportive husband? Why was she saying this? Catherine was in a daze, unaware now of her daughter's distress. Blood was pouring unabated from her and her screams were getting louder, but to Catherine, it was as though someone had placed noise-cancelling headphones over her ears. She was in a dull, soundless place, unable to comprehend what was going on.

Elizabeth, meanwhile, stopped writhing; stopped screaming. Her world was changing, too. She couldn't focus, her breathing was a struggle, her head spinning. She closed her eyes and wished everything would just go away.

*

Jack Hall drew up outside his house totally oblivious of the drama taking place in his kitchen. He'd had a good day in the office, a promotion was on the cards, it had been hinted. His designs for a big clients' new advertising campaign had been greeted with enthusiasm. He skipped from his car, carrying the large bunch of flowers he'd bought for Catherine. He knew she'd been having it tough recently and, as much he'd tried to help, there wasn't much he could do. He knew nothing about handbags. He'd offered to knock up some ideas for an advertising push on social media, but his wife hadn't taken up the offer yet, blaming being too busy. Hopefully the flowers, along with his news of promotion would put her in a good mood. Maybe they could go out for a meal, something they hadn't done since before COVID.

He was barely through the door before he saw Catherine racing towards him. He held out his arms, but the look in her face told him she was not looking for an embrace. He didn't see the knife until he felt it pierce his stomach.

'What are you…' were the last words he spoke as the knife penetrated his body, spewing blood across the broken flowers strewn around their feet. The knife perforated the body unceasingly for several minutes after Jack Hall was dead.

CHAPTER ONE

All Saints' church sits at the top of Maldon High Street, an imposing building originating from somewhere around the Anglo-Saxon period but rebuilt in the thirteenth century. It has a possibly unique triangular tower, and the great-great grandfather of George Washington is buried in the churchyard. In niches along the outside walls are carved statues of famous ancestors of the town of Maldon. It is still a working place of worship as well as a meeting-place where the community entertain many secular activities. The town's war memorial stands adjacent to the church. There is a food bank not far away and All Saint's often stored some provisions in the cool crypt in the depths of the building.

It was outside this church that Harry Ellis and Amelia Goddard were standing. They were young, seventeen and fifteen respectively. Harry was keen on Amelia but wasn't mature enough to use the word love, yet. He knew what he wanted. He wanted to explore feelings that were relatively new to him; feelings he didn't really have a full understanding of; feelings he wasn't completely sure about.

Amelia *was* in love with Harry, she was sure about that. She envisioned spending the rest of her life with the good-looking man by her side as they stood in front of the war memorial. They'd been for coffee after school at one of the several independent coffee-houses that had sprung up in recent years in the small market town. Amelia had paid as Harry had forgotten his wallet, he'd said. She didn't mind, she knew he was telling the truth. Money was one thing the Ellis's weren't short of.

Both she and Harry had exams coming up in the summer and, as they were both excellent students, they were expected to do well. They would often spend their time together quizzing each other about their specialised subjects. Harry's were more specific as he was due to take his A levels, whilst Amelia's general education had only evolved as far as GCSE's. Both were expecting a full house of top grades.

Harry was a very fit young man, spending his spare time in the gym as well as other groups. Amelia didn't begrudge him the time he spent working on his body, she liked the way he looked. He had been talking about heading off to university in the Autumn, and, much as she wanted him to do well, Amelia's mood had become melancholy as she imagined the two of them being far apart in the not-too-distant future.

'Where do you think you'll go?' she asked him.

He shrugged. 'Depends on my results, I suppose, but I've kept my applications to the Russell Group Unis at the moment. There's even a possibility of Cambridge. I mean, you might as well try for the best.'

Amelia smiled sadly. 'None of them are in Essex though, are they?'

He laughed. 'Not likely, I want to get as far away from Maldon as I can. There's nothing here for us young people. Cambridge isn't that far away, though.'

A tear escaped from Amelia's eye. 'I'll miss you,' she whispered.

He reached under her chin and lifted her head. 'Hey, it's not for ages yet. Besides I might not get into any of them. There's a lot of competition.'

She nodded, sadly. 'You will. You're a genius, remember?'

'Oh yes, I'd forgotten that.' A grin spread across his face and he tapped her nose gently with his finger. 'I'll still be able to come and see you, I'm not going to Mars. Anyway, you'll be able to come and join me in a couple of years.'

'A couple of years might as well be light years away.'

'Light years are a measure of length, not time, Amelia.' He wagged his finger at her playfully.

'I know,' she replied. 'And you'll be a long measure of length away from me.'

He put his arm round her and kissed her.

'Not here,' she said bashfully. 'Not in the street.'

He sighed. 'I wish we had our own place. Somewhere there were no prying eyes.'

Amelia looked down, slightly embarrassed. 'Maybe you'll have somewhere when you're at Uni and I can visit you?'

'I don't want to wait that long to show how much you mean to me.'

Amelia knew what he meant. He'd been coming on strong recently. Spring was in the air and the birds and the bees were getting ready, he'd told her – even though it was only February and not exactly Springlike weather. They'd been seeing each other for nearly a year, and he was what Amelia called her first proper boyfriend. When he'd asked her out it had sent shivers through her. New sensations she'd only dreamed about. She'd felt as though she was walking on air and all the other cliches she'd read about on teenage websites. Best of all, her friends had been jealous, although some of them pretended to be pleased for her. Just one or two had started to put bad stuff on social media so she stopped looking at them. She didn't need social media; she had Harry all to herself – at least she did for a few more months.

Her group of close friends had all made an oath that they wouldn't sleep with anyone until they were at least sixteen but, as Harry would be away before her sixteenth birthday, she was worried she wouldn't be able to keep her promise. She knew he wanted to make out with her, and it made her excited and scared. Was she ready? Would her friends find out? More to the point, would her parents find out? Her father had been wary of her going out with a boy nearly two years older than her, but once they'd met him, he'd charmed her mother, who was already talking wedding bells in the future. Amelia wanted the same but she knew it would be a while. Harry had to finish university and she wanted to further her education too.

Harry was wearing a sweatshirt under a leather bomber jacket, as he could wear what he liked at sixth form college. Amelia still had to wear her school uniform. The sun was setting and a chill was seeping into Amelia's bones as the sun went down. She was pleased that Harry held her close, keeping her snug. He was taller than her and she fitted neatly under his shoulder as they strolled away from the High Street.

'Have you ever been to the old leper hospital?' Harry asked her as they rounded the top of the High Street.

'Been past it in the car. You can't go in, can you? There's a padlock on the gates.'

Harry grinned. 'There's a gap in the hedge along the side. Come on.' He upped his pace.

'Okay,' agreed Amelia, cautiously. 'Can't be long, though. My tea will be on the table.' She laughed. It was a joke that they had about her parents being controlling.

They wandered up Spital Road until they reached the old ruins.

'Some people say there were underground passages between here and Beeleigh Abbey that the monks had used as they tried to escape the heinous acts of butchery inflicted on the occupants by Henry VIII's knights during the Dissolution,' Harry informed Amelia. 'Wouldn't it be great if we could find them?'

Amelia had no intention of digging around in the ancient grounds. Her heart was pounding as it was as they stood by the fencing outside the chapel. The main road ran close to the ruins, cars passing every few minutes, a few people walking along the pavement.

'I don't think we should go in, Harry. It's not allowed.'

There was a sign declaring visits could only take place by special arrangement of Maldon District Council.

'Come on,' said Harry, taking her hand and leading her down a path to the side of the site. A high hedge guarded the ruins but roughly halfway down the track, Harry stopped and pushed at the greenery. A narrow break in the hedgerow appeared.

'There's still a fence there, Harry.' Amelia pointed out the four-foot-high black railings that showed through the middle of the greenery.

Harry grinned, put his hand on the top of the fence and leaped over.

'I can't do that,' protested Amelia.

Harry reached over and took her under her shoulders. 'Put your foot there.' He indicated a crossrail. Amelia stepped up and with little effort he lifted the slight girl over the top.

She wasn't sure if her rapid heartbeat was caused by the proximity of Harry, the danger of being somewhere they shouldn't, or the expectation of what she was sure was to come.

'We shouldn't be doing this, Harry,' she persisted.

He grinned and pulled her gently towards an open archway. Through the crumbling bricks and stones were the decrepit remains of a room roughly twelve by ten. The roof and the two end walls had long since gone and a wooden framed doorway on the side was open to the elements, giving a view of the hedge.

Harry led Amelia to the doorway and sat her down on a stone jutting out near the doorway. The walls were at least three feet thick, providing a screen from the main road.

'This is really romantic, don't you think?' he whispered. 'No-one can see us here.'

Amelia wasn't so sure. The stone was cold and damp, lichen was growing out of the walls. She worried that her school uniform would show signs of her behaving in a manner which her parents, her father in particular, would certainly not approve. Harry's arm held her close, and she raised her head to allow his lips to meet hers.

'Someone might see,' she breathed.

Harry looked around. The view to the outside world was obscured by twelfth century brickwork. 'I think we'll be alright,' he replied, his hand moving down Amelia's body. She didn't resist at first, even though she wasn't confident it was what she wanted. Not yet. She put her hand on his as he moved it towards her lap.

'I'm not ready, Harry.'

'Come on. You love me, don't you?'

'Of course I do.' His hands were still moving all over her body. His breath was coming in short gasps. She tried to stop him lifting her skirt, but he was strong and as he started caressing her thigh, his lips found her mouth again.

Her head and her heart were in dispute. One saying no, the other desperate for him go further. A noise behind them distracted her.

'There's someone there,' she said, pulling away.

It happened so quick. She saw nothing other than a flash of light. Warm blood spattered across her face. Harry's body grew heavy in her arms. She screamed, leapt up, petrified as Harry collapsed to the floor, his hand at his throat, red liquid spurting from his neck in an ever-decreasing flow. She felt a hand grab at her blouse but saw no-one as she ran from the ramshackle house into the open grassy area between the ruins and screamed. A man was climbing over the fence by the road. Someone took her in his arms as the world went blurred and drifted away.

CHAPTER TWO

DS Alice Porter arrived first, followed swiftly by DI Anne Edwards. PC Ernie Kemp was already at St Giles and had informed the small Maldon CID team as soon as he'd seen the mayhem.

The girl was in the back of an ambulance with a silver blanket round her shoulders. More paramedics could be seen by the ruins of the old leper hospital. Anne sent Alice over to the girl, while she strode towards the paramedics. The sight that confronted her almost made her retch. A young boy, his throat badly cut, blood spatters over the ground and the ancient stones, his eyes staring up through the open roof of the building.

'Please don't touch him,' she asked the medics. 'This is a crime scene now.'

'We ascertained the rather obvious fact that he is dead but haven't moved him. It's terrible, isn't it? Here in Maldon. You don't expect this, do you?'

Anne had been in the police force long enough to always expect the worst, but she shook her head as she took her phone from her pocket and called Sarah Clifford, her forensics pathologist friend.

'I hope you're not busy, Sarah,' said Anne as the call connected.

'I suspect I'm about to be. What have you got?'

'Young male, throat cut.'

'Nice. Where?'

'St Giles Leper Hospital, Spital Road, Maldon. Do you need the post code?'

'I think I can find that. I'll be half an hour or so.'

Anne disconnected. 'Ernie?' she called the officer over. 'Keep everyone away from here, will you?'

'Yes, Ma'am,' he replied, looking over to the increasing crowd that was forming on the pavement.

*

Amelia Goddard looked like a zombie as she sat bolt upright on a gurney in the ambulance. She was in shock, not speaking and barely moving. Alice was told the girl was not in a state to be interviewed and that she was about to be taken to the hospital.

'Has anyone informed her parents or anything?' she asked the paramedic, who shrugged his shoulders.

Amelia's schoolbag was in the ambulance and Alice checked through it, finding the girl's phone but it was locked. There were a number of schoolbooks in the bag, all with the name Amelia Goddard on the front. 'Is your name Amelia?' Alice asked her. There was no response. 'Can you unlock this for me, Amelia,' Alice persisted, handing her the phone. 'We need to tell your parents, Amelia. Do you have their number?'

Amelia sat rigid, not moving, or speaking, clutching her phone in her hand.

'We need to get her to the hospital.' The paramedic had a kind face and Alice knew he would have other calls to attend to. The Ambulance Service had been under tremendous pressure during and since the pandemic and much as the man in green next to her was being patient, she knew he had to get the girl safely to A&E as soon as possible.

'Okay,' she replied. 'I'll let your parents know, Amelia.' An address was written on her bag which Alice assumed was her home. She took a photo of the address on her phone and radioed in to arrange for an officer to go round to the Goddard household as she wandered over to Anne. The sun was setting above the houses that surrounded the old hospital, red and gold spreading across the skyline. Alice looked up at it and thought how incongruous it was, such a beautiful natural phenomenon throwing its pale light over the macabre scene amongst the ruins. The boy was still spreadeagled across the stones by the crumbling walls of the archaic building, the cut on his throat showing white amongst the reddish-brown drying blood. The two paramedics stood silently outside the walls of the building.

'Anyone know what happened?' Anne asked as she stood in full PPE. Alice, was keeping her distance from the body so as not to contaminate the scene.

'No, the girl's in shock. Her name's Amelia Goddard. I've sent someone round to tell her parents. Do you want me to go to Broomfield Hospital? That's where they're taking her.'

'Might be a good idea. Someone should be there when her parents arrive. Try and find out who this boy is. Was he her boyfriend? Did they have a row? Did she kill him?'

'I'll try, Ma'am, but I doubt I'll get anything from the girl at the moment.'

Anne nodded. 'See what you can do. I'll wait here for Sarah.'

*

Sarah Clifford was there in less than half an hour. She shook her head as she looked at the prostrate body. 'So young,' she said to Anne. 'Any idea how it happened?'

'None at the moment. Don't even know who he is - sorry, was.'

Anne moved away while Sarah examined the body. Close examination of dead people, although a part of Anne's job, was not something she relished. It made her feel sick to think of another wasted young life. She looked around the ruins of St Giles and wondered how many other bodies had once lain in the same place as the boy, their bodies slowly decomposing as leprosy took hold and destroyed them. Several people in white Hazmat suits were dusting the time-worn walls and placing yellow markers around the area. She wandered over to the railings where Ernie Kemp was doing his best to keep the rubberneckers away. The gates were padlocked but the railings were not insurmountable to anyone who wanted to get into the site. The dead boy looked as though he had been fit and strong, he could easily have scaled the barrier and then helped the girl over. What were they doing there? She had a pretty good idea about that, she wasn't so old she couldn't remember having to find love nests away from prying eyes. But was there someone else there? Did the girl really slash his throat so violently, and if she did, where was the knife? She summoned a constable to search the hedge and surrounding area for a murder weapon.

She needed to find out who the boy was. She hadn't found any sort of ID on him, no bank cards, no driving licence, not even a wallet. Could it have been a robbery? She wandered back towards the gates.

'Anyone see anything at all, Ernie?' she asked as she reached him.

'I heard the scream,' said a middle-aged man in a smart, long coat and, incongruously, a baseball cap, standing behind the policeman.

'And you are?' asked Anne.

'Walter Mayfield,' replied the man. 'I was just walking past.'

'Did you see anyone?'

'Only the girl. She was standing in the middle of the field screaming her head off. I climbed over the railings and then saw the boy. He was obviously dead. I couldn't do anything for him. I phoned you and the ambulance.'

'Did you touch the body?'

'I checked his pulse,' Walter Mayfield showed the blood on his hands. 'He was still warm.'

'I'll need you to give a DNA test, Mr Mayfield, to eliminate you.'

'Of course,' he said.

'And there was no-one else around?'

'Not a soul.'

Anne turned to Ernie. 'There are some test kits in my car, PC Kemp. Could you get someone to do a DNA on Mr Mayfield and take his details?' She handed him her car keys and returned to Sarah, who was instructing the paramedics to take the body to Broomfield.

'Any idea about time of death?' she asked.

'Can't be exact but I'd say within the last hour or two,' Sarah replied. 'I need to get to the hospital, want to come with me?'

'To the autopsy? Not unless you really need me there.'

Sarah shook her head. 'I'll send you the results. Looks pretty straightforward, though. Sharp knife, not serrated, slashed across from left to right, carotid artery severed, death pretty quick, I would imagine.'

Anne sighed. 'Okay, send me the final analysis.'

Anne waited until the body had gone before checking with the officer searching for a murder weapon.

'No sign of anything, Ma'am. There's a load of weeds over there,' he pointed to a patch of green leaves behind the chapel. 'Couldn't see a knife or anything but someone could have got through here pretty easily.' He led Anne to the small gap in the hedge.

'There's a fence there.'

'Not a very big one though.'

Anne nodded. 'Go down that path. There must be a knife here somewhere.'

The officer wandered down the path to the side of the site.

Anne checked that Ernie had put up the police tape to detract intruders. 'You'll have to stay here for a bit, I'm afraid,' she told him.

Ernie's face fell. 'The wife's doing shepherd's pie, Ma'am.'

'I'm sure it'll keep. I'll get someone else here as soon as.'

Anne felt a small amount of guilt as she had arranged to meet Derek Clarke in The Queen's Head in less than half an hour and was wondering whether to cancel or not. Derek was a man she'd met at the beginning of the COVID pandemic. He'd had to leave his rented digs and moved himself onto her sofa for a brief while but that hadn't worked out and he'd found different accommodation. They still met up occasionally for a drink or a meal, but Anne was pretty certain the relationship couldn't go any further than that. He ran a Krav Maga class, a kind of martial art, and she knew he had a session that evening, hence the early drink. Ignoring her better instincts, she decided she wouldn't be missed if she spent an hour in the pub. She had to eat, after all. Sarah wouldn't be finished with the autopsy until much later, if she even got it done by tonight and Alice could handle the parents of the girl. Someone had to find out who the boy was pretty quickly, though. His parents would start to worry – and with good reason, sadly. She phoned in to the station and deployed a constable to try and find out the boy's name, sending a rather macabre snapshot of his face, before heading down to the quay and the pub.

*

Amelia Goddard was still in the back of the ambulance which was backed up in a queue outside Broomfield A&E when her mother arrived. Alice met her and took her into the main reception area, offering tea or coffee. Once informed she couldn't go into the ambulance as COVID rules still applied in hospitals and Alice's reassurance that her daughter was physically unhurt, she reluctantly agreed and followed Alice to one of the coffee bars that lined the main corridor.

'Allan works in London. I've told him but he won't get here for a while,' she said as they sat with coffees.

'That's okay, Mrs Goddard.'

'June. My name's June.' Alice noticed her hand shaking as she started to reach for her cup but then withdrew.

'Thank you, June. My name's Alice. Do you know why your daughter was in St Giles Leper Hospital?'

'The ruins? I haven't a clue. She said she was revising.' The corners of her mouth dropped and tears filled her eyes as she looked down at the table. 'Are you sure she's alright? I ought to be with her.'

'I'll be informed as soon as she's been attended to. I'm sure you'll be able to see her then.' Alice took a sip of coffee. June Goddard had still not touched hers. 'She was with a boy, June. Any idea who he might be? A boyfriend or something?'

June Goddard nodded. 'Harry. Harry Ellis.' She looked up. 'Is he alright?'

Alice chose not to answer. 'Do you know his address?'

June Goddard's face went white. 'He's dead, isn't he?'

'Why would you say that?'

'I just feel it.'

'I can't really confirm anything at the moment, I'm afraid. Would you have his address?'

June Goddard shook her head. 'Great Totham somewhere. I can't remember the exact address. What happened?'

'We don't know. That's what we're trying to find out. Had they been going out with each other for long?'

June clocked the past tense and shuddered. 'About a year, I suppose. He's older than Amelia but a lovely boy. Oh God!' The tears flowed from her eyes, the tension flowing out of her.

Alice remained quiet. There was nothing she could say.

'I'm sorry,' said June after a while. 'Can't you tell me what happened?'

'Somebody seems to have attacked Harry. Was there any problem between him and Amelia?'

June lifted her head and glared through her tears at Alice. 'You're not accusing Amelia?'

'No, June, I'm not accusing anyone, I'm just trying to get as much information as I can. We will have to talk to Amelia, though.'

June looked round towards the reception. 'Why are they taking so long?' Her voice was strained and high-pitched.

'They're very busy, June. At least it means Amelia's not in a bad way or they'd have rushed her through.' Alice hoped she was right with that assumption. 'If you're alright here for a minute, I'll see if I can find out how long she'll be. Your husband's coming here, you said?'

June's head nodded once. 'He's busy, as he always is. He'll be here as soon as he can, he says.'

Alice went towards the reception area. Were there marital problems in the Goddard family? Or was June just stressed and angry that her husband couldn't drop everything at a moment's notice. She had no intention of interrupting the overworked girl at her desk behind the Perspex screen, she'd been told she'd be sent a text as soon as Amelia was being triaged. She needed to give Anne the name of the dead boy.

*

Derek had ordered Anne a white wine before she'd arrived at The Queen's Head, which she gratefully accepted and sat opposite him in the back bar overlooking the River Blackwater.

'Tough day?' he asked.

'That obvious?'

Derek nodded.

'Dead boy found in the ruins of St Giles.'

Derek sighed. 'I don't know how you do your job, Anne.'

'Someone has to.'

'So how come you're here? You usually fob me off if a case comes in.'

'That's harsh, Derek. Anyway, there's not a lot I can do at the moment.' She lifted her glass. 'Besides, you're off to take your class soon, aren't you?'

He checked his watch. 'In an hour or so if you can spare me that long.' He reciprocated with his pint of beer.

'Should you be drinking before a session?'

'One pint won't hurt. I don't have to do the hard work.'

Anne shrugged. 'You were a complete fitness freak when I first met you. Drank orange juice, I seem to remember. What happened?'

'Apart from you? COVID happened.'

'I'm not sure how to take that.' Anne grinned. She knew he'd been in training for the London Marathon that didn't happen. She just wondered why he hadn't gone for it again. Not that she minded too much. Fitness was something a bit alien to her. Her phone rang and, checking the caller's name, answered.

'Hi Alice. Everything okay?'

'Yeah. Amelia's still in the ambulance in a queue. Her mother's here and we're waiting for dad to arrive from London. Amelia's boyfriend is called Harry Ellis, lives somewhere in Great Totham.'

'Harry Ellis,' Anne repeated, writing his name on a napkin. 'Thanks, Alice, I'll get someone to inform the parents. Do you have an address?'

'Negative. I'd better get back to Amelia's mother, she's obviously in a bit of a state. Shall I let you know when I'm done here?'

'Yep. I'll get onto finding the address and I'll do the informing. Hope you're not too long.'

'I'll let you buy me a drink if you're still in The Queen's.' Alice disconnected.

'Harry Ellis?' said Derek.

'Yeah, do you know him?'

'One of my students. What's he done?'

Anne was quiet for a moment. 'Er…I can't really tell you. You don't happen to know his address, do you?'

'It'll be in my files. I can send it you when I get to the gym.'

'Don't say anything, please. I just need to know where he lives.'

'Okay, is he alright?'

Anne didn't reply.

He nodded. He understood that Anne couldn't give him restricted information and she evidently needed the boy's address. 'Perhaps I should go now and I'll check his address for you. I'll text it over.'

'Thanks, Derek.'

'Is he..?'

Anne raised her hands. Derek knowing he couldn't ask more, downed his drink and stood up. 'I could see you later if you've time.'

'I would have liked that but…' Anne shrugged.

'See you soon, then. I'll send you that text ASAP,' he said and left the pub.

Anne sat feeling miserable, sipping her wine. She could quite happily have stayed here for the rest of the evening, getting drunk, but she knew that was not possible. She hated it when Derek left, they seemed to be still at that teenage awkwardness stage in their relationship. He'd never kissed her, not even a peck on the cheek, never made an advance towards her even when he was staying in her flat. She wasn't sure that's what she wanted really but the chance would be some sort of improvement on her currently dull existence.

The bar manageress, Charlotte Tibbs, plonked a glass of white wine next to her, and sat down. 'You look like you needed another one,' she said. 'It's on the house.'

Anne smiled. Charlotte was in her late twenties, a hard worker, who'd taken over the running of the pub, following the death of the previous manager – a murder case that Anne had worked on a few years ago. Her boyfriend and co-manager Ben and her had been through a rough time during the pandemic, trying to keep the business sustainable but it looked as though things were hopefully starting to get back to near normal.

'Thanks, Charlie. I shouldn't really but…' She finished her first glass and raised the new one.

'Something you can talk about?' asked Charlotte.

Anne laughed. 'It's not to do with Derek if that's what you mean.'

Charlotte raised her eyebrows.

'It's not, Charlie.' Anne phone pinged as Derek's text came through. 'Looks like I might have to go,' she said.

'Will you be back?' Charlotte wondered. 'I can put that glass in the fridge.'

'Not likely.' She downed the wine in one. 'If I'm back, I'll buy another one and get one for you too.' She stood up and wobbled slightly.

'Are you fit to drive?' queried Charlotte.

'I'm a DI,' was Anne's reasoning. 'I pity the poor bugger that tries to breathalyse me.'

CHAPTER THREE

Great Totham is a village a few miles from the centre of Maldon. It is split into two halves, North and South, which are roughly a mile and a half apart, which was annoying when you didn't know which half the address you had was in, as Anne was finding out. She had never been a great user of Satnav whilst travelling round her home district, she'd not believed it necessary – until now. To make matters worse, the Ellis's lived in an area called Beacon Hill, which she'd discovered too late, was to the west of Great Totham, nearer to Wickham Bishops, an easier route for the detective if she'd realised sooner. DC Abeer Kumar, sitting next to her suggesting she use her GPS app on her phone, didn't help. Not that this was an easy journey, anyway. She hated being the bearer of bad news, and there wasn't much news that was worse than informing a parent their child had been murdered.

They left the Colchester Road near Tiptree Heath and Anne reluctantly followed Abeer's phone GPS along Mountains Road towards Beacon Hill and Wickham Bishops.

'Legend has it that this area was a smugglers' paradise in 'the olden days',' Abeer informed her, reading from her phone.

Anne nodded imagining the late-night carts struggling their way up the hill to the Beacon. 'I wonder whereabouts they would hide the contraband,' she said, looking at the scrubland surrounding them.

'Presumably in some bigwig's house, who made huge profits from the illegal trade,' replied Abeer.

The Ellis house was probably one of them originally; a large Tudor building with a half-timbered frontage, looking as though it dated from the sixteenth century but had been added to and modernised over the years. Exactly the sort of out-of-the-way place to store barrels of brandy or whatever the smugglers were concealing from the authorities. Whatever, it was a very expensive dwelling and Anne could feel the anxiety building up inside her as she drove up the winding drive, past several mature trees and bushes, to the front door. Harry's parents were evidently very wealthy, the sort of people she always found it hard to communicate with. Whether it was her upbringing as a farmer's daughter or her own lack of money, her insecurity often overwhelmed her in 'posh' company.

She parked the car, took a deep breath and, stepping up to the door, rang the bell, Abeer waiting obediently behind her. She'd expected a butler or some member of staff to answer, but, instead, a genial man with longish grey hair opened the oaken portal.

'Hallo,' he said, a welcoming smile on his face. 'Can I help you?'

Anne swallowed, taking out her warrant card. 'My name is DI Anne Edwards, this is DC Abeer Kumar. Can we come in?'

'Edwin Ellis,' said the man, introducing himself as he opened the door wider. 'Should I call the wife?'

Anne nodded and they followed him through to the biggest lounge Anne had ever seen. There were two three-piece suites covered in what looked like genuine antique tapestry material, a large fireplace with a marble surround, landscapes and portraits on the walls. It reminded her of some stately home she'd visited on a school trip many years ago.

'Linda, there's some coppers here,' the man yelled as he offered Anne and Abeer a seat on one of the expansive sofas.

A woman came through wearing tight jogging pants and a t-shirt. She looked quite a few years younger than her husband; her hair was dyed blond and curled with long tresses falling over her shoulders. 'Can I help you?' she said.

Anne was slightly perturbed by the fact that neither of them appeared concerned that two detectives had turned up unannounced at their house. She took another deep breath.

'Are you the parents of Harry Ellis?' she started.

'What's he done?' replied the father, raising his eyes to the heavens.

'I'm afraid there's been an incident at the ruins of St Giles Hospital in Maldon.'

'What sort of incident?' At least Linda Ellis showed some sort of apprehension.

'I'm afraid Harry has been found dead.' There was no other way of breaking this sort of news. It couldn't be covered up in a fluffy blanket or made any less tragic.

'Dead?' said the father, all the colour draining from his face. 'Are you sure?'

Anne nodded.

'Oh God!' Linda Ellis collapsed on the sofa.

'What happened?' asked her husband.

'We don't know. It appears he was with Amelia Goddard.'

'Oh no, is she alright?' Linda sat up.

'She's in the hospital but seems to be okay.'

'But Harry...?' Edwin Ellis' voice was quavering. Anne shook her head. 'Excuse me,' he said and left the room.

Anne turned to Linda. 'I'm sorry. I have to ask you a few questions, is that alright?'

Linda Ellis nodded.

'Have you any idea why they would be in those ruins?'

'He was our only child,' she replied. 'We'd tried so hard to have him.'

Anne didn't know what to say. She could hear Edwin sobbing in the next room. Loud heart-wrenching cries. Linda was just staring into space.

'Maybe we should come back later,' said Anne.

'No. I don't know why they would be in those ruins. They were very close, always in each other's company. They were revising together. They both have exams coming up.'

'Harry didn't appear to have put up any fight. Can you think of anyone who might have killed him? Anyone he'd upset or didn't get on with.? Was he hanging about with any rough characters?'

Linda's face went completely bloodless and she shook her head.

There was a silence. 'Would you like me to sort out a family liaison officer?' Anne was looking to where the wailing was coming from.

Linda didn't reply. Anne realised she would get nothing of use from questioning either of them now, so she decided to leave the two of them to their sorrow and went outside, leaving Abeer in the sitting room. Taking out her phone, she moved around to try and get a signal, before calling to organise an officer to attend the house as soon as possible. Turning back to look at the closed front door, she got into her car and drove back towards Maldon.

*

The old Maldon Police Station had been closed down a few years previously and the force had since occupied part of the Maldon District

Council offices. From somewhere the money had been found to renovate part of the offices and turn them into a proper police station – complete with a blue lamp outside. There was a separate entrance up some stone steps that led to a brightly painted yellow door with an intercom attached and a key code. They even had a front desk now, mostly staffed by PC Ernie Kemp, even though he had his other duties to perform – as he insisted on pointing out as often as possible. There was a rumour that a full-time desk sergeant would be appointed in the near future but no-one was holding their breath.

Alice was in the office when Anne got back.

'How did you get on?' Anne asked her.

'Once Amelia actually got into A&E, they gave her the once over and let her go. She was given some tranquillisers, and her mother took her away. I told them we'd need to talk to her, but she wasn't keen at the moment, quoting the doctor telling her the girl needed rest and relaxation. I have their address and I've arranged a meeting for tomorrow.'

Anne wasn't too happy about that. If she'd killed Harry, she'd just been given a get-out and could disappear, but she shouldn't be taking up a bed in the hospital and Anne didn't think Amelia was the killer.

'How about you with Harry's folks?' asked Alice.

'Dad broke down in tears and left the room. Mum was quite stoic. Have they got an FLO, yet?'

'Got there eventually. Abeer's been waiting. They seem to be in short supply.'

Anne nodded. She pitied the family liaison officer, it wasn't a job she could do, sitting with a grieving family and helping them cope with the loss of their child – their only child, as Linda was keen to point out.

'So, what do we know about Harry Ellis?'

Alice looked at her notes. 'Seventeen; Pupil at the local secondary school; A* student, by all accounts; only child of Edwin and Linda Ellis. Harry and Amelia were inseparable. Abeer's on her way to the school's Headmaster's house now to interview him. How was Derek?'

'Fine, except Harry was one of his students at the Krav Maga classes. Really into fitness, he told me.'

'Anyone there he'd upset?'

'I'll get Derek to find out if he can. I've told him to keep it quiet at the moment. What do you know about St Giles?'

'Only what we were told at school. Ancient leper hospital.'

'Ever known of any trouble there before? Drugs, vagrants, vandals, that sort of thing?'

'Not really. Only the ghost.'

Anne glared at her.

'There's a ghost there, apparently. A hooded monk.'

'Great. Does he often go round slitting people's throats?'

'Not that I know of. Apparently, he just appears in a mist.' Alice started to wave her arms in the air before thinking better of it.

Anne sat heavily onto her chair. The last thing she needed was rumours of ghostly beings going round murdering young people. Her phone rang.

'No Felix, I don't have anything to tell you,' she said, speaking to the news reporter from the local newspaper.

'Come on, Anne. You must have something.'

'I wish I did, Felix. All I can tell you is that it has nothing to do with ghosts, so don't go spreading any nonsense like that.' Anne had closed her mouth too late. She'd just given Felix Corbett his next headline.

'As if I would,' he replied.

'I mean it, Felix. Don't do it.'

'Thanks, Anne. Fancy a drink anytime?'

Anne didn't answer.

'Oh well, no doubt I'll see you around.'

Alice raised an eyebrow.

'I know, I shouldn't have said it. Took me by surprise.' Anne was grinning.

'You did it deliberately, didn't you? Why?'

'It wasn't deliberate, actually, but if the killer suspects the general public think it's supernatural, the perpetrator may get a bit lapse.'

Alice was incredulous. 'You're not serious?' she said.

Anne shook her head. 'No, just desperate at the moment. Who in Maldon is likely to slit some youth's throat for no apparent reason?'

'I don't know. Could be any number of people I suppose.'

'So, we have to find a reason why someone wanted to slaughter an innocent boy?'

'If he was innocent.'

'You're getting there, Alice.'

Abeer Kumar walked through the door. 'Harry Ellis was one of the most popular boys in the school, according to the Head,' she announced.

'Funny how they always say that, isn't it?' said Alice.

'No, evidently, he was,' replied Abeer. 'Never in trouble; captain of the school football team; no enemies supposedly.'

'And someone all the girls wanted to go out with, no doubt.' Anne was deep in thought. 'I need you to go to the school in the morning, Abeer. Interview as many of the kids as you can. Someone must know who had a grudge against him.'

'Do you think it was a student who killed him?' Abeer seemed astounded.

'Who knows? We can't ignore anyone at the moment. Get home, Abeer. I need you at the school first thing.'

'Yes, Ma'am.'

'Just find out who he hung about with – apart from Amelia – and who might be jealous of him. Male or female. We can't rule anyone out, remember. Oh, and thanks for hanging about for the FLO.'

Abeer Kumar nodded and left the room.

'Might as well all of us call it a day. Alice, you're seeing Amelia tomorrow?'

Alice nodded.

'Same thing, then. Find out about their peers at the school and anyone who may have had a grudge.'

'Are you going back to the pub?' she asked Anne.

'Bit late. I'll phone Derek and see what he knows from the Krav Maga. There has to be someone who wanted to hurt Harry Ellis. I can't believe this is random.' She picked up her bag. 'Unless you fancy a quick one?'

Alice shook her head. 'Best not if I'm seeing Amelia's parents first thing, sorry.'

*

Edwin Ellis came through to the lounge, where his wife was sitting immobile on the sofa. Her face was like a stone statue, unmoving, unemotional, and alabaster pale.

Edwin sat next to her, his face red, his eyes puffy from sobbing. He didn't look at Linda, just sat staring at the floor. He took a deep breath, composing himself.

'Do you think it was him?' he said.

Linda slowly moved her head to look at him. He was still inspecting the pattern on the carpet.

'How would he find him?'

Edwin shrugged.

'We haven't heard anything from him since we moved,' continued Linda. She could hear Edwin's breath coming in short gasps.

He looked over to where the FLO was making tea in the kitchen. 'You didn't tell them, did you?' he said eventually.

'Of course not.'

CHAPTER FOUR

Agnes Waterhouse was a witch, a self-proclaimed witch. She had a website. Her real name was Harriet Adcock but she'd changed it by deed poll some years ago. She'd chosen the name Agnes Waterhouse in respect of a sixteenth century woman who had been the first person hanged for witchcraft in England. The execution had taken place at Chelmsford on the twenty-ninth of July 1566. Harriot Adcock had written several well-respected books about the absurdity of the Essex witch trials and was still attempting to clear the women's names nearly four hundred years after their deaths.

The current Agnes Waterhouse was sitting in a field near the River Blackwater, in a circle she'd created from small stones, waiting for Felix Corbett. She had agreed to be interviewed by the reporter about the death at St Giles Leper Hospital. She had been a great advocate for the recognition of the spirits of the slaughtered monks for many years but had been laughed at by the authorities. Now she would turn the tide and see who still wanted to ridicule her.

She'd known about the ghostly monk for ages. She'd had an encounter with him and discovered the reason behind his torment. All he wanted now was to be left in peace, lying safe in the consecrated ground surrounding the ruins that were once his home. He resented visitors coming to view the remains because they had no reverence for the holy place but his hauntings were intended to discourage more desecration to his beloved chapel, not to kill anyone.

*

Felix Corbett was miserable. There was a chill in the air, and it looked like rain. Why on earth he'd agreed to the crazy woman insisting they met in a field, he could no longer fathom. At the time he'd assumed he would have a photographer with him who could take atmospheric pictures to enhance the piece he was to write but, oh no, he wasn't deemed worthy enough to warrant the extra expense of an official photographer, he was expected to take some shots with his phone.

He could see the witch across the field near Limebrook Creek. The only way to reach her was by foot across damp overgrown meadowland. He looked down at his suede loafers and made a mental note to up his expense account. Normally he'd arrange his interviews in a pub where the said expense account could pay for something useful like a couple of pints but at this moment, with the wind whipping round his ears, all he wanted was a hot cup of tea and a scarf.

Agnes Waterhouse was sitting cross-legged on the ground inside the circle of stones. She was wearing what looked like a bunch of rags, held together by dirt and grime. The outer garment hung round her shoulders like a cloak, over a grubby long medieval style dress, a rope tied round her middle. Her head was covered with a cloth resembling a used tea-towel.

She hadn't turned to look at him as he'd approached. It was as though she'd sensed his presence, giving him the impression he'd been intruding on her contemplations.

'Good day,' she intoned. 'Step in.'

'Hi,' replied Felix.

'Not at the moment.'

The witch turned and grinned. Felix, never having actually met a witch before, had expected a long, hooked nose, almost meeting a pointed chin. There should have been warts on the cheeks and forehead and nose, surrounding black eyes, just a couple of yellowed teeth randomly showing on her gums. But this was no Disney witch. The analogy of a Disney princess would be more appropriate, even though this was not a young girl, she must have been at least sixty. Underneath the grungy costume and straggly hair, was the face of an angel. Smooth skin with no apparent make-up, piercing blue eyes behind long curling lashes. The nose not hooked, but small, slightly upturned, and definitely wartless. She had all her teeth which, although small, were perfect and white. Maybe there was something in this witchery.

'I suppose you want to talk about the hospital,' she said.

'Yes, I do.' Felix was feeling awkward towering above the woman. He sighed and sat on the damp grass. Agnes Waterhouse took a plastic sheet from a patchwork bag next to her.

'You'll get piles if you sit on the wet vegetation.'

Felix took the sheet and slipped it under him. It was already too late; he could tell his trousers were more than damp.

'The monk didn't do it if that's what you're thinking,' said Agnes.

'I wasn't really thinking anything,' admitted Felix. 'I was hoping you could enlighten me.'

'About what?'

Felix shrugged. 'I don't know. Ghostly goings-on? Supernatural happenings?'

She looked at him with a certain amount of contempt. 'I thought you'd want to talk about the stabbing.'

Felix nodded. 'That's what I meant.'

'Nothing supernatural there. Someone slit the boy's throat. He most probably deserved it.'

Felix was taken aback. 'Deserved it? Why?'

'The monk doesn't slit throats; he's a holy man. He tries to keep people away that shouldn't be there – like that boy and his girlfriend.'

'Do you think the monk was present?'

'He's always present.'

'When you contacted me, you said you had some information about the killing. What is it?' Felix was already fed up with this woman, not to mention the cold and wet.

'There's something in the air,' she said in her monotonous tone.

'Yes, rain,' thought Felix but didn't say.

'Let me put you straight. The apparition isn't actually a monk, he is Abbot Thomas, who became involved in a plot to dethrone the awful Henry IV in 1403.'

Felix's interest in medieval history was limited to say the least but he tried his best to show some enthusiasm. 'What happened to him? Was his throat cut and left to die in the old hospital?'

'He was pardoned but removed from the Abbey.'

'Are you sure he wasn't slaughtered by Henry VIII's soldiers during the dissolution of the monasteries?' he said showing off his knowledge of history,

Agnes Waterhouse gave him a look that made him feel like an ignorant schoolboy. 'That happened over a hundred and fifty years later and this wasn't a monastery. Abbot Thomas was most probably poisoned by one of the other conspirators. He died in Surrey.'

'So what's he doing here?'

'He objected to being removed as Abbot.'

'And came back?'

The witch nodded.

'Who poisoned him?'

'A man called John Ultyng was charged and acquitted. He later became Abbot of Durford.'

'So could this boy who was killed be an ancestor of this Ultyng bloke and Abbot Thomas has come back to gain revenge?'

Once again, the look of disdain was directed towards Felix. 'The Abbot didn't do it, I told you.'

Felix wasn't sure what to do next. He'd promised his editor a story, yet this strange woman didn't seem to have anything relating to the murder to tell him. He tried once more.

'Did you know the boy who was killed? He was local, I believe.'

'Great Totham. Not local.'

'But he went to school here.'

Agnes shrugged. She was staring across the river, her eyes taking a weird opaque hue now, not the deep blue but a hazy, creamy, green colour. Suddenly she stood and raised her arms. From under her long skirts, a black cat appeared, who spat at Felix. He kicked his foot towards the creature.

'Do not touch him.' Agnes turned to the journalist; her face contorted from angel to devil.

Felix felt his heart jump into his mouth. For a moment he couldn't breathe as panic overtook him.

'Calm yourself,' said the witch. 'Take slow breaths. In and out. Slowly.'

Felix looked at the woman, now restored to her former beauty. She was smiling.

'You're very gullible for a journalist, aren't you? I wouldn't look to the ghost for your suspect. I'd look to the youth of the town who are taking the wrong drugs.'

'The *wrong* drugs?' replied Felix, his breath restored, if not his perception.

Agnes smiled again. 'If you want to write a story, Mr Journalist, write about the evil monsters who are manufacturing narcotics and feeding them to our youngsters. There are plenty of herbs that will give the same effect without the damage.' She put her hand into a deep pocket in her coat and withdrew what looked to Felix like something he'd throw out on the rare occasions he actually weeded his garden. 'Try some,' she said.

'I don't think so,' he said.

'Scared, Mr Journalist?'

Felix stood up. 'No. Just cautious.'

She broke a stem from the bunch and held it before him. 'Just a little nibble.'

Not wishing to appear a wimp and being a gullible sort, he shoved the whole stem into his mouth. It was sweet, which surprised him.

'Very nice,' he said. 'What is that supposed to do to me, then? Turn me into a toad?'

Agnes Waterhouse laughed. 'We don't do that anymore. Well, not very often, anyway.' She turned and strolled back across the meadow.

'Wait a minute, I need a picture.' Felix attempted to take out his phone. He dropped it in the mud, bent to pick it up and collapsed on the ground. He was not hurt but his legs didn't seem to work very well. He started to laugh uncontrollably for no reason as he watched the witch disappear into the horizon.

*

In the fabulously refurbished Maldon Police Station, the CID had their own office, still not the largest room in the building but sufficient to ably fit the three women, Anne, Alice and Abeer – the A team as Anne had christened them.

'Who is Agnes Waterhouse?' Anne was reading the Maldon and Burnham Standard.

Alice grinned. 'You must have heard of our resident witch?'

'Enlighten me.'

'She's harmless enough. Bit of a nutter if you ask me. She calls herself Agnes Waterhouse after some witch from the past, her real name's Harriet Adcock. Does Tarot readings at the Carnival and contributes to a page in the Maldon and Burnham Standard, going on about healing plants and spiritualism.'

'Wellbeing?'

'She'd go mental if she heard you say that. She hates the word. And mindfulness before you try that one.'

'It appears she had a confrontation with our friend Felix Corbett. She seems quite upset that he wanted to blame the hooded monk ghost for the killing.'

'You read the front page I suppose?'

Anne nodded. '"Ghostly goings-on as phantom monk causes death of popular local youth", you mean?' She handed Alice the paper.

Felix had written his piece unaware that Agnes had already submitted copy for her column. The articles contradicted each other. He had gone ahead with his original idea that blaming the ghost would be a good story, using a made-up story about Harry Ellis being descended from the man who supposedly killed the Abbot, whilst Agnes had used her whole column to ridicule and diminish Felix, whilst promoting the leper hospital as a Holy place that should be revered.

'I always thought witches were supposed to be pally with the devil. Why would she care about the hospital being Holy?'

'I'm not sure fornication with Beelzebub is an essential qualification these days, Alice.'

She shrugged. 'Oh well, I'm heading off to Amelia's parents. Anything you want me to say – or not say?'

'Don't mention hooded monks,' was Anne's reply. 'Or having sex with the devil,' she called after her as she left the office.

*

Abeer Kumar was apprehensive as she approached the only secondary school in Maldon. Her parents used to live in the town and Abeer was brought up here, attending this very school. Her family had moved a few years ago because, according to her aunts – the matriarchs of the family – racism was rife in Maldon. Personally, Abeer had found more prejudice when she'd been working in Chelmsford which was where her family now lived. She liked Maldon and wished they'd never moved. Still, heading to her old school reception sent shivers up her spine. The headmaster, whom she'd spoken with the previous evening, was not the same as when she was there but seemed affable, wanting to do all he could to help the investigation into the death of one of his pupils.

'It's tragic,' he said as he welcomed her at reception. 'Such a good boy with such a future ahead of him.'

Abeer nodded, thinking would it have made a difference if he'd been a bad boy with little future. 'Can I speak to the students?' she asked.

'Yes. We've been in touch with all the parents of his group and we're having an assembly just for his year group. I'm not sure how much you'll get from anyone. They are all, obviously, terribly upset.'

'I understand. I just want to try and get an idea of what his peers thought of him.'

It wasn't that long ago that Abeer had attended the school and she was still feeling the same disquiet as she followed the Head up the stairs to the hall as she did at almost every assembly when she was younger. The hall was the same, a stage at one end of the room, it's long blue curtains drawn tight, rows of raked seats rising up towards the back of the room, in which sat roughly thirty young people in various states of tears and grief at the loss of one of their contemporaries alongside the ubiquitous teachers, also upset, who were positioned around the rows of seats. The Head took a short assembly before indicating Abeer.

'This is Detective Constable Abeer Kumar,' said the headmaster. 'She's one of our ex-students,' he added proudly – even though he hadn't been at the school at the time. 'She needs to ask you some questions to help with the investigation into the incident involving Harry Ellis.'

A wail emanated from someone somewhere amongst the seats. Abeer stood at the front of the hall, remembrances of speaking at school assemblies racing back into her mind as she cleared her throat.

'Good morning, everyone. Thank you for your attendance this morning.' She felt her voice wavering as she expected to be marked on her performance by some teacher. She took a deep breath. 'I understand this is a difficult time for you but anything you say to me will be confidential and will only be used by the police with regard to this investigation. It would help me if I could see you all individually but, if you feel you would like to come to me in small groups, I will understand.' This was one of the worst speeches she'd ever given. She was sure the headmaster would stop her any minute. 'I will stand here, by this piano and one of your teachers will lead you to me.'

Abeer took up her place by the grand piano to the right of the stage and waited. She had her notebook in hand ready to record the student's names and anything they had to say about Harry Ellis. A group of three girls was the first to join her. Two of them were too overcome to say much. Abeer took their names while the other shakily told her what a great guy Harry Ellis was. That group was followed by the rest of the year, either singly or in small groups. No-one had anything to say other than praise for the school football team captain.

Abeer thanked the students and, once again, commiserated. The headmaster informed them that a counsellor was available in First Aid if they needed to talk. Slowly the young people made their way out of the hall, directed by the teachers. Abeer became aware of a young man, holding back from the main group. He was looking in her direction. She quickly checked her notes, reminding herself of his name. She looked up. He was still watching her. She smiled and he looked away. Did he have something else to say to her? He had said nothing at all when he'd come to her with another boy who'd enthused about Harry. He was lagging behind and the teacher tried to hurry him along. Abeer made her way over to him and spoke to the teacher.

'Could I have a quick word with Michael,' she said quietly. The boy was called Michael Mooney according to her notes.

The teacher turned to him. 'Do you want to speak to the detective?' she asked him.

Michael looked down at the floor. 'Not here,' he muttered.

'Would it be alright if I went outside with him?' Abeer asked the teacher, who looked at her suspiciously. 'It's a nice day for February.' The teacher checked with the youth, who nodded his head.

'Well, everyone's supposed to go to the common room.' She looked at Michael again, who still seemed reluctant to follow her to join the others. 'But I suppose it would be alright if Michael's happy to do that.'

Michael made a barely perceptible nod.

'If you could stand near the main entrance, DC Kumar, we'll be able to see you on the CCTV, safeguarding you understand and Michael, you must return to the common room when the officer's finished with you.' The teacher smiled an irritated smile, before leading them down the stairs to the main entrance to the Academy. She hovered as if she felt her authority was being undermined.

'Thank you, Miss Deacon,' said Abeer.

The teacher looked at her closely.

'You taught me Geography, Miss,' explained Abeer.

'Oh yes,' she said in that non-committal way that teachers have of not letting you know whether they remembered you or whether they thought you were a good student or not.

Once the woman had left, Abeer turned to Michael. 'You can tell me anything, Michael. It'll be completely confidential. Take your time.'

Michael Mooney was studying the tarmac. 'The other students will know I'm speaking to you,' he said.

'They won't know what you've said to me, and I won't tell them.'

'But they'll know. Everyone thinks he was great. Goldenballs, they called him – after David Beckham?' he clarified, in case Abeer was not up on football.

'But you didn't think so?'

Michael shrugged. 'He was okay, I suppose.' He was looking up at the CCTV camera.

'Shall we move round the corner?' suggested Abeer.

'Miss said not to.'

'Blame me.' They strolled round to where there was no camera. 'So, Michael, you weren't that keen on Harry.'

'He was a bully. It was alright if you were part of the in-crowd, the sycophants that followed him around. If you weren't, he treated you like shit – sorry, I shouldn't say that.'

'I've heard a lot worse, believe me. You tell it how it is, Michael.'

'I used to go out with his girlfriend – before he did, I mean.'

'Amelia?'

He nodded. 'When she started going with him, Harry put a lot of crap on Facebook, slagging me off and making out I was no good at…you know.'

'Were you and Amelia sleeping together?'

Michael looked shocked and shook his head. 'She'd made a pact. She said that none of her gang would sleep with anyone before they were sixteen. She was barely fourteen when we were together, so I wouldn't have tried it on with her anyway – but Harry?'

Abeer waited.

'People were putting horrible things on Facebook, saying she was a great shag, if you know what I mean.' He blushed and looked at the floor.

Abeer controlled her laughter. She wasn't sure if his reticence was due to her being a copper or because she seemed old to him or because she was Asian – she knew a lot of people round here thought Asians didn't have sex. 'It's not that long ago I left school, Michael. Was he implying that they were sleeping together?'

He nodded.

'So do you know anyone else who wasn't over-enamoured with Harry?' Abeer asked him.

'Not at school.'

'Outside school?' Abeer knew that Michael wanted to tell her something more. She had to be careful, though. This was a boy whose girlfriend had been taken from him by Goldenballs.

'I shouldn't say, really.'

'It'll go no further,' reassured Abeer.

He raised his eyes and looked Abeer in the face. 'He broke someone's leg when he was playing for the school team. He laughed at the boy as he was writhing in pain, told him it was a man's game, and he should get up. Harry got a lot of abuse on Facebook after that from the other team. Threats and the like.'

'When was this?'

'Earlier this term.'

Abeer knew they were only a few weeks into the term, so this was recent. 'What sort of threats, Michael?'

'Someone said they'd break both his legs next time they played and if that didn't stop him, they'd…' he paused, scrutinising the ground again.

'They'd what, Michael?'

He looked Abeer in the eyes again. 'Slit his throat.'

CHAPTER FIVE

It was dark where she was. Dark and damp. She thought she could get used to the rats, although she still jumped when one appeared out of the blue. Gathering food had been the most difficult thing. She'd thought briefly about killing a rat with her knife and tried that but dismissed it pretty quickly. She'd never lived like this before. Before, everything had been provided. She'd had a nice house; a family; an account with the local supermarket who delivered food to her house. And now? Well, now there was nothing; no house; no happy family; and, most of all, no food.

She'd known all along she'd have to show herself at some point. She'd found her way in by accident, curiosity maybe, more like needing to find somewhere to hide, to get her head round everything that had happened. There appeared to be two entrances to the underground passage that she was now calling home, one at each end of the town. She had never known they'd existed when she'd lived here but it was evident that the passage had been around for a long, long time. The hardest part was knowing whether it was day or night. There were small holes in the ceiling where some light came in but only if it was really sunny, and at this time of year that was rare. She didn't know what day it was either. She'd never used a wristwatch, always relying on her phone but that didn't operate underground, and the charge had long since run out, so time was mystery to her. It was always night in her hobbit home. She'd had a torch, but the batteries were gone, and she hadn't worked out how to acquire new ones yet. She had no money and couldn't go into a shop when it was open anyway. Not after what she'd done.

It had been less than a week ago that she'd arrived here. At first, she'd snuck into the church and hidden behind some pews until someone came to lock up. They hadn't seen her. Alone in the old building she'd been cold. In a room at the back she'd found a long robe strewn across a chair, presumably belonging to the vicar or someone. It was black and long, like a cloak with a hood, and it was warm. She'd taken it and covered herself. It dragged along the ground and she'd had to hold up the bottom hem. If she'd been at her old home, she could have shortened it, but then, if she'd been at her old home, she wouldn't have needed it. She knew she had to find somewhere better to hide, she couldn't stay hidden in the church. She needed somewhere that they wouldn't find her. It was then that she discovered the entrance to what was now her home.

There was a foul smell in the passage but then she suspected that her fragrance wasn't all that savoury. She couldn't remember the last time she'd showered. She looked down at her hands. They were grimy, her nails ragged, her palms calloused, a small cut below her thumb was black but healing. She was amazed at how quickly the human body declined if it was not looked after. She needed to get some sustenance somehow. The day had been sunny, the dim light emanating from the ceiling had told her as much, so she'd waited until there was no light at all and then waited longer – she didn't know how long – until she'd hoped it was night-time. She'd donned the cloak, crawled along the passage using her hands to guide her, until she'd reached the end. Pushing upwards, a tiny aperture revealed no daylight. She pushed a little more, opening a slightly larger space, through which she crawled into the open air. It smelt good after the hobbit house. She'd timed it well. There'd been no-one around and it was pitch black, the streetlights were off. She'd made her way down the once familiar High Street, now much changed. The layout was the same just the shops that were different. She was soon to realise this was in her favour, as many of the old stores had become cafes, bars and eating places. Veering off the main street, she wound up behind one of the restaurants. Three large green bins were situated against the wall, overflowing with cardboard and leftover food. She'd lifted one of the lids and dug into a luxury meal of vegetables that were not good enough for the fussy customers who visited the sort of overpriced places she used to frequent.

She was gorging on a simple cabbage leaf when she felt a hand on her back.

'What you think you're doing?' came a gravelly voice.

She could smell the man even above her own odour. She remained still for a moment, contemplating her next move. She didn't have to wait long.

'Gerrout o' here, you filthy cow.' The man whispered in her ear, spitting something thick and wet onto the side of her face.

Calmly she'd climbed down from where she'd been perched on the side of the bin and turned to look at the piece of filth crouched next to her.

'This is where I eat. Fuck off,' he growled.

Totally composed, she'd smiled. 'I'm sorry. My mistake, I didn't know you had to book to eat here.'

The man had stared at her; eyes open wide. He'd tried to speak but could only spurt dirty brown blood onto the floor, as she hit him hard in the stomach. He'd grabbed hold of the side of the green bin, before collapsing onto the floor, next to the pool of pus emanating from his stomach.

She'd reached up and taken as much leftover food as she could reasonably carry from the waste bin before leaving the man lying on the ground in his own waste.

*

Sarah Clifford had ascertained that Harry Ellis had been killed by a single wound inflicted by a single blade – probably a kitchen knife –

that severed his carotid artery confirming that the boy's death would have been quick.

'Forensics also think there's someone else's blood on his clothes but haven't found a match.'

'Amelia's?' queried Anne.

'Could be. It is female apparently.'

'Thanks Sarah.'

'Oh, and some black threads, possibly woollen. They don't belong to him either. He didn't fight back, by the way. There was no DNA under his fingernails. It's not for me to say but he either knew his attacker or it was a complete surprise attack.'

Anne sat at her desk. Had the girl been attacked as well and made her escape? Where was the motive? If they knew the assailant, she must know whoever did it, surely. Unless she didn't see the person. She was wearing her school blazer which is black – which could explain the threads that had been found, presumably.

*

The team that Harry Ellis' school had been playing was from Hertfordshire in a place called Broxbourne and the boy with the broken leg was called Thomas Lloyd. Abeer Kumar couldn't understand why school football teams had to play quite so far away, although Broxbourne was only just over the Essex border. She actually couldn't understand why anyone wanted to play football anyway. Her interest in sport consisted of the odd game of chess.

She was currently sitting opposite Anne in the office in Maldon. Michael Mooney had sent her a screenshot of the some of the taunts about Harry Ellis from his Twitter account. It was just schoolboy banter really but the threat of slitting his throat meant it had to be chased up. She had managed to get hold of the headmaster of Badger's Sixth Form College, a Mr William Hinsworth, who'd told her that Thomas Lloyd was still not at school due to complications with his broken leg. He would not reveal the boy's address over the phone, claiming data privacy which meant a trip to the school for Abeer. The headmaster was not keen for her to visit during school hours so he couldn't possibly see her before 3.30pm. It was thirty-five miles to Broxbourne and would take over an hour at that time of day, according to Google Maps, meaning she wouldn't be home until well into the evening. Her parents were having a party and she was expected to be there. She'd have to pluck up the courage to let them know she'd be late.

'Is it vital I talk to this Thomas Lloyd today, Ma'am?' she asked Anne.

'I wouldn't say vital,' Anne replied without looking up from her screen. 'But it might be useful.'

Abeer nodded and picked up her phone. 'Is it okay if I just make a quick phone call?'

Anne nodded and Abeer went outside.

Anne was trying to find out about the original Agnes Waterhouse. Unbelievably, she had her own Wiki page. Born in Hatfield Peverel sometime around 1503 she was most probably a midwife and healer – someone who provided herbal remedies for ailments – but was accused of being the matriarch of a coterie of women engaged in devilish practices. She had a familiar, a cat called Satan, who later was apparently turned into a toad, who helped her commit terrible injuries and death amongst neighbouring livestock and people. Her sister, Elizabeth Francis, had given her the cat in exchange for a cake. Elizabeth was also accused along with Agnes's daughter, Joan. Joan was acquitted and Elizabeth was not executed at this time although she fell to the authorities several years later as the witch trials accelerated across the East of England.

None of this seemed relevant to the boy killed in St Giles but the local newspaper was printing a running battle between Felix Corbett and Harriet Adcock – AKA Agnes Waterhouse. DCI Horobin in Chelmsford wanted 'this nonsense to be stopped'.

Abeer Kumar entered the room like a child who'd been to see the headmaster, her head hung down, shoulders slumped, the weight of the world on her shoulders.

'Are you alright, Abeer?' queried Anne, looking up from her screen.

Abeer sighed deeply. 'Who was it that said your parents fuck you up?'

Anne smiled. 'I think you mean Philip Larkin's poem. "They fuck you up your mum and dad" is the actual line.'

'Yeah, well he was right.'

'Bit of trouble?'

'My mother's having a party tonight and wants to show me off. My aunts probably have a prospective husband for me. I told her I had to work, and mum went ballistic. I told her it's not my fault. One minute she says she's really proud of me being promoted to detective constable, then she resents me having to do my job.' She sat down heavily in a chair and folded her arms like a petulant child.

Anne smirked. 'You'll miss them when they're gone,' she said.

Abeer looked up shamefaced. 'Oh, I'm so sorry, Ma'am.'

'It's fine Abeer. My mother's death was what is called a blessed relief. She had dementia. And while we're in here, call me Anne, please. I hate this official crap. Save that for when we're in public.'

A smile made its best effort to spread across Abeer's face.

'What are you doing that prevents you going to your family party?' asked Anne.

'Questioning the head at Thomas Lloyd's school, the boy whose leg Harry Ellis broke. I have to wait till after three-thirty and it's in Hertfordshire.'

'I can do that if you want?' Anne had no plans for the evening – as usual.

'Oh, I couldn't Ma'am.' Anne gave her a look. 'Anne. I don't even want to go to the party. My family can be such a pain.'

Anne grinned. 'Go to your party this evening. In the meantime, try and get to see Agnes Waterhouse and ask her what the hell she thinks she has to do with our investigation.'

'The witch?'

Anne nodded. 'Do you have a problem with that?'

'No, I don't, Anne. It's just…'

'What?'

'I've wanted to do this job for some time and I feel I'm letting you down making you do my interview before I've hardly set foot in CID.'

'Don't worry, Abeer. I'll make sure you make it up to me in the future. This is a one-off.'

Abeer Kumar visibly relaxed.

'Where is this place?'

Abeer opened her laptop and sent Anne the details of the Badger's College. 'The boy's still not in school and the head would only give me his address in person – after 3.30.'

'So, I have to get the boy's address and then go and visit?'

Abeer nodded.

Anne was starting to regret agreeing to take on Abeer's job as she checked the details on her screen. She sent her subordinate off to find Agnes Waterhouse.

*

The Goddard house was on one of the new estates that had been built in Maldon in the last few years. June and her husband, Allan, had moved to the new house very recently. Both were from Maldon and had been living in a small, terraced house near the town centre. Allan worked as an accountant in the City but his salary was not so great to not have had to save hard to be able to afford one of the new three-bedroom houses next to the ring road on the east of the town.

Alice knew the estate well, her flat being in the next plot, but had no knowledge of any of her neighbours. It seemed like a whole new town had sprung up recently and more houses were being built, spreading out along the fields and meadows she'd happily played in as a child. She turned off the ring road and followed the snaking tarmacked road, parking in front of the address June Goddard had given her in the hospital.

Allan Goddard was not a handsome man. He was probably in his fifties, was wearing an expensive suit with a crisp white shirt and a silk tie. His dark hair was long on the top, the sides clipped almost to the skin, bushy eyebrows framed brown eyes, hidden behind tinted round glasses perched on a rather large bulbous nose.

'Can I help you?' he asked as he opened the door. 'We're not buying anything.'

Alice showed her warrant card. 'DS Alice Porter. I need to ask you some questions about Amelia and Harry Ellis.'

His mouth turned up at the side in a sneer. 'What for?'

'We're investigating a murder, Mr Goddard. We have to follow all the leads we can.'

June Goddard appeared at his shoulder. 'Oh hello,' she said to Alice. 'Would you like to come in?'

Allan Goddard glared at his wife as though she'd just pulled the rug out from under his feet but stepped back to allow Alice into the hallway. The house was like most new-builds on the estate. Rectangular rooms, painted white, the long living room opening out at the far end to a kitchen and a dining room, folding floor-to-ceiling doors giving the ability to close the area off if desired. Windows at either end, along with the light-coloured walls, gave a bright impression to an otherwise unimaginative plastered box. Alice reminded herself that her flat was basically just a smaller version of the same, but she had finally got round to making it more lived-in by adding throws and cushions to her second-hand sofa and hanging posters on her walls. This place was bare. New furniture that looked as though one shouldn't sit on it in case one made it dirty. No pictures anywhere; white wooden open cubes lined one wall, most of which contained nothing more than an artificial plant; thick-pile carpet sank beneath her feet as she followed the couple through to the kitchen area. The kitchen looked as though nothing had ever been cooked in it. There were many accessories sitting on the marble-topped surface that ran around three sides of the room, but all of them appeared to have just been taken from their packaging.

'Tea or coffee, DS Porter?' asked June.

'Tea would be nice, thank you.'

Allan Goddard pulled a high stool from under a breakfast bar and offered it to Alice who perched herself uncomfortably on it. He pulled another out and sat himself on it, leaving his wife to get her own.

June brought a tea service to the bar, three cups, a teapot, sugar bowl and a jug of milk. None of the items looked anything less than pristine.

'Have you lived here long?' Alice asked as June poured the tea.

June smiled. 'Is it that obvious?'

'Well,' replied Alice. 'Everything looks...'

'New,' interrupted Allan.

Alice nodded.

'We've only been here a month,' said June. 'We used to live on Wantz Road.'

'It became too noisy. Bloody drunks shouting as they staggered home from the pubs. You should do something about that.'

'I agree, Mr Goddard. Unfortunately, due to cuts, we have very few officers on the beat these days. Is Amelia in?' Alice looked at June, who looked at Allan, who shook his head.

'She's very upset, as you can imagine.' June sipped her tea.

'You said she'd been seeing Harry Ellis for about a year? Did they seem happy together?'

'Huh.' Allan Goddard shifted on his stool.

'They were very happy.' June Goddard's eyes were glistening as she fought back tears. 'He was a very bright boy.' June's voice was cracking.

'He was a bloody arrogant sod.'

'In what way, Mr Goddard?'

'Thought he was God's gift. Captain of the football team, A star student, thought the sun shone out of his backside.'

'Allan,' cautioned June. She turned to Alice. 'He wasn't like that at all, really. He was a charming young man.'

'He certainly charmed our daughter.'

'Did you not approve of the relationship, Mr Goddard?' It was a question Alice didn't need to hear the answer to but she remained looking Amelia's father in the eyes. Eventually he looked away.

'I didn't but I hope you're not making any kind of accusation, DS Porter.' He looked back at her.

'Of course not. Did Harry come round here very often?' Alice asked.

June glared at her husband, willing him not to speak.

'No,' she said.

'Any reason?'

June sighed. 'Not really.'

'What my wife is trying not to tell you is that I didn't like the relationship. Amelia's exams are important to her. She has to work hard at them, unlike him, and he kept insisting that they went somewhere to revise together. But, evidently, that's not what they were doing. It's not right.'

June looked shocked. 'It was. It was what they were doing, Allan.'

'In the ruins of the old leper hospital? I don't think so.'

There was a short silence. Alice took a swig of her tea. It was weak, insipid, as though a teabag had just taken a glance at the cup on its way to the recycling bin.

'Are you friends with Harry's parents, at all?' she asked.

Allan Goddard answered immediately. 'No.'

June's face went pale. 'We did meet up once when they first moved here.'

'But not anymore?'

'No,' repeated Allan, glaring at his wife again.

'I really would like a quick chat with Amelia if that's at all possible. You'd be welcome to stay, obviously.'

'I'll see if she feels able,' said June, getting up.

'No, I'll go.' Allan was off his stool and heading out of the kitchen.

'I'm sorry about Allan,' said June as soon as he was out of earshot. 'He's very upset.'

Alice nodded. She didn't think he seemed at all upset about Harry Ellis losing his life. He'd almost appeared jealous of the boy who was taking his beloved daughter away from him.

'Is Amelia a bit of a daddy's girl?' asked Alice.

June smiled sadly. 'He'd like to think so but I know she finds him a bit overprotective, if you know what I mean. Do you have children?'

Alice shook her head. 'Not yet.'

Allan Goddard appeared at the door. 'She doesn't want to see anyone,' he said.

CHAPTER SIX

To suggest that Abeer Kumar was scared of Agnes Waterhouse would be an exaggeration. It wasn't fear but a complete incomprehension of her lifestyle. Abeer's life was ruled mostly by her family. It was ordered. Strict, certainly, but at least she knew the rules and it was her choice whether she bent those rules or not – well almost. She had bent them on occasion but not very openly. Definitely not when there was any chance of her parents finding out. This witchy woman, though, didn't appear to abide by any rules at all, as far as Abeer could make out.

The outside of her thatched cottage was overgrown with weeds – well, they could have been weeds or maybe they were drugs of some sort, Abeer didn't know. The door opened before she could knock as if the witch knew she was there.

'Come in,' she said. 'I've been waiting for someone to call. I assume you're the police?'

'DC Kumar,' replied Abeer, showing her warrant card and stepping cautiously over the threshold.

The inside of the small cottage was completely different to the exterior. It was neat and tidy. A small two-seater floral covered 'country cottage' sofa was in the middle of the room, a high-backed armchair to its left. An old but well-kept pine sideboard stood along the wall under a window of leaded lights, a criss-cross of soft metal holding tiny panes of ancient glass, floral curtains hung on either side of the casement matching the covering on the sofa. The carpet, although not new, was clean and also patterned to compliment the rest of the fabrics. Small posies of wildflowers in petite cut-glass vases decorated the top of the sideboard. There was an aroma that Abeer could not put a name to pervading the low-ceilinged room.

Agnes Waterhouse indicated that Abeer should sit on the sofa, while she tucked her legs under her and wrapped herself into a ball on the chair. Abeer couldn't help but notice the woman's beautiful features. Her smile was radiant as she waited for Abeer to sit.

'You don't have to be afraid,' said Agnes.

'I'm not.' Abeer was sitting on the edge of the sofa. It looked the sort of furniture that sunk if you sat in the middle, and she didn't want to appear ridiculous when she had to get up again.

'You look stressed. I suppose you're here to talk about the boy?'

'Yes.'

The witch suddenly flung her legs out in front of her and stood. 'I'm sorry. Would you like some refreshment. How rude of me.'

Abeer shook her head. 'I'm okay, thanks.'

'I was only offering tea. Nothing spooky.' Agnes laughed.

'I've just had some coffee but thank you,' Abeer lied. There was no way she intended to drink anything brewed up by a witch.

Agnes went out of the room and Abeer heard a kettle boiling. A few minutes later a sweet smell preceded the witch into the room.

'I went for strawberry tea. Are you sure you don't want some? It's very relaxing.' She held up the teapot she was carrying along with two pottery mugs.

'I'm quite relaxed, thank you. What can you tell me about the boy?'

'About the boy?' She curled herself back into the chair. 'Nothing.'

'You seemed to be quite informed in the newspaper,' retorted Abeer.

'Not about the boy. If you want to know about St Giles Hospital, then I might be able to help you.'

Abeer looked at the woman, trying not to show her irritation.

'I spend a lot of time at St Giles. Did you know that they grew herbs there centuries ago? Herbs that heal. It was a hospital. Many of them still grow there if you know what you're looking for. Chamomile; feverfew; lady's mantle; even the humble marigold has many healing properties. Do you suffer with PMT?'

Unable to hide her shock at the question, Abeer almost shrieked. 'No!'

Agnes nodded knowingly. 'You should try chasteberry, also known as monk's pepper. It doesn't grow here really but I know the monks at the hospital had a ready supply – probably from the Mediterranean – it might take the edge off your sex life though so be wary as to how much you take.'

Abeer, embarrassed, could feel her skin getting hot.

'Have a tea,' said Agnes, getting up and pouring a mugful which she handed to Abeer.

Abeer, too flustered to refuse, took the warm mug in her hands. The fragrance was intoxicating.

'What's in here?' she asked, staring into the pinkish liquid.

'Just strawberry leaves really. The thing about St Giles is that it's not very secure. I see young people in there all the time. I find used condoms just left lying about on the sacred ground. Do you think that's alright?'

Abeer wasn't sure whether she meant leaving condoms around or the strawberry tea. She went for the former.

'No, of course I don't. That's not a police matter, I'm afraid. The ruins are the council's responsibility.' She took a sip of tea. It was sweet and quite refreshing. 'What do you do if you see any of these young people?'

Agnes grinned. 'I scare them away.'

'How?'

'That depends. Sometimes I just appear and shout at them. Sometimes I call upon Abbot Thomas.'

'Abbot Thomas?'

Agnes Waterhouse nodded. 'He was the abbot here in the fifteenth century.'

'Are you suggesting he is a ghost?' Abeer said.

'Well, he wouldn't still be what you would call living, would he?' She laughed.

Abeer put her mug on the sideboard. She appeared to have drunk nearly all of the strawberry tea. 'Do you have any information that may help us in finding the killer of the boy, Harriet?'

'Agnes. I only answer to Agnes.'

Abeer glared at her and stood up.

'Thank you for the tea,' she said as she made her way to the door.

'It will help you relax,' said the witch. 'I don't think the boy will be the last.'

Abeer stopped by the door. 'Meaning?'

'There is something bad going on, DC Kumar. Something very bad indeed. I'm not sure what it is yet but if I find out, I'll let you know.'

Abeer Kumar left the cottage feeling she had just spent a complete waste of time talking to a deluded nutcase. She sighed. However, much against her will, she was feeling strangely relaxed as she got into her car and drove off to prepare for a party with another bunch of nutcases.

*

William Hinsworth was sitting in his office at Badgers Sixth Form College. He was waiting impatiently for DC Kumar, who was late. She'd said she'd be there at three-thirty, and it was now a quarter to four. The receptionist, an older woman called Mary, was slowly typing something on her computer.

'Any sign of that policewoman, Mary?' he bellowed.

She carried on typing for a few seconds before turning to him.

'No sign, I'm afraid, Mr Hinsworth.'

He went back into his office, slamming the door. He knew what the law was here to find out. He knew about the threats on social media and had informed the culprits that they would be in serious trouble if he ever saw anything like that again. Part of him felt proud that the boys had stood up for one of their own who'd been abused by the Essex boy but he knew the reputation of his college was at stake. He also knew that Thomas Lloyd had an aggressive parent and had probably encouraged the online abuse, not that he would admit any such thing to DC Kumar.

Mary poked her head in the door. 'She's here, Mr Hinsworth.'

'Send her in.' He stood behind his desk and watched a short woman, not in uniform, waddle into his office. 'DC Kumar?' he said holding out his hand. 'William Hinsworth.'

'I'm afraid not, I am DI Anne Edwards,' said Anne, showing her warrant card as she took his hand.

Hinsworth frowned. 'A bit trivial for a Detective Inspector, isn't it? It was just a football injury, after all.'

Anne sat down on the hardwood chair in front of the desk. 'I'm not really interested in the football match, Mr Hinsworth. I'm interested in the exchange of comments on social media that followed.'

'Ah, yes. I put a stop to that as soon as I found out. You know what these young people are like.' He smiled.

'I do, Mr Hinsworth.' She studied the man in front of her. Even though he was seated she could tell he was a tall and thin man, his suit just slightly too large for his narrow shoulders. She guessed he was in his late thirties which seemed quite young for a headmaster – not that she had any idea how old a headmaster should be, they'd always seemed ancient when she'd been at school. His hair was swept back and stuck down either with hairspray or some sort of grease. His nose was long and as thin as the rest of him. He appeared to be a thoroughly weak man and she surmised the students would have him wrapped round their little fingers.

'I understand that Thomas Lloyd is still off school.'

'It's a college, DI Edwards, but yes, he is. It was a nasty tackle, leaving him seriously in danger of a permanent limp.'

'I'd like to interview him. Do you have his address?'

Hinsworth hesitated. 'Could I just ask what was supposedly said that demands the attention of a Detective Inspector. I read the threads, they were just youthful banter, surely.'

Anne waited without answering. Hinsworth shrugged and handed her a printed sheet he'd run off earlier.

'That's the address of the boy's parents. I have informed them someone may contact them from the Essex Police, so they are expecting you. I believe they may want to make a complaint against the boy who broke young Thomas's leg.'

'That might be a bit difficult,' said Anne, as she took the paper from Hinsworth before exiting the room.

*

The Lloyd family lived in a terraced house in the middle of Broxbourne. Thomas' parents were called Patricia and Robert. The window frames were in need of a coat of paint if not a complete refit and the front door was scuffed around the bottom as though it had been kicked often. Grubby curtains hung listlessly behind grimy windows. There was no garden, the entrance opening straight onto the pavement. The rest of the houses along the road did not look much better. Anne knocked at the door and waited. After a short while Thomas Lloyd's mother, Patricia, opened it and stared at Anne.

'You the police?'

'I am DI Edwards, yes.'

'About time.' She was wearing baggy jeans and a sweatshirt that hadn't seen a washing machine for some time. She stood back holding the door wide open. Anne could sense the curtains twitching opposite before Patricia yelled an obscenity in the general direction.

'Trouble with the neighbours?' said Anne.

Patricia didn't answer and stomped through to a grimy living room. A youth lay on threadbare sofa, his leg in plaster currently hanging on a makeshift A-frame made from scrap bits of wood and rope. He moaned as Anne entered the room, as if on cue. A man dressed in jogging pants that had never jogged and a tee shirt that didn't even try to hide his flabby belly, stood before an old gas-fire that most probably was dishing out carbon-monoxide by the barrowload. Anne declined the offer to sit on an equally filthy, shabby armchair.

'We want compensation,' the man said.

'That's not why I'm here, I'm afraid, Mr Lloyd,' said Anne.

'Shepherd. Bob Shepherd. I'm not his dad. His dad's a bastard,' said the man.

'As I said, that's not why I'm here, Mr Shepherd. Could I speak to Thomas in private?'

There was another on-cue groan from the sofa.

'I don't fink so,' said Bob Shepherd. 'There's nowt he can't say in front of us.'

Anne turned to the boy. 'How are you feeling, Thomas?' she asked him.

'How do you fink he's feelin'?' Bob Shepherd's voice filled the room. 'He'll probably never walk again, fanks to that bastard.'

'Did you instigate the threats on social media, Thomas?' continued Anne, ignoring the stepfather.

'It were nowt to do wiv 'im.' It was Patricia's turn to speak.

Anne remained looking at the boy. He grimaced to show the pain he was supposed to be suffering.

'Thomas, I need you to answer my questions. Are you able to talk?'

'Of course he's able. Depends what you're askin'.' Bob Shepherd took a step towards Anne, who turned to him.

'Have you read the stuff on Thomas's Facebook page, Mr Shepherd. The stuff directed towards Harry Ellis?'

'He deserves a lot more than that. If I see the little bugger, I'll beat the shit out of 'im.'

'A bit late, I'm afraid. Someone seems to have done that already.'

'I hope you're not blaming us,' interjected Patricia, her arms folded across her ample bosom.

'Have you been to Essex recently?'

'I don't like Essex.' Bob took another pace forward, towering over Anne.

'Thomas, have any of your friends been anywhere near Essex in the last week, do you know?'

'"Ow would he know? 'E's been laid up 'ere, the poor love.' Patricia moved towards the boy and put her arm round him. He tensed and tried to move away but was trapped between his mother and the back of the sofa.

'Do you have a car, Mr Shepherd?'

Bob looked at her warily.

'I can check, Mr Shepherd.'

'It's outside. It's taxed.'

Anne looked through the dirt on the window at an old Renault parked in front of the house. 'That one?' She pointed.

Bob nodded. 'It's insured.'

Anne doubted it was insured or taxed but that didn't bother her at the moment. 'I'll arrange for someone to come and pick Thomas up and bring him to the station in Chelmsford – that's in Essex – as I need to question him formally. I'll make sure they have a wheelchair. One of you may accompany him.' She went towards the door.

'You can't do that. You arresting him?'

'No, I'm not, Mr Shepherd, I'm asking him to help us with our inquiries at the moment. Of course, if he refuses...'

'I'll come.' They were the first words Anne had heard the boy say.

'Thank you, Thomas. Will tomorrow be alright? About ten?'

The boy looked at his parents. 'Yes,' he said. 'I'll come on my own.'

'I'll come wiv you, darling,' said Patricia. She glared at Anne. 'And I'm quite capable of driving him there, I don't want bloody police cars turning up 'ere.'

Thomas looked resigned and nodded.

'I'll see myself out,' said Anne. 'Look forward to seeing you tomorrow, Thomas. Hope you feel better soon.'

Anne took the registration of the Renault, before heading back to her own car and driving back to Maldon feeling extremely frustrated.

*

It was long past dusk and the late February sky was gloomy and overcast not giving any moonlight a chance to seep through. Amelia didn't know what she was doing or where she was going, she'd just had to get out of the house. Her mother had been overbearing in her attempts to be consoling and her father, although trying hard not to show it, almost appeared happy that Harry had died. In fact, she'd overheard him saying as much to her mum. She'd never experienced grief before. Both of her grandfathers had passed away before she was born and both of her grandmothers were still living, one in a care home, the other was in a nice retirement village in Devon. No-one close to her had died. No-one she knew had ever been murdered. The strange thing was she didn't know how she was supposed to feel. She didn't know how grief was supposed to represent itself in her. She felt sad, of course, but she also felt lost, alone, no idea which way her life was going to turn now. Not along the road that led to a pretty rose-covered cottage in the country – not that she ever believed that was any kind of reality but it had been a dream that had been taken away from her before its time. Now she was just drifting, not knowing where to go or what to do. She'd thought briefly about life after death and whether, if she died, her and Harry could be together again but it didn't last long. She had no illusions. Life was life and death was death. That was how it was, she was certain, but in the state of mind she was at present she couldn't see what her life had to offer anymore. No Harry. Harry was dead. Killed.

Without intention, her meanderings had brought her to the very place she had last been with Harry, St Giles Leper Hospital. She flicked the hood of her jacket up so that the policeman standing guard on the crime scene wouldn't recognise her and stood by the locked gates staring at the ruins, wishing they had never entered through the gap in the hedge. Why hadn't she said no? She knew why. She'd wanted to be alone with Harry just as she wanted to be with him now and she hadn't wanted to lose him. She wandered down the lane by the side of the historical site. It was almost as though the cleft in the hedge was opening for her, letting her into the place her love had died. She poked her head through the aperture and looked over to the gates. The policeman was leaning against the fence surveying something across the road, his mind not on the ruins and, under cover of the hedge, she climbed the fence into the hallowed ground.

Someone was there. Across the grass by the huge old tree, she could see a person bending over, scavenging in the earth. At least, she assumed it was a person. Someone in a long flowing cloak, scurrying around in the dark. Amelia hid herself behind a lichen-covered stone wall, peering through what had once been a window.

'Oi, you!' The shout came from the gates. The policeman. She ducked down behind the remains, trying to work out if she could get to the hedge before the copper got to where she was. She heard the keys opening the gate and the man's steps as he strode across the cobbled path.

'I've told you before,' he shouted.

'I have every right to be here.' A different voice. A female.

Keeping her hood tight around her face she shifted up slightly, peeping through the broken-down aperture again. The figure she'd seen digging around was standing up now. It was a woman she vaguely knew. The witch, they called her. She was a bit of a joke at school, the older girls using her to scare the kids just starting at the big school. 'The witch will get you if you don't do as I say.' No-one believed it after their first term but there was always the thought that maybe, just maybe, she really was a witch. Most people avoided her but Harry had once suggested going to one of the occult classes she ran at her house. There was no way Amelia was going to do that. She didn't know if Harry had or not. And now she was here before her. Amelia had never been this close before. She didn't really look like a witch. She stood there in her hippy clothes, bunches of weeds in her hands, defying the policeman.

'Come on, Harriet. You know this is a crime scene. Don't make me arrest you.' The policeman seemed very reasonable under the circumstances.

The woman gave him some of the weeds she'd procured.

'I'll be five minutes, Ernie. Make a tea with these when you get home. Help you sleep.' She was stroking his arm. 'And you know my name is Agnes, you naughty boy.'

The policeman smiled, removed her arm from his and said, 'Five minutes. I'll be at the gate, if you're not out by then, I'll have to arrest you.'

'I'll go now if you buy me a drink across the road. There's no-one about, Ernie.'

She reached up and brushed his cheek with the back of her hand before following the policeman back towards the gate. Amelia ducked down as they strolled past.

'Just a quick one, then,' she heard him say. She heard the padlock being locked on the gates as they disappeared towards the pub.

Amelia wasn't aware of anything untoward until she felt the hand across her mouth and she was lifted up. She struggled but a kind female voice in her ear whispered, 'Shh. I'm not going to hurt you.'

Was it the witch? Amelia couldn't turn her head. She'd seen the witch leave, hadn't she? She couldn't call out, the hand was covering her mouth and nose, making it difficult to breathe. She was feeling faint, her senses dulling. Slowly she felt herself falling, the world going dark and quiet. She fell back into the arms that held her and knew no more.

CHAPTER SEVEN

'Do you know someone called Catherine Hall?' Alice was logged on to her computer in the Maldon office, Anne sitting across from her.

'No, should I?' she replied.

'She's from Maldon.'

'So are a lot of people, Alice. I can't be expected to know all of them.'

'She's about your age.'

Anne was about to repeat that she couldn't know everyone her age from Maldon but thought better of it. 'Why are you asking?'

'Missive from the Met. Apparently, her husband and daughter were found dead in East London and she's gone missing.'

'And?'

'They think she might have come back to Maldon. Have you not looked at your emails this morning?'

'No, I'm trying to pretend they don't exist.'

Anne reluctantly brought up the messages on her screen. There was a post that DCI Horobin had forwarded. She opened it and started reading.

'Oh my God!' she said as a photo appeared in the script. 'That's Cat. Cat Willis. You're right I do know her – well I did. We went to the same school.' Anne carried on reading. 'This is terrible. Her daughter bled to death and her husband suffered multiple stab wounds. What happened to Cat?'

'I'm looking at the news reports. It seems the girl – who was only thirteen – was pregnant and haemorrhaged whilst miscarrying. She was in the kitchen and the husband was found in the hallway. No-one appears to know what happened. It seems your friend could either be a suspect or she may have fled the attacker,' Alice informed her.

'The Met want our help to find Cat but there's no reason to speculate that she returned to Maldon. She has no family here.' Anne carried on reading. 'Her parents emigrated to Australia and the Met don't look like they can find them.' She looked up from her screen. 'I expect they didn't try very hard.'

'What do we do about it?' asked Alice.

Anne thought for a moment. 'We can keep our eyes and ears open, but we can't really take on one of the Met's cases. We have enough on our plate as it is.'

Alice agreed. 'Do you want me in on your interview with the boy?'

'Thomas? Yes, please. I just hope his stepfather isn't with him. We're seeing him in Chelmsford.' Anne looked at her watch. 'If we head off now, we might have time to get a takeaway coffee from that new place by the market.'

'Really? Why would you want to pay twice the price of our usual café?'

Anne shrugged. 'Need to keep ahead of the times, Sergeant. Check out the new, you know.'

Alice shook her head. 'I hope you're paying, then.'

Anne grinned. 'I can probably run to a small latte for my faithful Sergeant.'

*

Someone was stroking Amelia's hair. She couldn't see who it was. They were behind her, and it was dark. Where was she? She hated the dark, it made her feel closed in, constricted, as though someone was sitting on her chest. She felt like she was waking from a deep, deep sleep, her thoughts muddled and confused. She reached up and pushed the hand away.

'Get off me,' she said.

'Elizabeth, you're awake.' A kind face moved through the gloom, close to Amelia's. She didn't recognise her.

'Who are you?' she said.

The woman smiled. 'I'm your mummy, Elizabeth.'

'You're not my mother. Why are you calling me Elizabeth?'

The woman was stroking Amelia's hair again. It was not comforting but Amelia couldn't move away. She seemed to be tied round her waist to something. She put her hands down and felt a thick rope which was cutting into her stomach every time she tried to get away from the woman.

'It's your name,' came the answer. 'It's your lovely, lovely name.'

Amelia tried again to move.

'Don't try and leave, Elizabeth. I'm not letting you go again. He can't hurt you while you're with me.'

Amelia held her breath. She tried all the meditation that Harry had taught her. Deep breaths now. Calm down. 'I think you're mistaken. I'm not Elizabeth. No-one's trying to hurt me.' Amelia was aware of her voice being tight and high-pitched. She was desperately endeavouring not to show her fear but however much she tried, her brain was not in her control. Her instincts were governing her now and they were furiously looking for some way for her to escape. She pulled at the rope around her middle.

The woman patted her arm. 'That's my brave girl. I've made a special meal for you. Stay there.'

The woman moved away. Amelia had no choice but to stay. She tried yanking at the binding, but it was tied tightly, and every movement felt like it carved a trench in her side. She still had no idea where she was. As her eyes grew accustomed to the lack of light, she could see that the rope was a dark colour and was silky smooth. She looked around her but all that was in her eyeline were slimy old bricks and a dirt-covered floor. It was a small space and it smelt like a sewer. Maybe that's where she was, in a sewer. Why would she be in a sewer? It couldn't be a sewer; it was dry and musty. The smell was earthy, grimy, dirty, but not sewery really. Where was she? And where had the woman calling herself 'mummy' gone? And why was she calling her Elizabeth? She put her fingers to her neck and stroked the locket that Harry had given her. How she wished he was here now. He would help her; he would be her knight in shining armour; he would save her. But he couldn't. He was dead.

'Here we are.' The woman arrived holding what looked like it had been a cabbage leaf once in a while, topped with what could have been chopped onion. She thrust it at Amelia, who turned her head. 'Come on Elizabeth, you must eat. You know what happened last time.'

Amelia didn't know what happened last time. She didn't know anything; she didn't know who this woman was who kept calling her by the wrong name; she didn't know where she was, and she didn't know what was going on.

*

Anne and Alice finished their takeaway coffees in the car outside Chelmsford Police Station. Alice looked sideways at her boss. 'Bit pricey for hot milk,' she observed.

'I'm sure there was some coffee in there somewhere,' replied Anne. Neither of them would be a frequent customer of the new coffee bar.

Interviews were still being held at Chelmsford as the Maldon rooms were not quite ready, they'd been told. They went into the station to be greeted by James Royley, the jolly desk sergeant.

'Your boy's in interview room one with PC Branstone' he said quietly. 'His mother's behind you.'

Anne turned round. 'Where the fuck have you been?' yelled the woman as she recognised the DI. Anne ignored her and went down the corridor towards the interview rooms, followed by Alice and a stream of verbal abuse from Patricia Lloyd.

'Nice,' said Alice as they reached the door.

'You should see her partner.' Anne opened the door. 'Hello Thomas,' she said as the two women took their seats opposite the youth, dismissing PC Branstone at the same time.

Thomas Lloyd was sprawled on the chair, his plastered leg out in front of him. He was wearing the same clothes as the previous evening, Anne noticed, a grubby pair of jeans cut up the side to accommodate his plaster cast and a stained tee shirt. He didn't speak. There was a woman in a suit next to him.

'Thanks for coming over today, Thomas. How's the leg?' Anne smiled at him.

Thomas shrugged.

'Must have been a nasty tackle,' Anne continued.

Thomas grunted.

Anne studied her notes for a moment. 'About these posts, Thomas. Why did you think it was okay to put them on your timeline?'

'I didn't.' The boy spoke but didn't look up.

'But they're on your timeline.'

'I didn't put them there.'

'Who did, then?'

Thomas shrugged again.

'Was it one of your teammates?' Alice suggested.

'No,' Thomas mumbled into his tee shirt.

'Who are you trying to protect, Thomas? These are malicious communications, and the perpetrator is committing an offence. It's against the law, Thomas. As things stand, because they are on your timeline, you are culpable. Do you understand what that means?'

Thomas looked up at Anne, who could see he was obviously scared. 'I didn't do it, though.'

The woman in the suit put her hand on his arm. 'Is my client under arrest?'

Anne glared at the woman. 'He's helping with our enquiries. I don't even know why you're here?'

'I believe it's called safeguarding,' she said condescendingly. 'He's a child and you are adults.'

Anne turned back to Thomas. 'They're on your timeline.'

'Someone else must have done it?' His face was drawn and pale, his breath coming in short bursts.

'We need to know who that might be, Thomas.' Alice smiled kindly at the boy.

Both she and Anne knew the boy had not deliberately broken the law but the posts were threatening and there was more than one. It would be up to Harry Ellis's parents to bring a complaint. All the detectives wanted to know at the moment was whether Thomas was covering for someone else.

'Who would have access to your account, Thomas?' asked Anne.

Thomas was back to shrugging. Anne leaned forward, her elbows on the table, her face close to where Thomas lounged.

'I don't want to have to arrest you, Thomas but I need to know who put up those posts if it wasn't you. A cybercrime has been committed and it's my duty to find the culprit. I believe you. I don't think it was you but if you can't at least give me a clue as to who would have access to your Facebook account, you will leave me with no alternative.' She sat back in her chair and folded her arms.

'He'll kill me,' muttered Thomas.

'Who will?'

'Bob.'

'Would that be your stepfather?'

'You can't tell him.' The boy looked close to tears.

'I won't tell him, Thomas,' confirmed Anne. Alice did not speak. The solicitor, or whatever she was, made some notes.

Thomas Lloyd looked at Anne. 'He told me we'd get compensation. I didn't want that. These things happen when you play football. I'm sure he didn't really mean to hurt me. When the first post went up, other people followed. It were horrible. I didn't want it.'

'Why didn't you stop it happening?' asked Alice.

'How?'

'Change your password?'

Thomas shook his head.

'Did you know that the boy who tackled you was killed not long after those posts went up?' Anne stared at the boy. She could tell by his face that he evidently didn't. He started to shake and a tear escaped from his eye.

'I didn't do nothing,' he whimpered.

Neither of the detectives answered.

*

'What you done to him?'

Anne and Alice passed Thomas back to his mother. He was sobbing into her ample bosom.

Patricia Lloyd spoke to the woman in the suit. 'We want compensation. This is police brutality.'

Anne and Alice smiled at her.

'Perhaps we could discuss that with your partner, Bob,' suggested Alice.

'Too right you will.'

'Could you ask him to come in?' Anne had pointed him out to Alice sitting in his car on a double yellow line as they'd finished their coffees.

Patricia Lloyd took out her phone. 'They want to talk compensation. Come in 'ere now,' she barked into the handset.

Less than a minute later Bob Shepherd stomped through the door of the station.

'I can help if you want,' ventured the responsible adult who'd been with Thomas.

Bob Shepherd looked at her. 'That'll cost. I don't need you.'

She shrugged and made her way out of the station.

'That bastard's got to pay. E's ruined my boy's career,' yelled Bob. His face close to Anne's, smelt of stale tobacco and alcohol – even though it was barely eleven o'clock.

'If you'd like to follow me, Mr Shepherd.' Anne led him down the corridor.

Once inside the interview room Anne and Alice resumed the seats they'd just vacated.

'Do sit down, Mr Shepherd,' said Anne.

He took his seat opposite them. 'Thomas 'as 'ad an offer from a top Premier league club which he can't take up now, thanks to that bastard. 'E would be earning upwards of ten grand a week as a youf player. Compensation's gonna run to a million or more. What you going to do about it?'

Anne pulled a face and looked to Alice. 'What do you think, DC Porter?'

Alice put on a thoughtful expression. 'I'm not sure we have the jurisdiction,' she said.

Anne turned back to Bob Shepherd. 'We're not actually here to discuss compensation. That would be for a court to decide. We would like to discuss Thomas's Facebook account.'

'What's that to do wi' me?'

'Where were you on February 19th?'

'What?'

Anne sighed. 'Where were you on February 19th?'

''Ow do I know? Why you askin' that?'

'Because, Mr Shepherd, on that evening, the young man who broke your boy's leg was murdered.'

'Not by me.' Bob Shepherd didn't seem at all shocked or surprised by the news.

'His throat was slit.'

Bob Shepherd shrugged.

'Have you read Thomas's Facebook page?'

'Nowt to do wi' me.'

'You see, on that page is a threat to slit the boy's throat. We don't believe Thomas wrote that, so we'd like to find out who did and whether they carried out that threat.' Alice rested her chin on her hand.

'Well it weren't me. 'Oo said it was?'

'No-one said it was you, Mr Shepherd. We're just trying every avenue at the moment to see who might have had a reason to kill the young man.'

'Probably anyone 'oo's played football 'gainst 'im.'

'Do you have access to Thomas's phone and laptop,' asked Alice.

Bob Shepherd looked at her with contempt. 'I 'ave access to the laptop. We only 'ave one. We're not like those rich buggers what can afford loads of tech.'

'And the phone?'

'I 'ave used it. Mine's very old and don't always get a signal.'

'Would Thomas's Facebook page be open when you use either device?'

'I wouldn't know.'

'Oh, I think you would, Mr Shepherd. Do you ever go on his page?'

'Nah. I'm not a kid. I don't do social.'

Alice assumed he meant he didn't do social media but couldn't be sure. She turned her laptop to face him. 'Who put this up, then?'

On the screen was a post with a video of Thomas Lloyd scoring what looked like a very good goal, although Alice couldn't be sure, knowing nothing about the beautiful game, followed by the words – 'Another cracker by my boy.'

'Maybe Thomas put it up?' replied Bob Shepherd.

Anne and Alice simultaneously lifted an eyebrow each.

'Well, yeah. I might've put that up. It's not illegal.'

'No, it's not, Mr Shepherd,' replied Anne. 'The thing is you told us you'd never been on Thomas's Facebook page.'

He didn't say anything, just curled his lip. Alice showed him another post.

'Did you also put this up?'

Bob Shepherd didn't look at the post. He knew which one it was.

'What if I did? 'E's ruined my boy's life.'

'There is a law against putting threatening posts on social media, and, in this case, it's a threat that has been carried out. So, I ask again. Where were you on the 19th February?'

'I were in the fucking 'ospital, caring for my boy.'

'Your boy, if you're talking about Thomas, wasn't in hospital on the 19th February. He was discharged nearly a week before that. So, where were you? Were you in Maldon in Essex?'

'I told you I don't like Essex.'

Anne sighed and put her hands flat on the table, resisting the urge to clench them into fists.

'Mr Shepherd. If you can't tell me where you were I am within my rights to arrest you on suspicion of murder. I don't really want to do that because it could be a waste of my time. I could also arrest you for driving a vehicle without an MOT or insurance but, like I say, I have more important things on my mind at the moment.'

'I 'ave MOT and insurance,' he blurted out.

'You may have a dodgy MOT, Mr Shepherd, but that heap outside your house was definitely not roadworthy and you don't have insurance. However, that's for my colleagues to deal with – if I tell them. I'm sending someone home with you and I want you to let us have Thomas's phone and laptop.'

'You need a warrant for that,' he sneered.

'Not if they are voluntarily offered which I'm sure you'll be happy to do.'

Bob Shepherd's lip curled some more.

'Or I could inform the traffic police…'

'I don't know where they are.'

'I'm sure Thomas does. Thank you for your time, Mr Shepherd.'

PC Branstone opened the door for Bob Shepherd.

'Take him home, PC Branstone. He will give you a laptop and a phone when you get there.'

The officer nodded his head and escorted Shepherd along the corridor.

Alice turned to Anne. 'Do you think he did it?' she said.

'No more than I believe that seventeen-year-old has had an offer from a top Premier League club,' Anne replied. 'Most kids are picked up by academies long before that age.'

'Well, I hope you're right, Anne. If he put that post up and then Harry Ellis died in exactly that way…?'

'Let's hope my instinct hasn't completely deserted me.'

*

Much as Bob Shepherd tried to stop him, PC Branstone manoeuvred his way into the shabby house where the family lived. Thomas was on crutches but seemed to be coping well with them. He didn't look like a boy who'd never walk again. Still, Branstone used the excuse of helping him into the house to gain his own entry. The boy went to the sofa and handed him his phone without any problem. PC Branstone put his gloves on and placed it in an evidence bag.

'And a laptop?'

'I don't know where it is.'

Branstone turned to Bob Shepherd, who shrugged his shoulders.

'I fink it's in our bedroom,' offered Patricia.

'Is it fuck,' yelled Bob.

'You were on it last night.'

'I 'aven't seen it for weeks.'

PC Branstone smiled at Patricia Lloyd. 'Could you have a look for me?' he said kindly.

'I'll go,' said Bob.

'I think Mrs Lloyd can manage, Mr Shepherd.' Branstone stood between the man and the door, while Patricia sheepishly left the room.

'There's nowt on it. I ain't done nowt.' Bob was glaring at Thomas who seemed to shrink into the sofa.

Patricia came back with an ancient looking laptop under her arm. She held it out to Branstone, who slipped it into another plastic bag.

'Is this the only one?' he asked.

'Yeah, don't damage it. It's all we can afford,' said Patricia.

PC Branstone turned to Thomas. 'Good luck, son. Hope you recover soon. That was a great goal on your Facebook page.'

The boy's face lit up.

'What about our compensation?' complained Bob Shepherd.

'Above my pay grade, mate, sorry.' He let himself out. As he looked through the grubby windows he could just about make out Patricia Lloyd protecting her son from any aggression that might come by way of his stepfather.

CHAPTER EIGHT

DC Doug Griffiths was a tall, good-looking man with curly blond hair in his late twenties. He'd had five years' service in the Metropolitan Police Force. He had a Professional Policing Degree and following his graduation was taken onto the Graduate Detective Program and was seen as a 'good worker and team member'. He was currently heading out to the sticks of rural Essex to help the local force look for Catherine Hall. He was convinced she had returned to the town of her birth, even though there had been unfounded sightings of her as far afield as Newcastle and Devon.

He was currently sitting in a traffic jam on the A12, a packed holdall next to his laptop bag on the back seat of his pride and joy – an ancient Volvo estate with a hundred and twenty-five miles on the clock. Having an old jalopy used to be an advantage in London as not even the most desperate car thief would bother to look twice at it. He didn't even bother to lock it in case some idiot decided to break a window and scour the glove compartment – which he always left open anyway to prove there was nothing worth nicking. However, since the mayor had brought in his ultra-low emission zone, he could no longer drive it in the capital without paying through the nose for the privilege, so he kept it parked on the outskirts of the zone these days.

Apart from a couple of holidays abroad he'd never felt the need to venture out of the capital city. He'd always loved London; the city life; the variety of entertainment; the pubs; the Thames; the history; the vibrancy of living in a diverse and exciting metropolis. He had no idea what to expect out in the wilds of the Essex coast. Probably a load of people chewing on straws and drinking some sort of homemade hooch.

A BMW blew it's horn behind him. He hadn't noticed that the traffic had moved about ten yards before stopping again. He didn't know where the driver thought he was going to go other than ten yards further along the traffic jam but he duly moved his vehicle closer to the stationary car in front and pulled on the handbrake.

*

Abeer Kumar's shift started at two o'clock but she'd come into the office at just after eleven, sitting alone at her desk. There was no-one else in. She was seriously considering how she could get out of living at her family's home. It wasn't that she disliked them or anything, she just found it oppressive. Although her parents were pretty cool and weren't controlled by the disciplines of outdated Pakistani traditions (they'd been born here and Abeer was third generation British Asian) they still kowtowed to her aunts; the ones who'd been born in the old country and refused to accept the more liberal attitude of modern British Asians and who were currently obsessed with why her parents hadn't found her a good husband yet. As she'd suspected, they had invited a young man to her parents' party last night.

'Such a good catch, Abeer. You wouldn't have to go out to work,' Khala Huma had told her. She'd smiled politely like a good girl and spent the evening being bored by the accountant her aunt wanted her to marry.

Abeer had spent the early morning scanning the internet for flats in Maldon but the rents were far too expensive for her at the moment. Maybe if she could work her way up to a detective sergeant, she'd be able to afford to move out of her parents' and away from her aunts. They weren't even her real aunts but were elders from the village her great-grandparents had lived in about a hundred years ago and considered themselves guardians of the old life.

A knock at the door made her jump and a tall golden-haired man stepped through into the office.

'DI Edwards?' he inquired.

Abeer smirked. 'Not me. I'm just a lowly DC.'

The man smiled. He had a nice smile, friendly. 'Me too. DC Griffiths, Met Police.'

'DC Kumar,' she replied. 'Abeer.'

He stepped forward, holding out his hand. 'Doug.'

'How did you get in here?' she asked.

'No-one on the desk.'

'What can I do for you, DC Griffiths?' inquired Abeer.

'Doug, please. I'm here about the missing Maldon woman?'

Abeer looked blank. She knew nothing of a missing woman from Maldon.

'You should have had a message.'

Abeer shrugged. 'Maybe DI Edwards knows about it but she's interviewing someone in Chelmsford at the moment. She should be back here later this afternoon if you can wait.'

Doug Griffiths sighed. 'Oh, I can wait. I've been booked into a hotel. I'm here for the week apparently.'

There was an embarrassed silence while Abeer decided whether she should ask the man to stay and wait or not which was broken by Doug.

'The hotel I'm booked into doesn't do lunch. I don't suppose you could recommend anywhere?'

Abeer breathed a sigh of relief. She didn't want this stranger hanging about the office. Even though he'd shown his ID she hadn't really checked him out. He could be anyone.

'There's a nice place on the quay if you're looking for a pub lunch. The Queen's Head,' she told him.

'Pub lunch sounds ideal to me.' Doug Griffiths grinned. 'Where would this establishment actually be? I don't know where the quay is.'

'Oh, sorry. Go out of here and back to the High Street. Turn right and follow it down to St Mary's church. Turn left. The quay's in front of you.'

'And this is a good pub, is it?'

'So I'm told. My boss swears by it.'

Doug smiled his nice smile again. 'That's good enough for me, then. Thanks.' He turned and left the office leaving Abeer feeling slightly bewildered. Who was this missing woman that the Met thought was important enough to send a detective constable out here for a week? And why wasn't Ernie at the desk?

*

Charlotte Tibbs was arguing with her cook. His name was Chris but only answered to Claude, as he believed his weekend Cordon Bleu course made him a French chef. He wasn't by any stretch of the imagination the new Raymond Blanc but he was generally reliable and his cooking was good enough for the riverside pub. His biggest trouble was insisting on writing new menus in his own version of the Gallic language, something Charlotte continually tried to stop him doing. This was once again the meat at the centre of their argument. The bars weren't busy yet. It was early and the weather wasn't conducive to sitting on a terrace by the river. There would be the few locals who came in for lunch and then a slow afternoon until the workers finished and came to whet their whistles around five o'clock. There were few if any tourists at this time of the year, so she was surprised to see the tall stranger come into the back bar.

'Do you do lunch?' he asked.

'We certainly do,' replied Charlotte handing him a menu.

'I'll have the fish and chips,' said Doug, perusing the fare on offer. 'I was recommended this place by the local constabulary. Is this the place they like to hang out?'

Charlotte looked at him warily. 'Some of them come in occasionally,' she said.

'Good. For the next week, I'm one of them.' Doug smiled. 'Seconded out here from the big city.'

'Chelmsford?' asked Charlotte, feeling rather put out by this man.

Doug hung his head. 'Sorry. That was quite rude of me, wasn't it. I've never been here before; it looks like a great place. Beautiful scenery,' he added looking out at the river through the windows.

Charlotte shrugged. 'It's okay, I suppose. Anything to drink?'

'I'd better just have a Coke, I'm on duty.'

Charlotte poured his drink, and he sat at a table by the window, admiring the view. Charlotte picked up her phone and rang Anne Edwards.

Anne and Alice were heading back to Maldon. As Anne was driving, Alice answered her phone.

'Do you have some bloke seconded to you from the big city?' asked Charlotte.

Alice looked at Anne, who shrugged.

'Not that we know of, why?'

'Someone is sitting in my pub saying he's been seconded to the local constabulary.'

Alice looked at Anne again, who nodded.

'We'll be there in about ten minutes.' Alice hung up. 'Who do you think that is, then?'

'No idea. Probably one of Horobin's plans to undermine us.'

*

Abeer was starting to wonder where Anne and Alice were, it was nearly one o'clock. She hoped that DC Griffiths didn't return before they did, she wasn't sure what she was supposed to do with him. The phone rang in the office.

'Abeer, did some bloke from London come into the office this morning?' said Alice.

'There was a man calling himself DC Griffiths asking for DI Edwards before lunch. I sent him to the Queen's Head as he said he needed to eat. I hope that was right.'

'Yes, we're on our way there now. Did he say what he wanted?'

'Something about a missing Maldon woman. Why would a DC from the Met come looking for someone out here?'

'Don't know. Can you hold the fort till we're back?'

'Yes. I'm not sure what to do, though.'

Alice checked with Anne. 'Anne says can you follow up anything on the witchy woman?'

Abeer felt a shiver go through her. 'Yeah. Okay,' she said, still not sure what she was supposed to do.

'We won't be long, hopefully.' Alice disconnected and Abeer replaced the receiver.

*

'He's by the window,' said Charlotte as Anne and Alice went into the 'Members' Bar' at the front of the pub. She indicated the man in the other bar working his way through an enormous plate of battered fish and home-cooked chips.

'Do you know him?' Alice asked Anne.

'Nope.'

'Good-looking,' observed Alice. Anne looked down her nose at her, a difficult thing to do to someone at least six inches taller.

They went through to the back bar and stood by DC Griffiths' table. He wiped his mouth on a paper napkin.

'DI Edwards?' he said to Alice, who blushed and nodded her head towards Anne.

He stood up, almost knocking the small table over, and held out his hand. 'DC Doug Griffiths,' he said.

'Finish your dinner, DC Griffiths. The food's too good here to waste.'

'It is very good. I'm glad your DC recommended it.' He sat awkwardly.

'When you've finished, you can come through to the other bar. It's quieter,' she said, indicating the toddler pretending to be an aeroplane, much to the joy of its proud mother.

'You blushed,' Anne said to Alice as they sat in the Members'.

'I thought I did. I could feel the heat on my face. I don't know why.'

Anne smirked and sipped her glass of wine.

It was less than five minutes before Doug Griffiths came through to the Members'.

'It's nice in here, you're right. Much quieter.' He looked at the two women's glasses. 'Are you allowed to drink on duty?'

'What are you here for, DC Griffiths?' answered Anne, ignoring the question.

'Oh, I've been asked to help you look for this missing woman.'

'We're not looking for a missing woman, DC Griffiths.'

He sat down looking confused. He sipped his Coke. 'Did you not get a message from us about Catherine Hall?'

'We did, didn't we, DS Porter?'

Alice was sitting staring at the man, seemingly unable to speak. She nodded.

'DS Porter is a little overcome at the moment,' said Anne.

'Oh no. What's the matter?'

'You are, I think.' Anne smiled. 'Tell me again why you're here.'

Doug Griffiths was even more confused now. He'd been told that rural policing was different to London but he hadn't expected these two odd women sitting drinking in a pub in the middle of the day. He had to admit that the younger one was quite attractive but seemed to be on mute. Maybe she wasn't allowed to speak in front of her evidently brusque boss. He took out a little black notebook, flipped a few pages and started to read.

'Catherine Hall's husband was brutally murdered at their home. Their daughter, Elizabeth, died from loss of blood whilst miscarrying, as far as we can tell. Elizabeth was thirteen! Mrs Hall has not been seen since the day before the murder. She originates from Maldon and my boss believes that she is most probably hiding somewhere here. What we don't know is whether she is the murderer or a victim.'

'Murderess,' corrected Anne.

'I'm sorry.'

'The feminine tense of murderer is murderess, DC Griffiths.'

'Right.' What was this woman on? Was she still living in the nineteen-fifties? No-one used masculine and feminine terms anymore, did they? 'Anyway, I've been sent here to try and find her.'

'Good luck with that.' Anne hoped she was making it obvious that they didn't have the time or the inclination to help the Met with anything.

'DI Edwards went to school with her,' butted in Alice.

'Oh, hello. Found your voice?' commented Anne.

Doug Griffiths looked excited. 'So, you'd recognise her.'

'It was a long time ago, DC Griffiths. I expect she may not be wandering around in school uniform anymore. Plus, I didn't know her all that well.'

Doug sat quietly for a moment. He wasn't sure what his best approach was, antagonising this woman more would not be much help to his assignment.

'I suppose we could check out some of her old haunts?' suggested Alice.

Anne glared at her. She knew what was going on, Alice had developed an instant crush on this urban Adonis. He was good-looking, she had to admit, but there was no time or money in her budget to look for a suspect/victim in another force's case, just to satisfy her junior's lust.

'If she is on the run, for whatever reason, I doubt she'll be hanging about at the local pubs, which is all I remember her doing.'

'Where did she live?' Griffiths asked Alice.

She looked pleadingly at Anne.

'Do we have a budget allowance from the Met for helping you out?' Anne rested her head on her fists.

Doug Griffiths smiled. 'I doubt it, but I could check.'

Anne remained staring at him.

'I can't do it now,' he protested.

Anne shrugged and raised her eyebrows. Doug took out his phone.

'No signal.' He looked surprised.

'We're in the country, Sergeant. Outside the front door's the best place.' Anne pointed through the windows to where several cars were parked against the pub's wall.

Doug stood up and went outside.

'Stop it, now, Alice,' warned Anne. 'He's most probably married.'

'I'm just trying to be helpful,' she answered, grinning.

*

Abeer Kumar decided she'd better visit Agnes Waterhouse's cottage again. She had no phone number for her, she suspected she didn't use anything as modern as a phone anyway, although she did have a website, she reminded herself. Whatever, she had no other way of getting in touch. She stood outside the quaint dwelling. There was a bell hanging from an ornate black metal hook in the shape of what Abeer assumed was a spirit of some sort. The bell itself had a bearded face cast into it, a metal ball hung on a chain inside it that Abeer used to make a clamorous noise that would most probably wake the dead – but then maybe that was the intention, she thought. A shiver went through her. This seemed to happen every time she thought about this woman. Taking a deep breath, she rang the bell again.

'You after the witch?' came a voice from behind her.

Abeer turned round and showed her warrant card. 'I'm looking for Harriet Adcock.'

'Ah, 'bout time too. Come to arrest her?'

Abeer was looking at a large man, his hair cut short, his belly hanging over his jeans and a short-sleeved tee shirt revealing a large tattoo on his muscly upper arm.

'Who are you?' she asked.

'Neighbour.' He moved closer to her. 'It were 'er what done it,' he whispered.

Feeling as though she was in a bad Agatha Christie movie, Abeer resisted the urge to laugh.

'Done what, Mr...?'

'Barber, Jed Barber. It were 'er what killed that kid.'

'What kid, Mr Barber?'

'Up the leper 'ospital. She's always 'anging about there.' He leaned into Abeer again. 'I seen that boy in 'er 'ouse.'

Abeer indicated the cottage and Jed Barber nodded.

'When was this?'

'She 'as 'em 'ere all the time. Youngsters. Don't know what they get up to but it ain't nowt good.'

'You mean she holds some sort of meetings?'

Jed Barber nodded again. 'In 'er coven.' He pointed to the cottage.

Abeer chose not to point out that a coven wasn't a place. 'Do you have a contact number, Mr Barber. I may need to talk to you again.'

'If it got 'er put away, I'd do whatever you want but I can't afford no phone. I lives just there.' He pointed to a ramshackle building a few doors away. 'She'll be over at the leper 'ospital now, I expect. That's where she 'angs out doing 'er evil deeds.'

Abeer thanked him and went back to her car. She could see Jed Barber staring at the cottage, a look of disgust on his face. She also noticed that he didn't go too near. What was he afraid of? Was this just superstition or did he have another reason to get Harriet Adcock 'put away'? He spat on the floor outside her gate and went back to his own hovel. Abeer followed him with her eyes. Could Abeer believe anything he'd told her? Did this witch have youngsters in her house, and if so, that wasn't illegal in itself, was it? Maybe they were interested in the supernatural or something?

She drove up to St Giles' leper hospital. Ernie Kemp was on duty there again as it was still a crime scene.

'Come to relieve me, Abeer?' he asked as she went over to him.

'Don't be silly. Why is this still a crime scene, anyway? Surely forensics have finished, haven't they?'

'I think I'm here more to keep people away. There's been reports of some odd characters hanging about.'

'Agnes Waterhouse?' suggested Abeer.

'She's the least of the problems. She's harmless enough, it's the bovver boys that want to cause…well…bovver.'

'Jed Barber, by any chance?'

'Oh, you know him, do you?'

'We've just been introduced. He thinks our Agnes murdered the kid.'

'I know. I can't believe that's true. She wouldn't hurt a fly – unless it was to put it into a cauldron with spotted toads.' He opened his eyes wide.

'Is she here?' asked Abeer, ignoring his childish behaviour.

'There's no-one allowed in,' said Ernie cautiously.

'Who's that then?' Abeer pointed to where Agnes Waterhouse AKA Harriet Adcock was stooping down by some bushes inside the grounds of the hospital.

'I've told her not to do that. Oi, Agnes.'

'It's okay Ernie. I'll go to her. Can you let me in?'

Ernie sighed and unlocked the metal gate.

'How does she get in?' asked Abeer.

Ernie shrugged. 'She's a witch.' He smirked.

'I'm not doing anything illegal, DC Kumar,' said Agnes without looking round.

'That's not strictly true but I need to talk to you again.'

She turned round, a small trowel in her hand. 'Go on, then.'

Abeer looked around. It was secluded and as this was not an official interview, she could see no reason not to talk here.

'Do you come here often?' she asked.

Agnes grinned. 'Are you chatting me up?'

Abeer didn't understand. 'No.'

'I do come here a lot. I have for many years.' She waved her hand across the bushes. 'These are my babies. My herbs. I'm carrying on the tradition started by the monks.'

'So were you here when the boy was murdered?' Abeer held her nerve and stared into Agnes Waterhouse's eyes.

A sly grin spread across her face. 'Are you accusing me of something, DC Kumar?'

'No. I'm looking for someone to help me find out what happened and why.'

'The boy – and the girl – were desecrating holy ground. They should have known better.'

Agnes's reverence to consecrated ground had been intriguing her since they'd met at Agnes's cottage. Surely a witch would be against anything holy.

'Why would that bother you? Aren't you a Pagan?'

Agnes laughed. 'It doesn't bother me but I'm not a Pagan and I don't dance with the devil.'

'So, were you here that day?'

Agnes gave the impression of thinking long and hard. 'I would have been here but earlier in the day. There was a strange atmosphere, I remember. I knew there was something bad going to happen, so I left.'

'Have you ever invited young people to your house at all?'

Another laugh. 'You have been talking to Jed, I see. Yes, I hold educational evenings for local people – young and old – who want to know more about witchcraft. You see witchcraft is not a bad thing. It's not evil. You're a woman, you must realise how our society puts us down. It's nothing new. James the First was scared of women and used the fear of witchcraft to suppress us. That's when the witch hunts started. But witches have nearly always been good people – midwives, healers – but certain men were afraid of us becoming more powerful, so they concocted stories about devil worship and the like. Any group of more than two women were seen as dangerous. Not much has changed, sadly. People like Jed Barber even blame us for COVID, can you believe?'

Abeer listened patiently. She could sympathise to a certain extent but found Agnes's claims hard to credit. 'Have you seen any other people desecrating this place?'

'All the time. Very few people have any respect these days.'

'But none of those was killed.'

Agnes grinned. 'That's very true,' she said.

'So why that young man, do you think?'

The witch shrugged. 'Bad luck. Wrong time, wrong place.'

Abeer studied the woman in front of her. She surmised she must be in her sixties but wearing extremely well for her age, her skin sleek with no wrinkles, a slight sheen on her cheeks. No make-up that Abeer could ascertain. 'You know you shouldn't be in here, don't you?'

Agnes raised one shoulder. 'I'm not hurting anyone. Someone needs to tend my plants.'

Abeer left the ruins. Ernie Kemp smiled as she left.

'I'll keep an eye on her, Abeer. She won't do any harm.'

Abeer couldn't be sure about that. She had a bad feeling about this woman.

'DC Kumar?' Agnes voice echoed round the remains of the old hospital. 'You might want to have a look at this?'

Abeer and Ernie both hurried over to where Agnes Waterhouse was standing pointing at a plastic carrier bag from a well-known supermarket.

'Can't do much about people dumping rubbish, Agnes,' said Ernie. 'That's the council's job.'

'Depends what's in it, I suppose,' said the witch.

Ernie reached over and picked up a handle of the bag. Brownish, red liquid spilled onto the ground, and he dropped it.

'That's blood, that is,' said Agnes.

CHAPTER NINE

Doug Griffiths stood by the door of the CID office at Maldon Police Station. There didn't seem to be anywhere to sit as DI Edwards and DS Porter were taking up the available chairs. DS Porter had offered her seat but he'd thought it appropriate to refuse.

DI Edwards looked up from her computer. 'The thing is, DC Griffiths, even with the few hundred quid you tell me the Met have deigned to afford us, we just don't have the manpower.'

'Womanpower,' said Doug.

Anne glared at him. 'We have a serious murder case on our hands, DC Griffiths. A young boy was stabbed to death. That is taking up all our time.'

'Maybe I could help you,' said Doug.

'I'm sure the Met would love that.' Anne looked back at her screen.

'The Met needn't know.' Doug took a step towards Anne's desk. 'I'm here for a week, whatever. I don't know if Catherine Hall is in Maldon or not but from what I can see it's not a very big place.'

'It's big enough for the people living here, DC Griffiths,' griped Anne.

'And getting bigger all the time,' added Alice, referring to the new estates that seemed to be springing up like some of Agnes Waterhouse's herbs.

Doug sighed. It appeared that whatever he said, DI Edwards would turn it against him. He could understand that she might feel undermined if the Met had expected her team to drop everything for their case but he could do without being put down every time he opened his mouth.

'That's not what I meant. Look, I know you're upset with me being here. I wouldn't want someone coming onto my patch and interfering which is why I'm offering to help.'

Anne looked over at Alice whose eyes were pleading with her to let Doug help. 'What do you think DC Griffiths could help us with, DS Porter?'

Excitement beamed over her features. 'I could show him the crime scene?' she suggested.

Anne's phone rang. Abeer Kumar's voice was agitated and she spoke rapidly. Anne listened patiently.

'Okay, I'll send someone over.' She put her phone down. 'Looks like your wish has been granted, DS Porter. DC Kumar seems to have found something at the crime scene. Maybe you could go and have a look?' Anne looked over to Doug. 'You're welcome to take DC Griffiths with you but try and remember you're working.'

Alice's cheeks turned a darker shade of pink as she stood up and manoeuvred herself round her desk. 'Would that be alright, DC Griffiths?'

He nodded. 'Doug,' he said. 'My name's Doug. Thank you…' He raised his eyebrows to Anne.

'Mine's DI Edwards,' she told him dismissively.

The two of them left, leaving Anne shaking her head. Her phone rang and her heart sank as she heard June Goddard's voice. On top of everything else, Amelia Goddard had gone missing. Her mother was understandably distraught. They hadn't noticed the girl's absence until that morning, thinking she had shut herself in her room, and she'd left her alone on her husband's advice. He'd said she needed time to get over Harry's demise. June Goddard was now not talking to her husband, blaming his lack of compassion over Harry's death being the cause of their daughter having gone missing. She was on her way to the police station.

Anne greeted the woman at the door, apologising for the lack of facilities at the Maldon office, before taking her through to her office.

'I can get a coffee from the council offices if you'd like,' Anne offered.

June Goddard shook her head. Her eyes were red raw, her face drawn, her hair limply clinging to the side of her face.

'So when exactly did you last see Amelia?' Anne had a notebook in her hand.

'The day before last. Well, morning, really. About eight o'clock. Do you know where she is?'

Anne looked up, confused. 'Why do think I would know that?'

June shrugged. 'I thought she might have come to you.'

'Why?'

'Do you know who killed Harry?'

The beseeching look in her eyes made Anne's stomach churn. This woman was suffering deeply. Anne hated having to deal with these situations. There was nothing she could do to offer any comfort. 'We don't know yet,' was all she could say.

'Reuben Elbrow.' June looked into Anne's eyes. 'Have you tried him?'

'I don't know who Reuben Elbrow is, June.'

'He's Harry's brother.'

*

Amelia did not have a clue as to how long she'd been in this place. She was still tied by the rope to some sort of metal ring embedded in the wall. Dignity was in her past. All her bodily functions had taken place in full view of this woman who was calling herself Mummy. She couldn't tell what this place was. The walls were studded with stones, boulders held together with mud, the floor just bare earth. Small areas of dim light emanated from the ceiling, which also let in some air, but the atmosphere was musty, and her chest felt like she'd been breathing nothing but car fumes. She felt dirty. She wanted a shower and a change of clothes. The skirt she was wearing was covered in mud and her sweater likewise. Her underwear had disappeared, taken away by the Mummy woman. She felt ashamed and cold. The nights were particularly cold and even once she'd let the Mummy woman hold her throughout the night, there wasn't a great deal of warmth. She'd cried out all the tears she had in her. The woman had just sat next to her being sympathetic. But it was her fault she was here, wasn't it? Maybe it wasn't. Maybe they were both prisoners here. Maybe this was some sort of gaol. It was the witch. She had captured them. What was she going to do with them?

The Mummy woman wasn't here at present. There were times when she disappeared. Amelia didn't know where to but she always returned with food of some sort and bottles of water. She didn't know where she got them from. Last time she had brought some candles but they weren't lit at the moment. Amelia hadn't been able to move more than the few feet her tether allowed. What did they want to do with her, whoever was keeping her in here? No-one had actually tried to assault her in any way – other than tying her to the ring in the wall – no sexual advances even though she was all but naked from the waist down. Her period had started and needless to say there were no pads or tampons anywhere. The soil next to where she was sitting was stained and wet. From somewhere, her eyes found tears again and she wept.

*

Doug and Alice arrived at the ruins. Ernie Kemp and Abeer Kumar were still there guarding the gates. There was no sign of Agnes Waterhouse.

'What have you found, Abeer?' asked Alice. 'This is DC Griffiths,' she added, indicating the man next to her that Ernie was eyeing suspiciously.

Doug held out his hand which Ernie took reluctantly. 'Hello,' he said.

Ernie didn't answer and let Abeer lead them across the ground to where the bloody carrier bag lay amongst the herb garden.

'Agnes Waterhouse says it's blood. I wouldn't know. I left it where we found it,' Abeer informed them.

'And where's Agnes now?'

'She had to leave.'

Doug was making his way through the longer undergrowth to the other side of the herb garden. He put on his nitrile gloves, got down on his haunches and, with a stick, lifted one handle of the bag. It wobbled precariously as he lifted it from the greenery and peered inside.

'It's just liquid. There's nothing else in there. No flesh or body parts,' he told Alice and Abeer.

'Is it blood?' asked Alice.

Doug looked into the bag, being careful not to touch it. 'Could be,' he said.

'Better get it over to Chelmsford. Can you manage not to spill it?' Alice looked at the bag tipping alarmingly.

Doug slipped his gloved fingers through the handles and made his way back across the herbs.

'How are you going to get that to Chelmsford?' asked Ernie. 'Wouldn't want it my car.'

'I have an evidence bag, it can go in that,' replied Alice.

Doug Griffiths carefully transferred the bag from his hand into the large evidence bag Alice was holding open for him, making sure to keep it upright.

'I'll hold it on my lap. Where are we taking it?' he asked as they got into Alice's car.

Alice had to think for a moment. Really, she ought to take it to Anne but it was so precarious to transport she decided to go straight to Chelmsford.

'Can you let Anne know what we're doing, Abeer?'

DC Kumar nodded. Doug sat in the passenger seat cradling the bag of blood and hoping that Alice was a careful driver.

*

'Linda Ellis told me Harry was an only child.' Anne hadn't a clue as to why June Goddard was suddenly bringing up a brother.

'They kept it quiet. I don't think the other one was their biological child. As far as I know they fostered this boy when they lived in London,' June explained.

'When was this, do you know?'

June shook her head. 'They moved to Maldon about seven years ago. The foster boy didn't come with them and they never speak about him, apparently. Harry had mentioned him to Amelia who told me with the strict proviso that I never told a soul. I thought I ought to let you know, though, in the circumstances.'

'Why do you think this boy…' Anne looked at the notes she'd made. '…Reuben Elbrow, killed his brother?'

'I don't know. Amelia said they hadn't got on when they lived in London. He was one of the reasons Allan and Linda moved.'

'And just left Reuben?'

'He was older than Harry, about seven or eight years older. Reuben would have been over eighteen when they left.'

'That still doesn't mean he's likely to come out to Maldon, find the boy, and kill him.'

'I don't know. I'm worried he's got Amelia now.'

'I'll see what we can find out about Reuben Elbrow, June but there's no reason to think he's had any contact with Amelia, surely. Had they ever met?'

June shook her head and sighed. 'I'm desperate, DI Edwards. I want to know where my daughter is.'

'Would you like to report her as missing?'

'I thought I'd just done that.'

Anne printed out a form and put it before June.

'Is there anywhere she would be likely to visit? A relative? Friend?'

June shook her head again, tears falling onto the report she was slowly filling in.

'Could you make a list, please. Anyone at all that you can think of.' Anne turned to her computer and put in a search for Reuben Elbrow. It didn't seem like a common name, and sure enough, there were two entries she could find – police reports from some years ago concerning fracas that had taken place in East London, both some sort of demonstration it appeared. Reuben Elbrow had been arrested for assaulting a police officer and had spent the night in the cells. No charges were brought in either case. She was pretty sure June was clutching at straws. But why had Linda Ellis said Harry was an only child? Strictly speaking, she supposed, Harry *was* their only child if Reuben was fostered. She suddenly became aware of June Goddard's head collapsing onto the desk, her shoulders heaving. Anne edged her way out from behind her desk and went over to her, putting her hand on her back.

'Are you okay, June.'

She threw Anne's hand from her and turned her head. 'Of course I'm not okay. My daughter's missing. Her boyfriend was horribly murdered and you don't seem to care.'

'I do care, June. I'm chasing up Reuben Elbrow right now but there's not much to go on. Was Harry still in touch with Reuben, do you know?'

June Goddard stood up, making Anne move out of the way. 'Just do your job and find my little girl before I find whoever's abducted her. Because, if I do, I'll be on a murder charge.' She stormed out of the office.

Anne sat on the chair June had vacated and put her head in her hands. When she'd first started in the force she'd wondered if she would ever stop feeling guilty but she'd known some time ago that the answer was no. Guilt was part of the job, she'd been told as much by her boss in Chester when she was on her first assignment as a lowly constable. Not much had changed she realised. There was no reason for her to feel this way, it wasn't her fault Amelia had gone missing. Surely as a parent you wouldn't let your distressed daughter shut herself in her bedroom for forty-eight hours without checking on her, would you? She couldn't be sure; she'd never been a parent but what about food? Were they happy for her not to eat for two days? Her musings were interrupted by the door opening and Abeer Kumar coming in.

'You look like you have the weight of the world on your shoulders, Ma'am.'

'I feel like I have, Abeer and it's Anne when no-one's around, remember.' Anne sat up. 'Amelia Goddard's gone missing and her mother's blaming Harry Ellis's brother who I didn't know existed. Can you organise uniforms to do a house to house, see if anyone's seen her,'

'Yes.' Abeer stood looking as though she had more to say.

Anne raised her eyebrows. 'Oh, what did you find up at the ruins?'

'It was a carrier bag with blood in it. Liquid blood, not just stains. DC Porter asked me to tell you they've taken it to Chelmsford.'

Anne sighed. That would lead to more trouble from DCI Horobin, no doubt. 'Has the Met officer gone with her?'

'DC Griffiths? Yes,' confirmed Abeer.

Anne went over to the whiteboard on the wall and took up her pen. A line had been drawn down the middle and, on the left side, HARRY ELLIS inside a ring in large letters; then a line across to another ring in which was written AMELIA GODDARD; near the bottom Anne added Reuben Elbrow in smaller letters.

'Who's Reuben Elbrow?' asked Abeer.

'Harry's supposed brother. His parents fostered him some years ago according to June Goddard.' She stood back from the wall. 'Who or what links these people?'

'Agnes Waterhouse?'

Anne included the witch's name, followed by THOMAS LLOYD and the names of his parents.

'Harry and Amelia's parents?'

Their names joined the others. On the right-hand side Anne inscribed the names of CATHERINE HALL/WILLIS; ELIZABETH HALL; JACK HALL and East London. She then drew a line from East London to Reuben Elbrow.

'Why?' asked Abeer.

'No reason really. Reuben lived in East London with the Ellis's.' Anne shrugged her shoulders.

'But the two cases aren't related, are they?'

'I doubt it but I'm sceptical as to why DC Griffiths has been sent here. I suspect something dodgy, probably emanating from DCI Horobin.'

Abeer grinned. 'I think you're being a bit paranoid, if I may say, Ma'am.'

Anne grinned back. 'You may not say, DC Kumar.'

*

Alice Porter had had a change of mind as she'd driven towards Chelmsford Police Station and detoured to Broomfield hospital. A hands-free phone call had confirmed that Sarah Clifford would be happy to look at the blood bag and let them know pretty quickly if it was human or animal.

'You're quite impressive, DS Porter,' said Doug Griffiths as Alice ended the call.

'Thank you, DC Griffiths,' she muttered, embarrassed by his compliment.

'Doug,' he said.

'Oh yes, sorry, Doug.'

'And you are Alice?'

She nodded.

'Do I intimidate you, Alice?' he said.

'No. I think you're very nice.' Alice could feel the blood rushing to her cheeks. Why was she behaving like this? She wasn't a teenager.

'Thank you. I reciprocate.'

Alice let out an involuntary giggle.

'See, I knew you had a sense of humour. Look, I'm here for at least a week. If you have an evening off, I'd love to share a drink or two with you. I'm likely to be a bit lonely.'

Alice almost crashed the car. 'Are you asking me out?' she said, controlling herself and the vehicle.

Doug laughed. 'I hadn't thought of it like that but I wouldn't mind getting to know you out of uniform, so to speak.'

'I don't wear uni…' Alice laughed and blushed some more. 'Let's get this blood to Sarah first,' she said and concentrated on her driving for the last few minutes as they approached the hospital.

Sarah was waiting in reception when they arrived. 'I don't have long,' she said. 'But I'll see what I can do. Should be able to tell if it's human.'

Alice followed Sarah into her lab, Doug bringing up the rear, carrying the bag of blood. Once in the lab, Sarah took a swab and dipped it into the liquid, before smearing some onto a slide, which she placed under a microscope.

'It's human I'm afraid but the colour is a very deep red, which is strange. I can do a test to check why.' Sarah took another swab and went to drawer which contained boxes of some sort of kit used for testing. She dropped a couple of drops of the blood onto a small plastic strip and waited for a few minutes, staring at it. Eventually she nodded. 'Shall I do a DNA on it?' asked Sarah.

'If you could.'

'It is related to an urgent case, I suspect.' Sarah raised her eyebrows. Alice smiled, noncommittedly. 'Tell DI Edwards that's a bottle of wine she owes me. I'll email the results as soon as I get them.'

'Thanks, Sarah. If Anne doesn't buy, then I will.'

Alice and Doug left the hospital and returned to her car.

'I'd never get away with that in London,' said Doug.

'Good job we're not in London then,' said Alice as she headed back towards Maldon.

'How about that drink? Are you finished now?'

Alice glanced at him. 'Don't you actually have any work to do here?' she inquired.

'Not tonight. I'm starting the hard bit tomorrow.'

'Which is?'

'Dealing with your boss?'

Alice grunted. 'Well, DC Griffiths, I'll have to check with my boss if I'm available tonight.'

Doug laughed. 'Well, I am if you are.'

*

Anne and Abeer were still in the office when Doug and Alice arrived back. Alice explained they'd got Sarah to test the blood. Doug still had the bag in his hands.

'Why have you brought that here?' Anne asked him.

'We didn't know what to do with it,' Alice answered for him.

'Stick it under the desk. It's cold enough in here. I'm through for the day. Who's coming to the Queen's?'

Alice looked at Doug.

'Am I invited?' he said.

'If you're here to work with us then yes, otherwise no,' replied Anne.

'He's been very helpful this afternoon,' chirped Alice.

Anne grinned. 'Better come along then, DC Griffiths. With your London Weighting it must be your round.'

They had been in the pub for less than an hour when Alice's phone rang. The blush in her cheek faded and her eyebrows lowered into a confused frown as she listened to Sarah Clifford.

'The blood in that bag is menstrual blood,' she said.

CHAPTER TEN

'Why would anyone leave a bag of menstrual blood in a field?'

Anne, Alice and Abeer were back in the office. They'd remained in the pub the previous night for only a couple of drinks – both rounds bought by Doug Griffiths' London Weighting – but the atmosphere was not really conducive to a good night out. Anne had instructed them not to discuss Sarah's news in the pub and the evening consisted mostly of Alice looking longingly at the 'Man from the Met', as Anne was now calling him. The bloodied carrier bag was still sat under Anne's desk; no-one had looked into it this morning.

'More to the point,' said Alice. 'No-one was supposed to be in the ruins.'

'Is it still a crime scene?' asked Abeer.

'No, but you need permission from the council to go through the gate.'

'We all know no-one takes any notice of that, Alice,' said Anne. 'Where exactly was this bag found?'

'Behind the tree, in the witch's herb garden,' Alice said.

It was a thought that all three of them had at the same time. They looked from one to another before Anne said, 'Bring the witch in, Abeer.'

'What arrest her?'

'No, ask her politely to help us with our inquiries.' Anne smiled.

Abeer felt the obligatory shiver go through her. Why was it always her who had to deal with Agnes Waterhouse? 'Do you want me to do it now?' she asked.

Anne nodded. Abeer slowly stood up and made her way out of the door.

Alice was on the internet. 'Menstrual blood can be used as a fertiliser; did you know that?'

'I haven't had a garden for over twenty years Alice, and if I did that's the last thing I'd put on it.'

'Maybe that's what Agnes Waterhouse was using it for.'

'I would suspect that Agnes Waterhouse is past the age of menstruation.'

'It can also be used as a potion to make someone fall in love with you?'

'What are you looking at?' Anne indicated Alice's laptop.

'It's the witch's website. There's all sorts of uses for menstrual blood apparently. Dabbing some on one's solar plexus can relieve tension; putting it in tea can calm the energy created by someone you've had a row with; and if you put some coffee beans up…oh no, I can't believe that.'

'And I don't want to know but if I find you offering young DC Griffiths some coffee in the near future…' Anne started to giggle.

Alice didn't join in. 'Stop it,' she said.

'Let me know when Agnes is available. I have to visit Great Totham again.

*

'I hear Amelia's gone missing now,' said Linda Ellis pouring tea from a china pot.

Anne nodded. They were sitting in the conservatory of the grand house. Edwin was out doing voluntary work and Linda was alone.

'How did you get on with her parents, Linda?'

There was a pause, Linda looking deep into her teacup. 'We used to get on well but things got a bit awkward.'

Anne raised her eyebrows and waited.

'Amelia's father didn't like Harry seeing his daughter,' said June eventually.

'And you were happy about it?'

Another pause. 'They were just kids. There was nothing serious going on.'

Anne doubted that but chose not to comment. 'Why did you tell me Harry was an only child, Linda?'

'He was,' she insisted.

'Reuben Elbrow?' queried Anne.

Linda physically slumped on the wicker chair. 'I don't know him,' she said.

'You do. You and Edwin were his foster parents.'

Linda put her head in her hands. 'We don't talk about him. He's in prison.'

'Where was he in prison, Linda, do you know?'

She shook her head. Her cheeks were wet as she looked up at Anne. 'He was a problem child. We did our best for him but he got in with a bad crowd – something political – I'm afraid we cast him out.'

'What sort of politics?'

'He was anti everything. Everything that we stood for, you know. Good living, working hard and improving one's life. A sense of ambition, aspiration, he had none of those things after all we'd done for him. All he wanted to do was to go on demonstrations. We tried to stop him but couldn't so as soon as he was old enough we let him go.'

'To where?'

Linda shrugged her shoulders. 'I think he found a hostel or something.'

'And you didn't care?'

She stared at Anne. 'Oh, we cared. We'd cared for him since he was a young child. We did our bit. He didn't want to know.'

'Do you have a picture of Reuben?' Anne asked her.

She shook her head. 'He's not in our life anymore.'

'How did he get on with Harry?'

There was a long pause. 'They hated each other.'

*

Agnes Waterhouse had no problem coming to help with Maldon Police's inquiries she told Abeer and was happy to accompany her to the offices at the council. Anne had arranged for one of the rooms to be used as an interview space. There was no official recording device, but CCTV was active in that room.

Alice and Anne were already seated and waiting when Abeer showed Agnes in. Anne dismissed the detective constable and invited Agnes to sit at the table. The only other things in the room were a few old grey plastic chairs, a filing cabinet and a bookcase that held several old-looking box files. The CCTV camera was high up in a corner of the walls.

'Thank you for coming so promptly. Harriet…'

'Agnes. My name's Agnes.' The witch interrupted Anne.

'Yes, sorry. We are not recording this but there is CCTV in this room, is that alright with you?'

Agnes nodded. 'I've nothing to hide.'

'You have a herb garden in the grounds of St Giles hospital, I believe.'

'I have a healing plant area, yes.'

'But it's private ground, you shouldn't really be able to come and go as you please. Do you have permission from the council?' Alice queried.

Agnes Waterhouse laughed. 'It's not private ground. It was given to the people of Maldon by Henry II. The council are just custodians, they have no right to prevent anyone entering with good intent.'

'Good intent?'

'An altruistic person. My healing plants are available for anyone to use, as long as they know how.'

'But you still need permission to go in there,' Alice persisted.

'Are you arresting me for trespass?'

'No, Agnes,' Anne pointed out. 'We're not arresting you for anything.' Yet, she nearly added.

'Do you use menstrual blood?' asked Alice.

Agnes grinned. 'For what?'

'I don't know. Love potions? Stress relief?'

Agnes laughed. 'You've been reading my website.'

'It is mentioned.'

'In the historical section, I think you'll find. Some witches still advocate using menstrual fluids, but I don't. Plus, with the greatest respect, I'm a bit past looking for a lover.'

'Can you explain why a carrier bag with menstrual blood was found in the middle of your herb patch?' Anne looked the woman in the eyes.

'You'd be surprised at the things I find besmirching that sacred ground,' came the reply.

'Did you know the blood in that carrier bag was menstrual?' Alice leant forward, her elbows on the table, her chin resting on her hands.

'No.'

'So you weren't thinking of using it for anything?'

Agnes laughed again. 'What are you accusing me of?'

The two police officers just stared at her.

Agnes stood up. 'Would you like me to strip naked so you can check for Devil's marks? Would you like to prick me to see if I feel pain? Throw me in the river to see if I float?'

'Sit down, Agnes. As I said, we're not accusing you of anything. We need your help. Why would anyone collect menstrual blood in a carrier bag, do you think?'

Agnes sat down and shrugged. 'Have you seen the price of sanitary products?'

'Do you use menstrual blood in any of your potions?' asked Alice, ignoring Agnes's remark.

'It's a very powerful fluid.'

'But do you use it?'

Agnes shook her head. 'It only really works if it's your own and sadly I'm dried up.'

'What about your students?' suggested Anne.

'I wouldn't know. All the women have the power if they know how to use it but to be honest, it's a bit too precious to put in a carrier bag and chuck it away. It can be frozen or dried for future use if anyone can be bothered. I wouldn't imagine any of my girls would.'

'What about any male members?' asked Alice.

'They tend not to menstruate.'

'But their girlfriends or wives presumably do. What if one of those wanted to make a potion with a girlfriend's fluid?'

Agnes shook her head. 'It wouldn't work so it would be pointless.'

'Which could be why it was thrown away?' ventured Alice.

'Harry Ellis used to come to your meetings, didn't he?' said Anne.

'He's unlikely to be the culprit, he is dead, in case you'd forgotten.'

Anne had an urge to slap the woman but managed to restrain herself. Agnes was right, of course, Harry couldn't have dumped the bag, it hadn't been there before.

'Did he attend your meetings, Agnes?'

'He came twice. He seemed to think it was funny to take the piss. When he turned up the second time, he wore a pointed hat and a mask with a warty nose and chin. As you can probably see, we don't look like that outside of Hollywood. I threw him out.'

'When was this?'

'A few weeks ago.'

Anne glanced at Alice.

'So not long before he was killed,' Alice said.

Agnes laughed again. 'If I killed everyone who thought witchcraft was a bit quirky, there wouldn't be many people left in Maldon.'

'Have you always lived in Maldon?' Anne asked.

'Born and bred,' replied Agnes.

'Did you ever know someone called Catherine Hall or Catherine Willis?'

'Cat Willis? Yes, she used to come to my classes but lost interest. Seemed to prefer The Girl Guides for some strange reason.'

'Have you seen her recently?'

Agnes smirked. 'Cat Willis? What would she be doing here?'

'She's gone missing.'

'Can't see her coming back here. She hated the place, couldn't wait to marry some rich bugger and get out.'

'Do you know someone called Reuben Elbrow?'

Agnes answered immediately in the negative.

Anne leaned forward and leant on the table. She sighed. 'Agnes, I'm going to ask you a question and I'd like you to answer it honestly, without any sarcasm.'

Agnes raised her eyebrows.

'Probably against my better nature, I'd like you to help us. I can arrange for you to attend your herb garden without being apprehended. Whatever you believe to be the case, as far as the law is concerned, that land belongs to Maldon District Council and you have been trespassing.'

'No, I have not.'

Anne ignored her. 'However, it would be good to have someone keeping an eye out for anyone who shouldn't be there. People with bags of blood, for instance, or sharp knives, or ghostly apparitions. Do you think you could do that for us? Keep watch over your sacred ground?'

Agnes looked suspicious. 'I can't be there all the time.'

'I know, but the times you are, could you let us know if there's anything happening that shouldn't be?'

Agnes smiled her assent.

'And, if you happen to see Cat Willis anywhere, which I know is unlikely, let us know immediately, okay?' Alice added.

'What do I get from it?'

Anne smiled. 'You get to attend your herbs without risk of arrest.'

*

'What were you trying to do, Anne?' Alice and Anne were back in the office with Abeer.

'Get some voluntary help?' Anne replied as she headed towards the whiteboard. 'Who had a reason to kill Harry Ellis? However obscure.'

'Agnes Waterhouse,' Alice and Abeer answered in unison.

Anne underlined her name in red.

'Is that it?' Anne turned to her colleagues.

'Well, no. There's Thomas Lloyd but I don't think it's him,' said Alice. 'Bob Shepherd?'

Both names were underlined.

'Reuben Elbrow?' suggested Abeer.

'Who is that?' Alice hadn't been present when Anne had added his name to the board.

'Harry's brother.' Anne also underlined Edwin Ellis and Amelia Goddard.

'You're not serious,' said Alice. 'His father and his girlfriend?'

'Until we have some evidence, we need to consider everyone.'

'Agnes Waterhouse suggested it could be drugged-up youths,' put in Abeer.

Anne drew another circle and added 'local junkies'.

'Anyone else?' asked Anne.

A knock at the door delayed anyone from answering as Doug Griffiths walked in.

'Good morning, all,' he said chirpily.

Anne looked at her watch. 'Do you only turn up when it's lunchtime?' she said.

Doug looked at his own timepiece. 'Oh, so it is. Sorry, I had a Zoom meeting with the boss.'

'Any progress?' Alice inquired.

Doug shook his head. 'No, and I'm stuck here until I find something positive, apparently. If I was paranoid, I'd say my boss didn't want me there.'

Alice couldn't help smiling.

'Well, lunch at the Queen's Head, then,' said Anne.

Doug shuffled on his feet. 'Er…my London Weighting isn't that big, you know.'

Anne grinned. 'Don't worry, Constable. We can buy our own. We're not total freeloaders out here in the sticks.'

*

Agnes Waterhouse wasn't sure what she'd agreed to. Fundamentally she was against fraternising with authorities of any kind and yet, here she was helping the police force, of all people. She'd spent the last hour cleaning the graffiti that had appeared on her front door – not for the first time – and was angry. She ought to report the vandalism to the police but she knew they wouldn't do anything about it.

However, helping the police with their problems meant she wasn't going to be bothered as she attended to her beloved plants and revelled in the peace she found in the ruins. It appeared that they wanted to stop the wrong people infiltrating the chapel of St Giles, which could only be a good thing. That's all that was left now, just the chapel, even though they still called it the leper hospital. Whatever remains there were of the leper hospital had long disappeared underground. She wandered up the High Street, along Spital Road to where Ernie Kemp still stood on guard.

'Don't you have anything better to do, Ernie?' she asked him.

'My life consists of doing what I'm told,' he replied.

'Open the gate for me, then, will you? I'm getting too old to leap over fences.'

'You're not allowed in, Agnes.'

'Oh, but I am. Ask your DI.'

Ernie looked at her quizzically.

'I'm helping with your case, constable.'

Ernie took out his radio, received confirmation of Agnes's new responsibility and was told to return to the front desk at the station as St Giles was no longer considered a crime scene.

*

In the pub across the road from the ruins sat three men, in a corner, under the dart board,

'She'll be over there now,' said one of them.

'I'm not sure,' said another.

'Scared?' said the third.

'She's a witch.'

The other two laughed. 'Have one more. Bit of Dutch courage, that's what you need,' said the first, and he went to the bar.

'What about the police?'

'It's not a crime scene anymore. I saw old Ernie Kemp taking down the police tape and going off in a huff.'

Less than an hour later, the three men entered the ruins of St Giles by way of the gap in the hedge.

CHAPTER ELEVEN

'Could I see Amelia's room, do you think?'

Anne was standing in the lounge of the Goddard house. She hadn't been inside any of the new houses, only Alice's flat and this house had no more atmosphere than that did. The estate had just been a field when Anne was growing up. She'd played in it with the few friends she'd had from Maldon. Now it was covered in breezeblock rectangles, all part of the expansion of the small market town.

'Do you have a warrant?' asked Allan Goddard.

'No, I don't, Mr Goddard. I'm looking for any reason your daughter may have gone missing and there could be something in her room to help. Does she have a laptop?'

June Goddard nodded. 'And a phone, which she hasn't taken with her, it's in her room.'

Anne waited for permission to go into the girl's bedroom. Eventually Allan gave way to his wife's angry stare. 'It's private. Even I don't go in there.'

'We need all the help we can get, Allan.' June kept staring at her husband, her hands on her hips. The tension between them was palpable.

He shrugged. 'I'll come in with you,' he told Anne.

'No problem,' she replied. Anne left her bag on the floor by the sofa and started up the stairs. She'd far rather Allan wasn't with her especially as he'd apparently never been in Amelia's room before – if that was true – as going into a teenage girl's domain might be a bit of a shock for him. He opened the door and let Anne and June go in. He stayed in the doorway. It was a clean, brightly painted room. There were no posters or anything decorating the yellow walls, which Anne found strange. When she'd been Amelia's age, her walls were covered with images of pop stars. Maybe the youth of today didn't do that. She had to admit, she couldn't even remember who the people were that she thought were so dynamic all those years ago, but it was part of growing up back then, there was no internet or phones. She looked around the room, aware of Allan Goddard's eyes on her. She noted that the books lying by her wooden slatted bed seemed to be all classic novels – Jane Austen; Virginia Woolf; The Brontës – no teen angst novels. The duvet was furry, spotted red and black, and a couple of matching cushions lay on top of the pillows. There was a wardrobe which was closed and a small computer desk underneath a window with curtains that matched the duvet set. A closed laptop sat on top of the desk, an iPhone next to it.

'May I?' asked Anne indicating the laptop. As no-one objected, she flipped the top open. The home screen was a view of the River Blackwater taken from the Promenade Park. Anne pressed the space bar, and a window came up asking for a password. 'Anyone know Amelia's password?'

Allan shook his head.

'Try Harry17*!'

Allan looked at June. 'How would you know that?'

She looked at him. 'I saw her put it in once and queried her about it. I told her it wasn't a very safe password. She may have changed it.'

Anne shook her head as Amelia's screen came to life. The icons showed several social media platforms and Anne double clicked the Facebook one. It went straight to Amelia's home page.

'No password there,' commented June.

'Looks like she just leaves it open all the time. Bit risky,' observed Anne. She scanned through the various pages Amelia had liked. There were the usual teenage sites here. She seemed to be signed up to several influencers as well as other celebrities. There was a link to one site that worried Anne, she knew all about it. It professed to be a page to help with teenage depression but Anne knew that it also led to pages about suicide and self-harm. She didn't open that page and closed the laptop. 'Would it be at all possible for me to borrow this for a few days?'

'Why?' asked Allan.

'Just to get my IT people to check it out. There may be something on here to help find out why Amelia went away and where to.'

'Someone took her,' said Allan.

'Did you see anyone, Mr Goddard?' Anne asked him.

He shook his head. 'She wouldn't just run away.'

Anne chose not to comment. She could think of many reasons Amelia might have run away and one of them could well be on that laptop. She hoped not because she knew that viewing sites like Amelia had been looking at did not usually end well. She hoped they were not now looking for a body as runaways came back within a day or two usually and it had already been nearly forty-eight hours.

'I'll really need to take the phone as well,' said Anne, picking it up from the desk. June nodded; Allan remained tight-lipped.

Anne put the two items in a large evidence bag before indicating the wardrobe. 'Could you tell if she took any clothes with her?'

June opened the wardrobe door and ran her hand through the jeans and skirts hanging from a rail. A couple of shelves held neatly folded tee-shirts and jumpers, a few pairs of shoes on the bottom. She started to cry, tears rolling down her cheeks as she looked at her daughter's clothes.

'What was she wearing the last time you saw her?' asked Anne.

'She had her school uniform on. She'd said she was going to go back to school but Allan stopped her.'

'She wasn't in any sort of state to go back,' said Allan, angrily. 'The girl was distressed.'

'I can understand that. Did you seek any medical advice?'

'No, of course not. She wasn't ill, she'd just had a bad experience.' Allan's face twisted in anger.

'Her boyfriend had just been murdered,' June said through her tears. Anne noticed that Allan did nothing to comfort his wife.

'And when you last saw Amelia, she was in her school uniform?' Anne tried to get back to the point. 'When exactly was that?'

'Two mornings ago. She got up to go to school, Allan told her she couldn't and she shut herself in her room,' June informed her.

'Did she not come down to eat lunch or dinner?'

June shook her head.

'We thought it was best to leave her,' said Allan.

'No, you thought it was best. There was no 'we' about it.' June's tears had started again. Allan just glared at her.

'Is her school uniform here somewhere?' Anne was searching in the wardrobe. She wasn't only looking through the clothes. She knew from her own experience that wardrobes had handy little nooks and crannies where all sorts of things could be hidden.

'I didn't see it,' said June.

'But she could be wearing something else. You can't see anything missing?'

June looked in the wardrobe again, her hands pulling at the clothes. Several skirts and blouses fell onto the floor along with their hangers. June threw several more angrily on top of them.

'I don't know,' she screamed. 'I don't know what she wore. Why didn't I take more notice?'

'It's okay, June,' Anne said comfortingly.

The wardrobe was against the wall opposite Amelia's bed. The slope of the ceiling meant there was a gap of about a foot to the left-hand side. From the gap, Anne withdrew a skirt, blouse, and blazer. 'Well, she wasn't wearing her school uniform,' she observed. June took the clothes from her and held them to her face.

'What about the rubbish that Harry bought her?' Allan was still standing by the door, looking as though it wasn't safe to step inside his teenage daughter's room. Anne raised her eyebrows questioningly at him.

June answered. 'Harry bought her an athletic top and leggings. There was also some sort of short skirt. Gym wear.'

Anne inspected the wardrobe again, picked up some black material that had fallen onto a pair of shoes. 'Are these the leggings?' Anne held them up and closed the wardrobe.

June added them to the pile of school uniform she was still holding to her breast.

There was no sign of the top or the short skirt but if Amelia had gone out in those she'd be freezing by now. It was only March and the weather had decided it still wasn't Spring yet.

'There was a sweatshirt as well,' said June. 'One of those sports brands.'

'What colour were they, June, can you remember?'

Remember? It was her daughter. It was almost as though this policewoman was talking about Amelia in the past. 'They were black,' she said. 'There may have been some pink on them. It had a hood.'

'Thanks.' Anne took her own phone out and made some notes in her Pages App, before going over to check Amelia's bed. It had been made properly, so it didn't look like she'd disappeared on impulse. Putting her phone on top of the bedclothes, she squatted down and looked underneath the bed but there was nothing there. Anne was surprised. Under her bed were boxes and books and God knows what else. Apart from the novels, the bedroom was quite sparse. There was no television, which Anne believed to be essential in young people's rooms these days. No video games. No entertainment at all. 'Where would her schoolbooks be?'

'In the dining room,' said Allan. 'That's where she used to work.'

'I'd like to have a look if I can,' replied Anne.

They went downstairs and into a square room at the back of the house. The windows overlooked a cramped but tidy garden, a dining table big enough to seat six comfortably took up the centre of the room but looked as though no-one had ever eaten there, a Welsh dresser with blue and white plates standing on shelves was along the far wall. The kitchen was through another door. Allan picked up a backpack from the corner by the dresser and dumped it on the table. Anne opened it and removed the books from the main compartment. She was surprised to learn that students still wrote in exercise books. She'd assumed everything would be done on tablets and laptops now. She skimmed through them. The handwriting was very neat, small, and not flamboyant. The schoolbooks didn't appear to be filled with anything other than notes and essays about things Anne didn't understand – she'd left school a long time ago. In a front pocket of the bag was a plastic container that had once held food, presumably a lunchbox, a couple of cheap ballpoint pens, a rubber and pencil sharpener – even though there did not seem to be any pencils. The rest of the backpack was empty.

June looked over Anne's shoulder. 'There's no trainers. She always took her trainers.'

'She's probably wearing them, then,' Anne noted. She patted her pocket with her hand, her shoulders sagged. 'Can't find my phone,' she said. 'I'll just check my bag.' She went through to the living room and picked it up. 'No, must be upstairs.'

'I'll get it for you,' said Allan.

'No, it's fine Mr Goddard, I remember where I left it now and the exercise will do me good.' Anne went up the stairs as fast her overweight body would let her, snuck into Amelia's room, opened the wardrobe, put an article that was hiding in the back behind a pair of shoes in her bag, picked up her phone from Amelia's bed and made her way downstairs. Allan was standing at the foot, his face showing no emotion. Anne couldn't work out whether he wanted to say something to her or not. She paused on the bottom step.

Allan looked towards the living room. 'He had some strange bedfellows,' he said quietly.

'Who did, Mr Goddard?'

'Harry. He was involved in the dark arts. I tried to tell her. I tried to stop her seeing him.' He looked pathetic, Anne thought. He looked like someone who was trying to absolve himself of blame for some reason.

'Where were you when Harry was killed, Mr Goddard?'

'I was at work,' he said. 'I work at Witheford's.'

'The accountants?

Allan nodded.

'Nice. Top people's accountants, aren't they?'

'I'm not on that pay scale, sadly. I tend to get the lesser ones, the stroppy ones, which is why I often have to work late.'

Anne remembered Alice saying he didn't make the hospital while she was there due to working late. 'Well, Mr Goddard, we will do everything we can to find your daughter and the person who killed her boyfriend.' She went through to the living room where June was sitting silently on the sofa staring at the wall. 'Thanks, June. I have officers doing a house to house, questioning to see if anyone's spotted Amelia and I'll be in touch if we have any news at all.'

June Goddard nodded but didn't look at Anne as the detective left the house.

*

'Well, well. The witchy woman. What a surprise, eh, lads?' Jed Barber stood next to the remains of the chapel, legs splayed looking like something out of the OK Corral, the setting sun on the ancient wall creating a shimmering effect on the stones behind him.

Agnes Waterhouse didn't bother to turn round. She knew who was there. Jed Barber was like a wasp, ignore his irritation for long enough and he gets bored and goes away.

'Cat got your tongue, Harriet?'

She remained silent for the moment, tending to her herbs.

Jed took a couple of paces towards her. 'Time for you to pay for your misdeeds, witch.'

Agnes turned her head and stared at him. He was flanked by two other men, one of whom had evidently had too much to drink. She smiled at them.

'What do you want?' she said.

'You, you evil bastard.' Jed drew a long knife from under his coat.

'What you doing?' yelled the drunk man.

'Leave it, Jed. No violence, we said,' added the other.

Jed turned to them. 'I never said no violence.' He moved towards Agnes.

'Stop it, Jed,' yelled the drunk.

'What's the matter. Still scared of the witch?'

All this time Agnes had been observing the three men. She knew she was in trouble here. She had no way of defending herself against a madman with a knife. She looked past Barber at the drunk.

'Do you know what happens if you attack a witch?' she shouted.

The drunk and his friend became visibly wary.

'I can turn you all into toads in an instant.'

She raised her hands above her head, her long cloak billowing in the breeze. The two men turned and ran, the drunk stumbling as they tried to leap the fence by the gap in the hedge. Jed Barber held his ground, his knife in his hand.

'You don't scare me, you silly cow,' he said. 'Turn me into a toad. Go on.' He stood with his arms out to his sides.

Agnes stared at him. As he brought the knife down in front of him, a shadow appeared from behind the chapel ruins. Agnes smiled. There was a flash of light as a blade cut the air. The next thing he felt was a sharp pain at the side of his neck.

'What the…' He put his hand to his throat, which was pumping blood onto the ancient stones. He was still holding his knife. He turned as his legs gave way. There was no-one in sight.

Agnes raced back to her herb garden. Jed vainly lifted his arm and tried to stick his knife in her as she returned to him. Grabbing the handle she wrenched it from his hand, throwing it across the ground. She put her hand on his neck, trying vainly to stem the blood. Jed's body was growing weaker, his eyes rolling, his breath coming in short gasps. She'd picked some fresh yarrow leaves and held them against the wound.

'Help!' she cried.

Ten minutes later, Jed Barber left this world.

CHAPTER TWELVE

Agnes Waterhouse was raving. She'd been thrown, almost literally, into a cell at Chelmsford Police Station and locked in. An officer was standing guard outside and doing his best to ignore her rantings. She could understand how the stupid policewoman who'd arrested her might think she was the killer of Jed Barber but she'd expected to be listened to rather than cuffed and thrown in here like some common criminal.

She was moved to a room with four chairs and a table, all screwed to the floor and continued her tirade until, eventually realising no-one was going to take any notice of her shouting, she sat herself down on one of the seats and waited.

Anne Edwards and Alice Porter were sitting in one of the offices.

'I knew it was her,' said Alice.

'On what grounds?'

'St Giles grounds,' Alice replied, grinning. 'Harry and Amelia had entered her hallowed halls, and now Jed Barber's done the same.'

'I don't think so, Alice.'

'But the knife has her prints all over it and she's covered in blood – presumably Jed Barber's.'

Anne could see Alice's point but she had seen no evidence that Agnes Waterhouse was the aggressive sort. Not to the point of slitting anyone's throat anyway. Also, she was the one who had alerted the poor member of the public who happened to be passing. It must have been a shock for the man having a witch covered in blood telling him to call the police. Abeer Kumar was currently dealing with him in the pub opposite the ruins.

'We'd better go in and see her,' she said, standing up.

Alice picked up her notebook and followed down the short corridor to where Agnes Waterhouse was waiting impatiently.

'About time,' said the witch as they entered the room.

Anne and Alice sat opposite her.

'You're entitled to a solicitor,' said Anne.

'Don't need one. I haven't committed any crime. I was trying to help you out if you remember.'

'We asked you to let us know if anyone suspicious was hanging around. We didn't tell you to kill them.' said Alice.

'I didn't kill anyone.'

'You were covered in blood.'

'Because I was trying to save the stupid man.'

'There were some herbs stuck into his wound,' said Anne. 'Did you put them there?'

'They're yarrow leaves, they help to stem bleeding, but it was too late for him.'

'So, Agnes,' continued Anne. 'If you didn't kill him, who did?'

Agnes sighed. 'I don't know.'

'Were you there?'

Agnes nodded. 'There were three of them. They'd come from the pub. They were yelling abuse at me. Two of them got scared and ran away but Jed Barber started to come at me with his knife. I turned away and then I heard him scream and he lay bleeding on the ground.'

'And there was no-one else there?' asked Alice.

Agnes shook her head. She'd seen the two others run away leaving Jed on his own. She'd seen the shadow run across him and she'd heard him scream. 'Maybe he killed himself?'

'That's not very likely, is it, Agnes?' said Alice raising her eyes to the ceiling. 'Maybe you put a spell on him. We'll check those leaves we found on him. Did you drug him?'

Agnes laughed. 'You are so naïve, aren't you?'

'The problem we have, Agnes,' said Anne. 'Is that you were found in the ruins with a dead body, covered in blood, a knife with your fingerprints on it, some leaves you admit to shoving into the cut on the guy's neck and nobody else in sight. What are we supposed to think, the ghostly monk did it?'

Agnes twisted her lip.

'We're going to have to keep you here, Agnes, while we try and work out what happened. If you can't tell us, you'll be sitting in a cell until you can.'

*

Abeer Kumar felt uncomfortable sitting in the pub. She was aware of being the only non-white person there and a number of eyes were drilling into her back as she sat taking details from Gary Chapman, the unfortunate passer-by who's been confronted by Agnes Waterhouse.

'I've never seen a dead body before,' he said, his hand shaking as he lifted his pint to his lips. 'It were horrible.'

Abeer nodded. 'You were just walking past, is that right?'

He nodded.

'Did you see anyone other than Ms Waterhouse who asked you to phone us?'

He shook his head.

'Would you like us to get in touch with anyone?'

'My wife's on her way,' he replied.

Two men were sitting at a table by the dart board. They both looked at each other but neither spoke. They finished their drinks quickly and left.

*

Agnes Waterhouse was cautioned and sent to the cells. Even though it was late, Anne didn't want to go back to her flat yet. There was a lot on her mind. She'd sent Alice home, gone back to the Maldon office and made herself a coffee. She hadn't had a chance to look at Amelia Goddard's computer, something she wanted to do alone. Her suspicions were just that – suspicions. The link she needed to look at via Facebook was probably innocent but she needed to check. Plus, she had what she'd basically stolen from the girl's wardrobe. A book. Just a teenage schoolbook, it's cover a youthful expression of swirling patterns and letters – very unlike the neat handwriting in her schoolbooks. Her name and Harry's surrounded by colourful hearts. A quick glance had revealed poems and diary entries. Anne sat at her desk and opened it.

*

'This is a nice pub.' The man was standing at the bar in the back room at the Queen's Head. He had long hair and a wide moustache over a neat goatee beard, pointed like some seventeenth century cavalier. He was wearing a Parka coat over a sweatshirt and clean jeans. Charlotte had served him a pint of lager but as there was no-one else in the pub she'd felt obliged to let herself be caught in conversation with him. 'Bit quiet. Is it always like this?'

'Until the summer. We don't get a lot of late evening trade in the winter.' She tried not to make it obvious that she'd rather be closing.

'Are you from here? Maldon?' he said slowly supping his pint.

'Yes.'

'Do you do accommodation?'

Charlotte shook her head. 'No, sorry.'

'Where's the best place to stay, then?'

Charlotte looked at him. 'All the hotels here are quite expensive,' she told him. 'Besides, they are usually full at this time of year with contractors from the nuclear power station being de-commissioned at Bradwell, a couple of miles down the coast. What sort of thing are you looking for?'

'Just somewhere for the night. I'm here to look someone up I haven't seen for a long time.'

'There's a Travelodge. They might have something.'

'I'll check them out,' he said, not taking out his phone.

'They have a website, I believe.'

'Yes, I've used them before.'

'Right.' Charlotte stood for a moment. 'Well, I'd better get on.'

He looked round the bar. 'And do what?' he laughed.

'Get ready to close.' Charlotte had had enough of this person.

'Close? I'd better get another in quick, then.' He handed his now empty glass to her. 'One for yourself?' She put his glass in the glasswasher tray and poured a fresh one, wondering how long she could reasonably wait to call last orders.

'I'm alright, thanks,' she replied. Strictly speaking they could be open for another hour yet but she didn't want to stand here talking to this solitary customer. Her fears were temporarily relieved as the front door opened and someone went into the 'Members' Bar' at the front of the pub.

'Hi Charlie,' said Alice Porter as she stood at the bar. 'White wine, please. Do you want one?'

'Better not.' Charlotte indicated the other customer. 'Maybe if he goes,' she whispered. She poured a large wine for Alice and put it on the bar. 'You look like you've had a bit of a day.'

Alice grimaced. 'You could say that.' She looked innocently around the 'Members' Bar'. 'I don't suppose DC Griffiths has been in, has he?'

Charlotte grinned. 'Rumours are true, then.'

'What rumours.' Alice could feel the heat building in her face.

'Oh, nothing.'

'Any chance of another?' The voice came from the other bar.

'That's his third in about five minutes,' said Charlotte quietly.

'Where's Ben?'

'Gym.'

'I'd better hang about then in case there's trouble.' Alice didn't need an excuse to carry on drinking. No matter how long she'd been in the police, dead bodies were something she'd never get used to seeing.

'You don't happen to know someone called Harry Ellis, do you? He lives round here, I believe,' said the man as Charlotte handed him his pint.

Charlotte shook her head. 'No, doesn't ring a bell.'

Alice's ears had pricked up as she'd heard him from the other bar. She wandered through to the back room and stood next to the man.

'Sorry, I couldn't help overhearing. Are you looking for Harry Ellis?' she asked him.

'Yes. Do you know him?'

'Why are you looking for him?'

The man stared at Alice. 'Why do you want to know?'

'Call it curiosity.'

He smiled and shook his head. 'Do you know where he is?'

Alice didn't reply.

He smiled again and turned to Charlotte. 'Travelodge. Where is it?'

'Go along the river to Heybridge. You can't miss it; it's in the new retail centre.'

The man sank his pint in one and left the pub, leaving Alice perturbed.

'Have you seen him before?' she asked Charlotte.

'No.'

The door opened and Ben came bouncing into the pub.

'Hello Alice. On your own?' he bellowed.

'Why wouldn't I be?'

Ben looked quizzically round the two bars. 'Has he stood you up?'

'Who?'

'The Man from the Met.'

Alice downed her wine and put her glass a bit too heavily onto the bar. 'I don't know who is spreading rumours but I was not meeting anyone in the bar tonight.'

Ben winked. 'I won't tell anyone,' he said, pouring her another wine.

'I don't want another drink,' said Alice haughtily.

'Ben's just teasing, Alice. It's on the house.' Charlotte held the glass up in Alice's direction. Alice paused for a brief moment before accepting the drink. 'Harry Ellis is that boy who was killed, isn't he?'

Alice nodded.

'And now his girlfriend's gone missing, hasn't she?' Charlotte showed the local newspaper's Facebook page on her phone, handing it to Alice. There was an article by local reporter Felix Corbett giving mostly false details about Amelia's disappearance as well as 'Breaking News' about Agnes Waterhouse being arrested for murder. 'And she's the witch, isn't she?'

'Yes, Charlotte. I don't know how Felix got hold of that information. Agnes is just under caution at the moment. A bit of an altercation over at the leper hospital.'

'You can't trust witches these days, can you?' joked Ben. Alice agreed, silently.

'Has she been arrested over the boy's death?' Charlotte inquired.

'No, Charlotte. We still don't know who did that and she hasn't been arrested.'

'Maybe it was that bloke who's just left. Come back to finish the job.'

'It's not a joking matter, Charlie.'

The front door opened again. 'Am I too late for a nightcap?'

Doug Griffiths looked a bit windswept as he came through to the 'Member's'. Alice's face went beetroot coloured. Ben, having the biggest grin on his face, only made things worse for her.

An hour after closing time, Doug Griffiths walked Alice back to her flat.

CHAPTER THIRTEEN

Anne had not been home. She'd dozed on and off in her office chair. Her head was lying on the table when Alice bounded into the office. She slowly lifted it up.

'You look pleased with yourself,' she said as Alice threw her coat onto her chair.

'You look like shit. Have you not been home?'

Anne ignored her. 'Get me a coffee,' she said and shook herself awake. Her computer was still on, although asleep, and an exercise book was lying open on her desk.

Abeer Kumar entered quietly.

'Alice is making coffee,' said Anne, shooing her out of the door to the kitchen. Alice was most probably right. She felt like shit, so her visage most probably represented her mood. Used as she was to sleeping in offices, no matter how many times she did it, it never got any better. Maybe she should get a proper job where she could go home at five o'clock every night. But then what would she do at home at five o'clock? Sit and watch television. She wondered for a moment whether she should invite Derek into her flat again, he'd be company at least but then she remembered how controlling he'd been and decided it was best to keep things as they were. Drinking buddies, basically.

She'd spent the night going through Amelia's laptop and diary before she fell asleep. The girl had interacted with one of the suicide websites which worried Anne. It seemed though, that she had been arguing that killing oneself was not the answer. The thread followed with several entries of people trying to prove her wrong. Anne couldn't believe these sorts of websites were even legal. In Amelia's diary, even before Harry's death, some entries were filled with insecurity and self-doubt but nothing verging on suicidal. Most worrying were the references to her father.

Alice and Abeer came in carrying a tray with three mugs of coffee on it.

'Right, sit down,' ordered Anne. 'What do you make of this?'

She showed them an entry in the exercise book.

"Dad's at the door again. He thinks I don't know he does it. I'm tempted to just throw all my clothes off and stand naked in front of him. I'm sure that's what he's looking for. I really should make sure that the door's fully closed but I'm scared to. I never close my bedroom door."

The entry was followed by a drawing of a scary monster's head peeping round the door of her room.

'Paedophile?' said Alice.

'More likely a voyeur, I think,' said Anne. 'He needs to be questioned though. I'll go back there this morning.'

'Are you fit enough for that?'

Anne glared at Alice. 'You don't actually look like you had much sleep either, DS Porter. What was his name?'

Alice blushed.

'I knew it. Who was it?'

'Just someone.'

Abeer looked embarrassed. 'What do you want me to do, Ma'am.'

'Someone has to question the witch, I suppose. We can't keep her without charging her.'

'Charge her, then. It's obvious she killed Jed Barber, at least.'

'There's no evidence, though, Alice,' Anne insisted.

'Her fingerprints were on the knife. There was no-one else there. She had blood all over her.'

'That's still not conclusive. She says she tried to stem the bleeding.'

'But there was no-one else there. She admits that.' Alice threw her arms wide in exasperation.

'She said there were two others with Jed when he arrived. Who are they?'

Alice shrugged.

'Would you like me to talk to Amelia's parents?' piped up Abeer. 'Then you can question Agnes.' Abeer wanted nothing more to do with the witch. Although she wouldn't admit it, the woman made her feel uneasy ever since she'd given her that herbal tea. Abeer was the sort of person who liked to be in control but it had been like that infusion had taken over her body – in a nice way, she had to admit – which scared her even more.

Anne looked at her. She wanted to go through Amelia's laptop again before talking to June but maybe Abeer could discover something she hadn't thought about. Sometimes a new face brought new information. She nodded. 'See if you can talk to June on her own. Hopefully her husband will be at work. See if she knows anything about Allan's behaviour towards their daughter. Try and be subtle, Abeer.' She handed her the notes she'd taken from the last interview. 'Get Ernie to go with you.'

Abeer tried not to show the relief she felt. Interviewing ordinary people was preferable to confronting the witch. 'Shall I go now?' Anne nodded and Abeer picked up her bag and made her way out, texting Ernie Kemp as she went.

Anne turned to Alice and stared into her eyes. 'So. Where were you last night and who with?'

Alice could feel herself blushing again.

'I just went to the Queen's. I was feeling a bit depressed after finding another dead body.'

'And?' Anne raised her eyebrows.

Alice sighed. 'Doug came in.'

'Did he? Walk you home?' Anne had a very wide grin on her face.

Alice's mouth dropped open. 'Oh shit. I forgot to tell you. There was a man in the pub asking for Harry Ellis.'

'What?'

'I asked him why he wanted to know and he left. Said he was going to the Travelodge.'

'And you didn't follow him?'

'I was off-duty, Ma'am,' said Alice, resenting Anne's attitude.

'And you were with a handsome man.'

'No, Anne, I wasn't. He came in later. Look, I'm sorry I forgot. I guess it's probably nothing anyway.'

'Nothing is ever nothing, Alice. I want to know who he is. As soon as we've finished with the witch, go down to the Travelodge and see who booked in late last night.'

'Yes, Ma'am.' Alice saluted her boss.

*

Agnes Waterhouse looked completely different as she sat in the interview room at Chelmsford Police Station. She was dressed in a baggy grey tracksuit that didn't fit very well. She had been showered and her clothes taken for forensics to look at. Her long grey hair fell lankly onto her shoulders and down her back.

'Who were the other two that came into St Giles with Jed Barber, Agnes,' asked Anne, having again checked she didn't want a solicitor and setting the recording equipment in motion.

'I don't know,' replied the witch.

'That's not very helpful, Agnes. As it stands you are the only person we know for sure was at the scene when Jed Barber was stabbed.'

'Well, obviously I wasn't because I didn't stab him. He was about to attack me.'

'Are you saying it was self-defence?' asked Alice.

'No. I'm saying I didn't stab him.'

'So who did?' Alice was leaning forward, her face close to Agnes's.

'I don't know but it wasn't me.'

There was a knock on the door. Alice went over and a constable gave her a note which she looked at and gave to Anne.

'Remind me,' said Anne. 'Were you in the ruins when that boy Harry Ellis, was killed?'

'You know I wasn't.'

'And had you ever seen him or his girlfriend in there at any time?'

'No.'

'Do you know his girlfriend? Her name's Amelia. Amelia Goddard.'

Agnes thought for a moment, then shook her head. 'No. Not one of mine.'

'Not one of your what?' queried Alice.

'Not one of my students. I've never heard of the girl.'

'Do you remember that bag of menstrual blood found in your herb garden?'

'Of course I do.'

'Any idea how it got there?'

Agnes shook her head.

'That blood belonged to Amelia Goddard.' Anne indicated the note she'd been given. 'Amelia Goddard is missing. Shall we try again. How do you know Amelia Goddard?'

'I don't.' For the first time, Agnes Waterhouse looked worried.

'So how do you think her menstrual blood ended up in your herb garden?'

'I don't know.' Agnes actually felt scared now. She could see that the evidence was stacking up against her and she couldn't see any way that she could convince these two detectives that they were going down the wrong road. The trouble was, she didn't know where the right road was. 'Lots of things end up in my healing garden. You should stop people doing it!'

'We'll need to search your house, Agnes. Are you willing for us to do that or do I need to get a warrant?'

'Go ahead,' she answered. 'It's not locked. There's nothing to steal and there are no illegal drugs there, so don't try and plant anything. All my herbs are completely natural.'

'In the meantime, you will stay here. If I were you I would ask for a solicitor.'

*

Abeer Kumar sat in her car outside the Goddard house studying the notes Anne had given her. There was no mention of taking the notebook, only a laptop and phone, so she thought she'd better not mention that. Anne had noted that Allan Goddard had seemed reticent to enter his daughter's bedroom, saying he'd never been in there. Ernie had not arrived yet and she knew she shouldn't go into the house alone but became aware of a woman looking through the window of the house at her car. She decided to venture up the drive. Ernie would be here shortly. She knocked on the door and the woman opened it an inch.

'What do you want?' she demanded.

Abeer showed her warrant card. 'DC Kumar. Are you June Goddard?' she said.

June looked warily at her. 'Why?'

'I'd just like to ask you some questions.'

'Have you found her?' June's lip was trembling.

'No, Mrs Goddard. Not yet.'

'Can I look at that?' She indicated Abeer's warrant card, which she held out to her. June studied it, checking the photograph against Abeer's face, before opening the door wider and beckoning her to follow into the kitchen. 'Unusual for you to come on your own, isn't it?'

'My colleague is on his way. I saw you looking through the window. I thought you might have been worried about someone sitting in a car outside your house.'

'Yes, I was. Sorry, I'm a bit nervous at the moment.'

'I understand that Mrs Goddard. Is your husband at home?'

June snorted and twisted her lip. 'Of course not. His work is far more important than his missing daughter.'

Abeer sat on the proffered stool. 'How was his relationship with Amelia?'

'Was? Is she dead?' June's face collapsed into tears.

'No, no, Mrs Goddard. I mean we don't know. There has been no news. I just wondered how your husband gets on with her,' she replied, stressing the present tense. 'Is there any animosity?'

June pulled herself together. 'He can be a bit strict sometimes,' she said, wiping her eyes.

'Strict?'

'He can be a bit possessive. He didn't like her boyfriend.'

'Harry?'

June nodded.

'Do they spend much time alone together? Amelia and her dad.'

June looked up at Abeer. 'What do you mean? What are you implying?'

'Nothing, Mrs Goddard. I'm trying to create a picture of your husband's relationship with her. You say it was strict. Has he ever hit her or anything?'

'Certainly not!'

'That's good. My father was strict too. He did smack me, I'm afraid, when I was little.'

'Allan's never laid a finger on her,' June reiterated.

'Or you?'

June paused before answering, 'No.'

'My colleague, DI Edwards said there was nothing missing and you thought she was wearing gym gear when she went missing. Is that right?'

'I think so but…'

Abeer waited, raising her eyebrows.

'Harry had given her a necklace – a locket on a chain – but Allan had told her she couldn't wear it. They didn't allow jewellery at school, you see. I can't find that so she might be wearing it now.'

'What sort of locket?'

'It was a heart shape,' she said. 'Allan went mad and nearly tore it off her neck. I think he was actually jealous of Harry.'

There was a knock at the front door.

'That'll be my colleague,' said Abeer. June let Ernie into the house.

'Would you like tea or coffee?' she said. 'I should have asked earlier.'

'No, we're fine,' said Abeer, ignoring Ernie's grumpy face. 'And you think Amelia may be wearing that locket now?'

June nodded.

'Was it silver or gold?'

'It was silver coloured. I'm sure it wasn't real silver. They were only kids.'

'Any engraving? It might help to find Amelia.'

'Help to identify her, you mean, don't you?'

'No. No, definitely not, Mrs Goddard. We could see if someone recognises anyone wearing that sort of locket.'

'I don't know if there was an engraving.'

'Do you know where he got it?'

'Off the internet, I would think.'

'Do you have a photo of it?'

Abeer clocked the pause before June answered.

'I might have somewhere. I don't have my phone handy.'

'Can you give me your number then I'll text you mine and you can send it to me, if that's okay.'

June reeled off the eleven digits of her mobile phone which Abeer put into her contacts.

'Thank you, Mrs Goddard. We will do everything we can to find your daughter. Just one thing, does Amelia keep a diary or anything?'

'No. She isn't that sort.'

Ernie Kemp followed Abeer out of the house. 'Well, thanks for that,' he said.

'What?'

'Going in without me. What was the point of me coming over? I'm here to safeguard you. If you just carry on without me, you could get into all sorts of trouble.'

'But I didn't.'

*

Anne and Alice were standing outside Agnes Waterhouse's cottage surveying the remains of red paint on the front door.

'What does it say?' Anne asked Alice, who was peering closely at the door.

'Looks like "Murdering witch"' she said. 'Or it could be bitch.'

They opened the front door and almost stepped on a lump of human excrement that had been posted through the letterbox.

'Who would do that?' said Alice.

'Someone who doesn't like witches, presumably.'

'Jed Barber?'

'If he was still alive. I suppose he could have done before he went to the ruins but someone has tried to rub the lettering off. Why would they leave the…poo.'

Alice put her gloves on and placed the excrement in an evidence bag. 'Can I put this in your car?' she checked.

'In the boot.' Anne went into the cottage. Everything inside the rooms was neat and clean, nothing appeared to have been disturbed. Alice joined her in the kitchen.

'Bit tidy for a witch, isn't it?' she said.

'I don't know, Alice. What is a witch's kitchen supposed to look like? Big black cauldron burning in the centre of the room? Ingredients like toads and newts hopping about?'

'I don't think newts hop,' replied Alice. 'I just didn't expect it to be so clean, that's all.'

'Look for a knife,' Anne told her.

'What, a knife in a kitchen? That would be unusual. Anyway, she had the knife in her hand covered in blood.'

'Look for a knife that might have killed Harry Ellis.'

'*You* think it was the witch as well, now, do you?'

'Just look for a knife.'

There was nothing to be found anywhere in the house that definitely connected Agnes to either killing, apart from the graffiti and the poo and that was consequential. Alice had bagged up every knife in the kitchen but they were all clean.

'If it was Jed Barber who posted the shit, maybe she took revenge?' suggested Alice.

'I don't think you kill someone for that, do you?'

Alice shrugged. 'Possible.'

'Let's get back to the office.'

Alice logged their findings and added POO in big letters to the whiteboard.

'Bit childish, Alice,' observed Anne. 'Do you have plans for tonight?'

'Yes,' came the curt reply.

Anne had arranged to have a drink with Derek at the Queen's Head and Alice had arranged to have a drink with Doug at a different pub.

'Better get going then. Switch the TV off,' said Anne, putting her coat on. The BBC News Channel was on permanently whenever anyone was in the office.

Alice thought about asking what Anne's last servant died of but decided against it and picked up the remote from her desk. Just as she was about to press the off button, the local news program started.

'This evening we talk to the mother of missing girl Amelia Goddard.'

'Anne,' yelled Alice.

Anne poked her head back in the door. 'What?'

'I think you might want to watch this.'

The picture had widened to include June Goddard sitting on the sofa next to the presenter.

'So, June. I know this must be the most terrible time for you.'

June Goddard nodded.

'What can you tell us about Amelia, June?'

Tears were in June's eyes as she spoke, looking directly into the camera. 'She was the most beautiful, lovely girl. She wouldn't just go away on her own. I think someone must have taken her.'

'Any idea who that could be?'

June shook her head. 'I just want her to come home. I keep the light on in the hall all the time, just in case.'

The presenter nodded. 'There'd been a very tragic event just a few days before she disappeared, hadn't there?'

June nodded again. 'Her boyfriend, Harry Ellis, was stabbed.'

'Yes, we reported on it at the time. He didn't survive, did he?' added the presenter.

June shook her head.

'And there's no news on his killer. Do you think there's any possibility that Amelia's disappearance might be related to that incident?'

'That's what I'm most scared of. No-one knows who killed Harry or why.'

'What do the police say?'

June scowled. 'They're useless. Amelia was very upset about Harry's death, obviously,' she continued. 'I hope she's just gone off somewhere on her own.' She turned to face the camera again. 'Wherever you are, Amelia, come home, baby. Come home.' June Goddard broke down in tears. The camera switched to a close-up of the presenter.

'Obviously this is a very distressing situation. We contacted Essex Police but they haven't replied.'

A picture of Amelia filled the screen.

'If anyone knows where Amelia is, please contact us here or at your local police station.'

The presenter stood up and moved to a different part of the studio to proceed with the rest of the program.

'Did you know about this, Anne?' asked Alice.

'No. She never mentioned it. Did anyone from Essex contact us about the interview?'

'Not me. Has she just done it off her own back?'

'Looks like it, Alice.' Anne punched her hand with her fist. 'Bloody Horobin. I bet they contacted him.'

*

No-one could ascertain when exactly the posters started appearing but suddenly they seemed to be everywhere. In shop windows, pubs and just about every lamppost on the High Street. Anne first noticed the one on the noticeboard at the Queen's Head that evening where she was meeting Derek. He pointed it out to her.

'Still not found that girl, then?' he said.

'What girl?'

Derek nodded his head towards the poster. 'I saw it on the telly. It's in the paper as well.'

'HAVE YOU SEEN THIS GIRL', read the poster, followed by a picture of Amelia Goddard and a directive to phone a mobile number.

'Had any response?'

'Not from that. That's not a police poster.' She stood up and studied it, noting down the phone number. She went over to the bar where Ben was looking bored due to the lack of customers. 'Who brought that poster in, Ben, do you know?'

'I wasn't here,' he told her. 'Terrible, though, isn't it. Her parents must be out of their minds.'

'Yes, they must,' agreed Anne. She went back to her table. 'I'll be back in a minute, Derek,' she said before storming outside to get a phone signal.

Derek looked at Ben and they both shrugged. Two minutes later Anne returned to the bar and threw the remains of her wine down her throat.

'Problem?' asked Derek.

'Yes. Out of wine,' she replied and went to the bar. 'Is Charlotte in tonight?'

'Yes, she's upstairs. Why?'

'Need a quick word.'

*

The Reverend Frank Thatcher was quietly contemplating in the front pew of All Saint's church. The lights weren't on but he had lit a few candles. He liked the atmosphere of the flickering illumination. It was late and, by rights, the church should be locked but Frank didn't believe in locking people out of God's house and regularly 'forgot' to turn the key. He was troubled. Not just with the state of the world, the poverty that forced people to have to use foodbanks but the fact that someone was stealing from the foodbank supplies, kindly given, that he'd been storing for the local charity. Maybe he should start locking the door after all. He was unsure who he should feel most sorry for. The ones who were going to have less to eat or the misguided thief. If he knew who had been taking the items, he would have gladly given them but he had no idea how they were being plundered. He guessed someone must be coming in during the night.

He was an old man now, nearing eighty, well past his three score years and ten. He'd been given this parish by the Bishop of Chelmsford who had told him it would be a good place to retire. But he had no intention of retiring. Clergy didn't retire. When one had the calling, it was for life. He'd done his best to increase the ever-depleting congregation and had achieved some success but it was not like when he was young. Then, nearly the whole of his village attended church every Sunday. Now, he was lucky if he made double figures sometimes. People had other things to worship.

As he always did when he was confused, he talked to God, asking for guidance. Which is what he was doing when the door opened and a woman entered apprehensively into the nave. He turned and smiled at her.

'Come in,' he said, looking at a worried face. 'Are you troubled?'

The woman stood at the back of the church. Frank Thatcher stood up and walked slowly towards her. 'Is there something I can help you with?' he asked.

The woman stared at him for a moment, then her eyes wandered around the dim church.

'I've never been in here,' she muttered.

Frank turned his hearing aid up. Her echoing voice was muted and he couldn't hear her clearly.

'You are welcome nonetheless,' he replied. 'Come and sit down.'

The woman looked warily at him but his kind face and smile convinced her to move closer. They sat on a pew at the back of the rows. She was still looking around her.

'It's a beautiful church, isn't it?' said Frank.

'I can feel her.' The woman stood up. 'She's here somewhere.'

'Who?' Frank asked.

'My daughter. She's here.'

'There's no-one here. Only God and us at the moment. What's your name?'

The woman looked at him as though he'd asked a difficult question, before replying, 'June.'

'And who else do you think is here, June?'

'My daughter, Amelia.' June Goddard stepped out from the pews and ran to the front of the church.

Frank's arthritis was causing him pain in his hips as he followed her, he limped towards where she was standing looking around her again.

'Would you like to pray for her?' he asked. He felt sympathy with her. It was always difficult dealing with people who'd lost a child which is what he assumed.

June stared into the old man's eyes. They were kind eyes, healing eyes. She'd never been religious, never been a churchgoer even as a child but there was something about this man that gave her comfort. 'Do you know where she is?' she asked him.

He took her hands in his. 'When did she pass away?' he said gently.

June snatched her hands from his. 'She hasn't passed away,' she snapped. 'I won't believe that.'

'Tell me about Amelia,' said Frank, gently.

*

'But surely it's a good thing,' insisted Derek. 'If you're looking for this girl, any help must be useful.'

'That's not the point, Derek. I don't know who's putting these posters up. It should have come through us. So should the TV interview.'

'But you didn't do it.'

'I know and maybe we should have found the time to. The trouble is, I'm going to have DCI Horobin on my back now. He'd love to make me look incompetent again.' Anne took a huge slug of wine.

'So, you're not annoyed by the fact the posters are there just that you didn't do it.'

Anne gritted her teeth. She knew Derek was trying to help but all he was doing was undermining her.

'Whoever did do it is only going to help you, surely,' Derek continued.

'No, Derek. Because if anyone has any information, that information will not come to us but to some unknown mobile phone number which didn't answer when I rang it. If we'd done it, someone would be monitoring the phone twenty-four hours. It doesn't help us at all.'

Derek quietly took a drink. 'Did Charlotte know who put them up?'

Anne shook her head. She was annoyed but it was unreasonable to take her frustration out on Derek or Charlotte. 'There was someone in here asking for Harry last night, long haired wearing a Parka. In his mid-twenties, she thought. Ring any bells? One of your students, maybe?'

Derek shook his head.

'Anyway, I've put Alice onto finding him. Right now, I just need another drink.'

Derek looked down his nose, stood up and went to the bar.

*

Frank Thatcher and June Goddard were in the vestry, a room off the main church where the vicar's robes were kept. Frank had a kettle in there and had made tea for June. They sat on two hard wooden chairs in the small space containing boxes of communion wafers alongside various accounting and religious books. Purple choir robes hung from a rail and there were a number of cardboard boxes filled with tins and cartons of food. A stack of bottled water and a couple of cases of red wine were next to them. Frank saw June looking at them.

'We store the food here for the food bank down the road, they don't have the room,' he explained.

'Doesn't look like you do either,' she observed, feeling quite claustrophobic in the overfilled room. 'What are those?' She pointed to some metal rings embedded high in the walls.

'This is a very old church,' said Frank. 'The religious communities of this country have not always been as beneficent as we like to think it is now. In the sixteenth century, after Henry VIII appointed himself Supreme Head of the Church of England, denouncing the Roman Catholic religion, many people still wanted to practice Catholicism. It's what they'd always known. However, many zealous followers of Henry punished anyone pursuing Catholicism by pillorying them – stringing them up, basically. After Henry's death, the young king Edward – he was only nine – carried on the Protestant way but, after his death, his half-sister Mary came the throne and the whole country became Catholic again. This time it was the Protestants who hung from those rings. Then we had Elizabeth the First who turned us all back to Protestantism. Thankfully, the church does not condemn people for their religious beliefs anymore.' He smiled at June. 'I'm sorry, I'm boring you.'

'No, it's interesting. There's rings on the floor as well.'

'That where their feet were tethered, while their arms...' he pointed to the rings high in the wall.

'But no-one's that tall, are they?'

Frank shook his head sadly. 'Can you imagine being stretched between the two? Just left there until you died?'

Tears were appearing in June's eyes.

'I'm sorry. You wanted to tell me about Amelia.' Frank shifted on the hard chair.

'She's missing. That's all I know, really.'

'For how long?'

'Three days. Her boyfriend was murdered. I'm so worried that someone has taken her.'

'Have you been to the police?'

June nodded.

'Then I'm sure they will be doing all they can to help you.'

June looked up at him. 'They've done nothing,' she said. 'I had to do my own posters.' She handed Frank one.

'I can put this on our noticeboard,' he offered. 'Would you like to light a candle?'

'Why?'

'To light a candle for someone indicates one's intention to say a prayer for that person and the candle symbolizes that prayer. If you write Amelia's name on the paper next to the candle other people will pray for her as well. Prayer can be very powerful,' he explained.

He picked up a small candle from a pile near his chair and held it out to her. She smiled.

'Does it work?' she asked.

Frank shrugged. 'I like to think so.'

'Can I pay you for this?' June took the candle from Frank.

'There's an offertory box next to the candle rack in the transept.'

'How much?'

'As much or as little as you can afford. It only goes to pay for the candles.'

'Are they expensive?'

Frank shrugged again. 'The cost doesn't matter. Although, someone seems to have taken a few recently. I hope they bring whoever it was comfort.'

'What? Stolen? From a church?' June looked shocked.

Frank smiled again. 'I'm sure they needed them,' he said. 'They took some of the food as well. It's a shame because if they'd gone to the food bank, they would have been able to meet other people if they're lonely. It's more than just a shop. It's a meeting place where people can get warm and talk to someone. There are many poor people in this world.'

June took two twenty-pound notes from her wallet and put them in Frank's hand.

He gave them back. 'That's too much, June.'

'I can afford it – unlike whoever needed to steal from you.'

'Put what you want to in the box, June. We will all pray for Amelia's safe return on Sunday. You'd be more than welcome to join us.'

*

Allan Goddard was alone in his house. He didn't know where his wife was but he was glad she wasn't here. He needed time to be alone with his thoughts. He was sitting on Amelia's bed stroking the fluffy duvet cover. He lay down and hugged one of the cushions by the pillows, kissing it, his tears dripping onto the faux fur.

'I'm sorry, Amelia,' he sobbed. 'I'm so, so sorry.'

CHAPTER FOURTEEN

Alice Porter was feeling guilty. She was happy. This was a feeling she hadn't experienced for some time. A rather handsome man was showing an interest in her. It had been fun until the doubts started to set in. Had she just had too much to drink? Was he really that interested or just taking advantage?

She was looking through the CCTV from the cameras on Maldon's streets, that had finally arrived from the council but found ir hard to concentrate. The council offices were in the same building. Why she couldn't just go and look at the discs there she couldn't comprehend. Protocol insisted that they were delivered to her and whoever had been charged with that task had been sluggish fulfilling it.

The evening that Amelia Goddard had disappeared had been dreary, yet the streetlights were not timed to come on until later, making the images in front of Alice grainy and unclear. However, she had spotted a girl wearing gym clothes walking up the High Street towards All Saints' Church. She hadn't entered the church but crossed the road and headed left. Unfortunately, that's where the CCTV cameras stopped. There was a gap between the church and the by-pass half a mile away. There had been no sign of the girl after she'd crossed the road.

Alice tried to picture where a fifteen-year-old girl would be heading. The High Street turned sharp left towards the old police station, but after that there were roads going in all directions. She could have turned back towards the estate she lived on; she could have turned right towards Beeleigh Abbey; she could have carried straight on, which would have brought her to St Giles Leper Hospital. Is that where she'd gone? The scene of her boyfriend's murder? There were no cameras there, the ruins were surrounded by private houses. She could check whether any of them had CCTV but she doubted it, this was Maldon, after all.

Anne came into the office. 'Found her?'

'Sort of. If that's her, she was on the High Street at 17.06 the day we think she disappeared. After that there's no sign.' Alice pointed to the screen.

'And no sign of her returning to the High Street?'

'Not yet. I still have quite a bit to go through.'

Anne nodded. Checking CCTV was a tedious business and she was glad that she wasn't having to do it herself. Her job looked like being equally tedious, though. She wanted to find out where Harry Ellis' brother, Reuben Elbrow, had been imprisoned – if he had, she only had Linda's word on that. She checked the databases but none of them showed Reuben Elbrow as a convicted criminal. It didn't look as though he'd ever been to prison. He had been held in a police cell twice following demonstrations but no charges had been brought. His address had been given as 'no fixed abode' but that had been a few years ago, there was no information as to his whereabouts now. Anne decided her budget didn't run to checking on East London hostels yet just because June Goddard was desperate.

'Did you find out who the mystery person in the pub was?' Anne asked Alice.

'No-one had checked into the Travelodge late that night,' she revealed.

'Presumably it was someone who didn't know Harry was dead. I checked with Charlotte but she hadn't seen him before or since,' Anne confirmed. 'What did he look like?'

'About my age. Long hair, goatee beard, Parka coat, clean jeans and trainers.'

Anne screwed her face up, thinking. 'I've told Charlotte to let me know if he comes in again. Did he seem suspicious?'

Alice thought for a moment. 'Not particularly. Didn't want to talk to me, though.'

'How's the Man from the Met?' Anne didn't look up from her computer.

Alice sighed. 'I'm a bit confused, to be honest. I mean, I've only known him for a few days and yet he seems to have wheedled his way into my whole life.'

Anne looked up. 'Your whole life?'

'Well, not really. I'm not used to people being nice to me, that's all.'

Anne put on a shocked face. 'I try my best to be nice.'

'That's not what I meant.' Alice smirked. 'I just don't know how far I should let this go on. I mean, he's going to go back to the Met at some point.'

'Well, if you're looking for an agony aunt, you're facing in the wrong direction. You know what my success rate with men is.'

Alice studied her screen again. She wasn't taking anything in that was in front of her eyes. The film from the CCTV cameras just washed over her.

'Is he really keen, then?' asked Anne.

Alice sighed deeply. 'I don't know, Anne. He was very keen the other night but…well…we'd had a drink or two.'

'Stay the night?'

Alice didn't answer. She wished she'd never started this conversation. Although she considered Anne her friend, she was also her boss and fraternising with another officer might not be looked upon too favourably. She was saved by Abeer entering the office.

'Are those our posters on all the lampposts in town?' she asked.

'The ones of Amelia? No. We have yet to find out who put them up. My suspicions lean towards Felix Corbett.'

'The journalist?'

Anne nodded.

'I think it's June Goddard.' Abeer showed Anne the number June had given her. It was the same as the one on the poster.

Anne blew her cheeks out. 'She must like the publicity. Can you get in touch and ask her to pass on any information she might have got?'

'Yes, Ma'am.' Anne glared at her detective constable. 'Sorry – Anne.'

'She's desperate, Anne,' said Alice. 'She must be going through hell.'

'I know, Alice, but taking it into her own hands doesn't exactly help us.'

'Where are we with the boy's murder?' Abeer was standing by the whiteboard. One of June's posters had been put up on it. The photo of Amelia showed her wearing a heart-shaped locket, presumably the love-token Harry had given her. Abeer tried not to be annoyed by the fact that June had not sent it to her as she'd asked.

'We're not anywhere with Harry's murder,' replied Anne. 'I need a break from somewhere. Someone who saw something; someone hanging around the leper hospital; someone other than the Lloyd boy who might have a reason to kill him.'

'Allan Goddard?' suggested Abeer. 'Even June admits he was jealous of Harry and when I asked about their own relationship there was a considerable pause before she told me it was fine.'

'I'm still going for the witch,' put in Alice. 'Is she still in custody?'

'Yes, but she's not the perpetrator of Harry's killing and I don't think she did Jed Barber in, either. Who did though, is anyone's guess. The trouble is there's not enough hard evidence to keep her locked up.'

'Knife dripping blood not enough, then.'

'It wasn't dripping, don't be dramatic,' replied Anne. 'Her cottage has been searched, there's nothing incriminating there. I don't know how much longer we'll be able to keep her. I don't want to charge her unless I have to.'

Alice stood up. 'Anyone want coffee?'

'Yes,' said Anne.

'Abeer?'

'Sorry, miles away. Yes please, Alice.'

Alice left the room.

'Something wrong, Abeer?' asked Anne.

'I don't know, Anne. There's someone missing from this wall, I'm sure about it. There has to be someone else and if we can find who that is I think we'll be a lot nearer finding Harry's murderer.'

Anne went over to the whiteboard. 'You're suggesting all these people are innocent?

'Not necessarily but something's niggling me. It's like there's a missing piece to the puzzle.' She studied the wall closely. 'Did Catherine Hall have any family here still?'

'Her parents emigrated. I wouldn't know about anyone else.'

'What about those men with Jed?'

Anne nodded and added 'two men' under Jed Barber's name. 'Maybe we need to find them somehow. The trouble is no-one saw them.'

'Except the witch.'

Alice came back into the office. 'I think we may have a problem on our hands,' she stated. 'There's a large group of people assembling in the park.'

*

After rain, there was a sweet smell in the tunnel where Amelia now resided. The small gaps where the light came in, also dripped rainwater, creating small puddles along the pathway. A few candles burnt further along the corridor, which gave off the sweet fragrance. The Mummy woman was chatting to her. It was inane talk and Amelia was ignoring it. In some way she had almost become resigned to her fate. She no longer felt scared. She was hungry and really wanted a proper meal but she knew the Mummy woman was doing her best to procure food of some sort every day. The tether that kept her tied to the wall had been extended and she was now able to move a few feet along the subterranean passageway, giving her a little privacy when nature called. There was a small nook where she could squat, rather than just soiling the ground next to where she sat.

'Can I go out with you sometime, Mummy,' she asked the woman. She'd accepted that she had to call her that in order to get any positive response.

'We'll have to see,' she said. 'It's still not safe yet.'

'Why is it not safe?'

'There are bad people out there, Elizabeth. You know what happened to you before.'

Amelia thought for a moment. She hadn't a clue what the woman was talking about. How should she play this? She needed information from this woman, who appeared to be completely delusional, but she had to be careful she didn't push her too far. At the moment, her compliance with her idea that she was called Elizabeth had meant she was at least talking.

'What did happen, Mummy? I can't remember,' she tried.

The Mummy woman put her arm round her. 'I know, darling. It was too traumatic. Your brain will have wiped it just as though you'd hit the delete button on your laptop. I won't mention it again.' She squeezed Amelia's shoulder. 'You know what day it is tomorrow?'

Amelia shook her head. She had no idea what day it was any day; what month it was; even what year it was. She had no concept of time anymore.

'It's your fourteenth birthday.' The Mummy woman smiled and gave Amelia a friendly shake. 'I haven't been able to get you much, I'm afraid. When this is all over, I'll make it up to you.'

Amelia knew she wasn't fourteen tomorrow, she'd been fourteen more than a year ago but then this woman seemed to think she was someone called Elizabeth. 'Maybe we could go out tomorrow somewhere for my birthday,' she said.

The Mummy woman let go of her. She stared at Amelia, her face twisted into a grimace. 'You can't leave here. How many times do I have to tell you.' She was yelling at Amelia, who backed away.

A wave of torpor came upon the girl. She wanted to cry but wouldn't show that woman her weakness. She leaned back against the stone wall. Her mind was in a whirl. What had she done to deserve this incarceration? Was it to do with Harry? Was it something he'd done? Is that what the Mummy woman meant when she'd talked about the traumatic experience Amelia had supposedly suffered? Seeing one's boyfriend die in front of you was certainly traumatic but it wasn't anything Amelia would delete from her memory. That image would be with her forever. Right now, all she felt was that she wanted to join Harry, to end it all here, this was no life, this was living like a rat. She wished she could get to her computer. She'd been looking at a site that helped with traumatic experiences. It hadn't done her much good, only depressed her more than she already was, but right now she needed someone to discuss things with and there were people on that site who were willing to do so.

The Mummy woman had disappeared along the tunnel. Amelia didn't know where she went but thankfully she usually came back with some sort of sustenance however meagre and unappetising. She looked at her surroundings, the darkness of the tunnel punctuated regularly by the candles and the small gaps in the roof. She wondered what was on the other side of the apertures in the ceiling. Obviously there was open air but where was it? Was it in Maldon? Had she been abducted and taken somewhere far from her home? She didn't think so. She remembered being in the leper hospital and then she fainted when the person grabbed her but surely she wasn't out cold for too long, was she? But if she was still in Maldon, whereabouts? Her first instinct had been the sewers or the drains, which would explain the grilled openings in the roof but they didn't appear to be big enough for roadside culverts, and the tunnels were basically dry. Anyway, as it was, it didn't really matter. She wasn't going to get out of here anytime in the near future.

*

'So what's happening wiv our compensation?' Bob Shepherd yelled at the young PC who'd returned Thomas's computer.

'I wouldn't know about that, sir,' he replied politely.

'Why not? What are we supposed to do, just sit 'ere and wait? My boy can't walk. Promising football career ruined. You need to do somethink about it.'

The constable didn't answer. Bob Shepherd slammed the door in his face and went through to the lounge where Thomas was playing on his old X-Box.

'This is shit, Bob,' he said. 'It keeps sticking.'

'You'll get a new one when the compo comes through. Anyway, you shouldn't be playing on it.' He pulled the plug out of the wall. 'You're supposed to be ill, remember.'

'It's my leg. That doesn't stop me playing video games.'

'If anyone sees you they'll talk. Get back on the sofa.'

Thomas sighed and edged back, putting his leg into the homemade sling. 'There's nothing wrong with my leg now anyway. I want to get this plaster off, it's driving me mad.'

Bob moved closer to him. 'You will keep that on until we have our compensation, son.'

Thomas turned his head away. He wanted to cry but knew that would only bring on another tirade from his stepfather.

'Leave him alone, Bob.' Patricia Lloyd had entered the room unnoticed.

Bob glared at her. ''E's got to play his part, Pat. We'll end up with nothink.'

'Just leave 'im be.'

He turned to his partner and scowled. 'I'm going out,' he said.

'Off to the pub again. It's no wonder we ain't got no money.'

'It's my money,' he replied. 'If you want some money go and earn some. Get a job.'

'Oh yeah and who'd look after 'im?' she pointed to Thomas. 'And who'd cook your meals?'

'I don't need looking after,' muttered Thomas. 'I could go back to school.'

'You ain't going nowhere till we've got compensation,' shouted Bob as he exited the lounge.

'My leg's fixed, mum. I really shouldn't be wearing this cast anymore; it'll be doing more harm than good.'

'You 'eard what 'e said,' replied Pat. 'You wear that till we've been paid.' She plugged his X-Box in again and left the room.

Thomas removed his leg from the frame and started up his game again.

*

There were probably upwards of a hundred people lined up along the Prom Park. A Police Sergeant who Anne didn't know was handing out Hi-Viz vests.

'What's going on here, Sergeant,' she said, holding up her warrant card.

'Looking for a missing girl, Ma'am.'

'And who authorised this?'

'DCI Horobin, Ma'am.'

Anne, feeling frustration starting to overwhelm her, bit her lip and turned to Alice. 'Looks like we've been dumped in it again by our lord and master.'

CHAPTER FIFTEEN

Sunday morning arrived with a bright sun. Spring hadn't exactly sprung and it was still chilly but the buds were beginning to appear on the large cherry tree outside All Saints' Church as June Goddard made her way across the High Street from the car park. She'd left Allan at home, they hardly spoke these days anyway, so she hadn't even bothered to tell him where she was going. He wouldn't approve of her going to church, it wasn't something either of them had ever done, but what he approved of didn't matter to her anymore. She felt quite awkward as she pushed the tall wooden doors open and entered the building. A woman aged about sixty handed her a hymn book, greeted her with a 'peace be with you' and introduced herself as Caroline. Peace is something June thought she may never experience again – certainly not while Amelia was missing and no-one seemed to be doing anything about it. The only messages from the posters had been from cranks, some of which were hurtful, some downright abusive. She'd heard nothing from the BBC. No-one had any information about her daughter's whereabouts.

Frank Thatcher caught her eye and smiled. He was dressed in a black cassock with some sort of scarf hanging round his shoulders, June didn't know what it was supposed to be or what it was called, it looked like part of some fancy-dress costume to her. She found herself an empty pew near the back of the church, there was barely a dozen people in the congregation but she didn't want to interact, didn't need anyone asking about her. She didn't really know why she was here. There was something soothing about the place and particularly Father Thatcher. He'd been kind to her, understanding, and something inside her felt an affinity of some sort – she couldn't explain what it was – and he'd instilled in her a want to help. There was organ music playing and a smell of incense burning. She couldn't tell where either were coming from; if someone was playing live or whether it was a recording but it had a calming effect which was strange as she'd never liked church music or incense before.

She sat quietly waiting for something to happen. The woman who'd greeted her came and asked if she'd like to move nearer the front but she told her she was quite happy where she was. Frank Thatcher, having paraded down an aisle behind a large crucifix, eventually started to speak. He had a microphone attached somewhere on his costume and his voice echoed round the stone walls of the half-empty church. He mentioned Amelia and asked the parishioners to keep her in their thoughts and prayers. A few hymns that June didn't know were sung and afterwards Frank said there would be tea and coffee served in the refectory. June watched as the people filed towards a room at the side of the church. Caroline was at her side again, urging her to join them for coffee. June was politely telling her she didn't have the time today when Frank appeared by Caroline's side.

'Hello, June. I'm so glad you could make it. Do come and join us in the refectory.'

June stood up and followed him along the aisle, leaving Caroline feeling slightly indignant that June was persuaded by the vicar and not by her.

*

The fingertip search lasting until after dark had made it even more useless than Anne had thought it in the first place. She'd felt obliged to stay until the end but had sent Alice home earlier. She had ended up standing in the murky light next to the officers Horobin had seconded to Maldon for the day. Everything the public had handed over to them sat in a pile on the grass, the officers studying the items by torchlight.

'Anything any good?' she'd asked.

'I don't think so, Ma'am.' The Sergeant had shrugged. 'Bit of a waste, if you ask me.'

Anne had agreed but hadn't said so. 'Well, thanks for your help. We're doing house to house as well. I'm pretty sure we'll find her.'

She wasn't sure but something in the back of mind told her that Amelia had just needed some time away from her family. She only hoped she hadn't done anything stupid. Right now, she had other things on her mind as she walked through the gloom up to the station.

*

Agnes Waterhouse was still refusing a solicitor. Her face was showing its age, the herbs she'd used daily to refresh her skin not being available in this place. She'd spent the night wracking her brains, trying to remember who those other two with Jed Barber were. They'd been wearing hoodies but the drunk one had slipped as he turned to run in his fright. Agnes was scouring the memory bank in her head to try and conjure a picture of the man's terror-stricken face and put a name to it. She'd seen him before, she was certain. He was one of Jed's cronies. She tried to remember everyone she'd seen going into his cottage next to hers, every idiot who'd stood near her own place shouting abuse. The clothes. They'd be a clue but all she could recall were dirty jeans and the hoodie – a plain hoodie, no slogan or anything. Then it came to her like a gift from the gods. The scar across his nose. It had looked like someone had tried to cut it off at some point. The scarred nose. Jesse Burton. Called himself Jesse James, like the outlaw, thinking it made him sound tough. One look at him and you knew he was really weak and vulnerable. She closed her eyes and concentrated her mind on the man. His hair was lank and unkempt – never seen a comb – and the scar from the bridge to his top lip. Jesse Burton. She banged on her cell door until the weary constable opened the flap. She demanded to see DI Edwards.

Alice was shocked to see the state Agnes's features had deteriorated to in such a short time. The blood vessels on her cheeks were showing through her fair skin and her hair was tangled and matted. Alice felt some sort of satisfaction. This was the real witch, the ugly witch. Not the Disney Princess they'd seen before.

'Finding it tough in here, Agnes?' she asked.

The witch ignored her and turned to Anne. 'Jesse Burton alias Jesse James,' she stated.

Anne stared at her expressionless.

'He was one of the other men.'

'And you've just remembered that have you?' asked Anne.

'I've been raking deep into my consciousness, DI Edwards. The two men were wearing hoodies but I caught sight of Jesse's face as he turned and ran like the spineless shite he is.'

'Where might I find this yellow-bellied outlaw?' Anne raised her eyebrows.

Agnes shrugged. 'He's usually with Jed Barber but obviously not at the moment.'

'Know where he lives?'

Agnes shook her head. 'Used to hang about at Jed's. He could be there? Or in the pub.'

'Did Jed live on his own?'

'No-one sensible would share with that piece of shit.'

Anne and Alice sat quietly for a moment.

'The problem I have, Agnes, is that you tell me these two men had gone by the time Jed was knifed. Are you suggesting that this terrified Jesse James came back and slaughtered his mate?' said Anne eventually.

Agnes sighed. 'I don't know. You asked if I knew who they were. I don't know who the other one was, he had his hoodie up all the time but a guy called Brad hangs around with him. I don't know if it was him, I couldn't see his face. Jesse has a scar across his nose if that helps you find him.'

Alice looked at Anne and dropped her head slightly.

'Tell me about the graffiti?' said Anne.

'Which lot? It happens regularly.'

'Why don't you report it, then?'

Agnes laughed. 'What's the point? You've far more important things to deal with – like locking up the wrong people.'

'We found some human excrement, posted through your front door, Agnes. Is that common too?' Alice said.

'Shit seems to be a way of some people trying to make a comment.'

'Someone had tried to remove the graffiti. Was that you, Agnes?'

She looked at Alice and sneered. 'Wouldn't you?'

'Yes, but I'd also remove the shit.'

'The shit wasn't there.'

'Any idea who did it?' asked Anne.

'Jed Barber.'

'But he was dead.'

'Not when I left the house. It was several hours later he turned up at St Giles'.'

'Doesn't it piss you off, Agnes,' said Alice, leaning towards her.

'Of course it does but like most things in this life, you get used to it. Can I go now?'

'You've nothing more to tell us?'

'Only to reiterate that I haven't done anything. I wouldn't kill Jed Barber because he shoved crap through my letterbox. I wouldn't waste my energy.'

'Well, you can go then,' said Anne.

Agnes stood up.

'Back to your cell.'

*

'Still no news?' Frank Thatcher was sitting next to June Goddard on the hard plastic seat in the refectory. There were five or six others dotted around the room drinking tea or coffee in a group by the windows that looked out over what was left of the graveyard. June hadn't joined them. She didn't want to chat and she certainly didn't want to view a graveyard. It only made her think Amelia could be dead. She shook her head.

'I'm sure you'll find her, June. I feel she is safe,' said Frank.

June looked at him and smiled. He was a kind old man but she knew he was only trying to give her some comfort. 'We scoured the Prom Park yesterday. Loads of local volunteers but there was no indication she'd been there. It all feels a bit hopeless.'

'There's always hope, June.' He held out his hand. 'What happened to your fingers?' he asked, indicating a swelling on June's knuckles.

She laughed. 'You won't believe this. I walked into a lamppost putting up one of Amelia's posters.'

Frank Thatcher didn't believe it but chose not to comment.

*

Anne arrived early at the station on Monday morning to be greeted by a young woman with red hair tucked into a police cap, sitting behind the front desk.

'Who are you?' she asked.

'Minnie Dawson, Ma'am. I'm the new desk sergeant.'

Anne looked at the girl. She looked younger than Alice. How had she risen to sergeant already?

'Pleased to meet you, Minnie,' she said.

Anne could see that Minnie was most inaptly named as she stood up. She must have been over six foot tall and built like a prop forward. 'Would you like coffee, Ma'am?'

Anne was warming to the giant. 'That would be much appreciated, sergeant. I'll be in my office.'

'CID?'

Anne didn't bother to answer. She spent the next hour going through the social media again in an attempt to find out more about Amelia Goddard's disappearance. She realised it was another burden on her small, overworked team yet here was a young girl who'd gone through a terrible trauma and was now missing. They had done a door-to-door all over the estate where she lived but no-one had any clue as to her whereabouts. There were quite a lot of posts about the missing girl from friends at her school and Abeer was questioning them this morning. The site that proposed to help teenage depression was still worrying her. Amelia had put up a few posts on her Facebook page, which she didn't seem to use very often, which had resulted in a lot of supportive replies, but there was nothing in the last few days, nothing since she'd disappeared. She knew Amelia didn't have her phone with her and she hadn't used her bank card either. Anne could only hope she was still alive.

Agnes was still in custody in Chelmsford and Anne knew she'd have to charge her with Jed's murder soon or let her go. They hadn't got any further with Harry Ellis' death. She spent an hour just staring at the whiteboard trying work out some connections between the names she had written up there but was getting nowhere. She'd rubbed out the POO, which had reminded her it was still in the boot of her car. She'd get forensics to come and pick it up.

'Think!' she said out loud, banging her fists to the sides of her head.

The door opened and Doug Griffiths wandered in. 'Hello,' he said.

'Ever thought of knocking?' replied Anne.

'Oh, sorry.' Doug tried to look suitably embarrassed.

'She's not here,' Anne said without turning from the whiteboard.

'I was looking for you.'

Anne gave him her attention. 'Why?'

Doug moved further into the office. 'I have a proposition. I'm due a month's leave and I thought I might spend it here, so I'd like to offer my services for free and help you with your case.'

Anne laughed. 'What makes you think we need your help, DC Griffiths?'

Doug shrugged. 'I'm not trying to suggest anything, it's just I'm going to take my leave, I like it here and I'm going to be around. I'm not the sort who's happy doing nothing so it would be doing me a favour if I could help. And now you also have this missing girl, it doesn't take much to see you're understaffed.'

'What about your case?'

'The Maldon connection has been closed apparently. They're concentrating their efforts elsewhere. Personally I think they're wrong but...'

'So you're still likely to be looking into that at the same time?'

He shrugged again.

'And you want to spend more time with my Detective Sergeant. Is that right?'

Doug didn't answer.

Anne sat at her desk and studied the man in front of her. Who was he? Why did she feel protective towards Alice? He seemed genuine and, although she'd never admit it, she could do with some help. 'Where will you stay?'

He smiled. 'I've already moved out of the hotel and have got myself a room at someone's house.'

'Anyone I know?'

He didn't answer.

'I'll need to check with your boss, of course.'

Doug's face dropped. 'I'd rather you didn't, DI Edwards, if that's possible. I know he won't take it at all well. If I'm to assist you, it'll have to be unofficial.'

Anne pursed her lips. 'How much do you know about my casework?'

Doug indicated if he could sit and Anne nodded.

'You have a young man whose throat was slit for no apparent reason apart from some spurious social media about a football injury. You have a woman calling herself a witch currently in custody regarding another slit throat at the same location. Now you have a missing girl who was going out with the dead youth and you have no credible suspect.'

'Is that Alice's analysis?' Anne said, trying to remain calm.

'Is it wrong?'

'Do you have a theory, then?' She raised her eyebrows and attempted to smile.

Doug stood up and crossed to the whiteboard. 'The main link seems to be the ruined hospital. The boy was killed there, the other man was killed there and it seems that the girl may have been heading there when she disappeared.'

Anne joined him at the wall. 'When Harry was stabbed, the only person there was Amelia, his girlfriend. When Jed Barber was killed, only Agnes the witch was present. No-one knows if Amelia vanished at that site or not.'

'The witch spends a lot of time there. How do we know she wasn't there at each event?'

'The knives we took from her cottage have been analysed but there's no unusual DNA.' Anne sighed. She knew this was coming from Alice who was convinced that Agnes was the killer. At the moment it was looking more and more likely but something told Anne the woman was innocent. Call it intuition or whatever, there didn't appear to be any reason why Agnes should suddenly become feral.

'Why do you have the Hall's up here? Is there a connection?'

'I didn't even know about them until you turned up.'

Doug stood thinking. Was there a connection between the two cases? 'What about this guy?' He pointed to Reuben Elbrow.

'Harry's foster-brother apparently. We don't know anything about him.'

Alice's head popped round the door.

'Come in, Alice,' said Anne. She turned to Doug. 'I'll let you know what help you can be DC Griffiths but for now, thanks for your insight.' She waited for him to get the hint.

'I'll...er...nip off, then.'

Anne nodded.

Alice stood back to let him through the door and remained there looking sheepish.

'Thanks, Alice.' Anne went back to her desk.

'I thought he could be useful.'

Anne slammed her hand on the desktop. 'Do you think I am so incapable that I need free assistance from the Metropolitan Police Force?' she said.

'No, of course not. I just thought…' Alice looked at the floor.

'You just thought, here's a handsome bloke who I wouldn't mind spending a bit more time with.'

'No,' protested Alice.

'You don't want to spend time with him, then?'

Alice blushed deeply. 'That's not the reason.'

'Of course it bloody is, Alice.' Anne woke her computer up and stared at the screen. She was angry with Alice but an extra detective she didn't have to pay for would be useful – if she could trust Doug Griffiths. There was something about him that made her feel uneasy. Was she jealous? Jealous of the attention Alice was getting? Alice was still standing by the door looking uncomfortable. 'For fuck's sake sit down, Alice,' she snapped.

Alice crept towards Anne's desk, slipping into the chair in front of it. 'I'm sorry, Anne,' she muttered. 'I guess I wasn't really thinking.'

Anne looked up at her and shook her head. 'How old are you, Alice?'

'Twenty-five.'

'So why are you behaving as though you're fifteen?'

Alice sighed. 'Look, Anne. You know what my love life has been like. No-one's interested in me once they find out I'm a copper. Never have been. Here's a bloke who seems to care – unlike anyone else round here. But you're right, I shouldn't have encouraged him to come and help us. I'll tell him to back off.'

Anne had always been aware that her lack of ruthlessness had held her back in her career. She ought to agree and let Alice get rid of Doug but she also knew that would only make for a sulky Detective Sergeant and bad feeling in her team. 'Tell him I'll give him a trial.'

Alice couldn't stop the grin appearing on her face no matter how hard she was trying. She pulled herself together. 'Any luck with the social media?'

Anne groaned. 'Not a thing. What the fuck do people see in this rubbish?'

'It's a young person's thing, I think.'

Anne glared at Alice for a moment but couldn't help her face softening into a smirk. 'You're a cheeky bugger, Alice Porter.'

Alice crossed to the computer on Anne's desk, peeking over her shoulder. Amelia's Facebook page was open showing a few threads from friends and acquaintances. 'What's that?' she said pointing to a thread posted by someone calling themselves 'Twinkle'. All it said was 'Bet im rite'. It had no direct relation to any of the other posts in the thread.

Anne shrugged. 'There's loads of stuff like that. No relevance. I don't know how these young people manage to understand it all.'

Alice almost commented but knew better.

'It's just teenage banter, isn't it?' said Anne.

'Could be truth amongst it somewhere even so.'

Anne shrugged.

'Right. You and your paramour can spend the afternoon looking for the other two who were with Jed Barber. See what you can find out. We know one of them is called Jesse Burton or Jesse James. Find him and get him to tell you who is pal is and what happened to Jed Barber. And Alice?'

'Yes?' She was already on her way out.

'Concentrate on the job in hand, please.'

Alice blushed and left the room. Anne went back to her computer.

CHAPTER SIXTEEN

Anne had given Abeer – a young person – the task of sending out pleas on social media for anyone who may have useful information about Amelia or Harry. She'd trusted her to be sensitive so Abeer had suggested that any replies should come through the direct messenger app. Consequently, Abeer's computer was now pinging every two or three seconds.

'Can you mute that, please, Abeer?' she demanded.

'Sorry. I didn't expect quite such a response.'

'Anything useful?'

'Not really yet. Stuff we already know. Glowing reports of what a great guy Harry was and how everyone is worried about Amelia.'

'Anything on her father?'

Abeer shook her head.

Anne wasn't surprised. There wasn't any social media when she was a teenager but it didn't stop the rumourmongers, they just did it less publicly. She'd heard nothing from Alice which again didn't surprise her. She had a pretty good idea as to how much work her and the Man from the Met were actually doing. Anne's problem was she was too soft, although no-one would believe it, but she remembered what it was like to be young and in love – just about – although Alice was close to stepping over the mark. There were still two murders and a disappearance to deal with – not even counting Doug Griffiths' East London case.

'It was the ghost, apparently,' said Abeer.

'Really?'

'According to, amongst others, BATTYBOOBOO69.'

'Is that her handle?' Anne raised her eyebrows.

Abeer smirked. 'Have you been revising, Ma'am – Anne?'

'I'm down wiv da kidz, girl.'

Abeer had to stop herself spluttering. 'She says she saw a figure in a black cloak with a hood hanging around St Giles around the time Harry was killed.'

'Bring her in,' said Anne.

'I don't know who she is.'

'Find out. Do you want coffee?'

Abeer nodded as Anne went to the kitchen.

A return message to BATTYBOOBOO69 brought a response which Abeer hadn't expected. She'd asked for more details about the ghost and BATTYBOOBOO69 had been more than keen to expound. Abeer's request for her to come to the station was agreed and BATTYBOOBOO69 would be there after school.

*

Jesse Burton was going through turmoil. He'd discussed Jed's death with Brad Jordan, the third member of the trio, yesterday and suggested they should go to the police. Tell them what happened.

'We don't know what happened, idiot, do we?' he'd replied.

'But there was only the witch there. We could get her locked up.'

'Unless she turns them all into toads and escapes through the cell wall.' Brad had leered at Jesse.

Jesse was now sitting under the dartboard in the pub opposite the leper hospital again, waiting for Brad to turn up for their usual morning libation. He only had enough cash for one pint until Brad arrived, so he was drinking far slower than he normally would. Jed's death had shaken him. He'd never expected the witch to actually stab anyone. Why would she when she could just cast a spell? Maybe it wasn't her after all. Maybe it was the ghost. He'd mentioned that to Brad as well, only to be greeted with derision. But he knew differently. He'd seen the ghost. More than once. Admittedly it was always after leaving the pub, but for several nights now he'd spied a hooded figure appearing out of nowhere and scrambling around amongst the ruins. One thing he was absolutely sure about was that he would not set foot in that place ever again, no matter what the circumstances.

He was starting to get stressed now. He had less than an inch left in his pint glass and there was still no sign of Brad. He eyed the dark brown liquid in the hope he might have been mistaken and there was still half a pint or more in the glass, only to be disappointed by the truth. His whole life was a disappointment. Jed had told him he ran the town when he'd first recruited him. No-one could do anything without his say-so. Not the shopkeepers; not the council; not even the police. It had been exciting. It was like joining the Mafia. Except it hadn't been. Jed Barber hadn't run anything. He'd been a fantasist. Jesse had no idea where he got his money from but it was certainly not by extortion. That's when he should have got out – when he found out Jed was a fraud – but he hadn't. He'd hung around. What else was he going to do? He fingered the scar across his face. He was proud of that at least. 'You should have seen the other guy', he used to tell people when they asked. The other guy had been dead. Jesse had spent five of a ten-year manslaughter conviction in prison, even though he hadn't been the killer. That was where he'd discovered there were bigger and tougher and certainly cleverer people than him. People he did not want to mix with; people who would throw him under a bus at a moment's notice. At least Jed wasn't like that. He wasn't really a gangster. Jed had looked after him. And now he was dead, Jesse hadn't a clue what he should do next.

The door opened and Jesse's heart rose. He downed the remaining inch of bitter and looked over to the door. The person who came in was not Brad Jordan but a tall man with fair curly hair. He was followed by someone he thought he knew. Wasn't she a female copper? He flipped his hood up and bent down to pretend to tie his shoelace. From under the table, he could see two pairs of feet approach and stop less than a yard away.

'Jesse Burton?' said the woman. He stayed couched down. 'Or should I say Jesse James? Looking for your six-shooter?'

Slowly Jesse rose to a sitting position and stared at the two people.

'Want a pint?' asked the man. 'You look a bit dry there. Bitter is it?'

Jesse's need for a drink made him nod his head slowly as the woman sat down opposite him. His eyes were scanning the pub.

'Don't look for an escape route, Jesse. We just want to have a quick chat.'

'What about?'

'Jed Barber,' she replied.

'No comment,' he said.

'No comment, no beer,' she responded.

'I wasn't there,' he tried, as Doug Griffiths put a pint glass on the table just out of his reach. Doug remained standing.

'Strictly speaking, you were,' stated Alice.

'Not when he got killed.'

'What were you doing there?' Alice's hand stopped Jesse reaching for the glass.

Doug put a small glass next to the pint. 'I got you a whisky chaser. Don't know if you drink the amber nectar in the morning or not.'

Jesse's lips were starting to dribble. 'What do you want to know?' he said quietly.

'Who did it.' Alice pushed the pint towards him but kept her hand clasped around the glass.

'I told you, I wasn't there.' Alice withdrew the glass. 'The witch was there. She must have done it.'

'She says she didn't.'

'She put a spell on us.' Jesse reached for the glass again.

Alice looked down her nose. 'A spell?'

'She must have done.' Both his and Alice's hands were on the pint now.

'Don't make me waste this, Jesse.' Alice shook the glass, spilling some on the table. 'Whoops.'

'Ask Brad,' asked Jesse. 'He'll tell you.'

'Brad?'

Jesse realised he may have spoken too soon. He'd assumed that Brad's absence was due to him having been questioned by this pair but the woman was looking as though she'd never heard of him.

'Brad who, Jesse?'

'I don't know.'

'Was he the other one at the leper hospital the night Jed Barber was killed?'

Jesse shrugged. He was still eyeing the bitter as though it was a crock of gold. Alice pushed it gently towards him.

'Tell me who Brad is, Jesse.' She tipped the glass slightly, a splash of beer landing on the table.

'Brad Jordan,' said Jesse. 'He didn't do it.'

Alice let the glass go. It wobbled as it righted itself. Jesse grabbed it and sank half of it in one go.

'What I don't understand, Jesse, is what you were doing there in the first place?'

Jesse wiped his mouth. 'We wanted to scare the witch,' he admitted.

'Why?'

'She's a pain.'

'Did you post shit through her letterbox?'

Jesse looked at the floor and mumbled something.

'Didn't quite catch that,' said Alice, reaching for Jesse's glass again.

He grabbed the pint and held it away from her. 'I said, that was Jed. He's done it before. I don't like things like that.'

Alice kept staring at him as he slurped the bitter. 'So what happened at the ruins?'

'She said she'd turn us into toads.'

Alice had to dig deep to stop herself laughing.

'Did she?'

Jesse shook his head. 'We ran away.'

'All of you?'

'Me and Brad. Jed stayed.'

'Who else was there, Jesse?'

He'd finished his pint and was looking at the whisky that Doug was still holding on to.

'Just the ghost.'

Alice covered her mouth to hide her smirk. This man was evidently an idiot.

'I seen him.'

'Who?'

'The monk. He wears a big black cloak with a hood and scuttles about over there.' He pointed through the wall towards the leper hospital.

'You've seen him before?'

Jesse nodded. 'A few times.'

'What sort of time?'

Jesse didn't answer.

'Wouldn't be closing time, by any chance?'

Jesse Burton leaned forward, his elbows on the tabletop. 'I know you think I'm stupid. Maybe I am but I knows what I seen and, if I were you, I'd look to the monk.'

Alice turned to Doug, who passed the whisky across the table. Jesse downed it in one.

Alice stood up and moved to Doug. 'Don't disappear, Jesse. We may need to speak again. Tell your friend Brad as well.' They went to the bar. Two minutes later they left the pub as the barman took another pint over to Jesse Burton.

*

'Brad Jordan is the name of the third man, and Jed Barber was the shitter.' stated Alice as she and Doug walked into the office. 'Jesse Burton says it's the ghost what done it.'

Anne and Abeer exchanged glances. 'Did he describe this ghost?'

Alice laughed. 'Oh yes. He says he wears a long black cloak with a hood – like a ghostly monk.'

'He's not the only person who's seen this figure,' said Anne, going over to the printer.

'I suspect if you tell enough people something some of them are going to believe it,' observed Alice.

Anne brought over a dark, blurry A4 print that could be a monk wearing a black cloak with a hood and put it in front of Alice. 'We have a girl called BATTYBOOBOO69 coming in this afternoon. She put this on a post about Harry Ellis saying she'd seen the monk in the leper hospital the day Harry was killed.'

Alice looked sceptical. 'There's no such thing as ghosts, you know that don't you, Anne.'

'How can you be certain, Alice?' piped up Abeer, who was still going through the social media posts.

Alice looked from one to the other. 'You're not seriously suggesting some sort of supernatural serial killer, I hope?'

Anne shrugged. 'Got a better idea?'

'You're winding me up, aren't you?'

Anne grinned. 'Only partly. These two are the only witnesses to a possible murderer. Someone in the right place at the right time. Did Jesse mention seeing the spectre being there when Jed met his end?'

Alice shook her head. 'Just the witch. Who is another witness – or perpetrator.'

'You really don't like her, do you?'

'I'm ambivalent.' Alice put her nose in the air. 'I just don't see the point of her, that's all.'

'Should we charge her?'

'Obviously.'

Anne sighed. 'If we get it wrong, she is the sort that could cause us a heap of trouble. I expect she's not exactly a big fan of the police and public opinion of the force is not very high at the moment.'

'But we can't keep her much longer.' Alice couldn't understand Anne's reticence at throwing the book at someone found at a murder scene with a knife and blood all over her.

Anne nodded, making up her mind, 'She's not really a flight risk, though, is she? I think I'll let her go, warning her we may need to speak again.'

'I'm sure that'll go down well,' said Alice. 'Make sure you hide her broomstick.'

Anne's phone vibrated on her desk. She picked it up and raised her eyes to the heavens. 'Not now, Felix. I'm a bit busy.'

'I have news for you.' Felix Corbett, the journalist for the local paper could almost be sensed gloating at the other end.

'That's your job, Felix. I doubt it's anything we don't already know.'

'Allan Goddard and the Ellis family.'

'What about them?'

'Meet me in the Queen's Head at seven this evening.' He hung up.

'What did he want?' asked Alice.

'He wants me to meet him in the Queen's later. Says he has some news for us.'

'That'll be the day.'

Anne looked at Alice. 'You're not on duty this evening, are you? Fancy a drink?'

'Well…' Alice hesitated.

'Okay.' Anne looked around the office. 'Where's lover-boy?'

'If you mean DC Griffiths, he's getting something to eat.'

'Queen's Head?'

Alice shrugged.

'I'm meeting Felix Corbett there at seven and I might need some back-up to stop me hitting him,' said Anne.

'Are you serious?' Abeer looked worried.

'No she's not, Abeer, but he can be the proverbial pain in the butt. Have you not met our local newshound?'

'No. I've read some of his stuff though. I think he just makes it up most of the time.'

'Of course he does, Abeer, he's a journalist,' remarked Anne, 'Anyway I have to meet him, see if he does actually have some news.'

Alice grinned. 'I suppose I could put myself out on my evening off to accompany you to the pub.'

'Don't accompany me, just be there in the other bar, just in case.' Anne looked over to her detective constable. 'Do you drink, Abeer?'

'You know I do – when none of my family are around.'

'You're welcome to join us if you would like to. Once I'm rid of Corbett, I think we deserve a night off.'

Abeer didn't really agree. It didn't seem they had got anywhere with any of the cases yet. Surely a night of boozing could wait at least until they had a lead but she chose not to contradict her boss. 'I'll see if I can slip away,' she said.

'Still not found your own place?'

Abeer shook her head. She knew there'd be no way she'd be going to the pub tonight.

*

BATTYBOOBOO69 turned out to be a teenage girl with dyed black hair, black eyeshadow and black nail varnish.

'Are you allowed to go to school like that?' asked Anne as she and Abeer sat opposite her.

BATTYBOOBOO69 shrugged. Abeer suspected she'd put her make-up on after she'd left school.

'So, what can you tell us about this person you saw at the leper hospital, Batty?' Anne didn't know what else to call her. 'Actually, what is your real name?'

'It's Melanie,' the Goth replied. 'It wasn't a person.'

'I suspect it wasn't a ghost, either.' Anne raised her eyebrows, waiting for a response.

'Whatever,' said Melanie. She was nervous now. The bravado she'd felt when she'd been asked to come in had all but gone. She'd thought the police would welcome her help but these two didn't even look like police, they weren't wearing uniforms. She felt stupid. They obviously didn't believe her.

'What sort of time was this, Melanie, when you saw the figure?' Abeer was asking the questions now.

'After school.'

'Did you think it was a bit strange?'

She shrugged again. 'I've seen it since then but it's usually later.'

'How much later, Melanie.' Anne intervened.

'About elevenish.'

'You're out at that time of night, are you?'

'Sometimes. My mum has to work nights.'

'And your dad?'

'Left.'

Abeer felt sorry for the girl. Home alone all night while her single mother had to go to work. What sort of chance did she have in life, she wondered. Much as she disliked the control her own parents exerted, at least they were there if she ever needed them. This kid was left roaming the streets when she should have been at home in bed.

'How old are you, Melanie?' she asked.

'Fourteen.'

'Is your mum at home now?'

Melanie shook her head.

'So, you knew Harry Ellis?'

Melanie nodded. She seemed to have lost her voice.

'And Amelia Goddard?'

Another nod.

'Have you seen Amelia recently, Melanie?' Anne was getting fed up with this. BATTYBOOBOO69 didn't have any news for them and she was pretty sure this interview would be on social media within minutes. Melanie getting her fifteen minutes of fame.

'No,' said the girl, finding her voice again. 'She's missing.'

'She is. Any idea where she might be?'

Melanie looked at the floor and mumbled something.

'Speak up, Melanie. I can't hear you.'

'I said, I hope the ghost hasn't got her.' A tear escaped from her eye, leaving a trail of black down her cheek.

'I'm sure he hasn't, Melanie,' said Abeer reassuringly. She looked at Anne, who was staring at the girl.

'Can I go now?' asked Melanie, her voice tight.

'Yes, you can,' said Anne. 'But I don't want to see any of this on any social media platform. Is that understood?'

Melanie nodded, another tear following the first. Abeer took her to the front of the station.

'Did I do wrong?'

'No, Melanie, you've been very helpful. Just keep this between us though. Okay?'

The girl headed off across the car park, Abeer watching her. Anne appeared at her shoulder.

'That's half an hour of my life I'll never get back,' she said.

'I thought you were a bit harsh, Ma'am. The poor girl was scared.'

'She had nothing to tell us Abeer but well done for bringing her in.' Anne turned and went back to the office, leaving Abeer trying not to feel as though she'd messed up. Minnie Dawson smiled at her.

CHAPTER SEVENTEEN

Felix Corbett was already there when Anne walked into the Members' at ten to seven. He was standing at the bar, a nearly empty pint glass in front of him.

'White wine, isn't it?' he checked with Anne.

'Orange juice, please. Some of us are here to work,' she replied curtly.

Felix shrugged, ordered himself another pint along with the orange juice. 'Shall we sit?' he said going over to the small table in the nook by the fire. There was no-one else in the Members' which Anne was happy about. Whatever Felix had to say ought to remain confidential. She spotted Alice and Doug entering through the terrace door and taking a seat in the back bar She nodded to them and followed Felix.

'Cheers,' he said, raising his glass.

'What do you have, Felix?' she replied not reciprocating the toast.

'How much do you know about the Goddard's and the Ellis's?'

Anne didn't reply.

'Okay. Did you know that Allan Goddard used to work for Edwin Ellis?' He smiled and took a sip of his beer.

This was actual news to Anne. If it was true, why did she not know about it? 'Go on,' she said.

'Edwin Ellis had a small company in London that made computer programs. He rode the bit.com revolution for quite a while before selling it for a fortune and moving out here to rural Essex. His accounts were done by a firm called Witheford's.'

'Yes, I know it. Allan Goddard works there.'

Felix nodded. 'He used to until about six months ago. They had to let him go it would seem.'

'Why?'

Felix shrugged.

'So, where does he work now?'

Felix shrugged again.

Anne was puzzled. Linda Goddard kept saying he was at work and often had to work late. Allan Goddard had implied he still worked at Witheford's.

Felix finished his pint and looked at Anne with a smile that signified he had more to say if his pint was somehow refreshed.

Anne went to the bar returning with a pint of bitter and a white wine.

Felix looked at her glass. 'Finished work, then?'

Anne didn't respond.

Felix sipped his beer. 'Edwin Ellis became quite pally with his accountant, it appears, having 'business' meetings,' he actually did air quotes, 'in a pub in Central London.'

'That's not unusual,' Anne was beginning to wonder if this was a waste of another half-hour or more.

'According to my source, which obviously I can't let you have, they chatted a great deal about Edwin's desire to father a child and how no amount of trying was resulting in any offspring. Allan apparently was not keen on having any children at that time, blaming not being able to afford the cost of bringing up a baby.'

'And?'

'Well, their relationship developed into Allan being invited round for dinner on regular occasions. It seems his wife, June, never attended for some reason.'

'Where is this going, Felix. I'm quite busy at the moment and all I'm hearing from you is gossip from some punter in a pub.'

'Have you met Linda Ellis?'

'I have, yes.'

'She's very attractive and quite a bit younger than old Edwin.'

Anne looked at Felix. A wry smile spread across his lips.

'Imagine what she must have looked like, say, seventeen years ago. That was around the time Mr Goddard regularly dined at the Ellis' house. Apparently, Edwin wasn't there on occasions and that was around the time he miraculously became virile.'

Anne sipped her wine. 'Are you suggesting that Allan Goddard and Linda Ellis had an affair?'

Felix shrugged. 'Who knows. Could just be a coincidence.'

'Yes it could, Felix. Do not try and print any of this. It's just gossip. Thanks for the heads-up, I'll look into it but having met all of the said parties, I think your theory is most unlikely. I also know that Edwin Ellis has a great deal of money and would not spare any of it pursuing you through the courts were you were to try and libel him.'

Felix slugged his bitter. 'I know, that's why I'm telling you. I only trust you will let me know if I'm right before any other hack gets their hands on the scoop.'

Anne smiled. 'You know you can trust me.'

Felix finished his drink, thought briefly about cadging another from DI Edwards, changed his mind and departed.

The second the door closed behind him, Alice and Doug came through to the Members'.

'Well?' said Alice.

Anne finished her wine and held up her glass.

'I'll get it.'

'Thank you, DC Griffiths.'

'Well?' repeated Alice, squeezing into the seat opposite Anne.

'Felix seems to think Allan Goddard might be Harry Ellis's biological father.'

Alice laughed out loud. 'You are joking. You've met Linda Ellis. Why on earth would she have a fling with a creep like Goddard?'

'To conceive a child?'

'That's a very scary thought,' said Alice seriously.

'What is?' Doug put refreshed drinks on the table.

'Conceiving children, DC Griffiths. Alice finds the thought scary,' said Anne. Alice blushed and threw a beermat at Anne.

Charlotte appeared at the bar, beckoning to Anne, who heaved herself up from her seat and went over.

'I think there might be someone in the other bar you were asking about,' she whispered.

Anne peered through to see a man with long hair and a goatee leaving the bar and finding a table by the window. Anne beckoned Alice.

'Is that him?' she nodded her head towards the table the man was now sitting at nursing his pint of lager.

Alice nodded.

'Okay, come on. Bring lover-boy.'

Alice glared at Anne's back but indicated that Doug should join them as they went through to the back bar.

Having three people suddenly standing by one's table was more than a little disturbing, especially as one was in a place one had never visited before. The man tried to ignore them, looking out over the river.

'Hello again,' said Alice, sitting at a chair opposite him 'We met the other evening.'

He looked at her. 'I don't remember.' His eyes flicked towards the other two. 'What do you want?'

'Nothing,' replied Alice. 'Just being friendly. You're not from round here, are you?'

He shook his head.

'Do you have a name?'

He went to stand up but Doug Griffiths took a step towards him, cramping him.

'What is this?' he said. He looked towards the bar but there was no-one in sight. 'What's going on?'

Anne stepped up to the table. 'We'd just like to know what your name is and what you're doing here, that's all. You were asking about Harry Ellis, I believe.'

'He's dead,' said the man, his head dropping.

'Yes we know.' Anne kept staring at him. 'He was murdered. Do you know who killed him?' No-one spoke. 'Was it you?' The man was breathing heavily, a small trickle of sweat showing under his hairline.

'What makes you think that?' He tried again to stand up, pushing Doug out of the way. The table wobbled and his pint fell to the floor. Anne stood in front of his exit and held up her warrant card. He stopped. Alice had risen and was next to Anne, her warrant card in her hand also.

'What's going on?' he repeated.

'We just want a quick chat, that's all. Sit down. DC Griffiths, go and get him another pint, please.'

The man realised there was nothing he could do but obey so he retook his seat at the table. A few drips of lager dribbled onto his leg.

'And a cloth, DC Griffiths,' yelled Anne, taking the seat Alice had vacated. 'So, let's try again. What's your name?'

'Why do you want to know?'

Anne looked down at the spilt beer that was creating a small river across the tabletop. Charlotte appeared with a cloth and started to mop up as Doug arrived with another pint.

'Thanks, Charlotte,' she said and turned back to the man. 'Why were you interested in Harry Ellis?' she asked him.

'I was supposed to meet him but he never turned up. I know why now.'

'Are you a friend of his?'

'Sort of.'

'Meaning?'

'I knew him some years ago.'

'How many years ago?' Anne had a theory working its way through her mind.

He shrugged. 'I don't know.'

'Shall we say about seven?' Anne tried.

'Could be.'

'Is your name Reuben?'

Alice looked at her and then back to the man.

'Look, what's going on?' The man's voice was tight, worried, scared.

'I think you're Harry's brother. Well, not his biological brother but someone his parents fostered before Harry was born. Am I right?' Anne said.

The man paused, staring at her, and then nodded his head.

'See, that wasn't too difficult, was it?' Anne reverted to her smiling face. 'So, why now, Reuben? Why try and make contact after all these years?'

'He wanted me to meet his girlfriend.'

'And did you?'

He shook his head. 'I told you, he didn't turn up.'

'Where were you meeting him?'

He turned towards the quay. 'Just there. By the boats.'

'They're barges but never mind. Look, Reuben, we really shouldn't be discussing this in the pub. Would you do me a favour and accompany us to the police station?'

'I haven't done anything. Are you arresting me?'

Anne held up her hands. 'No, of course not. I'm just making a request. Where are you staying?'

'A bed and breakfast in town,'

'Not the Travelodge, then,' said Alice.

He looked as though he'd forgotten she was there. 'No.'

'Hopefully we won't keep you long, Reuben. Finish your drink first.' She turned to Doug. 'Could you do me a favour and escort Mr Elbrow up to the station, DC Griffiths? You can take my car.' She handed him the keys. 'Alice and I will follow shortly.'

Reuben Elbrow looked up at Doug then at Anne. He sighed and stood up. 'You can keep your drink,' he said as he went to the front door with Doug.

Anne went to the bar. 'Two white wines, please, Charlotte.'

'What about him?' Alice pointed to where Reuben and Doug had gone.

'I don't think he wants a white wine. He didn't drink his lager.' Anne grinned.

'You just going to leave Doug to cope with him?'

'For a little while. He wanted to help, he said.'

'That's not fair, Anne.'

'I know,' she said, raising her glass and moving through to the Members' Bar.

'How did you know, anyway,' said Alice, following her through.

'What? That he was Reuben Elbrow?'

Alice nodded.

'I didn't but I deduced, Alice. That's what detectives do. I deduced that he was probably seven or eight years older than Harry was and I wondered why Harry would have an old friend that much his senior.'

'He could have been a friend from the gym?' suggested Alice.

'But he implied he hadn't seen him for years, which would mean Harry was a child when they last met. I guess I put two and two together and hit the jackpot.'

Alice sat down. She was still angry that Anne had sent this Reuben off with Doug. It wasn't his job to look after him. She wasn't even sure they had any right to apprehend him at this time of night for no reason.

'Why did you want him at the station?'

'So I could record him. Do you not think it's a bit of a coincidence that Reuben Elbrow, who hasn't seen Harry for years, turns up just around the time that the said Harry gets killed?'

'So why are we sitting in the pub and not getting answers from him?'

'Because we're off-duty. I don't want to overwork you, DS Porter.'

Alice was confused. Why was Anne behaving like this? It wasn't like her. Normally, she'd have been up to the station like a rocket trying to get information from this man. He could be the murderer and she'd let him go off with Doug on his own. 'Can Doug get into the station?' she asked. 'Minnie Dawson won't be there at this time of night.'

'Have you not given him the code, Alice?' Anne sipped her wine.

Alice sighed. That's what this was about. She knew this would happen. Anne didn't approve of her relationship with Doug. 'Me and Doug are not that involved, Anne. We're just having fun.'

'I know,' said Anne innocently. 'And a jolly good thing too. Get Charlotte to call a cab, will you?' She knocked back her drink.

*

June Goddard was sitting in her kitchen nursing a mug of coffee. Her fervour was diminishing the longer Amelia was not found. What could she do? She'd had no positive response from the posters or the TV interview or the so-called search party and nothing from the police.

Her husband, Allan, was useless. He was hiding in his work, she was aware of that. He had difficulty showing any emotion – other than the occasional angry outburst. Why had that policewoman asked if he'd ever hit her? Did she know something? He hadn't hit her but she'd been known to slap him down every now and then when he deserved it.

Apart from that big bonus he'd got just before they bought this house, she knew he found his work unsatisfying. He was still a junior after all these years. She knew other people had overtaken him, moved on to the bigger clients. He was useless that's why, too eager to please, which showed him up as a bit of a pushover and kept him in his lowly position.

He was working late again today, he'd said, which meant he'd come home having had too much to drink. She was sure most people would have taken time off if their daughter had gone missing but not Allan. He couldn't let his clients down, he'd told her. What about letting his daughter down? That didn't seem to matter. If she was truthful with herself, she didn't mind all that much. He was no use when he was here. They still hardly ever spoke, these days.

Her phone was on the tabletop next to her. She'd been staring at it night and day, hoping, longing for Amelia to get in touch. But she hadn't. She knew she wouldn't, she didn't have her phone but she just prayed that somehow she'd find a way. Every now and then the thought that she was dead crossed her mind and it was getting more and more difficult to dismiss it. The Reverend Frank Thatcher had been compassionate and caring. He'd made her feel somehow hopeful and more secure but when she was at her home alone, the old feelings started to take over. No-one had seen or heard anything about her daughter. She had literally disappeared off the face of the earth.

A text message came through and she leaped to read it. "Staying in town tonight. Early meeting." it read. June sighed. What was happening to her life? All the things she'd relied on were disappearing. Her daughter, her husband, everything. Now she was on her own in a kitchen she never used, in a house that didn't feel like a home. She threw the mug of cold coffee across the kitchen, a brown river spattering the white wall like a Jackson Pollock masterpiece. She laughed as she looked at the broken pottery strewn over the floor, before burying her head in her hands and sobbing.

*

Rueben Elbrow sat in the chair opposite Doug Griffiths. Neither of them spoke as they waited. Doug wasn't sure what his position was – whether he should say anything or not. This wasn't his case and it wasn't his police force. This was an Essex Police case. He hadn't expected DI Edwards to instruct him to take the guy up to the station. Was she testing him? He presumed that was the reason and he had no intention of giving her an excuse to get rid of him. He needed to stay in Maldon for a bit longer yet.

Rueben Elbrow was scrutinising him. 'I know you,' he said, eventually.

'No you don't,' warned Doug.

The door opened and Anne and Alice entered.

'Thank you, DC Griffiths. You can go now,' Anne informed him.

'Yes, Ma'am,' he said standing up.

'Alice is staying here with me,' she added, as she spotted the look between them. 'She may be free later.'

Alice grimaced as Doug left the room.

'So, Rueben,' said Anne sitting down and turning on an old-fashioned double tape recorder. 'Oh, I'm recording this, so I get everything right. Is that okay?'

Rueben nodded.

'Good.'

'Why am I here?' asked Rueben.

'Because you kindly offered to help with our enquiries into the death of your brother.'

'How can I help you? I wasn't here.'

'Where were you?'

'In London, where I live.' He was staring directly at Anne. No nerves, no fear – he'd done this before.

'But you're here now. You say you came here to meet your brother whom you have not seen for many years. Are you expecting us to believe that it's a coincidence? The timing, I mean.'

'Yes. It is.'

'When my colleague here asked you why you were looking for Harry the other night you upped and ran. Why was that?'

He laughed. 'I didn't up and run. I needed somewhere to stay.'

'Why didn't you tell DS Porter why you wanted to know about Harry?'

He sighed. 'Firstly, I didn't know she was the police and secondly…' he paused. Anne waited. 'I don't know how much anyone round here knew about my relationship with Harry's parents.'

'You tell me, Rueben. We know they fostered you.'

'They did.'

Rueben Elbrow sat back. He was resigned to giving them as much information as they wanted. He wanted to know what had happened to Harry. The stuff he'd gleaned from the newspaper hadn't made much sense to him. Stories of ghosts and ghoulies.

'I was six years old when Linda and Edwin Ellis fostered me. My birth mother was a junkie. I never knew my birth father but there had been several men, on a regular basis, who'd shacked up briefly with my mother, feeding her habit and treating me as an obstruction. When I was four the Social Services intervened and removed me to a Boy's Home. I hated it. I suppose I didn't understand why I'd been taken away. My behaviour became bad as I rebelled against the discipline I was now being subjected to. I was moved from Home to

Home as the authorities tried to decide what to do with me. Linda and Edwin Ellis had been trying to conceive a baby but without success. They were quite a laid-back, middle-class couple and it was suggested they might like to look at fostering to create a family. I was six when I moved into their house in the leafy suburbia that was Epsom in Surrey.'

'How was that? Being fostered, I mean.'

He smiled. 'For the first time in my life I realised I was happy and I turned from a potential hooligan to a model pupil at the local primary school. I discovered a talent for drawing, exceeding the efforts of many of the older boys and girls. Reading and writing was above the level expected and Linda and Edwin proudly displayed my artwork and naïve poetry on the door of their fridge.'

'So it was a typical happy family. What went wrong?'

'Harry. It wasn't his fault. Just before my eighth birthday Linda unexpectedly became pregnant, totally naturally, and was to bring a new baby boy into the household. I'd always wanted a brother or sister but once young Harry was born, my presence was not as all-consuming as it had been. Linda particularly spent all of her time with the baby, who screamed a lot, which seemed to make Linda depressed. She cried a lot – not when I was in the same room but I could hear her from my bedroom at night. Edwin had to spend more time at work – to pay for the new family, he said.'

'How did that make you feel?'

'More and more isolated. There were no more innocent little drawings on the fridge – my artwork had become less fanciful anyway, no more bright orange houses under bright yellow sunshine, everything took on a much darker tone, but no-one noticed. My foster parents didn't appear to have much time for me anymore. Everything revolved around the precious Harry.'

'How long did this go on for?' Anne was making notes all the time Rueben talked.

'Forever,' said Rueben.

'You got into trouble with the police, I understand.'

'You've been researching me, I see.'

Anne looked up at him. 'Rueben, I didn't even know you existed until a few days ago. Linda told me Harry was an only child.'

He laughed bitterly. 'Yes, she would. I was sixteen when I first got into trouble. There was a group of young men who hung around at the school gates, all dressed in military attire – camouflage fatigues and the like – and all had short hair. My hair was long, and I became an object of ridicule for the youths. Shouts of 'pouf' and 'girlie' resounded each time I left the school grounds. Some of my fellow pupils started to join in during the school day. A rumour began suggesting that my heritage was Jewish – being called Rueben – something the far-right youths despised for no other reason than they thought they should. Linda was at her wits end; scared that Harry would become embroiled in the brouhaha. Complaints to the school brought no results, the Headmaster claiming he had no jurisdiction outside of the school gates. It came to a pinnacle when I was finishing GCSE's. I'd just left after a two-hour English exam and was taking home a piece of artwork I'd prepared as part of my forthcoming Art exam. One of the ever-present Fascists grabbed the watercolour and having cast his opinion, tore the paper into small pieces which he proceeded to throw in my face. I ran at the yobbo, fists flying, catching him a smack on the chin, sending him sprawling onto the pavement. The others stood for a moment, shocked at the retaliation that had never come before. I jumped on top of the youth who'd ruined my work and laid into him with a flurry of punches, memories of my mother's boyfriends flicking across my brain. I knew how to fight; I'd seen enough of it as a small child. I just knew it didn't resolve anything. Eventually, the boots from the others forced me to stop, my senses blunted, face bleeding, my reasoning vanishing with each kick. A policeman picked me up and put me in the back of a car. I was vaguely aware of people surrounding me – I didn't know who they were. The Fascists had disappeared. Following a quick check-up at the hospital, showing there was no permanent damage other than cuts and bruises, I was taken to the local police station and charged with affray. No amount of pleading my innocence appeared to make any difference and I was thrown into a cell.'

'Are you telling us you have a bit of a temper, Rueben?' asked Alice.

'I'm telling you the opposite.'

'And yet, you have been involved in other altercations with the police.'

He smiled. 'After that incident, I spent a lot of time on the internet, trying to find out why those youths seemed to be able to carry on activities that were surely illegal without being arrested. Incitement to racial hatred was a crime but very difficult to prove it would seem. Beating people up was obviously against the law but again, someone had to witness and report it – not the person who was beaten, though, it turned out. I discovered a number of left-wing sites, organisations that fought against the sort of behaviour displayed by the yobbos and I became more and more interested in them, signing up for newsletters.'

'Communist websites?' asked Alice.

Rueben shook his head. 'Once exams finished, I had nothing to do over the long summer but wait for the results. I had no friends as such. No-one I could meet up with and do things with. I was Persona Non Grata in Epsom. Edwin had opened a young person's saving account for me some years before and, having earned pocket money cleaning the family car, washing up, keeping my room tidy and weeding the garden, I'd built up a small amount of funds that had remained unused in the bank. I was limited as to the amount I could withdraw without my guardian's knowledge but it was enough for me to travel to local rallies. I joined a group called 'For The People', a Socialist faction determined to try and turn the country away from Capitalism and right-wing influences. Linda and Edwin weren't bothered when I came home late from some meeting – it meant I hadn't caused any annoyance for Harry.'

'And you were still living at home at this time?'

'Yes. My results were due in August. Normally all the pupils attended the school to receive an envelope containing the keys to their future but mine had been sent through the post. I'd been ready to go to the school but Edwin had stopped me.

"They don't want you to stay on, Reuben," he said.

"Meaning what?" I replied.

"If your results are good enough to go on to 'A' Levels, you'll have to do them somewhere else."

"Where?"

'Edwin looked down at the floor as though he couldn't look me in the eyes. "Now you're past the age of sixteen – you're very nearly seventeen – we no longer feel able to care for you. In a year you'll no longer be the responsibility of the council but for that year we think it would be better if you went back into the system."

'I said nothing. I stared at the top of Edwin's bowed head for a moment before going upstairs to my room. There was no way I was going back into any sort of system. This was exactly the sort of thing 'For The People' were fighting against. Individual's rights being taken away. I was nearly an adult. I could look after myself. Being sent back into the care system would be disastrous. I opened my results and packed a bag. There was a march in Central London the following day, meeting at Covent Garden. I'd never been there but I had Google maps on my phone. I left for good first thing in the morning.'

He paused. Alice looked at Anne. She couldn't see where this was going and she wanted to remind Anne that she wasn't on duty and would far rather be sitting in The Queen's Head with Doug. Anne was ignoring her. Rueben carried on. It was like watching some sort of one-man show.

'I wasn't used to being amongst such a large crowd of people, I felt insecure. I couldn't see anyone from the local group. I wasn't sure

I was even in the right place. On the right march. A white girl with dreadlocks approached and asked if I was okay – she said later I'd looked like a rabbit in the headlights – and she took my arm, leading me towards a group holding some home-made banners. I stayed with the girl, her name's Fliss – short for Felicity – in a squat she shared with the rest for a year and a bit before we were busted.'

'So you were doing drugs?' Anne said.

'Nothing more than the odd joint for me. Somewhere deep in my memory I knew what hard drugs had done to my birth mother.'

'Is that when you attacked the policeman?' continued Anne.

'I didn't attack him. He attacked me and it was on a march, not at the squat.'

'Did Linda and Edwin know where you were, what was going on?' asked Alice.

'They made no attempt to find me it seems. I was sure they were more than happy for me to disappear before I corrupted their dear little boy.'

'What about the social services. Strictly speaking you were still their responsibility.'

'I suspect they couldn't be bothered either.'

'So where did you go after you were evicted from the squat?'

'Fliss invited me to live with her in a flat in South Kensington. It belonged to her extremely rich father, against whose Capitalist ideals she'd rebelled, hence living in the squat. He'd bought her the flat when she was still at school but she'd refused to live there until now. She's a year and a half older than me but we decided it would be a laugh to set up home together in the flat that was empty. Empty properties when there were so many homeless was against her principles, she'd reasoned.'

'Do you still live with Fliss? In South Kensington?' asked Anne.

He nodded.

'Not a very left-wing area, is it?' said Alice.

'Our rather extreme radical attitudes have tempered slightly. We rarely go on marches now but we still feel the same. I found a job as a commercial artist at an advertising agency. Fliss suggested that I should try and make my peace with Linda and Edwin but when I reluctantly turned up at the old house, I discovered they'd moved – no forwarding address. I wasn't inclined to delve any further.'

'Until now.'

Rueben sighed, 'Until now. Earlier this year, there was a knock at the door. I was working from home and when I opened the door I saw a tall young man standing there smiling. It took me a moment to recognise my erstwhile brother. Harry was on a school trip to the Victoria and Albert Museum – part of his 'A' Level course – and had slipped away to find me.'

'How did he know where you lived?' asked Alice, now resigned to not meeting up with Doug – it was nearly ten o'clock.

'The internet, he told me. He said he didn't believe it was really my address. Like you, he thought it was far too posh an area for a Communist.'

'So you are a Communist?'

'I'm a Socialist. I asked Harry what he was doing there? He said he wanted to see me and that he thought his parents had treated me badly. He said my name is never mentioned in the house and…and that he missed me. I didn't know whether to take that as Gospel or not. I'd barely thought of him for seven years. He was a snotty child of ten when I'd left, now he was a good-looking teenager, confident and assured. He told me they'd moved to Essex and that although he hadn't wanted to, if he hadn't he'd have never met Amelia. He talked a lot about Amelia. She must have been very special to him.'

'I expect she was,' agreed Anne.

'He told me he wanted me to meet her but there was no way she'd be allowed to go to London, so I told him there was nothing to stop me going to Essex; it wasn't exactly the other end of the earth. Harry's face had lit up at the thought of showing off his girlfriend to his newly re-found brother. I have to admit, I felt quite brotherly towards him for the first time in my life. We arranged to meet at a place called Hythe Quay in Maldon. Harry had not given me his address or his phone number, unwilling to take the risk of Linda and Edwin discovering we'd met up. I waited for hours for Harry to turn up but he didn't appear. I had no way of contacting him which is how I ended up in that pub, in the hope someone might know his whereabouts. I booked into a hotel – a bed and breakfast, not the Travelodge – and decided to try and get hold of my brother the next day somehow. I only hoped that Linda and Edwin had not found out and barred him any contact.' He sighed and looked down at the floor. 'The truth turned out to be far darker and distressing.'

'So you didn't try to find him?'

'How could I? Anyway, it turns out he was already dead.'

'What about Amelia?' Anne looked him in the eyes, trying to read this stranger.

'What about her?'

'Did you meet up with her?'

'I don't even know what she looks like.'

'Why didn't you go home after you found out Harry was dead?' asked Alice.

He shrugged. 'I don't know. I suppose I didn't want to believe it. If I turned up at the quay again maybe he'd come walking down the street or something – I don't know.'

Alice could see tears starting to form in his eyes. She looked at Anne again.

'Do you have any witnesses to say where you were the night Harry died?'

Rueben sniffed and looked up, the rims of his eyes were red. 'Fliss. We were both in.'

'How do you know which night I'm talking about?' Anne stared at him.

'The night he was stabbed.'

'You know a lot about it.'

'It was in the paper. There was a copy at the bed and breakfast.'

'I can't say you seem all that shocked.'

Alice was astounded. It seemed to her that the man was only just holding it together.

'Of course I'm shocked.' His voice was raised now. 'My brother's been killed.'

'A brother who you couldn't be bothered to see for seven years.'

'I couldn't. Don't you understand?' He was shouting now, standing up.

Anne sat back and remained quiet for a minute. Rueben controlled himself and sat down again.

'Are you sure you never met up with Amelia, Rueben?'

'I'm positive. I don't know the girl.'

'I'm only asking because she's gone missing. I wondered if you might have some idea where she is?'

Rueben looked shocked. He didn't know she was missing.

'You didn't see her mother's TV interview?'

'No.'

'Or one of these?' Anne took one of June's posters from a file in front of her and showed it to Rueben.

He smiled. 'She's a pretty girl but a bit young.'

'Fifteen.'

'Poor kid. Have you asked Linda and Edwin...sorry, of course you have. I can't really help you there, I'm afraid.'

Alice's phone buzzed. Anne looked at her.

'Where is he?' she said. Alice didn't answer. 'Well, Mr Elbrow. It seems my detective sergeant has another engagement, so we'll call it a day, or a night, really. I would be grateful if you could hang around Maldon for another day or two – I'm sure your employers will understand. Maybe Fliss would like to join you then she could confirm your alibi to us.'

'I can ask her.' He paused, frowning. 'Are you accusing me of killing Harry?'

'We're not accusing you of anything but we may want to have a bit of a chat with you again. Leave your details with my colleague.' Anne smiled and stood up, offering her hand. Rueben took it and they shook before Alice saw him out of the station.

'What was all that about, Anne?' she said as her boss joined her. 'Do you think he did it?'

Anne shook her head. 'No.'

'So why have I wasted my evening off?'

'Don't be angry, Alice. I'm sure Doug'll still be waiting.' She looked at her watch. 'You should get last orders if you're quick.'

Alice gritted her teeth, turned, and went to her car.

*

Doug Griffiths was sitting in the pub across from the leper hospital. He'd chosen there instead of the Queen's in the hope that DI

Edwards wouldn't want to venture to that end of town. He wanted to have a drink with Alice on their own. He also wanted to have another chat with Jesse Burton but he wasn't there. The landlord said he hadn't been in since the last time they chatted to him, but Doug didn't believe him. He'd finally received a reply from Alice saying she was on her way – alone, she'd put, with an exclamation mark. It seemed she was not too happy with her boss, either. He ordered her a white wine and sat in a window seat.

Alice parked her car along the road. The leper hospital wasn't quite visible from the pub and she wanted to have a quick look before she joined Doug. It was quite dark and the time was getting near to closing so she chose not to cross over. As she turned towards the pub, out of the corner of her eye, she caught something moving in the grounds of St Giles. She tried to focus. What she saw sent shivers through her and she ran to the pub.

'You look like you've seen a ghost,' said Doug, as she rushed in pale faced.

She downed her wine in one. 'I think I have,' she replied.

CHAPTER EIGHTEEN

Anne was down to her last bottle of wine. She hadn't had the time nor the inclination to visit the supermarket and had never signed up for deliveries. She was sitting in her kitchen gradually making her way through it. She was angry with herself. Why was she trying to humiliate Alice? Was she jealous? At her age? What was that about? Doug Griffiths – good-looking as he evidently was – was not her type and too young. Why was she feeling like this? She thought about phoning Derek but it was far too late and, the mood she was in, it could open a whole new can of worms, so she sat drinking alone.

Rueben Elbrow had intrigued her. She'd wanted him to be the killer but she knew he wasn't. She'd tried to provoke him and he'd ranted briefly but she was sure he wasn't really the aggressive type. She believed his story. Part of her even felt sorry for him. Linda had denied his existence. Did they know he was in Maldon now? And if they did, what would their reaction be? Anne had taken the address of the B&B he was staying at and also his home address in London. Was she being vindictive making him stay here for another couple of days? He didn't need to. He hadn't been charged with anything. He certainly didn't know Amelia, she could tell that from his reaction to her photograph. She was no further forward with Harry, Amelia or Jed Barber. What's more, Agnes Waterhouse was still in custody. She'd meant to release her yesterday but then Felix Corbett and Rueben Elbrow had taken up her time. It would have to wait till morning now.

She took out the notes she'd made from the chat with Felix. Could there be any truth in what he was suggesting? She needed to check if Allan Goddard was still at Witheford's or not. If he wasn't, how come he could suddenly afford a house on the new estate? Was it some sort of payment for fathering Harry. The boy had been about sixteen by the time they moved. But Alice was right, if Linda wanted to have an affair to try and conceive, why on earth would she choose Allan Goddard? Because he was available? If so, did Edwin know that Harry wasn't his child? Felix had said he was often not at the 'dinner parties' or whatever they were. How was she supposed to approach this? Also did June know? If Harry was Allan Goddard's offspring, Harry and Amelia were half-siblings which could be one of the reasons Allan was so against their relationship? June seemed to approve, so presumably she didn't know. Linda had just said they were kids, not serious. Was she being naïve? If she'd given birth to Harry…

She put the empty wine bottle in the recycling. Her head was spinning – not from the wine, she convinced herself – but from her feeling of a lack of self-worth. No relationship; no good at her job; no friends. And the one person she could call a friend – Alice – she was pushing away because she was jealous. She needed sleep but made a coffee and put one of her father's albums on. Janis Ian, 'Between The Lines.' It was an album she'd turned to many times in her teenage years. Times when she was feeling down, feeling insecure. It never made her feel better but gave her an opportunity to wallow, which is exactly what she needed to do now.

*

'It can't have been a ghost.' Doug was having breakfast in Alice's kitchen.

'Logically, I know that,' she replied. 'But it was a hooded monk figure, in the mist. When I looked again, he was gone. You explain it.'

They had gone over to the ruins from the pub the previous night. Doug had leapt over the railings and scoured the place with his phone torch. He'd gone right to the end, by the big oak tree, checked on Agnes's herb garden – which was starting to look a bit neglected – and around every bit of stone that was still standing. There was no sign of anyone having been there. There were a few depressions in the grass but they could have been there for ages, none of them looked like footprints and none appeared to lead anywhere specific.

'I can't,' he admitted. 'You were relatively sober.' He grinned.

'It's not funny, Doug. It really shook me up.'

He stood up and put an arm round her shoulder. 'Sorry,' he said. 'I suppose you ought to tell Edwards.'

Alice glared at him. 'Oh yes because she's going to believe me. I bet the first thing *she'd* ask is how much I'd had to drink.'

'You'll still have to tell her. It could have some relevance.'

'I know. She's behaving really strange at the moment, though. I don't know what I've done wrong.'

Doug pointed to himself.

'What's that got to do with her?'

He shrugged. 'Maybe she thinks I'm taking up too much of your time.'

'Well, she can think what she likes.' She moved closer to him and kissed him. 'What time is it?'

Doug grinned. 'Time for you to go to work, unfortunately. Don't want to upset your boss any more than I already seem to have done. I'll wash up and then go and have another look round the leper hospital. Text me if she'll let you out for lunch.'

'I'll decide if I'm available for lunch,' she said, putting on her coat.

*

'How much had you had to drink, Alice?' asked Anne, after Alice had told her about the vision she'd seen at the leper hospital.

'It was before I even got to the pub because I was incarcerated here interviewing Reuben Elbrow, if you remember.'

Anne nodded. 'Yes, I'm sorry about that. I didn't keep you here deliberately. I've told him he can go home. We don't need to see his Fliss for an alibi.'

'So it was a complete waste of time,'

'Who knows. Where's DC Griffiths?'

'He's gone to look round the ruins again. We couldn't see anything last night, it was dark.'

Anne went to the whiteboard. 'So, that's you, Jesse Burton, Battybooboo69 all claiming to have seen this ghostly figure at the leper hospital.'

'And Agnes Waterhouse. Has she been charged yet?'

'No, she's been released.'

Alice sighed. There was no point in asking why. 'So maybe there's something in this ghost, if so many people have witnessed the phenomenon.'

Anne sucked her lip. 'You could be right but I don't think it's anything supernatural.'

Alice looked at her quizzically.

'These sightings only seem to have taken place after Felix Corbett wrote that article in the paper.'

'BATTYBOOBOO69 said she saw it on the evening of Harry's murder.'

'True but she didn't say she had until later. There was nothing on her social media until well after Felix's article. Like you said, Alice, if you tell enough people something enough times, they'll start to believe it.'

Alice gave it some thought. She was pretty sure she had not been hallucinating last night and she was pretty sure it wasn't suggestive thoughts put into her head by some local hack. 'It looked pretty real to me, Anne,' she said.

'Of course it did. Because it most probably was real. But not a ghost.'

Alice frowned. 'Are you saying it was a person?'

Anne nodded. 'Someone dressed up.'

Alice pulled a disbelieving face. 'Why?'

'To distract from the actual murderer. If someone can make us think it was a ghost what done it, we'll stop looking too closely at the real villain.'

Alice sat down. 'Anne,' she said. 'Are you feeling alright?'

'I have a bit of a headache, apart from that, perfectly, thank you.'

'Do you want me to check on all the fancy dress shops?' said Alice, not trying to hide her sarcasm.

'No. I want you to go to all the local churches. See if there's any robes missing.'

'Vicars don't wear cowls, do they?'

Anne shrugged. 'I don't know. Maybe. While you're doing that I need to have a rather difficult chat with Linda Ellis.'

*

Alice went to the leper hospital first and met up with Doug. He was studying the fence by the gap in the hedge.

'It looks as though several feet have trampled the grass near here,' he told her.

'I think it's a well-known route into the ruins,' Alice said. 'It's a nice, secluded place for a bit of hank-panky.'

'What are you suggesting, DS Porter,' said Doug, attempting to look shocked.

'I'm suggesting that young people still living at home might want somewhere to express their feelings for one another.'

'Oh.' He put on a disappointed look.

'I don't live with my parents, DC Griffiths.'

He went to hug her but she put her hands up to stop him. 'Not at work, Doug. Like you say, I don't want to antagonise my boss.'

He sighed theatrically. 'So you think these footprints are made by local youths looking for somewhere to…?'

She nodded. 'I think that's what Harry and Amelia were doing before they were interrupted.'

Doug nodded.

'And, anyway, ghosts don't leave footprints, do they?' she added.

'I've been all round here again this morning. Apart from the trampled grass, there's no sign of anyone being here and if the grass is always like that…?'

'Anne thinks it's someone dressing up as the ghost to put us off looking for the real culprit.' Alice's expression showed what a ridiculous idea she thought that was.

But Doug thought about it. 'It's possible,' he said. 'I worked on a case where someone dressed as a clown, pretending to entertain children, when he was actually sexually abusing and killing the mothers.'

'That's completely different, Doug.'

'Not if it's the murderer who's dressing up as the ghost. There's been two people killed here, hasn't there?'

Alice agreed.

'Both with their throats cut. Harry was a fit young man, went to the gym, and Jed Barber was a big man and yet there doesn't seem to be much of a struggle put up in either case. If they were mesmerised by seeing what they thought was a ghost, they may have frozen for long enough to have their throats slashed.'

Alice shook her head. 'There was someone else there in both cases. Amelia and Agnes. Neither of them admits to seeing a ghost.'

'Hmm.' Doug rubbed his chin. 'Maybe I ought to do a bit of ghostbusting.'

'Later. I want you to accompany me to the church, first.'

Doug grinned. 'Shouldn't one of us have gone down on one knee and produced a ring or something?'

Alice's face went scarlet. 'I didn't mean…' She looked at the smirk on Doug's face, hit him playfully in the chest and left through the front gates. Doug followed, locking them behind him.

'Where did you get those keys?' Alice asked him as they walked down towards the High Street.

'Ernie Kemp.'

*

Anne sat outside the perimeter of the Ellis house for a few minutes. She wasn't sure of the best way to handle this. If Edwin wasn't there it would be easier. She could talk woman to woman or whatever they called it but if Edwin didn't have any idea about Linda's affair or if – which was highly likely – Felix was completely wrong with his theory, she could set off all sorts of fireworks. She took a deep breath and started up the drive leaving her car on the road. A car headed towards her and stopped, the window went down and Edwin Ellis's head popped out.

'Hello,' he said. 'Any news?'

Anne shook her head. 'Sorry Mr Ellis. We're still trying, though.'

He nodded sadly. 'Are you here to see me?'

'I'm quite happy to talk to Linda if that's okay. Nothing important really, just getting as much info as we can.'

'I'll be back in about an hour, if you do need me.'

Anne put her thumb up and Edwin drove off, leaving Anne more than relieved.

Linda brought tea in a couple of mugs and they sat in the living room. It was clean but untidy. How unlike the Goddard's, she thought. June had brought out the best china and the place was pristine, not a thing out of place. She supposed that was the difference with always having money and being new to it – as appeared to be the Goddard's case.'

Anne sipped her tea and smiled.

'How can I help you, DI Edwards?' said Linda.

'How well do you know the Goddard's, Linda?'

'Not that well, really. Allan did some accounts for Edwin when he had the company but I guess we've only seen them a couple of times since we moved here.'

'How did you feel about Harry and Amelia's relationship?' Anne bit her top lip.

'They were just kids, I wouldn't call it a relationship.'

Anne took out a notebook. 'You'd been trying for a family for some time before Harry came along, hadn't you?'

Linda raised her eyes to Anne's but didn't answer.

'That's why you fostered Rueben, isn't it?'

'I think I told you, Rueben was nothing but trouble. We don't speak about him.'

'But he was only trouble after Harry was born, wasn't he?'

'Who told you that?'

Anne didn't reply.

'Rueben was a mistake but once we'd committed ourselves, it was difficult to get out of it.'

'You could have done,' said Anne.

Linda sighed. 'But we didn't.'

'So Harry must have been a surprise?'

'Where is this going, DI Edwards?'

Anne shrugged. 'I'm just a bit intrigued.'

'Harry has been murdered. Is this your idea of offering comfort?' Linda's face was going red, her anger building up.

Anne seemed to be making everyone angry at the moment. She took a large gulp of tea before looking up at Linda. 'Was Harry Edwin's child, Linda?'

Linda turned instantly from crimson to a whiter shade of pale. 'Of course,' she said unconvincingly.

'Would you let me take both your's and Edwin's DNA?' Anne took a test kit from her bag.

'No! Why would you need to? I've told you. Edwin was Harry's father.'

Anne stroked her chin. 'I do have Allan Goddard's DNA,' she said, even though she hadn't.

Linda was silent for a moment and then burst into tears. 'Get out!' she yelled through her sobs.

'I don't really want to do that, Linda. I'd like you to tell me what happened in confidence. I don't have to tell Edwin or anyone else at the moment but I need to know.'

Linda's head was in her hands. She was still sobbing. Anne sat and waited.

'Do you know what it's like to want a child and be told you'll never be able to have one?' Linda Ellis and Anne were still sitting in the kitchen. Anne had offered to make more tea but Linda had fetched a bottle of Scotch which she was now doing her best to empty. Anne had refused the glass that she placed in front of her.

'No, I don't, I'm afraid, Linda.'

'It's like someone has sucked the life out of you. It's being told you're useless as a woman. You're no good. Barren. Destined to be an old maid, lonely and sad.'

'You have a husband,' said Anne.

Linda smiled sadly. 'Poor Edwin. He tried to understand. He refused to see a doctor but I went to see one – privately, without Edwin knowing – who told me there was no reason I couldn't get pregnant. I couldn't tell Edwin it was him firing blanks. I wanted to console him, make him believe it was me not him, but...' She finished her glass and refilled it. 'It was Allan's idea. He'd been round for dinner and the conversation had turned to our lack of children, Edwin going on and on about what a failure we were. The next day I had a phone call from Allan saying he could help. I thought he'd meant some sort of sperm donation but he didn't.' Linda shuddered. 'Anyway, he started visiting me while Edwin was at work and Rueben was at school and...well, you know. I hated it. I was cheating on my husband and with a man I was finding increasingly repulsive.'

She put her hands to her eyes and rubbed so hard, Anne thought about intervening before she caused herself damage.

'It took about six weeks – I don't know how many times, it was a business deal. I gave him some money – not much – and he gave me a baby. I thought that would be it but he wanted to carry on. I told him no and threatened to tell his wife. We didn't see him for a long time after that. Harry was born and Edwin sold his business. He was so happy. It made me sick to watch him, to be honest. I'd lied to him. He really thought a miracle had happened.'

'Did he find out, Linda?' Anne asked gently.

She shook her head. 'Almost. We'd just moved to Great Totham and Allan turned up at the door one afternoon. Edwin was out, I think Allan must have known that. Harry had met Amelia. It was quite by accident. They were at the same school. Allan threatened to tell Edwin, stop the kids seeing each other, ruin all our lives basically. I begged him not to. He suggested renewing our 'relationship' as he called it. I told him never.'

'Did you give him some more money, Linda?'

She shook her head.

'How do you think he could suddenly afford to buy a new house?' asked Anne.

'Maybe he won the Lottery.'

Anne waited. She could see Linda going through turmoil.

Eventually, Linda nodded. 'I had a legacy from my father which I'd intended to keep for Harry when he went to university but...anyway, he won't now, will he?' She burst into tears again.

Anne didn't quite know what to make of the whole situation. She couldn't work out if she was annoyed about the fact that Felix Corbett had been right or whether she was angry with Linda and Allan and their little scheme that had backfired spectacularly.

'Don't tell Edwin. It'll kill him. He's never going to get over Harry's death as it is.'

'What about you, Linda? How are you coping with Harry's death?'

Linda sank some more Scotch. 'Honestly?'

Anne nodded.

'I think it may be a blessing in disguise.' She finished her drink and emptied the remains of the bottle into her glass. 'He shouldn't have been born.'

'Do you need someone with you?' checked Anne.

Linda shook her head. 'Edwin will be back soon.'

Anne saw herself out.

CHAPTER NINETEEN

'It's funny you should say that DS Porter,' said Frank Thatcher. 'I do seem to have mislaid a piece of clothing.'

'Would it be a cassock with a hood, by any chance?' Alice inquired.

Frank smiled kindly. 'Cassocks don't have hoods,' he said. 'It's a cloak I've mislaid and it does have a hood. I'm sure it's around here somewhere.'

'How sure?' checked Doug.

'Could I ask why you are inquiring? Have you found one?'

'Possibly,' said Alice. 'Would it be a dark colour?'

Frank nodded. 'Black.'

'Woollen?'

He shrugged. 'I suppose so, something like that. I'm not great on textiles.'

'And when did you mislay this item of clothing?'

'Oh, I don't know. Some time ago, I suppose. It doesn't get a lot of use these days.'

'Do you think it was stolen?'

Frank sighed. 'People do take things from God's house sometimes but it's usually money or sometimes the food we store here for the foodbank. I can't imagine why anyone would take my cloak unless they needed the warmth it gave, in which case they are welcome to it.'

'Did you not report the theft?'

'What theft? If my cloak has gone missing, then whoever took it most probably needed it. That's not a theft, it's a need. There are a lot of people in need at the moment.'

'What do you know about ghosts, Father Thatcher?' Doug asked.

Frank chuckled. 'Is this about the Friar at the leper hospital, by any chance?'

'What do you know about him?'

'I don't really have an opinion about ghosts.'

'You know a young man was murdered at St Giles?'

'Yes, so sad. And now his girlfriend has gone missing I understand.'

'I saw you had a missing poster on your noticeboard.' Alice had spotted it as they'd entered the church.

'Yes, her mother brought it in, poor lady. She's at her wit's end but we all pray together which I hope helps her.'

'Is she one of your parishioners?' June Goddard didn't appear to be a churchgoer to Alice.

'She has been attending recently and she drops in occasionally for a chat with me. I hope I give her some comfort. I suppose there's no news as to where the girl might be?'

Alice shook her head. 'Not yet. How do people manage to take things from the church, Father Thatcher? Would they not be seen?'

Frank nodded slowly. 'I'm supposed to lock the church at night but I don't believe in shutting anyone out from God's house. One never knows when one may need the sanctuary it offers.'

Doug looked at Alice. 'So you sometimes leave the church open all night?'

'Often.'

'So, someone could have come and taken your cloak?'

'It is possible. Likely even.'

'Where do you keep it, Father,' asked Alice.

'In the vestry. I can show you if you like. I suppose you'll want to spray all that fingerprint dust everywhere but I'm not reporting a robbery.'

'There'll be no fingerprint dust,' said Doug as Frank Thatcher led them through a small door at the back of the church and into a room that was filled with foodbank supplies and a clothes rail of surplices and cassocks. 'Is this where it would have been hanging?' Doug indicated the rail.

'I doubt it. I expect I'd have just thrown it over a chair or something. I'm not the tidiest person on God's earth.'

Alice looked round the room. It was chock-a-block with boxes, a few hymnbooks and what looked like cases of wine. There was barely a square metre to stand in. As they left to go back into the church, Alice's foot caught on a metal ring cemented into the floor and almost tripped.

'Careful,' said Frank. 'There's many a trip hazard in these old churches.' He saw them to the door and waved as they went back to the High Street.

'I always feel weird in a church,' admitted Alice.

'You get used to it, I suppose.' Doug was looking back at the building. 'It's quite an impressive edifice, isn't it?'

Alice followed his eyes. 'I suppose so,' she answered. 'Do you think Anne might be right, then? I mean, if Father Thatcher's lost a black cloak with a hood, maybe it's making appearances on the back of a ghostly monk?'

'Anything's possible.'

*

Anne, Alice, Abeer and Doug Griffiths were in the Maldon Police Station office. Anne was at the whiteboard, pen in hand. She'd put a red ring round Allan Goddard's name.

'Do you really think he'd kill his own son?' asked Abeer. They'd all been filled in about June and Allan by Anne and Alice had updated them on the missing cloak.

'I intend to ask him that very question. The trouble is, if he did, why did he then go on to kill Jed Barber?'

'He didn't. That was the witch,' Alice spoke up.

'It wasn't, Alice. But I do think it was whoever stole the vicar's cloak.'

'But why, Anne? Jed had been threatening Agnes, hadn't he, Abeer?' Alice looked at her colleague.

'He did seem to have something against her,' she admitted.

'That doesn't mean she killed him, though.' Anne was certain the witch was not the killer.

Alice pulled a face to show her disdain.

'Alice, if you can find some evidence to convince me, I will arrest her but until that day, please try and concentrate on finding out who did commit the crime.'

'Is there any way we could find out who stole the vicar's cloak?' suggested Abeer.

'That could be difficult. The vestry is packed with crap, and I expect many people have passed through there since it went missing. Father Thatcher doesn't even know when it disappeared. He reckons he might have just mislaid it.' Alice raised her eyes to the heavens. She didn't have a very high opinion of the vicar of All Saints' Church – or any vicar for that matter.

'I've been thinking,' said Doug suddenly. 'The missing girl's father is also the dead boy's father, we think. The mother seems to be spending a lot of time in the church all of a sudden. The girl's father, also her boyfriend's father, and the girl's mother seem to have hit a bit of a rough patch in their marriage.'

'Where is this going, DC Griffiths?' asked Anne.

'I don't know, yet. If the mother wanted to keep the daughter away from the father – who, we know from her diary, might be a bit of a pervert – maybe she might have sought sanctuary in Father Thatcher's house of God. The two people who've been killed have both been slaughtered in the ruins – probably by someone dressed in the vicar's cloak. Allan Goddard, because he'd fathered Harry and didn't want him anywhere near his daughter maybe wanted to scare him and it all went wrong.'

Anne ran her tongue round her teeth. The others all looked at her.

'That is probably the biggest load of rubbish I've heard in my whole career, DC Griffiths,' she said.

'What's your theory then, Anne?' Alice found it hard to disguise her annoyance with her boss.

Anne looked at the board, then at her colleagues, then shrugged her shoulders, 'I don't have one,' she admitted.

'What about some sort of late-night vigil?' suggested Abeer.

'Meaning what?' said Anne.

'If this ghostly figure appears late at night...' she began.

'...yes after closing time at the pub opposite,' said Anne.

'I just thought maybe we could wait and see if it turns up.'

'When we're not on duty?' Alice had had enough of working unpaid overtime.

Abeer nodded her head slowly. 'Yes, you're right. It was just a thought.'

'It's a very good thought, Abeer,' said Anne. She turned to Alice. 'I have a proposition. It would be completely voluntary, of course, but we could meet and have a drink or two in that pub first.' Anne smiled.

'We'll definitely be seeing things then,' Alice observed.

'Like I said it'd be voluntary but I'll get the first round in at about ten o'clock. In the meantime, Abeer, you can come with me to talk to Mr Allan Goddard.'

*

June Goddard was in the church again. Frank was sitting next to her in the pews.

'Do you think she's dead, Father?' she said quietly.

He took hold of her hands. 'I really don't know, June. All we can do is pray that she's safe somewhere.'

'I'm losing hope,' she said.

'Never give that up, June.'

'Hope's such an awful thing, Father. It's like you're in a long tunnel with a little light at the end and the further you go down the tunnel, the further away the light gets, until you know you're never going to reach it.'

'You will reach it, June, one way or another. There's always hope, that light never goes out.'

She smiled sadly, wishing she could believe him, wishing she had some sort of faith to support her. Suddenly she looked up. 'Is there someone else here, Father?' she asked.

'Only God. He's always here, June.'

'I thought I heard something. A sort of scraping noise.'

Frank looked around, there was no-one in the church. 'I probably wouldn't hear it anyway,' he said pointing to his hearing aid.

June stood up and crept to where she'd heard the noise. 'I think it was in the vestry,' she said, opening the door.

Father Thatcher followed as quickly as his arthritis would let him. Inside the room, some of the boxes of food had evidently been tampered with, a few fallen onto the floor.

'Oh dear,' said Father Thatcher.

June was searching the room. 'How did they get in?' she said.

'I don't know,' he replied.

June was climbing over the rubble to get to the windows. 'This one's open,' she said.

Frank nodded. 'Most of them don't shut properly,' he admitted. 'We can't afford to get them secured.'

'That's terrible,' she said, climbing back down to the floor. 'What have they taken?'

Frank shrugged. 'Nothing important. Well, not important to us. I expect it is food again.'

The case of communion wine had been opened and at least a couple of bottles had gone. June's eyes were moist as she moved one of the boxes and sat down on a hard chair.

'The world's a terrible place, isn't it?' she said.

Frank smiled. 'No it isn't, June. There are things that are sent to test us but we mustn't give in. Whoever has taken these things needs them and we should be grateful that we were able to provide them.'

'And Amelia?'

Frank looked down. 'That is one of the hardest tests, June. Not knowing takes a lot of strength.'

June's eyes finally gave way to the flood of tears that had been building up as she lent forwards and broke down.

*

Allan Goddard opened the door. 'Have you found her?' he said.

'No, Mr Goddard, I'm afraid not. Could we come in?'

'June's not here,' he replied.

'It's you we wanted a chat with, actually,' Anne put her hand on the door and Allan gave way, letting the two women past.

They went through to the immaculate kitchen. Allan pulled out a couple of stools but they remained standing. No tea was offered.

'You implied you weren't very keen on Amelia's relationship with Harry Ellis. Could you expound on that?' asked Anne, her notebook in her hand.

'What do you mean?'

'Didn't you like him?'

'No, I didn't.'

'Do you know where Amelia is, Allan?' Anne stared at him.

'Of course I bloody don't.' Allan looked bewildered.

'Have you spoken with Harry's parents at all?'

Allan Goddard's mouth turned up on one side. 'No.'

'Didn't you like them either?' said Abeer.

'When did you last speak to them?' continued Anne.

He shrugged. 'I don't know. Not for years.'

Anne's eyebrows raised. 'Really? Years? How many years?'

'I don't know. We didn't get on.'

'But you used to. You used to get on very well. Especially with Linda Ellis, I'm led to believe.'

Allan's forehead creased. 'Who told you that?'

Anne remained staring at him.

'I think you should leave now,' he said.

Anne and Abeer stayed where they were.

'Did you hear what I said?'

Anne sat down on one of the stools. 'I'm not going anywhere unless it's down to the station with you. Or we could, of course, just carry on our conversation here. It's up to you.'

Allan Goddard laughed. 'Are you threatening to arrest me?'

Again, Anne and Abeer remained silent.

'I used to do Edwin Ellis's accounts,' he said quietly.

'Oh yes, that was when you worked at Witheforde's, wasn't it?'

Allan nodded.

'Where do you work now?'

'Same place,' he replied.

Anne turned to Abeer who read from her iPad. '"Mr Goddard left our employment some time ago." That's an email from your former employer, Mr Goddard.'

'So where do you go when June thinks you're out at work, Allan?' added Anne.

'What I do for a living is none of your business,' he said.

'That depends on what the business is, I suppose. You were aware of Linda and Edwin wanting a child, weren't you?'

Allan shrugged.

'It was you who came up with the solution, wasn't it? She's very attractive, Linda Goddard, isn't she?'

It was Allan's turn to keep quiet.

'Maybe it was a favour you intended, you know helping a friend out, giving them an opportunity to realise their life's dream. Maybe you were happy for them, watching their little baby boy grow up. Maybe you even suggested they move nearer to you so you could see him grow as well. Or maybe you just enjoyed your relationship with Linda, even though she didn't? Who knows? The thing is, Allan, Harry was your son and yet you didn't seem at all upset when he was stabbed to death.'

Allan's face was slowly turning scarlet, his breathing shallow. 'Get out!' he yelled.

Abeer flinched but Anne held her ground.

He took a step towards them, his expression angry, his nostrils wide, mouth twisted. He raised his hand towards Anne who stayed sitting exactly where she was.

'Don't do something you'll regret, Allan,' she said.

He stopped inches from her, thrust his face into hers and shrieked. 'Get out of my house!'

Abeer already had her handcuffs out but Anne shook her head.

'Mr Goddard, I am asking you nicely for the last time. Answer my questions here or I will arrest you.'

'What for?' he barked.

Anne blew her lips out. 'Threatening an officer in the course of her duty; blackmailing the mother of your illegitimate child; possible abduction of your legitimate daughter. Can you think of anything else DC Kumar?'

'I'm sure I could if I tried,' she replied, still swinging the cuffs.

Allan turned and walked over to the other side of the kitchen, leaning on the worktop.

'What do you want me to say?' he said quietly.

'Just the truth, Allan. Do you know where Amelia is?'

'No.'

'You bought this house with money you extorted from June Goddard after threatening to tell Edwin that Harry wasn't his son. Is that right?'

'Yes,' he muttered.

'I can understand your reluctance to allow Amelia and Harry's relationship to develop, they were brother and sister even though neither of them knew that. I assume June doesn't know?'

He shook his head before turning it towards the officers. His eyes were red, his cheeks blotchy. 'You can't tell her,' he pleaded.

'How did you lose your job, Allan?'

'I was accused of something I didn't do.'

'Fiddling Edwin Ellis's accounts?'

'It wasn't a fiddle. It was legitimate tax evasion. Perfectly legal.'

'I don't really care about that, Allan. But I do care about your wife and your daughter. I need to know your part in their turmoil.'

'I'd never hurt them,' he said.

'That's not strictly true either, is it? What sort of thrill do you get from spying on Amelia in her bedroom?'

'I don't.'

'You do, Allan. I could take you away now and have you locked up for a long time but I'm not going to.'

Abeer looked at her.

'I think you're a really sad man, Allan. I'd like to believe you were just helping out with the Ellis's procreation problem. You weren't to know that bringing them near to Maldon might mean your two offspring might meet and be attracted to each other. The thing I can't forgive you for is coercing a frightened woman into paying you off. Edwin adored Harry. For him to find out the boy wasn't his – even worse that he was yours – would have destroyed him.'

'Just as he destroyed me.'

Anne looked at him, waiting for an explanation.

'It was him who lost me my job. It was his idea for me to hide some of his large income – and yes, it was fraud. I knew it was but he paid me well. I was a fool to let him persuade me.'

'So you saw a way to get some recompense? Why didn't you just tell him who Harry's real father was?'

Allan let out a brief laugh. 'He wouldn't believe me. I was just an accountant to him. A nobody. Someone he could manipulate the same as he manipulated everyone. That's how you get to be rich.'

Anne was silent for a moment, weighing up this new information.

'I'm cautioning you, Allan Goddard. I want you to tell June about your affair with Linda…'

'It wasn't an affair. It was a business deal.'

'I want you to tell June that you were Harry's biological father. When we find Amelia, I don't want you to go anywhere near her bedroom. And I want you to apologise to Linda Ellis.'

Allan Goddard didn't reply. He gripped the side of the worktop and lowered his head.

'Tell all of those women to get in touch with me if they need any help. Don't try and bluster your way out of this Allan. It's redemption time.'

Anne stood up and went to the door, indicating that Abeer should follow.

'Was that safe?' asked Abeer, as they got into Anne's car.

'I don't know, Abeer. I hope so.'

'He might attack June?'

Anne smiled. 'I think it would be the other way round, if I'm not mistaken.'

'You could have arrested him.'

'I could have but I chose not to. Are you coming tonight?'

'Yes, I've told my parents I'm working. They weren't happy about it but I really don't care.'

'We need to find you somewhere else to stay, don't we?'

Abeer smiled. 'I'm working on it,' she said.

'I'll see you later then.' Anne put the key in the ignition and started the car.

'What are you doing now?' Abeer asked quietly.

'I have something to do at the office, why?'

'Just didn't fancy going home.'

'You're welcome to come to make me coffee and join me in a takeaway,' Anne said.

She looked back at what she knew was to become an even sadder house than it already was and hoped that they would find Amelia soon, preferably alive. Although what sort of life she would have from here on, who knew?

CHAPTER TWENTY

Alice and Doug sat on a bench in the Prom Park. They were eating chips from one of the kiosks and looking out over the lake at the birds scavenging on the far bank of the river. The tide was low which meant the River Blackwater was little more than a stream running down the middle of two vast mudbanks which would be completely covered in a couple of hours as the tide made its way back upstream.

'I'm really confused, Doug. I know Anne's my boss but I thought she was my friend as well. She seems to have become a different person just lately.'

'I can't say I've found her the friendliest of people, myself,' said Doug, slipping a chip into his mouth.

'Well, she was. She's always had a bit of a way about her with some people but never with me. It was her who got my promotion fast-tracked.'

'Maybe she'll change when I've gone back.'

A shiver went through Alice. She didn't even want to think about Doug going back. 'When will that be?' she asked tentatively.

'I don't know, to be honest. I'm not sure when my leave runs out.' He popped a chip into Alice's mouth. 'I suppose I could go tomorrow if I'm no help here.'

'Oh you are, Doug. Don't worry about Anne.'

'It's not Anne I'm worried about.'

Alice frowned.

'I don't want to ruin your career.'

Alice laughed. 'You won't do that.' She looked across at the birds again, who were still scratching for food before the waves covered up their dining tables. 'I'd like you to stay,' she said quietly.

'Would you?'

Alice turned her head back to him. 'Yes, Doug. I really would.' She leaned forward and kissed him.'

'Bit vinegary,' he said grinning. Alice punched him playfully. Doug put his hand in his pocket and drew out a small tissue-wrapped parcel. 'I got you something for letting me stay at yours.'

'You didn't have to do that. I wanted you to stay.' Alice took the parcel and unwrapped the paper revealing a small heart-shaped pendant on a chain. 'What's this?'

'Don't you like it?' he said pulling a sad face.

'It's lovely but I can't…'

'Yes, you can,' he said, taking it from her and putting it round her neck. 'It wasn't very expensive if that's what's worrying you.'

Alice tried unsuccessfully to stop the tears leaking from her eyes. Doug took his handkerchief and mopped her cheeks.

'Alice, I've enjoyed my time here. Far more than I expected. I thought I was coming to some backwoods where everyone walked around with a stick of straw in their mouth…'

Alice gave him a look.

'…but it's not like that at all. I've never really ventured out of London before and, to be honest, this is much preferable. The fresh air, the birds – the feathered variety, I mean – the more relaxed way of life. If I could I'd get a transfer.'

Alice grinned. 'That would really please Anne,' she said. She looked down at the pendant. There was a small stone set in the middle of the heart shape. 'Is that a diamond?'

Doug laughed out loud. 'Not for the price I paid. It was just something I saw on the internet and made me think of you.'

Alice took his hand. 'It's a very nice thought, Doug.'

'It certainly is,' he said, grinning again.

*

Doug and Alice scanned the pub as they arrived. There was no sign of Jesse Burton. Anne and Abeer were already there, sitting in the window seat in the main bar.

Anne beckoned them over. 'I have a tab set up, order what you want,' she said. 'As long as it's no more than a pint and a wine.'

Doug went to the bar and ordered while Alice sat at the table. Anne was staring at her.

'What?' said Alice.

'Nothing,' replied Anne. 'Sort of surprised you could find the time to turn up, that's all.'

Alice looked at Abeer who looked back sympathetically. Doug returned and sat next to Alice.

'Should we take turns,' said Abeer.

'To do what?' said Anne.

'Look for the ghost.'

Anne turned to Doug. 'What do you think DC Griffiths?'

'Me? I don't know. It's usually seen after closing time but Battybooboo saw it in the early evening she said. It could appear at any time, if at all.'

'Very true, DC Griffiths.' Anne took a drink from her glass which was nearly empty. 'Who wants to do the first shift, then?'

'I don't mind,' said Doug.

'No, I think maybe Alice would like to. Ten minutes each I think then we'll all go over there at closing time.'

Alice glared at Anne. 'I'm not on duty, remember.'

'Then why are you here?'

Alice threw her wine back and stood up. 'Ten minutes,' she said and left the pub.

'What's your problem, DI Edwards?' said Doug.

'Me? I don't have a problem. I'm just trying to solve a crime.'

'Alice wondered if you had a problem with me,' Doug continued.

'Shall I get a round in,' suggested Abeer, feeling embarrassed by the atmosphere.

'White wine,' said Anne.

'Doug?' asked Abeer.

'I'm alright, thank you.'

Abeer went to the bar.

'So, do you?' said Doug.

'What, have a problem with a Met police officer being thrust upon me who has then proceeded to take up all the time of my Detective Sergeant? No, no problem at all.'

'I'm not taking up Alice's time. She is allowed the odd evening off, you know.'

Anne tapped her head. 'You're taking up her mind, DC Griffiths.'

Abeer came back with three wines and a pint. 'I got you one anyway,' she said, putting the glass in front of Doug next to the one that was still nearly full. He smiled his thanks.

'I'm just trying to help, DI Edwards. If I'm not, I can go home now. Well, as soon as I've finished this pint your DC has kindly bought me.'

'You don't need to go. I'd be grateful if you did help. Whether you will or not seems to depend.'

The three of them sat silently for a while.

'Shall I go next?' asked Abeer, desperate to be away.

'No, I'll go,' said Doug. 'Just trying to be helpful,' he added not trying to hide the sarcasm.

Alice looked like a drowned rat when she returned. 'It's pissing down,' she announced.

'I got you a wine,' said Abeer.

'Probably need a hot chocolate. It's bloody freezing.' Alice sat down and sipped her wine, nevertheless.

'See anything?' checked Anne.

Alice shook her head, small drops of rainwater splashing onto the table. Doug stood up and pulled the hood of his jacket up. 'Good job I came prepared,' he said and went out.

'You ought to go and dry off in the Ladies. The hand drier moves round so you can direct it to your face.' Anne informed her.

Abeer was staring at Alice, her mouth was wide open.

'What?' said Alice.

'Oh sorry, nothing,' replied Abeer, closing her lips.

'What is it with everyone tonight?' said Alice and stomped off to the toilets.

Abeer turned to Anne. 'Did you see what Alice had round her neck?'

'No. It wasn't my hands, was it?'

Abeer frowned. 'She was wearing a locket.'

Anne shrugged. 'She's not on duty, as she keeps reminding me.'

'It's a silver locket.' Anne pointed to one of the ubiquitous missing girl notices on the wall. 'Like that one round Amelia's neck.'

Anne looked over to the poster. She hadn't noticed Alice wearing a locket, she'd check when she came back.

Alice was feeling despondent as she tried to dry her hair with the hand drier in the small Ladies toilet. She didn't know how much longer she could put up with Anne constantly having a go at her. It was her own decision with whom she had a relationship. Admittedly, it was a bit difficult because Doug had attached himself to the Maldon CID. Maybe she could persuade him to stay away from Anne, see if that helped. Perhaps it was a mistake coming on this wild goose chase looking for ghosts, even though she was pretty sure she'd seen the figure herself last night. She took a deep breath and ventured back to the bar.

Anne smiled as she sat at the table. 'Nice necklace,' she said.

Alice looked down. She'd forgotten she was still wearing Doug's pendant. 'Yes, sorry. Doug gave it to me this afternoon. I'll take it off.'

'No, leave it on. You're not on official duty. Just be careful in case the ghost takes a liking to it.'

Alice sighed irritably. Abeer looked at Anne, who smiled back at her.

Anne looked out of the window. 'Rain's stopped. Maybe we should all go over and give DC Griffiths a hand,' she said, putting on her coat. The clouds had dispersed allowing a full moon to give the ruins a suitably eerie vista.

'I'll join you when I've finished my drink,' said Alice.

Abeer didn't know what to do. She still had half a glass of wine in front of her and wasn't used to knocking alcohol back quickly.

'Okay, you girls stay here and finish your drinks. I'll be across the road when you're ready.' Anne went to the bar and paid her tab before heading over towards the leper hospital.

'Where did Doug get your locket?' asked Abeer. 'Do you know?'

Alice shrugged. 'Don't you start.' Alice calmed down and smiled. None of this was Abeer's fault. 'Off the internet apparently. It didn't cost him much, he said. It was just a friendly gift, nothing more.'

Abeer smiled and finished her drink.

*

Although the rain had stopped there was still a cold wind blowing across the grounds of St Giles Leper Hospital as Anne joined Doug near the gates.

'Nice necklace you bought my DS, DC Griffiths?' she said, pulling her hood around her face trying to shield herself from the wind.

'Is that not allowed?' he asked.

'Of course it is. It's a nice gesture. Where did you get it?'

'Why?'

'Thought I might buy my niece one,' Anne lied. She didn't have a niece.

'The internet. I could let you have the site if you want.'

'I'd like that, thanks. Who are you DC Griffiths?' Anne was staring into his eyes, looking for any hint of him lying.

'What do you mean?'

'I've been in touch with the Metropolitan Police this afternoon. They don't have a Detective Constable called Griffiths.' Anne waited for his reaction. His face was giving nothing away.

'They must have been mistaken. There's a lot of people in the Met. Who did you speak to?'

'Does that matter?'

'It might. There's quite a few there who shouldn't be in any police force, let alone the biggest in the country.'

'Including you?'

'No. I still don't know what your problem with me is but if you'd like me to leave now, I will.'

'I'm sure that would upset my Detective Sergeant.'

Suddenly Doug turned to his right. 'There's someone moving over there?' he whispered.

Anne looked across the grounds. Doug quietly unlocked the gates and entered the hospital grounds, silently moving through the shadows created by the hedge. Anne followed.

As they reached the large oak, Anne grabbed hold of Doug's arm. 'Stay here. I haven't finished with you, by the way,' she murmured and went towards the far end of the grounds. She grabbed hold of a figure who was kneeling amongst the undergrowth.

'For fuck's sake, Agnes. What are you doing here?' she said.

'Have you seen the state of this?' the witch said, indicating her herb garden. 'It's Spring and they're starting to reproduce. If you hadn't locked me up for no reason I wouldn't need to spend my evening tending to these poor things.' She lifted a wilted leaf and let it drop to the ground again. 'What are you doing here, anyway?'

'Looking for the ghost,' said Doug, who'd joined them.

Agnes laughed. 'Not likely to find him now.'

'Why?' asked Doug.

'Wrong time of year. He doesn't like the cold.'

'That's not the information we have, Agnes,' said Anne. 'There's been at least three sightings recently.'

Agnes waved her hands at them. 'Well, you've got wrong information then.'

'I'd like you to leave, please,' Anne told her.

Agnes sighed. 'Are you on a ghost hunt?'

'Something like that.' Anne spotted Alice and Abeer at the gates and beckoned them to join them. 'We have three witnesses that reckon they've seen a hooded figure in these grounds, late at night. Some of the sightings coincide with the two murders that occurred here, one of which you are still suspected of, if you remember.'

Agnes shrugged.

'What's she doing here?' said Alice as the others joined the group.

'Tending my garden,' replied Agnes.

Abeer held her hands up. 'Hush,' she said. 'Listen.'

The five of them fell silent, their ears pricked. A scraping sound could be heard somewhere between the oak and the gates. At Anne's insistence they hid themselves behind the tree. In the moonlight they could see part of the earth between the chancel and the chapel was moving. A small circle of cobblestones was turning. Doug took a pace forwards but Anne held him back. The circle of cobbles lifted an inch into the air and turned again before moving seemingly on its own and softly landing a few feet away, leaving a dark area where it had been. Through the darkness they saw a hood appear from the ground, followed by a figure slowly crawling its way out of the earth. Gradually the figure stood upright, its head turning right and left before relacing the cobbles and hurrying towards the hedge.

Doug ran from behind the tree and rugby tackled the figure. It was solid. This was no ghost. They fell to the ground in a heap. The others raced towards them, arriving just as Doug pulled the figure's hood down. He stopped, shocked before leaning in closely to the revealed face.

'You!' he shouted as his hands clutched the figure's neck.

The figure was evidently a female and her face showed as much shock as Doug's. 'Get off me,' she growled in a deep rustling voice.

'I'll fucking kill you, you bastard!' Doug was still yelling, still attempting to strangle the woman.

Anne, Alice and Abeer all took hold of Doug, pulling at him.

'Stop it,' Anne was shouting but he kept pressing his fingers into the frail neck. The woman's face was turning purple.

'Stop it, Doug,' said Alice. 'Please stop.'

Doug's fingers relaxed slightly but kept hold of the woman.

'Who are you?' Anne asked her. She stared back at her bewildered.

'Catherine fucking Hall,' said Doug.

Anne stared at the dirty specimen lying in front of her. She smelt foul, grime and dried blood on her hands and face. She looked and smelt as though she hadn't washed in weeks. 'Cat?' she said.

Catherine Hall focussed her eyes on Anne. 'Little Annie,' she said and spat towards Anne's face. Anne pulled her head back out of the way.

'Cuff her,' she told Alice. 'And leave her alone, DC Griffiths.'

Doug removed his hands. Catherine Hall looked confused. 'What did you call him?' she said, her voice grating.

No-one replied. Alice placed the handcuffs round Catherine's wrists and got her to a standing position with Abeer's help.

Anne was keeping Doug away from her. He was seething and still trying to get to Catherine. His face was twisted in the most horrible way, teeth bared, eyes screwed up.

'Take her away,' said Anne to Alice and Abeer, who started to manoeuvre her towards the gates. 'And radio for a car. Take her to Chelmsford. I'll follow shortly.'

'I'm going as well,' said Doug.

'No, you're not,' said Anne, physically holding him back. He pushed past her. Quick as a flash, Anne had her handcuffs out and cuffed one of his wrists. The surprise stopped him. She grabbed his other hand and cuffed it also.

'What are you doing?' he yelled.

'Stopping you doing something you might regret,' answered Anne. 'You stay here with me.'

Agnes was standing several feet away, unsure of what had just happened. She took a tentative pace forward. 'I'll...er...I'll get off then,' she said.

'No, you're staying as well. You're a witness.'

Anne was stressed. She hadn't expected anything to happen tonight, no ghost, no witch, no altercations, and yet somehow all those things seemed to have occurred. Now she had someone claiming to be in the Met CID handcuffed and standing in a field.

'So tell me now, who are you really?'

A police car drew up and Catherine Hall was bundled into the back. Alice and Abeer went in the vehicle with her to Chelmsford.

Doug sighed. 'Take these off,' he said waving his shackled hands in the air.

'Not until you tell me who you are.'

He looked at Agnes.

'Agnes, you can tend to your garden if you can see anything in the dark. Just don't go anywhere else.'

The witch went back to her herbs.

'So. Who are you? I won't ask again.'

'I am a Detective Constable in the Metropolitan Police Force.'

'No you're not.'

'I am. I'm just not called Doug Griffiths.'

Anne waited.

'My name is Gerald Hall. I am that bitch's brother-in-law.'

'Catherine Hall?'

He nodded. 'Jack was my brother.'

CHAPTER TWENTY-ONE

Catherine Hall had been booked into a holding cell at Chelmsford Police Station. The jolly Desk Sergeant James Royley had taken the details and a constable had escorted her along a corridor to the cells.'

'What is she, a tramp?' asked Royley.

Alice shook her head. 'She might be a murderer.'

'Murderess,' corrected Abeer, grinning.

The two detectives went through to the refectory and grabbed a couple of what were supposed to be hot chocolates from the vending machine and sat at a table.

'Do you know who Doug is really?' asked Abeer.

'What do you mean?'

'Ah.' Abeer drank some chocolate.

'What do you mean "ah"?'

'It turns out he's not who he seems,' said Abeer.

Alice's pulse rate increased. 'Yes, he is.'

'Not according to Anne. She got in touch with the Met. They don't have an officer called Doug Griffiths. Sorry, Alice.'

'When did this happen?'

'This afternoon.'

'Well it's bollocks. Anne's lying. She's never liked him and she resents the fact that he likes me. Don't believe her, Abeer.'

Abeer nodded. 'I was there, though. In the office. I heard what they said.'

Alice's hand went to her pendant, gripping it in her fist.

'When did he give you that, Alice?'

She looked down at the silver heart in her hand. 'This afternoon,' she said as a tear dripped down her cheek.

'Did you know it's the same as the one Amelia Goddard was wearing when she went missing?'

'What?'

'It's in the picture on those posters her mother put up.'

'Why are you doing this? Has Anne put you up to it?'

Abeer shook her head. 'I'm sorry, Alice. I thought you should know.'

'Yes, well, thanks.' Alice crushed her empty plastic cup in her hand, a small dribble of chocolate running across the tabletop. 'For nothing,' she added, getting up from the table. 'I'm in the loo if anybody wants me for something sensible.'

*

Anne stood in front of Gerald Hall who was leaning against the old oak, his hands still tethered.

'I really am a DC,' he told her. 'If you'd looked at my warrant card, you'd have seen my name. I was pretty sure you wouldn't – no-one ever does, especially not other police officers. I've been on compassionate leave since my brother and niece were killed by that slut, but I couldn't stay in my little flat on my own getting more and more frustrated. I wasn't allowed to be on the case myself, obviously but I wanted to find that evil cow. I knew she came from here; she'd often talked about it. Mostly she'd said what a great place it was and what a great life she'd had before she met my brother and had Elizabeth. She'd never worked until she'd suddenly decided she could be a designer handbag manufacturer – that's what she called herself. Jack had spent all his time and money trying to encourage her, make her life better but she didn't appreciate him. She just blamed him – and Elizabeth. He couldn't see it, of course. He adored her but Elizabeth was different. She didn't like her mother at all.'

'Did you know your sister-in-law was in Maldon?'

'No. I was working on a hunch if you like. After the first week I thought it was a waste of time but it turns out I was wrong and then…well, Alice happened.' He held up his cuffed hands. 'I know you don't approve. I don't know why but I would like to say that none of this is Alice's fault – or mine really. I didn't mean to fall in love.'

Anne spluttered. 'Are you really saying to me that you're in love with DS Porter?'

He smiled and nodded. 'Ridiculous, isn't it?'

*

In her cell in Chelmsford, Catherine Hall was nonplussed. Where was she? How did she get here? She had a vague sense of her brother-in-law Gerald, of all people, holding her round the neck and little Annie Edwards from school being there holding him back. What were they doing there? And why was she sitting in this room? She'd gone on her nightly foraging but hadn't made it to the town centre and the big green bins, she knew that much. Someone had thrown her to the ground. Was that Gerald? She wasn't breaking the law, all she was doing was keeping her daughter safe. Elizabeth! Where was she? Why wasn't she here? Oh my God! She raced to the door of the cell and banged on it. 'Where's Elizabeth?' she yelled. 'Where's my daughter? You can't keep me here. My girl needs me. She'll be hurt again. Help! Open the door.'

No-one came.

*

Agnes had moved from her herb garden and wandered over to where Catherine Hall had appeared from out of the ground. On the floor lay a wooden circle with metal studs in it. It was like a manhole cover and on the top several round stones were attached. Next to it a hole had appeared, roughly three feet in diameter. Agnes knelt down and stuck her head in but could see nothing, it just seemed to be a dark smelly hole. 'Hello?' she said, expecting an echo. None came, the sound presumably soaked up by the earth. She had started to stand when she thought she heard a small voice answering. There was an echo. It took a long time to come back, meaning there must be some sort of long tunnel, perhaps some sort of ancient sewer, she surmised. Then the voice came again. 'Mummy?'

Agnes ran over to Anne and Doug. 'There's someone down there,' she said.

'Where?'

'Where that woman came from.' Agnes pointed to the hole on the ground.

Anne had been distracted and hadn't even considered where Catherine Hall had appeared from. She and Doug raced towards the gap.

'Take these off,' Doug ordered, holding his cuffed hands up.

Anne released him. 'Don't you dare do anything stupid,' she warned.

Doug slithered down the hole, followed by Anne. It was a tight squeeze for the Detective Inspector but she managed and, taking out her phone shone the torch along a dank corridor.

'Mummy?'

The voice was faint and some way in front of them. The tunnel was low and even at five foot three, Anne had to bow her head. Doug was on his hands and knees. There appeared to be some flickering light up ahead.

'Be careful,' said Anne. 'We don't know what we're heading for.'

Gerald Hall turned to her. 'You can go back if you want,' he said.

'Not bloody likely.'

The two of them crabbed along the narrow tunnel. The smell was almost overpowering, urine and faeces mixed with the odour of damp earth. Gerald was a few feet ahead of Anne and he stopped suddenly, Anne almost smashing into him.

'Oh my God,' she heard him say.

There in front of him was a young girl, half undressed, filthy like some urchin from a Victorian etching, scared, shivering, eyes wide with fear, cheeks streaked with grimy tearstains. She was sitting in human excrement and blood.

'Amelia?' said Anne.

The girl burst into tears.

*

Anne and Gerald followed the ambulance with Amelia inside. She hadn't cuffed him again but she was still wary. She hadn't liked Doug Griffiths and now he was Gerald Hall, she liked him even less. She wondered if Alice knew his real identity and if she did, why she hadn't told her. Neither of them spoke during the journey to Broomfield Hospital The ambulance was backed up when they arrived but Anne used her authority to bypass the queue and get her straight into a private room.

They waited for over an hour before the doctor told them they could have five minutes with her.

'I'll go in on my own thank you, DC Hall. Just stay here until I come out. You and I need to have a long talk at some point.' She went into Amelia's room.

The girl was connected to various machines by tubes and wires. They'd cleaned her face but she still didn't smell particularly good.

Anne smiled. 'Hello, Amelia. I'm DI Edwards, Anne.'

'Where's my mum?' she asked, her voice soft and barely audible.

'She's on her way.' Anne had informed June that her daughter had been found safe and she was on her way to Broomfield. She just hoped she could get some information before the girl's mother arrived.

'And the other one? The one called 'mummy'?'

Anne leaned closer in order to hear the girl's croaky tones. 'Is that the one who kept you prisoner, Amelia?'

'She was keeping me safe, she said.'

'She's been taken to the police station.'

'She called me Elizabeth, do you know why?'

Anne put her hand on Amelia's. She felt her tense but didn't move it. 'I think she's a rather sick woman, Amelia. Can you tell me what happened? How you ended up in that tunnel?'

'I don't know,' she said. 'I was in the ruins – I don't know why, I suppose I just needed to get away from home.'

'Why was that?'

She closed her eyes. 'It was oppressive. Dad kept…he kept asking about Harry. What we'd been up to and that. I couldn't cope so I snuck out and went for a walk. I suppose I wanted to be where I was with Harry when he…' Tears started to erupt from her eyes, streaking down her cheeks and dripping onto the bedsheets. Anne gripped her hand tighter and waited. 'Anyway,' she blubbed. 'I was there one minute, the next I was in that place. It was dark and damp, I don't know how I got to it and I was tied up.' She lifted the covers. 'Am I still filthy?' she asked.

'I've seen worse,' said Anne, smiling. 'And you'd never seen this mummy woman before?'

Amelia shook her head.

'Can I have a shower?'

'I'm sure they'll let you soon. They just need to check you're okay first.'

She nodded slowly. 'Why have they taken my locket?'

Anne's heart rate increased. 'What locket, Amelia?'

'Harry gave me a locket. It was heart shaped. I had it on in the tunnel. I kept holding it, it gave me comfort.'

'Do you know when you lost it?'

She shook her head. 'It was there yesterday, I'm sure.'

'I'll check with the doctor. Maybe they had to take it off.'

'I don't want to lose it. It's all I have left.' The tears started again.

The door flew open and June Goddard rushed into the room, followed by a nurse. She clasped Amelia round the neck and hugged her.

'Be careful, Mrs Goddard,' warned the nurse.

Anne realising she was now in the way, left the room.

*

'She's screaming her head off, apparently,' James Royley had come through to the canteen where Alice and Abeer were sitting.

'Not much we can do until DI Edwards arrives,' said Alice.

'Just thought I'd let you know. The duty constable's getting fed-up.'

Alice shrugged and James went back to his favourite front desk where he felt more at home.

'What do you think you should do about Doug?' asked Abeer.

'London's not that far away, is it?' Alice replied. 'I'm sure we will still see each other.'

'But if he's lied to you…'

'He's not the liar, Abeer. Anne's had it in for him ever since he arrived here. He's definitely a copper, he knows too much about how we work.'

'But why would Anne lie to you?'

'She doesn't approve. She thinks he's taking up all my time. It's like I'm not allowed to have a personal life. Just because she wants to spend all her time pretending to solve crimes, she thinks everyone else should. I'm not even supposed to be here. I'm not on duty. Nor are you.'

Abeer nodded. 'So why are we?'

Alice's shoulders sunk. 'I don't know Abeer. I really don't know.' Her phone rang. Her lips became a tight line as she stood up. 'I'll take this outside.'

'Is it Anne?' asked Abeer but Alice was through the door.

*

'Anne's in with the girl now,' said Gerald. 'She seems to be a bit obsessed with that pendant I gave you. Any idea why?'

'Are you a police officer with the Metropolitan Police, Doug?' said Alice. She held her breath. She wasn't aware of Anne ever lying to her before.

'You've been told then?'

'Told what, Doug?' Alice's breath was coming in short bursts.

'That I'm not who you think I am?'

Alice tried hard to stop her tears. She couldn't answer him.

'I was going to tell you, Alice, honestly but I couldn't. Not until now. The woman we caught in the ruins is my sister-in-law. Jack Hall was my brother. My name is really Gerald Hall.'

Alice couldn't take it all in. Anne was right, he had been lying to her. Why? What could he gain from it? She knew nothing about Catherine Hall.

'I don't believe you,' she said.

'I will explain everything. I'm not playing with you, Alice. I didn't know this would happen. You are the most amazing woman, a great copper, and I don't want you to hate me. More than anything, I don't want you to hate me. Please.'

Alice disconnected and went to the Ladies. She took a handful of tissues, locked herself in a cubicle and sobbed.

*

Anne sent Alice home as soon as she saw the state she was in. Gerald had tried to comfort her but Alice had snubbed him, tears still streaming down her face as Anne held the man back.

'I want you to stay here, Gerald Hall. Don't do anything stupid. Don't make me have to cuff you again. And don't go near my Detective Sergeant,' she said, taking Abeer into the interview room where Catherine Hall was waiting, refusing to sit down and aggressively stamping her feet like a child.

'It would be better if you took a seat, Mrs Hall,' said Anne as the two detectives sat down.

'Where my daughter?' demanded Catherine.

'She's...' started Abeer. Anne put her hand on the constable's arm, stopping her.

'You tell us, Mrs Hall,' Anne responded.

'She was there with me. She'll be scared and hungry. I need to go to her.'

'You'll not be going anywhere for some time, I'm afraid.'

The woman leaned on the table, her face close to Anne's. 'Don't tell me what I will and won't be doing, little Annie. Who do you think you are?'

Anne moved her head away. 'I'm the arresting officer, Mrs Hall.'

Catherine sat down heavily and laughed. 'You're not the police,' she said. 'You're a farm girl, a dirty, little farm girl.'

'Things have moved on since you last saw me, Mrs Hall.'

Catherine sat back in her seat. 'I want my husband here. He'll sort you out.'

Abeer and Anne exchanged glances. 'Where do you live, Mrs Hall?' asked Anne.

Catherine looked confused. 'Where I've always lived. Here, in Maldon.'

'With your husband?'

'And my daughter. Where are they? She's in danger.'

'I'll see what I can find out,' said Anne standing. She paused the interview and left the room with Abeer. A constable came and stood by the door.

'Is she joking?' asked Abeer.

Anne shook her head. 'I don't think so. She seems to believe that her husband and daughter are still alive and living in Maldon. I'm assuming this isn't true as we have the report from the Met to the contrary. She's going to need looking at by someone who knows more about PTSD than I do. We'll keep her locked up for tonight and carry on in the morning if I can get hold of someone. You go home and get some sleep. There's a long way to go yet I think and Alice is likely to be worse than useless at the moment.'

*

Alice was feeling worse than useless. She was sitting in the kitchen of her flat, a half empty bottle of wine next to her. She'd stopped crying and felt drained and exhausted but couldn't go to bed. Her brain was not going to switch off. She reached out and grabbed the bottle, refilling her glass. Her head was throbbing and she was trying to convince herself that drinking more would take the pain away.

There were four missed calls from the man she'd known as Doug Griffiths. She couldn't talk to him now. Not over the phone. What she really wanted was for him to come round and tell her that none of it was true; that he really was called Doug Griffiths; that he wasn't Catherine Hall's brother-in-law; that he loved her. He had said that. He had said he loved her but was that just another lie? Those nights they'd spent locked together, were they just part of her fantasy, part of his deception? She'd removed the pendant he'd given her and thrown it onto the ledge that the estate agent had laughingly called a breakfast bar when she'd bought the place.

Her head had fallen onto the ledge and there was a ringing in her ears, cutting its way into the nebulous mess her mind had somehow turned into. She raised a bleary eyelid. The ringing had stopped. A hand was on her back, gently caressing. It felt nice, lulling her senses.

'You didn't answer the door,' a voice said softly in her ear.

She lifted her head and tried to focus. There was a man in her kitchen, a tall man with blond, curly hair. Abruptly she came to and sat up. Doug Griffiths was standing next to her. She shook her head, trying to make sense of what was happening.

'What are you doing here?' she managed to slur.

'We have to talk, Alice,' he said, his hands on her shoulders.

'What? More lies?' Alice was wide awake now.

'No more lies, Alice. Only explanations. Shall I make some coffee?'

'Yes…No. What are you doing here? How did you get in?'

Gerald Hall held up the set of keys Alice had had cut for him only two days ago. He put them gently next to her. 'I guess you don't want me to have these anymore,' he said.

She looked at them as if she'd never set eyes on them before. Her heart-shaped pendant was lying next to the keys. She picked it up and swung it from her finger. 'Is this Amelia's?'

'What?'

'Amelia was wearing one exactly the same when she went missing.'

Gerald nodded. 'That explains DI Edwards interest. No, Alice, it's not hers, it's yours. I didn't know Amelia had one. I bought it off the internet.'

Alice looked at him.

'I need to explain lots of things to you, Alice. You have every right to be angry with me but I want you to understand before I go.'

Alice looked up. 'Go?'

'Back to London. I have to see my boss, he's not very happy with me either, apparently.'

Alice nodded slowly. 'When do you go?'

'Today.' Gerald was standing near to Alice's stool not knowing whether he should touch her or keep his distance. He wanted to hold her, to make everything alright but he suspected that might not be possible. She solved his dilemma by taking his hand in hers.

'Tell me why?' she said gently, not looking at him.

He pulled out another stool and sat next to her. 'When I heard Jack was murdered, I knew it was Catherine that had done it. She'd threatened him before but he just thought she was joking. I never thought she'd let poor Elizabeth die, though. She was the sweetest girl, everyone loved her. I had to identify the bodies. It was the hardest thing I've ever had to do, Alice.'

She squeezed his hand slightly.

'They told me to take compassionate leave. They said I couldn't go back to my post for at least three weeks, so I decided to do a bit of detective work for myself. Catherine was forever going on about Maldon and how she'd still be living there if Jack hadn't made her move to East London. I put two and two together and thought that if she was on the run maybe this is where she would come to hide.'

'But surely people would know her here,' said Alice. 'If she was on the run she'd want to be somewhere no-one knew her, presumably.'

'No-one did know her, did they? Or if they did no-one said they'd seen her. Did you know about those tunnels under the town?'

Alice shook her head.

'I think maybe Catherine did and that's why she came here. I thought Maldon Police could help me which is why I introduced myself. Obviously I couldn't admit who I was, that would only arouse suspicion, so I came up with a pseudonym. I'd been at school with a Doug Griffiths.' He smiled and put his hand on Alice's hair, stroking it gently.

'You didn't have to lie to me. Was I just part of your plan?'

Gerald put his arm round Alice's shoulder and hugged her. 'You were never part of any plan that I'd devised. You are the only good thing to come of all this. You are a wonderful woman, Alice Porter, and I only wish we'd met under different circumstances. I also can only pray that one day you'll forgive my deceit and let me into your life again.' He kissed the top of her head.

Alice didn't know what to say. She wanted to tell him he was forgiven that it was all a misunderstanding but could she trust him again? Would he lie to her again? Was he lying now? He'd gone over to the coffee machine, placed a capsule in and switched it on. Alice heard the steam frothing its way into a cup, which Gerald brought to her.

'Drink some of this, Alice,' he said.

'I don't know what to do, what to think anymore, Doug – Gerald. Is that what I call you now?'

He nodded. 'Or Gerry, if you like.'

Alice smiled. 'Gerry Hall? Like Mick Jagger's wife?'

'Ex-wife. And they were never actually married. She was then married to Rupert Murdoch. She must like rich men – unlike me. I'm not rich at all.' He stroked her hair again. 'But I am a lot richer in many ways because I met you.'

Alice looked away. 'So, what happens when you go back to London?'

'I get a ticking-off and go back to work, I guess.'

'Will you ever come out this way again?'

'Would you like me to?'

She smiled. 'You once said you'd like to transfer to Maldon.'

'And you said your boss wouldn't be very happy about it. I think she'd be even less happy now.'

Alice nodded.

'I guess I could always get you a transfer to the Met, if you fancied it.'

'Me in the Met?' said Alice incredulously.

'You're a good detective, Alice. You helped us find Catherine.'

'But the Met?' she looked up at Gerald. He lowered his head and they kissed.

CHAPTER TWENTY-TWO

The Metropolitan Police Force was sending over a small detachment to take Catherine Hall back to their territory but Anne wanted more information about Amelia's kidnap, so, first thing in the morning, she and Abeer Kumar were sitting in an interview room at Chelmsford once again, Catherine Hall opposite. Although she had evidently been showered she still looked bedraggled, her eyes red and staring blankly in front of her.

'Tell us how you snatched Amelia Goddard, Catherine?' said Anne.

'I don't know anyone called Amelia Goddard,' she said.

'Okay, let's stop this now, Cat,' said Anne. There was not enough time to play about.

Catherine Hall looked at her, surprised. 'Don't call me Cat,' she said.

Anne looked down at her notes. 'Where were you on the evening of February 19th?'

'I don't know. I've been away.'

'Yes, you have Catherine. You've been living underground with Amelia Goddard as your prisoner.'

Catherine sniggered. 'Prisoner? No. I was with my daughter, protecting her. And now something bad will happen to her again.'

'Again? What happened to her before?' Abeer was on track.

'I can't tell you.'

Abeer looked at Anne, who nodded.

'Shall I tell you, then, Mrs Hall?' Abeer said.

Catherine frowned. She looked scared. 'Who are you?'

'DC Kumar. Your daughter died, Catherine, didn't she?'

Catherine started rocking in her seat, back and forth, her head nodding wildly.

'So did your husband, Mrs Hall. He was stabbed with a knife very similar to the one you had in the sleeve of your stolen cloak when you were arrested.' Abeer kept her eyes on the woman who was still hurling her body about wildly. Abeer was worried she would knock herself out on the table. Anne just stared at the woman. Suddenly she stood up and went round to her, grabbed her shoulders, and shook her.

'Stop it!' she yelled.

Catherine Hall stopped instantly as though shocked. She sat upright on the hard chair not moving. Anne resumed her seat.

'Why did you do it, Catherine?' Anne leaned towards her.

She stared back at her with her blank eyes.

'Why, Catherine?' Anne reiterated.

'Jack was screwing her,' she said in a monotone.

Anne didn't need this information. That wasn't her case.

'I meant, why did you take Amelia Goddard into that tunnel?'

'It was Elizabeth.'

'It wasn't, Catherine,' Anne shouted at her. 'It was an innocent girl whose boyfriend had just been killed…'

Catherine gasped. 'Boyfriend?'

'How long were you underground?'

Catherine didn't answer. Anne had worked out that it must have been soon after Jack Hall had been murdered, which was shortly before Harry Ellis was killed in the same place Catherine Hall had emerged the previous night.

'How often did you come out into St Giles Hospital's ruins, Catherine?'

'I had to eat.'

The tunnel had been searched and another exit revealed that led into the vestry at All Saints' church.

'But you'd been taking food from the church, hadn't you?'

'I needed air.'

'What about your captive? Didn't she need air too?'

'It wasn't safe.'

'So you kept her tied up, sitting in her own waste. How long did you think that could go on for, Catherine?'

'She was bleeding like before. I thought she'd die again.'

'You only die once, Catherine. That was not Elizabeth there with you. You knew that.'

Catherine slumped in her chair, her head banging on the table.

Anne called the duty officer in and let him deal with her. She went with Abeer to the canteen and bought them both coffees.

'I think she may be suffering with her mental health,' said Abeer as they sat at the Formica-topped tables.

Anne agreed. 'Doesn't help us much, does it? Do you think Jack Hall was actually screwing his thirteen-year-old daughter?'

'Men do.'

Anne nodded sadly. 'And she evidently thought Amelia was Elizabeth – even though she seemed to be aware that Elizabeth was dead.'

Abeer sat quietly for a moment. 'You think she killed Harry Ellis, don't you?'

'Pretty sure of it. The trouble is, once the Met have got her, our case will just be ditched. She'll be sent to a secure unit and two families – and one girl in particular – will be left devastated.'

*

Gerald Hall left Alice's flat and got a cab to Chelmsford to meet up with his Met colleagues to return to London with Catherine Hall. He would not be allowed near her he knew that which was probably a good thing. He'd gone close to ruining his career as it was without adding assaulting a prisoner to the list.

He'd gazed wistfully at Alice before he'd driven off. He'd wondered if it would ever be possible for them to keep up their relationship. Alice had not resisted him once he'd explained to her. He'd left her asleep, dressed himself and slipped out leaving her a note.

He vaguely knew the two officers sent to take Catherine Hall back to London and nodded as they all met up in the reception area in Chelmsford.

'Someone's bringing her up now,' said James Royley from behind his desk.

'You'd better make yourself scarce, DC Hall. We're to make sure you have no contact,' said one of the Met officers.

'You can go through to the canteen, if you want,' suggested Royley.

'Thanks.' Gerald made his way out of reception and headed for the canteen. The two Met officers looked at each other and nodded.

Abeer's face dropped as she saw Gerald Hall walk boldly into the room. She indicated with her head to Anne, who turned round and glowered at him.

'Look what the cat's dragged in,' she said loudly.

Gerald shrugged and sat at a table next to them. 'I know you hate me, DI Edwards but you'll be pleased to know I'll be out of your hair in less than half an hour.'

'And out of my Detective Sergeant's also, hopefully.'

He scratched at his chin. 'I think Alice is old enough to make her own decisions, don't you?' he said.

'Depends,' replied Anne turning away.

'Do you think Alice will be okay.' Abeer muttered quietly.

'She's not stupid,' said Anne.

Abeer sighed. 'What are we going to do about Catherine Hall?'

'I expect there'll be DNA somewhere that matches. That's the best we can hope for, really.'

'Do you remember that tramp who came in complaining about being attacked by the ghost? Do you think that was her too?'

'Yep. Maybe we should learn to listen better. I think that may have been a case of judging a book by its cover. Dirty old man rambling when he was actually giving us a lead we didn't choose to take.'

Two uniformed officers entered and went over to Gerald.

'Ready?' he said.

One of the officers took his handcuffs from his belt. 'Gerald Hall, I'm arresting you on suspicion of having sexual relations with a child. You do not have to say anything but it may harm your defence if you do not mention when questioned something which you later rely on in court. Anything you do say may be given in evidence.'

Gerald stood up. 'You are joking, I assume?'

'I'm afraid not, sir.' The officer held the cuffs on the end of his finger. 'Will you come with us, please?'

Gerald looked bewildered. 'What's going on?'

'Could you hold out your hands,' said the officer.

'Don't be ridiculous. I haven't done anything.'

The other officer grabbed Gerald and held him while the cuffs were attached round his wrists behind his back. The two officers led him away.

Abeer's eyes were nearly popping out of her head. Anne grinned at her.

'Seems he was nowhere near what he seemed to be. I wonder if Alice knows.'

'Don't, Anne. None of this is Alice's fault.'

Anne smirked. 'I know. We'd better get back to Maldon, looks like all the fun's over here.'

*

Alice Porter woke to an empty bed. Her pillow was wet with tears and she felt like shit. She dragged herself to the bathroom and gazed at an old woman staring back at her in the mirror. 'Oh shut up,' she said to her reflection.

Washed and dressed she went to find her laptop, only to discover it wasn't in its usual place in the kitchen. She searched the lounge and the bedroom. No sign of it. Dredging her memory was bringing no results. The last time she remembered having it was in the office when Anne was being childish and bellyaching about Doug – or Gerry as he now was. Thoughts of him set her anxiety off again. What was she supposed to do? He'd explained to her and it had all made sense in the early hours of the morning but now he was gone…She was confused. Head and heart. They needed to work together. Head said let him go, heart said no. She grabbed her car keys and hoped her laptop was still in the office. She had an important letter to write.

*

The printer was in full swing as Anne entered the office. She'd dropped Abeer at the local café to get some decent coffee. Anne hadn't expected Alice to be in but she was sitting at her desk, her head down looking at her laptop screen.

'What's printing?' asked Anne. 'Our printing budget's not for private stuff, you know.' Anne didn't want to be harsh with Alice but somehow every time she spoke to her recently she sounded like some old harridan.

Alice didn't comment so Anne went over to the printer and removed the top sheet. What she saw made her shiver. 'What's this?' she said.

'It says at the top,' said Alice quietly.

'You can't resign.' Anne tore the sheet into bits and threw them in the bin.

'It's still on here,' said Alice pointing at her laptop.

Anne sat opposite her. 'Why?'

Alice laughed. 'Why? Don't you know?'

Anne shook her head. 'No idea.' She could make a good guess. Her behaviour towards her DS had been appalling. She hadn't expected this, though.

'Then there's no point in discussing it further.' Alice closed her laptop and started to put it in her bag.

'Stop, Alice. I'm sorry.'

Alice did stop. She sat, her bag on her knee, the laptop half in, half out. 'Is that it? Sorry? Does that make it alright?'

Anne sighed. 'No, of course it doesn't. I know I've not been the best boss just lately…'

Alice snorted.

'…and I don't really know why.'

'Is my work not up to standard?'

Anne nodded. 'And beyond.'

'So?'

Anne didn't answer.

'What did I do wrong, Anne? I thought we were more than colleagues. I thought we were friends.'

'We are, Alice.' Anne put her hand across the desk. Alice ignored it.

'Then why have you been so vindictive towards me? Is it because I fell in love?'

'Don't say that, Alice.'

'Why? Don't you like it? What's the matter? Are you jealous?' Alice was shouting.

Anne suddenly felt tears in her eyes. She gritted her teeth willing them away. She couldn't cry. Not now. Not here in front of Alice. She looked down at the floor. 'Yes,' she mumbled. She looked up again, unable to stop the drops that had found their way onto her cheeks. 'Yes Alice, I am jealous.'

Alice was standing now, her fists clenched on the desktop, anger showing in her twisted face. 'What right have you to be jealous? What right have you to try and stop me having a life. Just because you have nothing other than this shit job, it doesn't mean we all have to be slaves to it.'

Anne nodded. 'I know,' she said, her voice barely audible. 'I'm sorry.'

'It's not fair, Anne. You're not being fair.'

'I know,' repeated Anne. She looked up into Alice's face. 'Please don't go.'

Alice looked at her tear-stained face and sat down again. 'I have to.'

The door opened and Abeer came in with a cardboard tray holding two coffees. 'Oh, hello Alice. I didn't know you were here or I would have…' her speech slowed like a car braking steadily as she looked at the two women. 'What's going on?'

Neither of them answered.

'Anne? Ma'am? Are you alright?'

Anne sat up. 'Alice has just handed in her notice.'

Abeer stared at Alice. 'You haven't, have you?'

Alice nodded. Abeer sat across the room at her own desk. 'Would you like my coffee, Alice?'

Alice shook her head. The room was silent.

'What are you going to do?' Abeer asked her.

'I'm putting in for a transfer,' Alice replied.

'To where? You've got a flat here.'

'I'll sell it to you if you like,' she said. 'You're looking for somewhere, aren't you?'

Abeer made a decision. 'I don't think you'll want to transfer, Alice. I assume you're thinking of the Met?'

Alice didn't reply. Anne looked warily at Abeer, shaking her head.

'Your boyfriend won't be there, Alice. He's been arrested.'

Alice's mouth dropped open. 'What?'

'He was taken from Chelmsford in handcuffs,' said Anne. 'I didn't want to tell you.'

'Why?' Alice turned on Anne. 'Did you do this? Did you think you could get to me by arranging for him to be locked up? You are an evil woman, Anne!' Alice left the office.

'Stop her, Anne.'

'No, let her go. She's right.'

*

Outside in the car park, Alice's phone went straight to Gerald's voicemail. Had he really been arrested? What for? Falling in love? Was that a crime nowadays? Was it something to do with Catherine Hall being his sister-in-law? Voicemail again. 'Answer the phone, Gerry. I need to speak to you,' she said but she somehow knew he would not reply. Not now. Maybe never. Was she the stupid one? Was he lying to her all along, even last night? It had been his idea to apply for a transfer so they could be together. She was going to stay at his flat, just the two of them. She banged her fists on the low brick wall that surrounded the car park and burst into tears.

Anne's hand gently touched Alice's shoulder. 'Come inside, Alice. Please. Let's talk.'

'Go away, Anne. This is all your fault.'

'Not all of it,' she replied. 'What did Gerald say?'

'Why do you want to know? So you can tell me it's all lies? He loved me.'

'I know. I think he really did. But you don't know the whole truth about him. Maybe none of us does.'

'I'm going home,' said Alice.

Anne paused. 'I'd rather you didn't.'

'You can't stop me,' Alice started to move.

'Strictly speaking, DS Porter, you are still at work. You are serving your notice. I am your superior officer and if I say you're not going home, you're not going home.'

Alice turned round and stomped like a schoolgirl back into the office. Anne followed feeling desolate.

'I don't want to discuss Gerry,' Alice said as Anne followed her into the office.

'Okay. Do you feel up to questioning Father Thatcher again?' replied Anne.

Alice took a deep breath. 'Of course. I'm working my notice,' she said, picking up her bag and heading for the door.

'You can go home after you've seen him and fill us in in the morning, if you like.'

Alice didn't answer and exited.

Abeer looked up from the screen she'd been hiding behind. 'Is she really going to leave?' she asked.

Anne sighed. 'I hope not, Abeer. I don't think she's sent her letter to Chelmsford yet. Hopefully it's just her trying to get revenge for something she thinks I've done.'

'You were a bit down on him.'

'With good reason it would seem.' Anne picked up her phone and punched in the number for the Metropolitan Police Force.

*

Alice had to drag herself out of bed the next morning. She used to look forward to going to work but now it had become a chore. She didn't know what sort of mood Anne would be in, Abeer was evidently trying to keep out it and the love of her life was no longer here. She wasn't sure she'd done the right thing writing that resignation letter. That had been Gerry's idea. He'd promised he'd get her a transfer but that was looking unlikely anytime soon. At best, they would have to wait until everything had been sorted out over his brother's murder. Why had he been arrested? An awful thought crossed her mind. He hadn't committed the murder, had he? He'd said it was Catherine, his sister-in-law. Surely he wasn't an accomplice, was he? Is that what they think? She'd tried ringing him again but it still kept going straight to voicemail. Whatever was happening, it wasn't fair.

She'd been to see Father Thatcher last evening. He was quite upset when he'd realised he'd been unwittingly harbouring a murderess underneath his church. The metal ring on the floor was attached to a stone cover, similar to the wooden one at St Giles which had been lifted revealing the tunnel. A search had revealed that it ran from the vestry right under the town to the ruins. There also appeared to be another passage leading off from the main one but that was blocked up by many years of rockfalls. A number of church candles had been discovered along with the remains of food stolen from the food bank's supplies in the vestry.

'I really didn't know,' he'd told Alice. 'If only I had, everything could have been sorted a lot quicker. That poor girl and her poor mother have suffered needlessly.'

'It's not your fault, Father,' she'd assured him.

'Is the girl alright?'

'She will be, I'm sure, thanks.'

'I'd like to meet her when she's better.'

'You'd have to talk to her mother.'

Father Thatcher had nodded. 'Poor woman. She is a very kind person. She came to see me often when Amelia was missing. I hope she'll still feel she can.'

'I'm sure she will.' Alice had not been in the mood for more misery. She'd had enough of her own for one day.

Father Thatcher had agreed to go up to the station and give a full statement as soon as he could and Alice had left him to his supplications or whatever he'd been doing.

She looked at the empty wine bottle in her kitchen. Had she really done a whole bottle again last night? She made a vow to not allow alcohol into her flat while she was so depressed and confused.

She decided to walk to the police station. If she needed to drive anywhere, they'd have to provide a car for her. She had no intention of giving anything to her soon to be ex-employers. It was a sunny morning but there was a cold wind blowing the detritus left by the revellers at the Rabbit the night before. Crisp bags and empty cigarette packets were racing each other along the gutters as she passed by. She pulled her collar tighter and strolled up the High Street.

'Don't take your coat off,' said Anne as Alice entered the office. Abeer was hiding behind her computer screen again. 'You're with me this morning.'

Alice looked at her boss. Normally she'd feel good about heading off with Anne but today, with all the things that had gone on between them, she felt her energy drain from her body. 'Where are we going, Ma'am?'

Anne noted the official title and sighed. 'London,' she said.

CHAPTER TWENTY-THREE

'Why am I here, Ma'am?' asked Alice. They were at Scotland Yard, standing in a gallery looking at some monitors that showed various angles of an empty interview room.

'I need you to see this, I'm afraid,' said Anne not looking at her.

There were two other senior police officers in the balcony room who weren't acknowledging them.

'Is this Doug's interview?' Alice felt a shiver of nerves run through her. She did not want to witness this.

Anne didn't answer. On the screens the figure of Gerald Hall appeared. He was wearing jeans and a sweatshirt and looked as though he hadn't slept. He had a solicitor with him and they both sat at a table in the middle of the room.

'We shouldn't be here,' said Alice. 'This is not our case.'

One of the other officers looked over at them and appeared to agree. Anne had spoken to one of their superior officers the day before, explaining her interest and it had been agreed that she could view the first interview with DC Hall. She remained silent as the screen showed two detectives come and sit opposite Gerald and the solicitor. They did the introductions for the recording.

'Do you know why you've been arrested, DC Hall,' asked one of them who'd introduced himself as DS Gary Swanwick.

Gerry nodded. 'You're wrong, though.'

'You are Jack Hall's brother, is that right?' asked the other, who'd introduced herself as DI Emily Berrington.

'Yes,' Gerry replied.

'And Elizabeth Hall's uncle?' she continued.

He nodded.

'You were quite close as a family, weren't you?' stated Swanwick.

'We were.'

'Meet up regularly?'

'Yes.'

'Did you babysit Elizabeth at all?'

Gerry paused.

'Did you, DC Hall?'

'Occasionally.'

'Recently?'

'No.'

DI Berrington looked at her notes. Alice knew she was playing for time, waiting for Gerry to speak. It was a tactic both she and Anne used all the time.

'So not in the last three months, say?' she said eventually.

'I don't think so,' said Gerry.

'Think a bit harder,' she said staring into his eyes.

Gerry shrugged. 'Not that I remember.'

'You were there on your own with Elizabeth just before Christmas, weren't you?'

'I don't know.'

'Is this relevant, DI Berrington?' butted in the solicitor.

She turned to him. 'Of course it's relevant or I wouldn't be asking, would I?' she snapped.

The solicitor looked suitably chastised and sat back in his chair.

'On the 20th of December last year, your brother and sister-in-law went to Jack's company's Christmas party. You stayed in with Elizabeth.'

'Maybe.'

'No, not maybe, DC Hall. We have a witness. Jack and Catherine's neighbour...' she looked at her notes again. 'A Mrs Ann Newton. Do you know her?'

'Vaguely.'

'You wished her a happy Christmas as Jack and Catherine left in a taxi.'

Gerry shrugged again. 'It was Christmas.'

'And then you went inside.'

'I suppose I would. It was probably cold,' he said, grinning.

'It's a nice house, isn't it?' Swanwick took over.

'I suppose so, if you like that sort of thing.' A bead of sweat appeared on Gerry's brow. He wiped it away.

'I do. I'd love a house like that. Must be worth well over a million.'

'Are you accusing me of killing my brother in order to inherit his house?' Gerry said incredulously. 'If that had been the case, wouldn't I have made sure his wife was also dead?'

The two detectives looked at each other.

Berrington turned to Gerry again. 'We're not accusing you of anything of the sort, DC Hall. It's your niece we're interested in.'

Gerry wiped his face again. 'What about her?'

'Were you close?'

'Of course. I loved Elizabeth.'

'Quite liberal with your love, aren't you, DC Hall?'

'What the hell does that mean?' Gerry's voice was raised.

'I don't know. You said you loved some Detective Sergeant over in Maldon I believe, when you were on the run.'

Up in the gallery, Alice let out an involuntary yelp.

'I was not on the run.'

'But you were in love, weren't you?'

'She was useful to me; helping me find the murderer of my brother.'

Alice's knees gave way. Anne held on to her and one of the other officers helped her to a chair.

'I don't want to see any more,' she whispered to Anne.

'I'm sorry, Alice,' she replied and turned back to the screen.

'Elizabeth died haemorrhaging whilst miscarrying. Did you know she was pregnant?' asked Berrington.

Gerry's face went white. 'She was thirteen.'

Berrington nodded. 'We have DNA, DC Hall. And we have a match.'

'To Jack?'

'Why do you say that?'

'They were very close.'

'There's a match, yes, to one of your family.'

Gerry looked bewildered. 'Well, it must be Jack, then.'

Berrington shook her head.

Swanwick took over again. 'So your brother and his wife went off to their Christmas party. What did you and Elizabeth do?'

'I don't know. I suppose we watched television. That's what we'd usually do.'

'Before you put her to bed?' DS Swanwick stared at Gerry.

'Yes.'

'As you said, she was thirteen, DC Hall. Couldn't she go to bed on her own?' said DI Berrington.

'Yes, she did. That's what I meant.'

'Maybe she was a bit cold. Needed a cuddle to help her get to sleep?' Swanwick said.

'No.'

'You never cuddled your niece?'

'Of course I did. Not in her bed.'

'No?'

There was a silence. Anne looked down at Alice. Tears were streaming from her eyes. Much as she wanted to, Anne couldn't intervene. Not yet. There was more Alice had to hear, however painful for her.

'I told you we have DNA, DC Hall,' said Berrington. 'Your brother was a close match but not as close as you.' She paused. Gerry sat like an automaton. 'What was it, a split condom? I'm sure you didn't intend to make her pregnant.'

Gerry didn't respond.

'Was it just the once, DC Hall, or are you a serial rapist? A bit unlucky, if it was just the once, eh?' said Swanwick.

'I didn't…' Gerry's head was hanging.

'Didn't what, DC Hall?'

'I didn't mean…'

'You didn't mean to get her pregnant? Your thirteen-year-old niece?'

'I…I…didn't…'

'You keep saying you didn't but you don't tell us what you didn't, DC Hall.'

Gerry was shaking. 'I didn't…rape her. She didn't say no or tell me to stop. She loved me.'

'She was thirteen! You were her uncle! What did you expect her to say?' yelled DI Berrington.

The two detectives sat staring at him. The solicitor seemed to be no help. Gerald Hall put his head in his hands. He was a broken man.

*

It was a long drive back to Maldon. Neither Anne nor Alice knew what to say. Anne knew it had been unkind to force Alice to watch Gerry's confession. She only hoped it was the right decision. Her instinct had told her right from the start that the man called Doug Griffiths was a bad 'un. She couldn't explain why and there hadn't been any clues. She was aware that Alice had become besotted very quickly, he'd virtually moved himself into her flat, although he'd denied it. He'd seemed charming and was certainly good-looking but something underlying had made Anne doubt him. Then she'd doubted herself. She was jealous. This man had been taking up too much time from one of her best colleagues. She'd been sure he'd been twisting her mind. She'd also been jealous that Alice appeared to be so happy. Happy to be in a relationship – blindly in love – something Anne hadn't experienced for years. She looked over at Alice still sobbing in the passenger seat.

'I'm sorry, Alice,' she said again. Alice did not reply.

Not another word was spoken until they were driving into Maldon.

'Would you like me to drop you at home, Alice?' suggested Anne.

'Why?'

'You're upset.'

'Of course I'm upset. That's what you wanted, isn't it?'

Anne turned into a supermarket car park and stopped. 'No, Alice. That is the last thing I wanted but I thought it was necessary, I'm afraid. I had to prove to you what sort of man your Gerald Hall actually was. If I'd told you, you would have accused me of lying to you. You needed to hear it from the horse's mouth.'

'She was thirteen,' muttered Alice. 'He tried to throw his dead brother under the bus.'

Anne nodded.

'He told me he loved me.'

'I know.'

Alice's breath was coming in short bursts. She was desperately trying to stop her tears.

'What should I do, Anne?' she asked, her voice squeaking.

Anne put her hand on her arm. 'It's up to you but the first thing I'd do is delete that resignation letter.'

Alice tried to smile and nearly succeeded. 'I'm not sure I can…'

'Up to you. I think you should and I think you can. You are the best DS I've had. I apologise for my behaviour, I should have handled it better but…I think I'd find it hard to carry on without you, to be honest.'

Alice nodded and wiped her eyes with her sleeve. Anne took a box of tissues from the glove compartment and gave them to her.

'Thanks,' she said.

'So, shall I drop you home?' asked Anne.

Alice shook her head. 'We still have work to do, don't we?'

*

Father Frank Thatcher had been into the station and given a statement to Abeer. There was no reason to believe he was culpable in any way, he didn't even know about the tunnels apparently, but he'd brought in a book he'd discovered in the vicarage, a history of All Saints' Church, which mentioned the legend of escape routes from St Giles. Apparently, the blocked up tunnel headed to Beeleigh Abbey and was used during the dissolution of the monasteries, but the author of the book stated nothing had ever been excavated and that he doubted their existence.

'Maybe I should have been more inquisitive,' he'd told Abeer. 'That poor child and that poor woman, down there in the dark and damp. If I'd only known.'

Abeer had assured him it hadn't been his fault.

*

Alice went straight to the Ladies when they arrived at the police station, to freshen up – as Anne had called it. She washed her face and reapplied some make-up. Looking in the mirror, she convinced herself she appeared almost human and went to the office.

Anne was reading Father Thatcher's statement. He'd mentioned that June Goddard had visited the church on several occasions and that she had appeared distraught over her missing daughter. He'd hoped that God had given her some comfort. He'd also said he hoped that the food taken from the food bank supplies had helped to keep Catherine and Amelia in better health than they would have been without it. 'It's what food banks are for,' he'd put. 'To help those who can't help themselves for whatever reason.'

'We'll need to speak to Amelia. Is she still in hospital?' Anne asked.

'No, she's at home,' said Abeer. 'Would you like me to go?'

Anne shook her head. 'It ought to be me, really.'

'Can I come?' asked Alice.

Anne looked at Abeer. 'I've got a lot to do here, Anne,' she said.

'Come on then,' Anne said, leaving Alice to follow.

They went to the Goddard house in Anne's car. As they parked on the road outside, Alice took hold of Anne's arm and indicated towards the front of the house. Allan Goddard was banging his fists on the door and screaming to be let in. There were several black bin liners strewn across the small lawn, some with clothes seeping out of them.

Anne opened the car door and stepped towards him. 'Is there a problem, Mr Goddard?'

Allan turned to her, his fists still clenched. 'A problem?' he yelled. 'Of course there's a fucking problem. A problem that's all your doing.' He took a pace nearer to her. He was staggering slightly.

'Stay where you are, Mr Goddard if you don't want to be arrested,' she said, her hand on her lapel radio.

'She won't let me see Amelia. Why did you have to tell her about the Ellis's?'

He was standing in the middle of the lawn, his hands out at his sides, looking like someone being crucified, which in some way Anne thought, he probably had.

'I think maybe you should pick up your things and leave for now, Mr Goddard,' said Alice, who had come to join Anne.

Allan looked daggers at the pair of them before kicking one of the black bags, sending more clothing across the garden and stomping off unsteadily to where he'd parked his car. He appeared to have been drinking. Anne and Alice watched him go before strolling up the path to the Goddard house. They rang the bell without any expectation of anyone answering. They knocked on the door and shouted through the letter box. There was no response. Anne took her phone out and punched in June Goddard's number. It took three calls before they heard a small voice behind the door.

'I can't let anyone in,' it said.

'It's DI Edwards and DS Porter, June. We need to speak to you. Allan has gone.'

The door opened a crack, revealing June's left eye. Anne smiled. June cautiously opened the door a bit further.

'It's not a good time,' she said.

'We'll try not to be long,' Anne answered.

The pristine house that Anne had visited previously was almost unrecognisable. Furniture had been tipped over and the few ornaments lay broken on the carpet.

'Do you want to report anything?' asked Alice surveying the state of the living room.

June shook her head.

'Can we speak to Amelia?' asked Anne. 'Is she here?'

'She's in her room,' replied June.

Anne started to go to the stairs, holding her hand out to stop June following. 'DS Porter will stay here with you, June. I need to speak to Amelia on her own.'

'But…' June's body slumped. She was a woman who'd had enough arguing. Alice took her back into the living room.

Amelia looked scared as Anne viewed her through the semi-open door to her bedroom. She was lying on her back on the bed, hugging her knees. Anne knew she was breaking safeguarding rules being on her own with the girl but she took a deep breath. 'Hello, Amelia. It's Anne Edwards. Is it okay if I come in?'

Amelia didn't reply but eyed her with suspicion.

'How are you feeling?' Anne asked her, still standing in the doorway.

Amelia's tense shoulders rose slightly.

Anne indicated the end of the bed. 'Is it alright if I sit?'

Amelia just stared at her but Anne went in and sat anyway.

'Can you tell me what happened, Amelia?'

She looked down at the spotted duvet cover. 'I don't really know,' she said.

'I just need to fill a few bits in,' explained Anne. 'You went out for a walk – to get some air, didn't you? I understand that. Sometimes parents can be a bit overpowering, can't they?'

Amelia raised her eyes to Anne's.

'You went to the ruins?'

Amelia's head nodded slightly.

'And then what? Did someone attack you?'

Amelia looked down again. 'I wasn't attacked.'

'Did you go willingly with someone? The one you called Mummy?'

Amelia's eyes were flicking from side to side. She was in a state of panic. Anne decided she had better leave her for now. She put her hand gently on the girl's leg and started to stand.

'I didn't go with her. I was in the ruins one minute and then I was in the dark place. Why did she call me Elizabeth?'

Anne slowly sat down again. 'Unfortunately, the woman you called Mummy lost her daughter recently and this made her mind do strange things. I think she thought you were her daughter and she wanted to keep you safe. Something really bad happened to her daughter and she blamed herself.'

'The poor woman,' said Amelia.

Anne was amazed at the kindness of this girl. Catherine Hall had kept her tied up in a dank tunnel and yet, she felt sorry for her captor.

'What will happen to her?' Amelia asked.

'I don't know, Amelia. She lives in London so they're dealing with her at the moment.'

'Can I see her?'

Anne paused. 'Not just yet, I'm afraid.' Anne put her hand in the bag she'd brought with her and drew out a book. 'I think this is yours, Amelia,' she said, handing her the journal.

Amelia's face went crimson, her eyes bulging. 'Where did you…'

'I found it in your wardrobe, Amelia. No-one knows I took it but it was helpful.'

'You read it?' Her eyes widened even further.

Anne smiled and nodded. 'It's okay. No-one else did.'

Amelia opened the book and looked at the pages.

'It's all there, Amelia.' Anne studied her. 'What can you tell me about your father?'

Amelia looked at her, scared to speak.

'It's okay. Just between you and me.'

The girl still didn't speak.

'Did he ever try it on with you?' Anne held her breath.

Amelia almost laughed. 'No,' she said. 'He'd be too scared of Mum.'

'Do they row a lot?'

Amelia laughed. 'A lot? How much is a lot? Every day? Yes.'

'Do you know what they argued about?'

The girl sighed. 'I think it was me mostly. Dad didn't want me seeing Harry – well, he's got his way on that, hasn't he? – and Mum…well, I don't really know what her problem is.'

'Did you ever meet Harry's parents?'

'Yes, they were lovely.'

Anne spotted a tear in Amelia's eye and changed the subject. 'I'll have to take a statement from you about where you've been and they might want one in London as well.'

'London? I'll never be allowed to go there.'

'You won't have to go, hopefully. They can do things remotely now.'

Amelia looked wistfully out of the window. 'Harry wanted to take me to London. He wanted me to meet his brother.'

Anne nodded.

'They wouldn't let me,' she indicated downstairs. 'He was going to come out here but it never happened.'

'He did come out, Amelia. He was a very nice, young man.'

'You met him?'

Anne nodded again. Amelia's shoulders sagged. 'Did he look like Harry?'

'A little bit.' Anne didn't know how much Amelia knew about Rueben.

The girl looked up at Anne. 'I really miss him,' she said.

'I know. It's hard but it gets easier.'

'I won't forget him.'

'You won't. He'll always be a part of you.'

*

Downstairs, Alice was helping June to straighten the mess in the living room. There was no blood and no marks on June so Alice decided forensics wouldn't be interested as June was not making any official complaint.

'What happened here?' Alice asked.

'Allan happened.'

Alice straightened the cushion on the sofa she'd picked up. 'Why did he do this?'

'He didn't. I did.' June was standing in the middle of the room. 'I hate this house. I hated it before I knew how he got the money to buy it. I hate it even more now.'

'Did he threaten you, June?'

She laughed. 'Him? He couldn't threaten a fly.'

'Does Amelia know?'

'Not unless your DI has told her which I suppose she has by now. It'll destroy her even more.'

'Shall I make some tea?' Alice suggested.

June shrugged and sat down on a chair. She looked as though her world had fallen apart. Alice went through to the kitchen. The stools from the breakfast bar were strewn across the floor, broken pottery – presumably cups or mugs – and one of the drawers had a handle hanging by one screw. She picked the stools up, searched the almost empty cupboards, found two unbroken mugs and a pack of teabags, filled the kettle and switched it on. One of the metal stool legs was bent and the seat wobbled. Alice decided to try and bend it back into shape but it was solid and wouldn't move. She went back into the living room.

'Bit of damage to your stools,' she said.

'His stools. Nothing in this house is mine.'

Alice squatted next to June so their eyes were level. 'Did he hit you, June?'

She shook her head.

'Was Amelia here while all this was going on?'

'She was in her room.'

'So there was just you and Allan down here?'

June looked at Alice with a puzzled face. 'What are you trying to say, DC Porter?'

'I'm just trying to find out what happened. Allan was pretty aggressive when we arrived.'

'I won't make a complaint,' she repeated.

'Are you sure, June. There's a lot of help out there these days.'

June smirked. 'You have no idea, have you?'

Anne came into the living room. 'Amelia's a bit upset,' she said, stating the obvious.

June stood up and went towards the door. 'I'll go up to her.'

'I think she wants to be on her own for the moment.' Anne barred her way.

'Are you her mother? How do you know what she wants?'

June pushed past Anne and went upstairs. Anne shrugged and indicated to Alice it was time to go.

'I made tea,' said Alice.

'I expect it'll get cold, then.' Anne went out of the front door, Alice following slowly.

'How was Amelia?' asked Alice as they walked towards Anne's car.

'She's a very sensible girl. Unfortunately her parents aren't.'

'Should we get hold of Social Services?'

Anne thought for a minute. 'Not yet.'

They sat in the car with their own thoughts for a while.

'Did you notice any cuts or anything on June Goddard?' Alice said eventually.

Anne looked at her quizzically.

'Only, one of the kitchen stool's legs was bent and when I tried to bend it back, there was a smear of what could have been blood on the end.'

'Do you think he hit June with the stool?'

'No. She implied Allan was a bit of a wimp.'

'Whereas she could be quite a handful if riled, I would suspect.'

'Do we need to go back in, Ma'am?'

Anne tapped her fingers on the steering wheel. 'Any idea where Allan Goddard might have gone?'

Alice's eyes opened wide. 'Oh my God,' she said, as Anne started the car.

CHAPTER TWENTY-FOUR

Gerald Hall was being questioned by DCI George Archer. The interview was not being recorded.

'I must say I'm both surprised and disappointed, Gerry,' said Archer. 'What were you thinking?'

Gerry looked down at the table. 'I don't know.' He looked up at George who was still officially his boss. 'I didn't think she'd get pregnant.'

'Does that make a difference? You'd still have carried on? How long did you carry on? How many times, Gerry?'

'It was just that Christmas time.' He sighed deeply. 'I'd known her all her life. We were like best friends.'

'She was thirteen, Gerry.'

'I know. It wasn't planned, you know. It just happened.'

'You mean you just took advantage.'

Gerry shook his head. 'No, it wasn't like that. We'd had a drink. It was Christmas, she was excited. She kept clinging to me, stroking me, you know?'

'She was thirteen,' Archer reiterated.

Gerry sat stroking the stubble on his face. 'What's going to happen?'

'I think the best thing for you would be to resign.'

'Will I be charged?'

George Archer looked away. 'Maybe.'

'Meaning?'

'As I see it, Gerry – just between you and me – the only person to bring a charge would be your sister-in-law and I can't see her being anywhere other than a top-security hospital. No-one would accept a charge from her. The girl's dead, the father's dead and the mother's mental. There is no-one else.'

'So do I still have to resign?'

George Archer looked at him pitifully.

*

They recognised the car in the long driveway that led to the Ellis' front door. It was parked erratically, slewed sideways, the stone chippings piled against the tyres on one side. Anne and Alice drew up behind it and went towards the open front door.

'Hello?' called Anne.

There was no answer. Cautiously they went into the hallway. Voices could be heard through the kitchen as they ventured further into the house.

'Hello?' Anne called again.

Edwin Ellis appeared in the doorway. There was blood on his hands and face. 'Thank God,' he said, holding onto the doorframe to keep himself upright.

Alice rushed to him. 'Are you alright?'

He gazed at her confused. 'Me? Yes. Yes, I'm alright. It's Linda.'

Anne pushed past them, through the kitchen and onto a stone patio at the back of the house. Linda was kneeling next to the prostrate body of Allan Goddard. Blood was seeping from a head wound. She looked up at Anne.

'What happened here, Linda? I warn you, you are under caution.' Anne hadn't cautioned her – yet.

'I don't know,' said Linda, her face white and scared.

Anne knelt next to Allan Goddard. 'Have you called an ambulance?'

Linda didn't answer, she just stared at Anne, not understanding. Allan Goddard was still breathing – just – and he had a faint pulse. Anne radioed for the paramedics and went back to where Alice was holding Edwin up as he leaned against the doorway.

'What's going on, Ma'am?' Alice's voice was shaky.

'Don't know yet.' Anne turned to Edwin. 'What happened here?'

Edwin squinted at Anne. 'He came in like a madman, ranting and raving. He said he was going to kill Linda.' He was speaking at a rapidity that made it impossible to breathe.

'Okay, Edwin, calm down. Take a breath.'

As he filled his lungs he started to sway.

'Sit him down somewhere, Alice.'

Between them they moved him into the kitchen and found a chair. Linda was still on the patio next to Allan.

'Go and see what you can do out there, Alice,' instructed Anne. 'Did you strike Allan, Edwin?'

'No. He pushed me out of the way and found Linda in the kitchen. I went in as he was chasing her onto the patio. I followed and arrived just as he collapsed.'

'Did Linda hit him?'

He shook his head. 'Just as I got there he fell over. I don't know if he tripped or what but Linda was nowhere near him. I tried to help him but he was a dead weight.' He looked down at his hands and recalled as if noticing the blood on them for the first time.

Alice put her head into the kitchen. 'Where's the ambulance, Ma'am? He's not looking good.'

'It's on its way. I'll radio again.'

Anne had just connected with her lapel radio as two paramedics entered.

'On the patio,' she told them. 'Did Allan speak to you, Edwin?'

'He just said "Where is she? I'm going to kill her." No reason or anything. He was mad, insane, waving his arms around and staggering.'

Linda walked into the kitchen like a ghost. Alice had never seen anyone so pale and still alive. Edwin stood up and hugged her. The two of them rocking in the middle of the room like the last couple in a dance marathon.

Anne left them and went out to the patio. The two female paramedics had attached a fluid bag via a catheter to Allan's arm, one of them holding it up in the air, the other pumping his chest. Anne left them to their work and went back to the kitchen. Alice had put the kettle on to make sweet tea. Anne went up to the couple and touched Linda on the shoulder.

'Are you able to talk to me, Linda?' she said gently.

Linda Ellis looked at her as though she'd never seen her before. 'What?' she said, her voice barely a whisper.

Anne drew her away from Edwin's hold and made her sit on a chair. 'I need you to tell me what's happened here, Linda. Did you hit him?'

'No. He was shouting at me. I don't know what he was saying and then he just collapsed.'

One of the paramedics flew through the room returning shortly with a gurney. 'Excuse me,' she said politely.

They made room and a minute later the two medics ran through with Allan's body, still attached to the fluid, and rushed out to the ambulance.

'Follow them, Alice,' instructed Anne.

'I don't have a car.'

'Take mine, I'll get a cab. Keep me informed.'

'Yes, Ma'am.'

Edwin was hugging his sobbing wife. They had both had a shock. Anne had no doubts as to why Allan had gone for Linda. Whether either of them had told Edwin the reason or not she didn't know.

'Have you spoken to Allan's wife?' she asked the couple.

'June?' said Edwin. 'No, why?'

'She seems to have thrown him out. I just wondered if you could throw any light on the reason?'

Edwin shook his head. He was calmer now that Allan had been taken away and Linda seemed safe. Anne looked at Linda who looked back with terrified eyes.

'Do you need anyone to come over?' said Anne.

'No, we have each other,' answered Linda.

'And that's all we need,' added Edwin, hugging his wife tighter.

'Then I'll leave you. You have my number. I'll need a statement from the two of you, maybe tomorrow, if you feel up to it.'

Neither answered and Anne left the room.

*

Allan Goddard was in intensive care. Alice had been told there was no point in waiting and that she would be informed if there was any change. He was unconscious and most probably wouldn't come round for a while, if he survived. She'd phoned Anne who'd told her to go home and get some rest. Which is where she was now. Sitting in her kitchen again, drinking wine again.

Her anxiety levels had risen steadily since she'd arrived home. She didn't know what she was supposed to do. There was no-one to tell her. She'd thought about talking to her parents but their attitude, whenever she'd had a problem, had always been ignore it and it will go away. This wasn't going to go away. Not on its own anyway. Doug – or Gerry – had gone away, at least bodily but he was still there in her head. Her sheets still smelt of his aftershave. She could almost feel his arms around her as she sat alone and empty. She'd been so sure about him. He was charming and loving. How could he have violated that poor thirteen-year-old girl? His niece! She didn't want to believe it. And yet she'd seen him confess to it. She'd seen him accuse his dead brother. She'd heard him say that she was just a means to use for his own ends. She'd also seen the way he'd attacked Catherine Hall in the ruins. He'd never shown that sort of violence before. She believed he would have killed her if they hadn't pulled him off her. But there was no point in talking about before. How long had she known him? She had no idea what he was like before. He'd raped a thirteen-year-old, of course he was violent. And yet, he'd been so tender and loving with her. She supposed it showed how wrong you can be.

And then there was Anne who'd been so horrible to her. It was like a favourite teacher had suddenly started dishing out detentions to her. She'd admitted to being jealous which Alice had found odd. Jealous of what? Had she fancied Gerry? No, she'd been rude to him from the start. She poured another glass of wine. That was something else. She'd never drunk wine at home before she'd met Anne. Was she turning into her? Sitting at home alone getting drunk night after night? No, she wouldn't let herself. Maybe she did have to get out of the Maldon CID. Maybe it just wasn't good for her. She flipped her laptop open and brought up her resignation letter. She'd just started to re-read it when her phone rang. The name on the screen said 'Doug'.

'Hey,' he said as she answered. 'How are you?'

'How do you think?'

'I can only apologise for those over-officious animals who decided to arrest me. It was all a mistake.'

Alice didn't answer.

'I was expecting to be praised for bringing a murderer in but instead I got nicked.' He laughed. 'There's no justice in this world, is there?'

'I'd like to hope so,' said Alice.

'Anyway, I've some surprising news for you. I've decided on a career change.'

'Have you?' Alice knew that hadn't been his decision. 'What are you going to do?'

There was a pause. 'Haven't really thought that out yet. I wondered if we could make that decision between us.'

Alice couldn't believe what she was hearing. Her heart was quivering, her hands so shaky she almost dropped the phone.

'What do you think?' he continued. 'Are you still going to apply for that transfer? Just because I'm leaving the Met doesn't mean you can't join it.'

Alice looked at the resignation letter on her screen.

'Why did they arrest you, Gerry?'

'It was all a misunderstanding. Poor Elizabeth, my niece, died from a haemorrhage whilst miscarrying a baby. She was thirteen. Can you believe that? Pregnant at thirteen. And it gets worse. They had DNA which was a close match to me. They tried to make out I'd been screwing my niece, which obviously I hadn't. It turns out, which in some ways is even sadder, that it was my brother screwing his own daughter. It makes me feel sick just to think about it.'

'I know what you mean,' said Alice, truthfully.

'Anyway, it was all cleared up but I felt I couldn't stay in a force that didn't trust me and I resigned there and then.'

'Is that true, Gerry?'

'On my mother's grave,' he said.

'Is your mother dead?'

'Well, no. It's just a turn of phrase.'

'A lie.'

'No.'

'So why did you confess,' she said, trying to keep her voice steady.

'Don't listen to what DI Edwards says, Alice. You know she hates me. She's just making things up if she told you that.'

'She didn't have to tell me, Gerry.'

There was silence from the other end of the phone call.

'You're the one that's been lying to me all along...'

'I explained that. I had to pretend to be someone else in order to track down Catherine.'

'Why are you still lying to me?'

'I'm not. I swear.'

'On your mother's grave again?'

'Look, I don't know what your boss has said but I did not confess and I was acquitted, charges dropped right there in the interview room.'

'No they weren't, Gerry. You confessed to having sexual relations with your thirteen-year-old niece. You even said you didn't rape her because she didn't say no. What sort of man are you, Gerald

Hall?' Alice's breath was coming in short bursts. She knocked back her glass of wine and refilled it.

'That's just rubbish, Alice. It's Edwards trying to turn you against me.'

'I was there.'

There was a very long silence. Alice wondered whether he's disconnected. Eventually he spoke.

'I don't think you were, Alice, I'd have noticed.' His tone had darkened. He sounded angry.

'I was in the gallery. I saw the whole thing on the monitors, Gerry. You tried to blame your brother but it was the other way round, wasn't it? The close match was with your brother, the exact match was with you, wasn't it, Gerry?'

'It was all wrong,' protested Gerry.

Alice shook her head. 'It's you that's all wrong, Gerry. I feel sorry for you in a way. You're a lost boy. Jealous of your brother to the point of blaming him for your misdeeds even after he was dead – which is also down to you. Catherine believed it was Jack who'd made Elizabeth pregnant, didn't she? That why she killed him in a fit of rage. Does she know the truth now, Gerry? Has anyone told her how you destroyed their lives, do you think? I'm not applying for a transfer. I don't want to come and live with you and help you sort your future out. I never want to see you again, Gerry.'

'You've got it all wrong, Alice.'

'No, what I got wrong was letting someone like you into my life. Do not phone this number again or I will make sure someone who is still in the police force pays you a visit and that won't be me. Oh, but I expect it will be somewhere at Her Majesty's Pleasure, won't it?'

'No, it won't. Alice, I wish you'd let me explain.'

'Go to hell, Gerry.' Alice disconnected and burst into tears.

*

Anne wasn't sure who she was supposed to feel sorriest for. There was June, stuck in a marriage with a possibly disabled man, if he survived, one that patently wasn't working even before. Linda, living with a secret she couldn't tell anyone. Edwin, still believing Harry was biologically his son. Cat Hall, who'd killed the wrong brother. And poor Alice who'd been duped by a rogue. She was somewhat pleased that her instinct hadn't let her down. She'd been unsure of the man calling himself DC Doug Griffiths but she should have checked him out before letting him temporarily join the team. He'd been right, no-one had looked very closely at his warrant card. One thing she was sure about was that she didn't feel sorry for him. She hoped he got locked up and they threw away the key. She also hoped he received the sort of treatment reserved solely for police officers in certain prisons.

She refilled her wine glass and tried to work out some sort of order for the things she had to do next. Who had attacked Allan Goddard? Linda? Edwin? Or, most probably, June. They should have checked that blood on the stool leg. That's at least two things she'd missed so far. She took a slug of wine. Had Allan threatened Linda? Had she hit him in self-defence? And where had Amelia actually been at the time? And then there was Allan's rather unnatural interest in his daughter. Had he committed a crime there? They'd have to talk to June again.

Was she going to be allowed to interview Catherine Hall again? She was part of one of her cases – the abducted girl – but she was in the custody of the great Metropolitan Police Force now. Were they going to let her have access? Doubtful she assumed but she put it on her list.

Thomas Lloyd. She decided she could forget about him, he'd done nothing wrong. His stepfather might still try for his compensation but he wouldn't get very far.

And then there was the witch, Agnes Waterhouse. Jed Barber had probably been killed by Catherine Hall but no-one had seen her and unless Anne could get a confession out of her – if she was allowed to see her – then Agnes was still the main suspect. Had she done wrong letting Agnes out? Was that another mistake she'd made?

She looked round her flat. There was a sofa no-one had sat on since Derek had used it as a temporary bed, a coffee table no-one ever bothered to use and her beloved record player. Nothing else. No person to share it with. Just an empty shell – a roof over her head to keep the rain out. Alice had suggested that she had nothing in her life other than her shit job. That had hurt – mostly because Alice had been right. She had no friends as such, rarely went out unless it was with her work colleagues. Even the rare occasions she and Derek met up were getting very few and far between. It must be her fault. She had to try and be nicer to people, more friendly. She didn't want to turn into some dreadful old spinster watching TV and drinking herself to an early grave. She reached for her phone.

*

Alice pulled herself together. Anne was right, it was time for her to grow up. She flicked through her iPad until she found the piece of music that she'd always used to relax and let it play loudly through her Bluetooth speaker. She woke up her laptop and looked again at her resignation letter. She hadn't sent it to Chelmsford yet. She assumed it had to go to DCI Horobin but she didn't know, she'd never resigned before. It was probably the right thing to do, the adult thing to do. Anne evidently didn't like her anymore and working closely together would be intolerable now. This afternoon hadn't been too bad but there was still an atmosphere. She'd just ordered her about like some lackey. It hadn't been enjoyable like before. Even going to the worst of crime scenes had been tempered with the knowledge that Anne was there and that they were friends. She'd admired her since before they'd worked together. She'd almost forced herself onto her team, and Anne had reciprocated by insisting she was fast-tracked to DS level, way before her time. She looked at the letter again. She would miss the work here plus, as Abeer had said, she had a flat here, something she'd worked hard to afford. Some of her friends were still living with their parents in their mid-twenties. The music rose to a crescendo. Alice took a deep breath and tried to relax.

She only just heard her phone over the loud music.

'Hi,' said Anne, sounding jolly.

'Oh, hello,' replied Alice, unsure of what else to say.

There was a noticeable pause. 'Alice, I've been thinking…'

'Yes?'

'Fancy going to the Queen's?'

'What now?'

'Yes, it's only nine o'clock.'

Alice looked at the half empty bottle. 'I've been drinking.'

'So have I but drinking alone is boring. I'd like some decent company if you're up for it.'

Alice felt a smile start to form on her lips. 'I don't know, Anne. Is it right?'

'Too bloody right it's right. What's that music I can hear?'

'It's Albinoni's Adagio. I put it on when I'm a bit depressed.'

'Bloody hell.'

'What do you play if you're feeling down?'

'Janis Ian.'

Alice didn't know who that was.

'So, Queen's? I think I owe you a drink as an apology if nothing else.'

'Apology for what?'

'Being a shit!'

Alice took another deep breath. 'Okay, race you there,' she said failing to stop the grin on her face as she grabbed her coat, stopping only to press the delete button on her laptop.

CHAPTER TWENTY-FIVE

Allan Goddard did not know where he was. He was lying down, he knew that much, in a tiny cubicle with blue curtains around it. There was a man leaning over him and saying something he couldn't quite comprehend.

'Can you tell me your name?' The man seemed to be speaking very slowly.

'Of course I can, why do you want to know,' is what Allan wanted to reply but what came out sounded like some jungle animal. A grunt, a slurred, moaning sound emanated from his lips.

'Can you hear me?' said the man.

Allan tried to nod but his head seemed lopsided, heavier on one side than the other. He attempted to sit up but nothing was moving properly. Panic started to set in. What was happening? Where was he?

As if reading his mind, the man said, 'I'm a doctor and you're in a hospital. You've had an accident. Do you understand?'

He was talking as if to a small child, everything slow and overenunciated. Allan wanted to ask what kind of accident but his brain would not connect with his mouth. The man turned away and spoke to a woman in a blue dress with white piping around the collar – a nurse presumably but Allan couldn't hear what was being said. He realised he had some sort of mask covering the lower half of his face. No wonder he couldn't speak, but try as he might, he could not find the strength to lift his hand to remove it. The nurse came over to him as the man left.

'How are we feeling? All a bit of a shock, I expect,' she said in the same sing-song voice as the doctor.

Allan managed a slight unbalanced movement with his head, desperate to communicate that it was more than a shock.

'Well, often people recover quite well from a stroke, so try not to worry. It'll just take time.'

A stroke! He'd had a stroke? When? How? He struggled to remember what had happened. He had a vague recollection of being with June. She'd told him to leave, hadn't she? Then what? He had no idea. How long ago was that? How long had he been in this place?

'We'll get you onto a ward as soon as we can. You'll be comfier there,' said the nurse. 'I'm Julie, by the way.'

Allan looked around him as much as his eyes would let him. He could barely turn his head. There was strip lighting up in the rafters that hurt if he focussed on them. A lot of extraneous noise, banging, rattling, people shouting.

'You'll be going for another scan soon,' Julie was still talking, didn't she have anything else to do? Hospitals were supposed to be overrun and understaffed, weren't they? Why was she hanging around? It wasn't as though they could have any sort of conversation. Allan looked at the girl, probably not more than early twenties, dark hair tied up in a bun under some sort of hat. She was studying a monitor that he seemed to be attached to now which was making beeping noises. A nice trim figure, he noticed.

A man in green overalls entered the space, pulling a trolley behind him.

'Hello, old man. Let's get you over to radiology,' he said, carefully removing the bedclothes, exposing Allan in a checked gown, before gently lifting him onto the trolley. Allan wasn't the smallest person but this man was like some sort of giant. He hoisted him up as though he were little more than a child.

'There we go,' he said. He waved his fingers at the nurse, who blushed slightly, and pushed Allan out of A&E.

*

The Queen's Head was quite busy when Anne arrived. She'd rushed there to beat Alice as she wanted to make sure she bought the first round. She'd made it by a matter of minutes.

'I bought a bottle,' she said as Alice came and stood next to her at the bar. There were no seats in The Members' but the couple on the table in the nook had very little left in their glasses and Anne hoped they didn't want a refill. The two police officers stood at the bar, eagerly eyeing the couple, who eventually took the hint and left. Anne almost sprinted to the table before anyone else could take it and sat down. Alice followed more slowly, unsure how to react to Anne. She took the couples' empties back to Charlotte at the bar, before coming back and sitting opposite her boss.

'You're not really going to resign, are you?' Anne looked at the tabletop. There was a small puddle of liquid that was running towards the window. Anne put her finger in it and started to doodle, a series of concentric circles in the middle of the light brown wood.

'I suppose I haven't decided yet,' Alice replied.

Anne looked up at her. 'Please don't.'

Alice looked up at the ceiling. 'Is that why you asked me for a drink? To try and persuade me?'

Anne smiled. 'No…well…partly, I suppose. The thing is, Alice, I've grown used to you…no, that came out completely wrong. I don't feel that I have many friends. The ones I grew up with here, I've grown apart from, you know, the ones that stayed here and never travelled further than Heybridge.'

'I've never really travelled. Only on holiday.'

'But you've lived, Alice. You're full of life. You're enthusiastic. And you're a bloody good detective. Also, I'd have to find another recruit whose name began with an A.'

Alice looked confused.

'Anne, Abeer and Alice. We are the 'A Team'.'

'Because all our names begin with A, I see. You could always replace me with Agnes Waterhouse. She might be the sort that would shave her head and grow a beard.'

'I'm surprised you remember the 'A Team.''

'There's such a thing as the internet, Anne. I watch a lot of those old cop shows. I see it as part of my job – to see how not to do it.'

'Anyway, I can't have a witch on my team, so you can't resign or we'll be an 'A' minus.'

Alice attempted to stem the warm feeling flowing through her veins. She knew she wasn't going to resign – she'd deleted the letter that had taken her ages to compose and she didn't intend to start again – but she needed to know that Anne really wanted her to stay. Not because she was a 'good detective' or because her name began with an 'A' but because she wanted to work with her, like before, without jealousy rearing its ugly head.

'On top of all that,' continued Anne. 'Drinking alone is a bad habit I don't want to get into.'

Alice smiled. 'You could stop drinking.'

'Now you're just being ridiculous.' Anne refilled their glasses. 'Don't you like working here?'

'I do. Well, I did before Doug/Gerald came on the scene.' She took a deep breath. 'The thing is, Anne. I'm very fond of you, we've always had a good rapport but you say I'm full of life and some of that life is outside of Maldon Police and I have to be able to live that life without feeling awkward about it.'

Anne nodded slowly. 'Of course,' she said. 'I suppose I'm about old enough to be your mother but I shouldn't interfere. I'm not your mother, though I hope I am your friend but I agree, it was none of my business.'

'Even though you were right?'

'I wasn't going to say that.'

Alice grinned. 'You thought it though.'

Anne took a long drink. 'Why don't people like me, Alice?' she asked.

'They do,' assured Alice. 'But...'

Anne looked up at her.

'Well, sometimes you can be a bit officious and you don't take criticism very well.'

'I'm not and I bloody do.'

Alice grinned. 'Case proven m'lud.'

'You know, sometimes you can be a bit too clever for your own good.'

'Yes, Ma'am. I know. Maybe we'll just end up a couple of old spinsters. I guess I'd have to be your carer.'

'Fuck off! I'm not that old.'

'Yes you are – mum.'

Alice laughed and Anne joined in eventually.

'That's what I like most about you, Alice. No sense of decorum.'

'True. I'll get another bottle.' Alice wobbled slightly as she went to the bar.

*

Allan Goddard's new surroundings made him feel worse than before. He was in a part of the ward where the sun refused to shine. The windows where the bright light shone through, appeared to be miles away. There were several other beds in the ward, all containing men with ages raging from mid-twenties to about a hundred by what he could see. Some were chatting to their neighbours and one or two were just moaning. Allan hated self-pity. He bet none of them were as bad as he was but he wasn't moaning. He wasn't chatting either. He couldn't. Would he ever be able to speak again. It was strange that his brain seemed to function inside his head but the channels to his mouth just weren't there, all that came out were animal noises. He lay back on the pillow – he couldn't do much else to be honest, his body didn't have any coordination.

He heard June before she came into his restricted vision. He wasn't sure how she was going to react or how he should react to her – if he was even able to. She looked at him as though she'd seen a ghost. He could see the shock on her face. If he'd been able to he'd have yelled at her, telling her that this is what she'd done to him but there was no point in even attempting it.

'How are you?' she said, her voice harsh.

He smiled his lopsided smile. There was someone else with her but he couldn't see who it was. It was a female, he could hear her whispering to his wife. She leaned towards him again.

'They tell me you can't speak.'

Was that a smile on her face?

'That's the good news. They're also telling me you're going to be my responsibility once you get out of here.'

He grunted, saliva dribbling down his chin. 'You reap what you sow, I suppose,' he thought.

A head appeared around June's shoulder and stared at him. He tried to smile at his daughter but she just kept staring, showing no emotion. He'd hoped she'd at least be upset but there was nothing. She turned away and he heard her footsteps leaving the ward.

'I'd better go after her.' June started to follow her daughter before turning back to her husband. 'Thanks for fucking up her life – and mine.'

The ward's visitors looked suitably shocked as they watched her leave.

*

Anne's head was throbbing as she sat behind her computer terminal in the Maldon office. She and Alice had left the Queen's Head well after midnight. Charlotte and Ben had joined them for a few drinks that neither of them really needed. It had seemed a long walk home. Alice was not in yet but Abeer had greeted her in what appeared to be a particularly loud voice. She'd sent her to get decent coffee.

She looked up at the whiteboard and wondered about all the names they'd written up. Catherine Hall had just been a bit part player somewhere near the bottom of the bill and yet, it looked like she'd turned out to be the killer of at least two of the victims, her husband and Harry Ellis – and most probably Jed Barber as well. Anne was left with a dilemma. What to do about Agnes Waterhouse. She'd emailed The Met requesting an interview with Catherine but hadn't had a reply as yet.

The door opened and Agnes stood there, a bunch of what looked like daisies held out in front of her. 'I brought you these,' she said.

'What are they?'

'Chamomile. Good for hangovers.'

Anne looked at her with her red eyes. 'What makes you think I might have a hangover?'

'Saw you leave the pub.'

Anne sighed. 'Why are you here? Apart from being a quack doctor?'

'There's no quackery in herbalism. It's been around a lot longer than the NHS, you know.' Agnes smiled and sat in front of Anne's desk. 'So, what's happening?'

'What do you mean?'

'Well, you've nicked that woman. Has she confessed to killing Jed Barber?'

'I can't tell you that,' replied Anne.

'That's a no, then. Am I still a suspect?'

'Did you see that woman at any time?'

Agnes shook her head.

Anne shrugged. 'You know she's your ghostly monk, don't you?'

Agnes laughed. 'If you say so.'

'Did you know about the tunnels?'

Agnes thought for a moment how best to answer. 'There'd always been rumours but I didn't know they actually existed, no.'

'You'd never noticed a manhole cover in the middle of the ruins?'

'Had you? You'd spent a lot of time there since the boy was killed.'

That was true. Anne hadn't noticed something that had been hiding in plain sight. A circle of cobblestones that appeared to have once been part of a patterned floor.

'I assume you've questioned Jed's cohorts?' continued Agnes.

'We have but they weren't there, you said.'

'I think I said I didn't see them. It was dark. Them and the woman might have been there for all I know.'

Abeer came into the office with two cardboard coffee cups. She looked at Agnes, then at Anne before sitting at her desk.

'Coffee's bad for hangovers, you'd be much better with a chamomile tea.' Agnes put the bunch of herbs on Anne's desk and left.

'What was that about?' asked Abeer.

'I don't know,' answered Anne, truthfully. She had no idea why Agnes had decided to pay them a visit.

'No Alice?' Abeer made a point of looking round the room.

'Not yet.' Anne went over to the whiteboard and started erasing names just as Alice turned up.

'Afternoon,' said Anne.

'Sorry,' Alice mumbled. 'Why are you doing that?'

'There are innocent people on here.'

'Are you sure?'

Anne turned to Alice. 'Meaning?'

'I've been thinking. Do you really consider it's a coincidence that Allan Goddard had a stroke just after his wife had kicked him out?'

Anne grabbed her coffee from Abeer's desk. 'Go on.'

'The leg of that stool in their kitchen was bent. I tried to straighten it but it wouldn't budge. I suspect June smashed it hard over Allan's head giving him a bigger headache than I have right now.' Alice sat down and massaged her temples.

'I think, Alice, if your supposition is correct. I surmise that June will be paying for it for some time yet.'

'But that's not fair, Anne.'

'Justice often isn't.'

'So you're just going to leave it?'

Anne shrugged. 'Not part of our investigation. If someone was to make a complaint…'

'What about Amelia?'

'In the hands of a reputable therapist, I believe.'

'Linda and Edwin?'

'They refused therapy.'

Alice looked at the whiteboard. 'I see you've left the witch.'

'I don't have closure on Jed Barber's murder yet.'

Abeer spoke up. 'Has anyone spoken to Brad Jordan?'

Anne looked at Alice who shook her head. 'He'd left by the time Jed Barber was killed, though.'

'How do we know that?' asked Abeer.

Alice looked abashed. 'The witch said.'

'Anyone know where he lives?' asked Anne.

Abeer held up a piece of paper. 'I have his address here. Would you like me to go and see him?'

'You'd better not go alone, he's a nasty piece of work, by all accounts.'

Alice looked pleadingly at Anne. 'Sorry, Alice. It's got to be you. Try the pub first, see if he's with Jesse. You could have a hair of the dog while you're there.' Anne smiled.

'Is the pub open?' said Abeer.

Anne checked the clock on the wall. 'By the time you've walked up there it will be, and if I'm not mistaken, one of those two will be banging on the door.'

*

The landlord was unlocking the doors to the pub as Alice and Abeer arrived.

'Oh God. Why don't you just shut me down?' he said.

'What do you mean?' asked Abeer.

'Half of my customers won't come in because they think there's going to be coppers here.'

'You should get a better class of customer then,' said Alice.

'I had customers who paid good money before you lot started sniffing around.'

'I suppose that depends on how one defines good money. Anyway, it's one of your customers we need to speak to.'

'Jesse's not here. It's a bit early even for him.'

'We need to speak to Brad Jordan,' Abeer informed him.

'Haven't seen him for over a week. Nor has Jesse apparently.'

'Is he not at home?' Alice assumed Jesse would have gone to his house.

'I dunno. He's not here filling my coffers, and Jesse's tab is getting bigger daily, that's all I know.' The landlord turned and went back into the pub. Abeer looked at Alice, who shook her head painfully.

'Let's check out his house. I hope it's not far.'

'The walk'll do you good.' Abeer grinned.

'You're as bad as the boss,' replied Alice.

Brad Jordan lived in a run-down bungalow next to the by-pass. It was little more than a shack really and looked as though it ought to be condemned. Nothing had seen a coat of paint for years by the looks of it. Alice rapped on the front door, flakes of green paint sticking to her knuckles. There was no answer. She tried again as Abeer went to look through one of the grubby windows.

'No sign of anyone,' she said coming back to Alice.

Alice hammered harder on the door, which creaked open an inch. She looked at Abeer who nodded before she pushed it open further. Rubbish and junk mail was trying its hardest to restrict entry, so Abeer put her shoulder to the door, forcing it wider. There was a foul smell emanating from somewhere inside, a bit like rotting food or maybe just somewhere that hadn't ever been cleaned smelt like that. Alice went first, calling Brad's name. The door opened straight into the living room, which held a filthy sofa, an overfilled ashtray cascading dog-ends onto the stained and tatty carpet, a few empty beer cans, crushed, lay around but no Brad Jordan. The bedroom door to the left was missing, an unmade bed taking up most of the space. Abeer poked her head inside.

'No-one in there,' she told Alice.

A door at the far end of the room was hanging off its hinges and the two women ventured steadily towards it. A kitchen could be seen on the other side of the aperture, detritus in the form of pizza boxes and more beer cans strewn across the floor. Alice carefully pulled the broken door towards them and squeezed through the gap.

'Oh shit,' she uttered.

Abeer followed her, her hands went straight to her mouth.

CHAPTER TWENTY-SIX

'No wonder he hadn't been to the pub,' said Anne, surveying the scene.

On the kitchen floor lay Brad Jordan, a dried-up brown laceration across the left side of his neck, a stain that had once been a pool of blood spread out to his side; spattering formed a pattern on the grimy sink and a dirty kitchen knife was in his hand. Anne had phoned Sarah Clifford who was on her way. There was nothing they could do until Sarah and the forensic team arrived.

'Coffee?' said Anne.

Alice and Abeer looked round the kitchen.

'Not here, you fools. Someone go and get some takeaways. Get one for Sarah too. Take my car if you have to.'

Abeer agreed to go as Alice was probably still over the drink-drive limit – even though that hadn't stopped Anne driving up here.

'Who did it, do you think? Jesse?' asked Anne.

'Unlikely, I'd have thought. Brad appeared to have been his main source of alcohol.'

'Burglary?'

'Not much to nick, is there?'

'Who knows? If there was, I suspect it has gone never to be found.'

'He has a knife in his hand.'

'I'm sure he didn't slit his own throat. Do you need to sit down, Alice. You're looking a bit pallid.'

Alice looked at the grimy kitchen chairs. 'I'm fine, thanks,' she said. However, the last thing she needed to look at with a hangover was a dead body. The smell was making her nauseous. A clean seat would have been welcome. 'How come you don't get hangovers?'

Anne grinned. 'Practice makes perfect.'

The back door of the kitchen was open but it wasn't reducing the putrid aroma.

'That how they got in, do you think?' Anne surmised.

'Could be but the front door wasn't properly shut either.'

'What do we know about Brad Jordan, Alice?'

Alice shrugged. 'I'm not sure we've really followed that up, to be honest. He's a petty villain. Bit of thuggery, bit of fraud, I expect, maybe a bit of protectionism. Always seemed to have plenty of cash on him.'

Sarah called from the front of the house.

'In here, Sarah,' yelled Anne.

The kitchen was a small extension attached to the original cottage. There was a sink under the grimy window and an ancient and rusting gas cooker that had never seen a cloth, let alone any cleaning fluid. A fold-down table had two broken chairs next to it, the floor was covered in grease and bits of food. The forensic doctor came through, scanned the scene, and started to don her PPE. 'You should do the same, really,' she told Anne and Alice.

'We're going outside and leaving you to it,' grinned Anne. 'I think Abeer's getting you a coffee.'

'Great, keep it warm for me.'

It was barely fifteen minutes later that Sarah joined the officers outside the front of the building. One or two onlookers had asked what was going on and been sent on their way. The 'A Team' were leaning on Anne's car, its roof making do as a coffee table.

'Probably been dead for at least two, maybe three days, can't say exactly until I've had him on the table. Jugular sliced through, can't see any other injury but I guess it wouldn't be needed. The rest of the team should be here shortly.' She picked up her coffee. 'Who do I owe for this?'

'It's okay,' said Abeer.

Sarah smiled. 'You'll be broke before long. I hope you're claiming expenses.' She turned to Anne. 'Who was he?'

'Brad Jordan, local petty crim. He was at the ruins when Jed Barber was struck, though.'

'Which was a similar stabbing?'

Anne nodded.

'Same perp?'

'I really don't know to be honest, Sarah. Similar to Harry Ellis, by any chance?'

Sarah thought for a moment. 'Similar but not the same, I would say.'

Anne raised her eyebrows. 'Meaning?'

'Harry Ellis was cut from behind. The other two were both frontal assaults.'

'How can you tell?' asked Abeer.

'In a slicing movement, the point of entry is narrower than the point of exit. Hence one can usually ascertain which direction the knife travelled.' Sarah demonstrated.

'But that's not absolutely conclusive, is it?'

Sarah smiled. 'Nothing ever is, I'm afraid, DC Kumar.' She finished her coffee and picked up her bag containing her PPE. 'Tell them to send him over to me ASAP. I don't want to be working all night.'

They waved Sarah off in her car. 'What do we do?' asked Abeer.

'Think,' replied Anne.

Alice posed like Rodin's thinker for moment before saying. 'It's the witch.'

'How did you work that out, Alice?'

'She had the motive.'

'Which was?'

'Brad Jordan saw her kill Jed Barber and she needed to shut him up.'

'Brad Jordan wasn't there when Jed was killed though.'

'So the witch says.'

'And Jesse James.'

'Oh well, I'm sure he's a very reliable witness.'

'I agree, Alice, but you can't just decide that Agnes Waterhouse is going round slitting people's throats.'

Alice shrugged.

'Catherine Hall hadn't been arrested three days ago. She could have killed Brad,' suggested Abeer.

'Why?' protested Alice.

It was Abeer's turn to shrug as the rest of the forensic team turned up, Anne informing them to release the body to Broomfield as soon as they could.

'Alice, you're with me. Abeer go back to the office and try and get hold of the Met, see what the situation is with Mrs Hall – whether she's confessed to anything and whether we can go and interview her about our ongoing case. I suspect you won't have much luck.'

*

Catherine Hall was sitting in an interview room in a police station in London. She didn't know which police station; in fact she didn't really know much at all. Everything was still a blur. There was a woman sitting next to her who she didn't know but had been told was her solicitor. She'd spoken to her briefly in her cell that morning but Catherine couldn't answer her questions very well, her head was muddled. Opposite them sat two police officers, one man and one woman. They were staring at her.

'Tell me again, Mrs Hall. You say your daughter is still alive?' the woman said.

'She is.'

'What about your husband?'

'Oh no, he's dead. I killed him.'

The solicitor put her hand on Catherine's.

'I did,' she repeated. 'He had raped his own daughter. He deserved it.'

'So, let me get this straight, Mrs Hall,' said the man. 'You found out that your husband had impregnated your daughter…'

'…she wasn't pregnant. She was having her period.'

'So you stabbed your husband violently to death.'

'I don't think violently is necessary,' said the solicitor.

'I would say thirty-two stab wounds is pretty violent but I'll let that pass. You killed your husband and left the house. Is that right?'

Catherine nodded. 'I think so.'

'And your daughter. Where was she whilst all this was happening?'

Catherine looked at the table, wracking her brains. 'I can't remember.'

'Did she come with you when you left?'

'No, I don't think so.'

'So you just left her dead.'

Catherine looked up. 'She wasn't dead. She isn't dead.'

'She would have been pretty traumatised,' said the woman. 'Why didn't you go to her, comfort her or something?'

'I don't know. Maybe she did come with me.'

The two officers looked at each other.

'You went back to your hometown of Maldon in Essex. Is that right?'

Catherine nodded. 'It's where I live.'

'With Elizabeth, your daughter.'

'She was there but not with me. She was with him,' she scowled.

'Who?'

'That boy who was trying to attack her. She was thirteen. She's fourteen now. We had a party.' A smile spread across Catherine's face.

The male officer looked at his notes. 'This attack took place in the ruins of St Giles' Leper Hospital in Maldon, yes?'

Catherine looked blankly at him.

'What were you doing there?'

'Protecting my daughter.'

'But your daughter was already dead back in East London, Catherine,' the man said forcefully.

Catherine sat back in her seat. 'Then how come she's spent the last I don't know how long with me in our little hobbit home?'

'That wasn't your daughter, Catherine,' said the woman.

Catherine laughed. 'Do you think I don't know my own daughter?'

'I do think that, yes,' said the man.

'Well, you're more stupid than I thought, then.'

The solicitor put her hand on Catherine's arm again. 'My client can't answer any more questions, I'm afraid, until we have the psychiatric report.'

'And when will that be?' said the man, not trying to hide his irritation.

The solicitor smiled. 'I don't know. He's your psychiatrist.'

*

'Don't go anywhere, Jesse,' barked Anne as they walked into the pub. Jesse Burton had tried to surreptitiously slip away as he saw them enter. He wasn't in his usual table by the dartboard, Alice noted but near the far door – presumably to help him make his quick exit. He stopped, his hand on the door, thought about doing a runner, then remembered the big guy who was with the copper last time. If he was outside, he didn't fancy a rumble with the likes of him.

'I ain't done nothing,' he stated proudly from the doorway.

'Come and sit down, Jesse. Give him a pint, Landlord.'

'Are you paying?'

'I am. The way you're losing customers you need the money.'

The landlord looked at her suspiciously and poured a pint of bitter.

Alice escorted Jesse to a table far enough away from the door to prevent any attempt at escape. Anne joined them with two wines and the pint on a tray.

'Are you sure, Ma'am,' said Alice, eyeing the alcohol as a certain level of nausea rose in her stomach.

'Do you good. Hair of the dog and all that.' Anne handed Alice a glass, and Jesse his pint before raising her glass. 'Here's to poor old Brad Jordan,' she toasted.

Jesse looked at her warily before he too raised his glass. 'Why are you toasting Brad?'

'Because that's what you do at wakes, isn't it? Let's face it, this is nearest he's likely to get to one.'

Jesse's face showed nothing but confusion.

'He's dead, Jesse, in case you didn't understand.'

Jesse's face visibly paled. Anne wasn't sure whether he was sorry for his friend or his friend's purse.

'So, who's going to pay for your drinks now, then?' she said.

'I pay my own way,' he muttered.

'No you don't, Jesse. You rely on your friend Brad. What I don't understand is what you had over him to make him do that.'

'Don't know what you mean.'

Alice was fingering her glass, wondering if taking a sip would make her throw up or not.

'Just drink it, Alice.' Anne turned back to Jesse. 'You were in the nick together, weren't you – you and Brad?'

Jesse Barton's face remained passive.

'I've been doing a bit of research, you see. You were convicted on a charge of manslaughter, weren't you, Jesse?'

No response.

'Yet Brad, who was with you when you supposedly assaulted the young gentleman, was only convicted of theft and GBH. Was that right, Jesse? With his record he'd still be inside if he'd been done for killing someone. Did you take the rap for him?'

'You don't know what you're talking about. I never done nothing.'

'And yet you spent five years inside.'

'I were framed.'

'By Brad Jordan? Is that what you had over him? Did he kill the young man?'

'I don't know. It weren't me, that's all I know.'

'We'll never know now, I suppose. Why didn't you go round to his house when he didn't show up here?'

'Never been there, didn't know where it was.'

Alice took a deep breath, glared at Anne and threw the whole glassful down her throat. Anne grinned. Alice took a moment to make sure it didn't have an adverse effect, thrust her head in the air, and went to the bar.

'How did he die?' Jesse mumbled.

'Do you care?'

'Not really. He probably deserved it.'

Anne laughed. 'Honour amongst thieves, eh?'

'I'm not a thief, though.'

'What exactly are you, Jesse? You haven't really crossed my path before.'

'I'm just a bloke minding his own business.'

'Like when you attacked Agnes Waterhouse in the ruins?'

'The witch? Didn't attack her. I'm not stupid.'

'Scared?'

Jesse Barton smiled. 'Yes. She's evil.'

Alice arrived with another tray of drinks. 'The landlord wants to know if we'll pay Jesse's tab,' she stated.

Anne looked at Jesse. 'What do you think, Jesse?'

He shrugged.

'Who do you think might have killed Brad? Any idea?'

'Could have been anyone.'

'Yes, it could. I'm doubting it was you as he was your main source of income, it would appear. However, in the absence of anyone else…'

'You can't pin that on me.'

Anne stared at him. His hand shook slightly as he picked up his beer.

'What do you think DS Porter?'

'Looks to me like he could have done it. Maybe he robbed him at the same time.'

'If so, he can pay his own tab.' Anne had not taken her eyes from the pathetic specimen sitting opposite her.

'Do you think I'll be next?' he said quietly.

'You tell me, Jesse.'

'She'll come for me.'

'Who?'

Jesse looked around the empty bar. 'The witch.'

Alice raised her eyebrows at her boss.

'You fink it was the witch wot done it?' Anne said in her best Dick Van Dyke Cockney. 'Why would she do that?'

'Because she killed Jed.'

Alice couldn't help grinning.

'How do you know that?'

'Because we seen her.'

*

The only suspects' names left on the whiteboard were Catherine Hall and Agnes Waterhouse.

'What about Rueben Elbrow? Why have we removed him?' asked Abeer.

'Because we're pretty sure that Catherine Hall killed his brother, Harry Ellis.'

'How do we know he didn't kill Jed Barber, though? Maybe he thought Jed and Brad were responsible for his brother's death and decided to seek revenge.'

Alice looked at Anne and grinned. 'You've been reading too many trashy novels, Abeer.'

'It's a thought, though,' admitted Anne, putting Rueben's name back on the board.

'Come on, Anne. We don't need any names other than Catherine Hall and the witch. Catherine killed Harry – the witch did the rest.'

'We have one unreliable witness, Alice. I'll keep my options open.'

Anne's phone rang.

'You need to get over to the ruins, Ma'am,' said Ernie Kemp. 'Agnes Waterhouse is here and she's not at all well. I've called an ambulance but she's insisting on seeing you.'

'What's the matter with her?'

'I don't know, Ma'am. I found her lying in her weeds.'

'We'll come over.' Anne looked at Alice. 'Your witch is in a bad way, it seems,' she said and beckoned them to follow her.

Ernie Kemp was kneeling next to the prostrate body of Agnes Waterhouse as Anne's car drew up. She put her hazard lights on as she parked on the double yellow lines in front of the railings by St Giles' Leper Hospital. The gates were open and they walked over to Agnes's little herb garden. The witch was on her back, looking even paler than she normally did, her usually sharp eyes, dull and lifeless. Ernie was holding her shoulders up and her head was bobbing on her long neck.

'Glad you could make it,' said Agnes in a monotone.

'What's going on, Agnes,' said Anne as she knelt beside her.

'Deathbed confession,' said muttered.

Anne looked at Alice.

'You're not dying, Agnes. There's an ambulance on its way.'

'Too late for that.'

Anne studied Agnes, looking for any wounds or blood but could see nothing, she just appeared pallid.

'What's all this about, Agnes?' Anne was confused.

'Aconitum Napellus,' breathed the witch. She weakly raised her arm. In her hand were some blue flowers. 'They are beautiful, aren't they.'

Anne went to take then from her.

'Don't touch them.' She lowered her arm. 'You found Brad Jordan, I suppose.'

Anne didn't answer. Alice and Abeer stood silently next to her.

'I shouldn't have killed him. I didn't mean to. He attacked me.'

'Why were you there, Agnes?' Anne turned to Alice. 'Where's that ambulance?' she whispered.

'I just wanted to scare him.'

'What about Jed Barber, Agnes. Did you kill him?'

Agnes's head bobbed. 'He came at me with a knife. If I did it was self-defence.'

'Why did you deny this before?' Anne was trying to work out if Agnes was telling the truth or not. No DNA matched she seemed to remember. 'Are you covering for someone?'

Alice looked aghast. 'Who would that be, Ma'am, the ghost?' she said. She was angry that Anne could not accept what she'd been telling her all along.

'Cover my grave with these flowers.' Agnes still held the blue posy. 'They're called Monkshood. Did you know that? Quite appropriate, isn't it?' Agnes's voice was getting weaker.

'Where's that bloody ambulance?' yelled Anne. 'I'm not letting her die.'

As she spoke, they heard the siren. The ambulance ejected two paramedics, who attached bottles of something to Agnes's arm, before removing her to the hospital.

Anne glared at Alice. 'Don't say it,' she said. Alice did her best to look innocent.

*

'We didn't have Agnes Waterhouse's DNA when we got the knife,' explained Sarah Clifford over the phone. 'They're doing another check now but I don't know how long they'll be.'

'Thanks, Sarah.' Anne was back in the office. Abeer had phoned the Met but had got exactly nowhere other than the direct number of the officer in charge – a DI Ellen Cooke – and she hadn't been able to speak to her. Anne had sent Alice and Abeer to Broomfield hospital with instructions to let her know if and when the witch regained consciousness. The information she'd got from Broomfield had been sketchy. They suggested she had ingested poison, probably from the Aconitum Napellus she'd still been clutching – a poisonous plant that was once used on arrow tips apparently but was rarely dangerous these days unless a large amount had been ingested. They'd pumped Agnes's stomach and bunged her full of antibiotics. Now they just had to wait, she was told.

Anne wasn't sure what she'd do if Agnes didn't recover. The only proof she'd got that she was the killer was a drunken tale told by a petty criminal and a confession from a woman calling herself a witch who'd apparently tried to poison herself. She needed to get a confession on tape, at least. No-one was going to get convicted on hearsay.

'Don't you dare bloody die, Agnes,' she said out loud and put her head in her hands.

CHAPTER TWENTY-SEVEN

'How is he?' Alice asked as she spotted June Goddard leaving Allan's ward.

'Alive unfortunately,' came the blunt reply.

'Quite a crack over the head you gave him, wasn't it?'

June froze. 'I don't know what you mean? I was nowhere near him when he had his stroke. He was at *her's.*' Her face twisted as she mentioned Linda.

'He was at yours just before that, though. The place was a mess I seem to recall. The legs on those kitchen stools are really hard to bend.'

'He threw it at me. It missed fortunately or it would be me lying there.' She indicated the ward she'd just left.

Alice smiled. 'You were lucky, then.'

June nodded slowly. 'Not so lucky. I now have an invalid to care for. One that I'd been quite happy never to see again a couple of days ago.'

'Justice comes in many forms,' replied Alice.

June scowled and started to walk away.

'How's Amelia?' Alice said.

June turned. 'How do you think?'

Abeer had been standing not far away. She touched Alice on the shoulder as they watched June retreat. 'That was a bit harsh, Alice.'

'Was it though? She should be on a domestic violence charge at least. Much as I didn't like Allan Goddard, I don't agree with anyone taking things into their own hands like she did. The trouble is, Allan Goddard's not likely to file a complaint, is he?'

'But like she said, she's got a worse sentence than any court could have given her.'

'Looking after someone with a disability shouldn't be a punishment.'

Abeer shrugged. 'I guess it is if you detest the person because they cheated on you.'

Alice didn't reply but accosted a woman in a white coat who'd just left Agnes's room. 'Any news?' she inquired.

The woman shook her head. 'Too early to tell. She was very poorly when she was brought in. Where did she get those plants?'

'She grows them.'

'Why?'

'She reckons she's a witch.'

The woman raised her eyes and went on down the corridor.

Abeer joined Alice as she leaned against the wall. 'How long do we have to wait?' she asked.

'As long as.'

*

'I shouldn't really tell you, DI Edwards,' said DI Cooke. 'I know Catherine Hall may be involved in your investigation but I'm under instructions to keep this in-house at least until we get the psychiatric report.'

'I just need to know if she's admitting to killing Harry Ellis,' said Anne irritably.

There was a pause. 'Is that the boy in the ruins?'

'Yep.'

'She may have indicated that she did, if that helps.'

'Is it on tape?'

'Yep.'

'That's great, DI Cooke…'

'Ellen.'

'Thanks, Ellen. Sorry if I was a bit stroppy. You'd think the powers that be would encourage us to cooperate with each other, wouldn't you? My name's Anne, by the way.'

'You would, Anne, but there's still a lot of competition amongst the forces. Particularly with the men. I have to say we didn't get much help from your bloke.'

'Horobin, by any chance?'

'That sounds like him.'

'It certainly does. If there's anything I can do, phone me direct. I'll deal with DCI Horobin later, if I have to.'

'Thanks for that. Can't really give you any more I'm afraid. It is a confession but our hands are tied until we get that report.'

'Hmm. I think the poor woman's mind might have gone AWOL, don't you?' suggested Anne.

'I'm not allowed to have an opinion on that.'

'Hey, if they ever let me come and interview Catherine Hall, fancy meeting up for a drink?'

There was a pause. 'Let's see if it happens.' DI Cooke disconnected.

Anne sat back in her chair. Was it her? She'd never even met Ellen Cooke, yet here she was point-blank refusing a social meeting. Maybe she sounded desperate. Needy. Maybe she was. Even though they'd spent a night in the Queen's, she knew she'd almost alienated Alice, who was one of the few she actually had a social life with. Perhaps she should encourage Abeer to come out more but she was very much under the collective thumbs of her family it seemed. She went over to the whiteboard and rubbed out Rueben Elbrow's name. She knew she'd only put it up there because it would irritate Alice. It was petty and childish.

*

Agnes Waterhouse was being wheeled away for a complete blood transfusion. Alice and Abeer were told they would not be able to speak to her for at least twenty-four hours but the doctors were hopeful she would recover.

'I'm glad it looks like she'll live,' said Alice.

Abeer looked at her suspiciously. 'Really?'

'Wouldn't want her to escape justice. Do you need a lift?'

'Wouldn't mind if that's okay. I hear you're not thinking of transferring now,' she added.

'Madam Edwards been shouting her mouth off?'

'No. Difficult to keep things secret, though, isn't it? I'm sorry about Doug if that's any consolation.'

Alice smiled. 'It's not really but thanks. And his name was Gerald. I've always hated that name. Where do you live?'

'The other side of Chelmsford, I'm afraid, near the cricket ground. I must try and get somewhere nearer Maldon.'

Alice was quiet for a moment as she drove off towards the address Abeer had given her. 'Look, I don't want to speak out of turn or anything but...well...I have a spare room and the cost of my mortgage is likely to rocket when my current rate expires. If you fancy it, I wouldn't mind having a housemate to help pay it.'

Abeer's face beamed. 'Are you serious?'

'Yes. It would suit us both if you could put up with me.'

Abeer laughed. 'You might have to put up with an inspection from my aunts.'

'Bloody hell. Is that dangerous?'

'No, and I'll make sure it'll only be the once.'

'Done deal, then. Let me know when you want to move in.'

*

'DNA's sketchy, Anne. There's a match with Agnes but it's not conclusive. She did say she took the knife off Jed Barber, so it could have been contaminated then,' Sarah Clifford said over the phone.

'She's implying it was self-defence.' Anne could sense Sarah shrugging. 'Nothing matching Catherine Hall?'

'Not a thing on that knife but convincing evidence from her own one. It was almost definitely the knife that killed your boy.'

'Thanks. That will help if I can ever get to see her. I don't even know if The Met have charged her with that murder, they're just interested in her husband and daughter.' Anne paused. 'Are you coming over this way anytime soon. I probably owe you a drink.'

'Can't see me getting any time off at the moment. Late nights, early mornings, you know how it is.'

'Yes,' said Anne, as Sarah disconnected. Another rejection leaving her feeling flat. She went to the whiteboard and drew a red line from Harry Ellis to Catherine Hall. Her pen hovered over Jed Barber's name. She ought to connect Agnes to him as well as Brad Jordan but she still didn't want to admit that Alice had been right all along and replaced the pen on the small shelf beneath the board, desperately trying to convince herself that it was because they didn't have conclusive proof yet.

Alice wandered into the office. 'She's a big girl, isn't she?' she said, throwing her bag onto a chair.

'Who?' said Anne turning round.

'That one on the front desk. Enough to scare anyone off.'

'What Minnie? Surely not.'

'She's about ten feet tall. I hadn't seen her standing up before. Scared me.'

'Keep the riff-raff out hopefully, then. She plays rugby, I'm told.'

'Any news?' Alice slunk into her chair and switched on her computer.

'Not really. DNA on Jed's knife inconclusive.'

'What a surprise.'

Anne looked over at her. 'There's no need to be bitter, Alice. We're still working on it.'

'What about her deathbed confession?'

'Turns out it wasn't her deathbed or a confession. She's regained consciousness and we're off to pay her a visit. Where's Abeer?'

'Day off.'

'Do we have days off? That's a new one on me,' said Anne her mouth forming a straight line across her face. She picked up her bag.

'She's preparing her family for the news that she's moving.'

'Oh, good news. Where to?'

'My flat.'

Anne stopped and turned to Alice. 'But you're not resigning, you told me.'

Alice stuck her head in the air and sniffed. 'You shouldn't believe everything anyone says.'

Anne glared at her. 'Please tell me you're joking.'

'No, Abeer is moving into my flat.'

Anne crossed the room and stood next to her Detective Sergeant. 'You can't do this to me, Alice. I thought we'd sorted it out.'

Alice turned and grinned. 'Abeer is moving into my spare room. Of course I'm not resigning. Not now that I know you couldn't cope without me.'

Anne gave her a playful slap. 'Don't push your luck, you cheeky bugger.' She went towards the door. 'Good news about Abeer, though. Seems like an excuse for a party.'

'Don't hold your breath. I have to be vetted by her family first. Don't want any sign of alcohol or drunken Detective Inspectors.' Alice went past her. 'Look out for the honey monster,' she whispered as they approached Minnie at the front desk.

*

'Because I'm an adult.' Abeer was pleading with her aunt.

'But you are unmarried. You should not leave your family home until you have a husband to care for you.'

Abeer desperately wanted to ask her if that was why her aunt was still living with them – because no man wanted to come near her; not even for money – but chose instead to turn to her mother.

'You understand, don't you, mother? My job is in Maldon and Alice is a lovely girl. I'm really lucky that she's offering me her spare room.'

'I don't like the idea of you sharing. How do I know what this Alice is like?'

'Because you're going to meet her. If you don't like her or her flat, I won't move in.' Abeer had her fingers crossed behind her back – something she'd done since she was a child when lying to her parents.

'We'll see what your father says,' said her mother, making sure Abeer knew that was the end of the discussion.

Abeer went back to her room and continued the packing she'd already started.

*

Agnes Waterhouse was lying in her hospital bed, a drip attached to her arm and something taped to her finger that appeared to be making noises emanate from some machine. She had a face like thunder. She'd removed the drip twice already, only for an eagle-eyed nurse to replace it.

'I don't want any of your drugs. That's not what I need,' she told the young girl.

'I don't care whether you think you need them or not,' the nurse had replied. 'You're getting these drugs to make you better, like it or not.'

'They kill you, drugs, you know,' continued the witch. 'Nothing natural coming out of that bottle.' She pointed at the plastic pouch hanging above her.

'Whether it's natural or not, it's saved your life. You should be grateful.'

'What if I didn't want my life saved?'

'Then you'd be doing me out of a job.' The nurse wrapped more tape than was necessary around the catheter, cutting the roll with a small pair of scissors before tucking the sheet tighter around Agnes and leaving the room just as Anne and Alice arrived.

'Oh God,' said Agnes. 'That's all I need.'

'Feeling better, then,' said Alice as the two women sat themselves down on the chairs next to Agnes's bed in the private room they'd managed to procure.

Agnes didn't answer.

'It wasn't a deathbed confession it turns out,' said Anne.

'It would have been if you lot hadn't interfered.'

'What I don't understand, Agnes, is why you wanted to top yourself anyway.'

'Seemed the right thing to do.'

Anne and Alice remained silent.

'I didn't mean to kill either of them. I don't agree with taking anyone's life, so I should take my punishment.'

'Your punishment should be many years in prison.' Alice said through clenched teeth. She was worried that Anne was going to let the witch off again. 'Why did you kill them?'

Agnes lay back on her pillows and gazed round the room. 'Nice here, isn't it?'

'Agnes, you told me that you'd killed both Jed Barber and Brad Jordan. Why did you do that?' asked Anne.

'Do you know what it's like to be constantly vilified by thugs like them? Have you any idea? Shit pushed through my letterbox; obscenities painted on my front door; abuse shouted at me whenever they saw me, do you know what that's like? The only thing that stopped them physically attacking me was their own fear of what they thought of as the supernatural. I only had to raise my arms in the air and they'd run a mile. I was used to it. It was like a game where we knew all the rules. But Jed broke the rules. He entered the chapel with his cronies.'

'And didn't leave?' asked Anne.

'The cronies ran when I threatened to turn them into toads but not Jed. He came at me with his knife, swearing and blaspheming right next to the chapel wall. I grabbed his arm and then…'

'Then what?' said Alice.

Agnes breathed deeply. 'Abbot Thomas was there.'

'The ghost?' Alice was staggered. 'The ghost was Catherine Hall, coming out of the catacombs to supposedly protect her dead daughter.'

Anne frowned at her.

Agnes was shaking her head. 'Cat Willis wasn't the ghost. Abbot Thomas guided my hand as it sliced into Jed Barber's throat. I was stunned. I couldn't believe the Abbot would do that. I had no intention of killing him, I just wanted to stop him hurting me. I rushed to get some yarrow but there was no point.'

'So are you pleading self-defence?'

'Or spectral intervention,' added Alice.

Agnes shrugged. 'You'll never understand.'

'What I do understand is that at least two people have had their throats slit by you, which is murder, and I intend that you go down for a very long time.' Alice was leaning over Agnes, their noses almost touching.

Anne stood up and pushed Alice back. 'Go outside DS Porter, please.'

Alice glowered at her boss 'But…'.

'Out.'

Alice left the room.

'She's very good,' said Agnes when the door closed.

Anne took a deep sigh. 'What am I supposed to do with you, Agnes?'

'Let me die?' she said pulling at the tape the nurse had used to stick the catheter to her arm.

Anne stopped her and held onto the witch's arm. 'You haven't said what happened with Brad Jordan. Did you go to his house?'

'You've been to my cottage.'

Anne nodded.

'And found the shit and the rest.'

Anne nodded again.

'There was a note along with the turd, written in red permanent ink. It said "I seen ya kill Jed. I want money or I torch this dump". Well, I didn't really want my cottage burnt to the ground. Apart from being my home, there's a lot of history in that place. It once belonged to Alice Chaundeler. I don't suppose you know who that was?'

'She was a witch, tried at the Moot Hall in Maldon and hanged.'

Agnes smiled. 'You have been doing your homework. That cottage has survived for over four hundred years. I wasn't going to let that idiot burn it down, so I went to see him.'

'You knew where he lived?'

Agnes didn't answer.

'What happened?'

'I tried to talk to him.'

'Why wasn't he scared of being turned into a toad, like before?'

'Oh, he was. He tried to run out of his back door but I'd had enough. I dragged him back into his kitchen. He was kicking and screaming like a baby. I told him to leave me alone and left him whimpering on his filthy kitchen floor.'

'Dead?'

'Not then.'

Anne raised her eyebrows indicating that she needed to know more.

'He came at me with a kitchen knife. It hadn't been washed – ever, I would imagine – and waved it at me. I told him to grow up, put it down and wash it, but he moved nearer. I raised my arms and he froze, totally petrified. But as I went to take the knife from him he slashed at me. I grabbed his arm, felt Abbot Thomas go through me again and slashed back at him. He collapsed on the floor. I'd had no intention of killing him.'

Anne sat back in her chair. 'Are you blaming Abbot Thomas again?'

'The Abbot is not to blame. It is only me.' Agnes looked tired. Her confession had evidently taken a lot out of her. She lay back on her pillows and closed her eyes.

'Harriet Adcock, AKA Agnes Waterhouse, I am arresting you on a charge of the murders of Jed Barber and Brad Jordan. You do not have to say anything but it may harm your defence if you do not mention when questioned something which you later rely on in court. Anything you do say may be given in evidence. Do you understand, Agnes?'

Agnes didn't answer.

'Why did you throw me out?' asked Alice as Anne joined her in the corridor.

'For your own good, Alice. You'll be pleased to know I've charged her. We'll do it officially when she's out of here.'

Alice nodded.

'And Alice?'

'What?'

'Don't get cocky because you were right and I was wrong.'

Alice grinned. 'As if I would, Ma'am.'

'Coffee?'

'Shouldn't we get back to the office, Anne?'

'I need to speak to the doctor. There's a Costa franchise round the corner in the main corridor. Get me a flat white.' Anne went off to find a doctor while Alice wandered towards the coffee shop.

Inside her private room, Agnes had managed to painfully tear the tape from her arm and remove the drip. She lay back in her bed and apologised to Abbot Thomas.

Anne came into the coffee bar and sat next to Alice, gratefully accepting the flat white sitting temptingly on the table in front of her.

'We may have time for another one. The doctor is very busy, I was told.'

Barely had the cup touched her lips before a siren was heard coming from the corridor leading to Agnes Waterhouse's room. Anne and Alice exchanged glances, stood up and headed to the corridor, only to be met by an officious-looking woman in a blue dress that was too tight for her.

'You can't go down there, there's an emergency.'

Anne flashed her warrant card.

'I don't care,' replied the blue crone. 'No-one's going down there unless they are medically trained.'

'Can you tell me if the emergency is in Ms Waterhouse's room?'

'No I can't.'

Anne and Alice started back to their coffees. As soon as the woman moved, they both shot down the corridor to Agnes' room.

The witch's room was full. Several nurses and someone who looked like a doctor were crowded round the bed. Blood had spattered across the bedclothes and up the wall from somewhere near Agnes' head.

'You can't come in here,' said one of the nurses, a young man who looked a shade of green.

'I fucking can,' replied Anne flashing her card again. 'That woman is a murder suspect.' She pushed past the man.

'I don't think she'll be much use to you now,' she heard him mutter as he left – presumably to throw up.

On the bed, in a pool of gore, lay Agnes Waterhouse, pretty obviously ex-witch. A small pair of scissors were being removed from her throat, the tube from her catheter swinging menacingly at the side of the bed. Her mouth was twisted into a grotesque smile, her hair two-tone – white and red – almost as though she'd dyed it.

The doctor turned and ushered them out. 'I'll talk to you later. Right now, here is not the place for you.'

Anne was about to protest but Alice took her arm and led her back to their now cold coffees.

CHAPTER TWENTY-EIGHT

The mood in the office was sombre. Anne was annoyed with Agnes, while Alice was livid with both the witch and her boss.

'You knew she'd do that, didn't you?' she said.

'No, Alice. I didn't. I wanted justice just as much as you did. This way no-one wins.'

'Except the witch.'

Abeer was sitting at her computer feeling left out. Even though it was supposed to be her day off, she'd been so sick of her family's constant questioning about moving out that she decided to come to work. Minnie had told her that the rest of the team were at Broomfield, so she'd sat and contemplated why life was so complicated. Why did Catherine Hall kill her husband? Why did she kidnap Amelia Goddard? Why did she kill Harry Ellis? And then there was the witch. What was she about? Potions and things. Strawberry tea that makes you feel...well, good actually. Did she kill Jed Barber and Brad Jordan, like she'd said she had? And then why did she try and poison herself? And now, apparently, she'd died.

'What happened?' she asked.

'The bitch topped herself to evade a trial,' snapped Alice.

'Agnes found some scissors that a nurse had forgotten to take with her and stuck them in her neck. It was not pretty,' said Anne.

'I bet she put a spell on the nurse, making her leave the weapon.'

'Stop it, Alice. Go and get us coffees from the new coffee machine,' demanded Anne.

'That means passing the honey monster.' Alice put on a scared face as she left.

Abeer looked quizzically at Anne.

'It's Alice's name for Minnie. She can be very childish sometimes.'

'What's a honey monster?'

'You're so young.'

Anne's phone rang. 'Oh God. What a surprise,' she said as she looked at the screen. 'Yes, sir.'

DCI Horobin's voice could be heard by Abeer across the room. 'What on earth did you think you were doing, DI Edwards? That's two suspects you've managed to lose on one case.'

'Looks like carelessness, sir.'

'What?'

'Misquoting Oscar Wilde, sir.'

'What are you doing about the woman who killed the boy?'

'I'm waiting on The Mighty Met, sir.'

Horobin harrumphed, which Anne found amusing as she didn't realise people actually did that.

'Get on to them and demand you see her right now. I need this sorted. The father has been on to me.'

Anne recoiled. 'Edwin?'

'Mr Ellis, yes. He says nothing is happening. He wants something done. Sort it out, Edwards. I have other things to do rather than babysit Maldon CID.' He disconnected.

'What a shit,' said Abeer.

Anne's eyes opened wide. 'Are you disrespecting our esteemed boss, DCI Horobin BEM, DC Kumar?'

'Yes. What's the BEM mean?'

'British Empire Medal. The monarch gives it to worthy people.' She raised her eyes.

'Some things are really wrong in this world, aren't they?'

'They certainly are but always remember there is good and bad in everything and mostly, the good can tip the balance if you let it.'

Abeer smiled. 'You're being very philosophical, Ma'am.'

'I like to surprise people sometimes.'

Alice entered with three mugs of coffee. 'What is the point of a coffee machine that only half-fills the mug?' she said putting them down on Anne's desk.

'Obviously not designed for caffeine addicts. Edwin Ellis wants something done. What are the chances, do you think?'

Alice just laughed.

'That's what I thought.'

Alice took Abeer's coffee to her. 'How did you get on telling your family?'

'I think I've persuaded them I'm nearly an adult,' she said, grinning.

'So?'

'If you're alright with it, my whole family are coming round at the weekend.'

Alice grimaced. 'Better get cleaning, then.'

'It's good news, Abeer. Glad you're going to join us in the metropolis of Maldon.' Anne picked up her phone. 'Wish me luck.'

*

'Do you really think it will help, Edwin. The woman has evidently lost her mind.' Linda was in the living room caressing a glass of red wine.

'It might help me if I can talk to her or something, Lin. I think it would help you too.'

'I don't know. Just the thought of it scares me.' She took a sizable mouthful of wine. 'We really need to discuss it, Ed.'

'That's what we're doing, isn't it?'

Linda sighed. 'Not really. You seem to have made up your mind.'

Edwin sat down next to his wife. He'd been pacing up and down all the time they'd been talking. 'You don't have to go through with it but I really think I need closure.'

'Surely they won't let you, anyway, will they?' A tear escaped from Linda's eye. 'This is really difficult, Edwin. I don't want you to hate me. I love you so much.'

Edwin frowned and put his arm round Linda. 'What do you mean? I couldn't hate you. I've always loved you.'

Linda took a deep breath. 'I have something to tell you that might make you hate me.'

Edwin stood up and started to pace again. 'Don't Linda. You don't need to say it.'

'I do, Edwin. It's time I unburdened myself. I'm so, so sorry.'

Edwin went through to the kitchen, returning immediately with the wine bottle.

'I don't have to have a drink to say it.'

'I know. I know what you're going to say and it's alright, Linda.'

She looked up at him. Did he know? Had he known all along?

'You're going to tell me Harry wasn't my child.'

The tears exploded from Linda Ellis' eyes. 'I'm so sorry.'

'No, don't apologise. I know why you did it and it's okay. The doctor told me I was firing blanks. There was no miracle. I knew I hadn't suddenly become some macho beast.'

'I did it for you.'

'I know, Lin. I've always known.' Edwin refilled Linda's glass.

'But you don't know...' She downed the glassful in one and held the empty glass for Edwin to replenish.

'I don't need to know.'

Edwin sat next to his wife and put his arm round her. She lay her head on his shoulder and sobbed.

*

Anne had managed to get through to DI Ellen Cooke without too much trouble. It was extremely unlikely Edwin would be allowed to speak to Catherine Hall. It seemed the woman was not in a fit state to do very much at all. They were getting very little more response from her and expected the psychiatric report to confirm what they all thought.

'Poor woman,' said Anne.

'Yes, but she has murdered at least two, maybe three, people,' replied Ellen. 'Their families deserve some sort of closure and that woman being in a secure unit won't make them feel any better, I expect.'

'Which is why Harry's father wants to meet with her, I suppose.'

'I'll see how the land lies, Anne but I wouldn't hold your breath. This case is slipping down the priority order, I'm afraid.'

Anne knew The Met had far more problems than Catherine Hall to deal with but that didn't help Edwin and Linda. She left Alice and Abeer discussing their own domestic arrangements and drove over to Great Totham.

Linda Ellis looked as though she hadn't slept in weeks. Anne hadn't seen her for some time due to the other developments in the case and was quite shocked. She appeared to have aged several years.

'Is it okay to come in, Linda?' she checked.

Linda nodded and opened the door wider. 'Edwin's out,' she told her. 'Would you like coffee?'

'Thanks.' Anne followed her through to the kitchen.

'Is this about that woman?' Linda put the kettle on.

'Looks like it'll be some time before anyone can have contact, I'm afraid, Linda, if at all. It seems Catherine Hall is likely to be under medical supervision for the foreseeable future.'

Linda nodded her head. 'Do you think it would be a good thing for Edwin to talk to her?'

Anne blew out her lips. 'I don't know, Linda. I'm not really an expert on restorative justice if that's what he's thinking. It's not something I've had anything to do with before.'

'I told Edwin about Harry.'

Anne waited while Linda put a mug in front of her.

'How did he take it?'

'He already knew.'

'He didn't hear it from us, Linda.'

She smiled. 'I know, I wasn't accusing you.' She sipped her coffee. 'He knew all the time, he said. I wish he'd told me.'

'It must have been hard for both of you keeping that secret all these years.'

'How's Amelia?' said Linda, changing the subject.

Anne considered what to say. 'You know about Allan's accident?'

She laughed. 'Accident? Is that what they're saying? Yes. You can't help but hear things in this community. Everyone knows everyone's business. I sometimes wish we still lived in London; one can be inconspicuous there.'

Anne took a swig of coffee. It was hot and quite bitter but she didn't complain. She felt sorry for Linda, holding in all that knowledge for years, building up the courage to tell her husband his dead son was not his, all the while not knowing that he already knew.

'Can I be there if he does get to speak to her?' Linda's voice was tight as though she found it hard to speak.

'Of course. You're as involved, he was your son.'

'Could you be there?' Linda looked despondent. 'I don't think he'd be able to go through with it on his own with just me, I mean. I think it's a big thing for him that he feels he needs to do.'

'And you're not so sure?'

Linda shrugged. 'Maybe it's the closure he needs.'

'I'll see what I can do, Linda, but I can't promise anything at the moment.'

Linda nodded. 'I know you'll do your best.'

*

Abeer was alone in the office when Anne got back.

'Where's Alice?'

'She went home, Anne. Didn't feel well. Her cheeks were bright red. I think she's going down with something.'

Anne sighed. 'Great. Let's hope we don't get busy.'

Abeer frowned. 'It's not her fault if she's not well, Anne.'

Anne sat at her desk. 'I know, I'm sorry. There's not a lot to do for the time being, anyway. Let's hope she feels better soon – like tomorrow. When are you moving in?'

'Not yet. Family inspection at the weekend. I said I'd help Alice get the place spotless if she's feeling alright.'

Anne waited for her computer to boot up. It really was time they replaced some of these old machines but what with the cuts, it was unlikely to happen any time soon.

'How do you feel about moving in with Alice, Abeer?'

'I'm looking forward to it.'

'Will it pass inspection, do you think?'

Abeer laughed. 'Buckingham Palace wouldn't pass inspection, Anne, but I don't really care. I'm not a child, whatever they think. My parents will be okay and my aunts can go…'

'…don't say it, you might regret it.'

'I don't think I would. What's the situation with Agnes?'

'I think we have enough evidence but you can't convict a dead body. Any news on Jed and Brad's families?'

'Jed has a daughter who is the only living relative as far as I can tell. When I informed her of her father's death she said, "Good riddance!". She's going to identify him tomorrow.'

'Nice.'

'Can't find anyone for Brad, though. I suppose we could get an identification from Jesse.'

Anne nodded. 'Stupid really, isn't it? We know who these people are but still have to find someone to tell us we're right.'

'It's the law, Anne.'

Anne leaned towards her. 'The law is an ass,' she said.

CHAPTER TWENTY-NINE

It was a Friday morning in early June. The sun was doing its best to shine and warm the streets and rivers of Maldon, particularly the riverside next to The Queen's Head, which irritated Anne no end. It meant the pub was full most of the time and while she was obviously pleased for Charlotte and Ben it was annoying for regulars like her who had to wait to be served, let alone be lucky enough to find a seat.

Fortunately, no-one else had been murdered since Brad Jordan which was particularly fortunate in Anne's eyes as Alice had been regularly taking time off for the last two months. She assured Anne that there was nothing seriously wrong with her, just some sort of sicky bug that wouldn't go away.

Abeer had moved in with Alice, which gave Anne concerns as she couldn't deal with both of her staff being off with a bug. The dreaded inspection by her family had gone pretty much as expected except Abeer's parents had both actually backed her against the aunts and agreed to give Abeer her space at last. Anne had waited for the housewarming invite but it hadn't arrived, so in the end she organised it herself. Sadly, it looked like Alice's bug was going to scupper things as it was supposed to be taking place that evening. Anne had bought presents and copious amounts of wine – red, white, and sparkling – and made sure that Abeer's family knew nothing about it. The thought of spending the evening in the company of strict teetotallers, giving her the heebie-jeebies.

Alice arrived at the office looking sheepish. She was late but at least she was here.

'So, I will be at your flat precisely at seven o'clock. I have arranged a surprise,' said Anne as her detective sergeant sat at her desk. 'I hope you're feeling up to it?'

Alice smiled. 'I will do my best, Ma'am.'

'Excellent. I've had news from The Met. Our friend and boss DCI Horobin has somehow arranged it that Edwin Ellis *can* meet up with Catherine Hall. It seems that *she* has asked for a restorative justice meeting – presumably through her solicitor as it might reduce her sentence, although pigs might also fly – and we're to send someone with the Ellis's to London Town.'

'What has it to do with DCI Horobin?'

'It appears he's a friend of Edwin Ellis's solicitor, who is a friend of Mrs Hall's solicitor. And Edwin Hall is also a benefactor of the Essex Police Force.'

'I always thought he was a bit of a hippy.' Alice observed.

'Even hippies need the police every now and then, Alice. So, I've arranged for you and me to go on a little trip to the Big City on Monday morning, if you're fit enough.'

Alice took a deep breath. 'Yes, Anne. I will be fit enough. I'm sorry I've had so much time off but I think I'm getting better now.'

'Is it okay to leave you in charge, Abeer?' said Anne.

'I'm sure the honey monster will keep me safe, Ma'am.' Abeer saluted.

'Good. Right, the next thing is to get ourselves glammed up for the party tonight.'

Abeer grinned. 'I've made sure that my family don't know anything about it.'

Anne smiled. She'd noticed Abeer's confidence growing steadily over the time she'd been away from her family. Much as she'd loved her own mum, she was eternally grateful that she hadn't tried to stop her from moving away when she was younger. The thought of being in her twenties and living at home was anathema to her.

'Excellent,' she said. 'I have wine, so it looks like we're in for a long night.'

Alice was fidgeting in her chair and rubbing her stomach.

'Are you alright, Alice?'

'Yes, Anne.' Her face was alight with a radiant smile. 'I've never felt better. Really looking forward to tonight. What's the surprise?'

'If I told you it wouldn't be a surprise, would it? Just don't prepare any food.'

*

Anne arrived promptly by taxi at Alice and now Abeer's flat. It wasn't a long way to walk but carrying a case of wine, several wrapped parcels and a bunch of flowers made it something Anne was not prepared to even attempt. Alice and Abeer eagerly opened the housewarming presents as though they were kids. None was particularly special; a framed print of Hythe Quay, with the Queen's Head in the background; a pottery vase to hold the flowers; and a set of crystal wine glasses – to hold the wine.

'Is that the surprise?' asked Alice indicating the gifts.

'Partly. Is that not enough?'

'Oh God, Anne. It's more than enough.' Alice hugged her boss, Anne's face turning red.

'Get off, you daft bugger.'

The doorbell rang.

'Oh no, don't let that be my parents,' said Abeer, looking at the mess of wrapping paper all over the floor and the unopened case of wine.

Alice answered the door to a man holding a large, insulated container, which he brought into the room. He was followed by another young man, carrying a large flat cardboard box, out of which he withdrew a white linen tablecloth and napkins. He threw the cloth in a professional manner over Alice's kitchen table, laid the napkins, plates and cutlery next to them, while the other man served hot dishes of various curries onto a hotplate that had appeared in the middle of the table.

'Ladies,' he said, indicating that they should sit. He took a bow and informed them he would return for the accoutrements in the morning, before bowing again and leaving the flat.

Alice started crying.

'What's the matter?' asked Abeer.

'I'm happy. I'm sorry, I just feel really weepy at the moment.'

Anne looked at her. 'Is there something you're not telling us?'

Alice stared at her for a full minute, before she left the kitchen, returning shortly holding a small plastic stick in her hand.

Anne looked at it. 'Please tell me that's a COVID test,' she said.

Alice shook her head. 'I'm going to be a mummy.'

'Oh My God!' Abeer hugged her flatmate, then let go and took a pace back. 'Does this mean I'll have to move out?'

'No, Abeer. Not until the little one needs their own room anyway and that'll be ages yet.'

Alice was aware that Anne had not said anything. She looked at her. 'I know what you're going to say, Anne.'

'What?'

'I won't take all my maternity leave, don't worry. My mother's only down the road. I'll be back at work as soon as I can.'

Anne remained looking at her.

'Anyway, there's another six months before I sprog.'

'What a horrible expression,' said Abeer.

'Do I know him?' said Anne.

Alice didn't answer.

'Does he know? You'll have to tell him, Alice.'

'Don't spoil it, Anne. I know there's difficult times ahead but I want this baby.'

'Then that's great.' Anne hugged her. 'Congratulations.'

'Do you really mean that?'

'Too bloody right I do. And if I'm not Godmother I'll be extremely pissed off.'

Alice and Abeer laughed. 'Aren't Godparents supposed to be responsible for a child's moral upbringing?' said Abeer.

'There's nothing immoral about me, young lady. Now start eating before this gets cold, while I open the bubbly.'

Alice grimaced. 'I can't drink alcohol for another six months.'

'Never mind. The baby's Godmother will drink yours for you.' Anne handed Abeer a glass and raised her own overflowing glass of sparkling wine. 'To my new Godchild.'

Alice sipped a glass of juice. 'This is not about you, Anne,' she said.

Anne grinned. 'You're going to be missed in The Queen's Head.'

'Then you'd better make sure Charlotte has some non-alcoholic wine in, Mrs Godmother.' Alice tucked into the curry.

It was late in the evening when the three of them were well-fed, two of them well-wined and one well-juiced. Abeer had insisted on washing the dishes, even though Anne had told her the restaurant would only wash them again and Alice was sitting on the sofa feeling overfull.

'Are you sure about this, Alice?' said Anne holding the younger woman's hand.

'I am, Anne. It was difficult at first. I couldn't tell anyone. I think I hoped there was some mistake and I wasn't really pregnant but once the doctor confirmed it yesterday, I am really happy, yes.'

'And Doug or Gerry or whatever his name is?'

Alice went quiet, looked down at her stomach and rubbed it gently. 'I don't know how to feel about him, Anne. I don't really want him to even know.'

Anne nodded. 'He'll have to, though.'

'Why? He lied to me. I don't ever have to see him again, hopefully. He has no right to my child.'

Anne smiled sadly. 'He does, Alice.'

'But only if he knows and I'm not going to tell him.'

'What about when the child grows up?'

Alice didn't reply.

'Will you be able to cope, do you think?'

Alice grinned. 'With the help of my child's Godmother, how could I not?'

Anne hugged her again. 'I so wish you could join me in some of this really expensive wine I bought from the supermarket,' she said raising her glass.

'Fuck off, Godmother,' said Alice raising her orange juice.

*

Anne and Alice stood at the station waiting for the London train. It was quite early and Alice had already thrown up once in the station toilets.

'You don't have to come, Alice. I didn't know you were pregnant when I asked you.'

'It's okay, the vomiting stops in about half an hour usually.'

'Great. It's times like this I'm glad I never wanted children.'

Alice had to visit the loo on the train only once and was feeling fine by the time they pulled into Liverpool Street. They took the circle line on the tube to Westminster station and then walked over to New Scotland Yard, where they were met by DI Ellen Cooke, who turned out to be a woman aged roughly around forty, Anne surmised, tall, with a blonde ponytail – something Anne thought was wrong on a woman of her age but had to admit suited the Detective Inspector. She was in full uniform which made Anne feel underdressed in her trousers and shirt. The weather was hot and she was impressed with DI Cooke's calm, cool demeanour. Anne kept her arms by her side to cover the underarm sweat marks she was sure were showing prominently. Alice, however, was looking remarkably serene and tranquil. She was wearing a flowery dress over her little bump, that flowed as she walked and she looked blooming, Anne believed was the expression. Ever since Friday night when she'd revealed her pregnancy, Anne couldn't help noticing that Alice's midriff had an obvious and significant bulge in it and she wondered why had she not noticed this before?

'We're meeting in that hotel across the road,' said Ellen Cooke, leading them towards a large imposing building.

Edwin and Linda Ellis were already in the reception of the hotel and they rose to greet The Met officer and the two Maldon detectives.

'How are you feeling?' asked Anne.

'Good,' said Edwin positively. Linda didn't look quite so good.

They went down a corridor into a room with soft furnishings where a man and a woman sat at a long table.

'Margaret Barker,' said the woman, standing up and proffering her hand. 'I'm from The Restorative Justice Council.'

The man also stood. 'Daniel Sheppard,' he said. 'Also one of the councillors.'

After the introduction, Edwin and Linda were shown to two seats near the middle of the long table, Alice and Anne relegated to the side.

'I'm quite happy for you to attend but you won't be able to speak at all,' Margaret told them. 'These things can be very difficult for the participants. It's an emotional experience and if at any time you don't want to carry on, I can terminate the interview,' she said to the Ellis's. 'Mrs Hall will appear by video.' She pointed to a large screen on the wall. 'She is not a well woman. Personally I don't think she should be doing this really but she seems keen to talk to you. Please help yourself to the water on the table in front of you.'

There was one other chair at the table which was currently empty. Anne had a horrible feeling she knew who it might be for. She looked at Alice, who appeared unaware and decided not to voice her suspicions. The screen lit up, showing a room with a table with no-one seated at it, a bottle of water standing forlornly in the centre next to a plastic glass. There was no sign of any people.

'We're just waiting for one more person before Mrs Hall arrives,' said Margaret Barker, looking at her watch impatiently.

Alice's face lost all its colour as the door opened and a tall, blond, curly-haired man entered.

'Sorry I'm late,' announced Gerald Hall as he sat on the vacant chair next to the Ellis's.

Anne took hold of Alice's hand. 'Do you want to go?' she whispered. Alice shook her head.

'Hello, ladies. Didn't expect to see you here?' said Gerald jollily. Neither of the Maldon girls spoke.

Catherine Hall was led into the room on the screen by a prison warder. She was followed by a man in a smart suit and a kind-looking middle-aged woman.

The woman spoke. 'Testing. Can you hear me alright?'

'Yes, thank you,' said Margaret. 'Once we've all introduced ourselves, we can get on. I'm Margaret Barker.'

Daniel Sheppard, Edwin and Linda Ellis and Gerald Hall followed with their own introductions.

'DI Edwards and DS Porter are from Essex Police and are here solely to observe. They will not enter into any discussion. If anyone feels uncomfortable with their presence I have the authority to ask them to leave,' announced Margaret Barker, leaving Anne and Alice wondering why they were here at all.

'Thank you, Margaret,' said the woman on the screen. 'My name is Selina Lewis. I am the designated Restorative Justice Facilitator. Prison Officer William Spratt is also present.' She turned to the others at the table.

'Good morning. Frederick Stevens, Mrs Hall's solicitor.'

Catherine Hall looked into the camera. Her eyes were half-closed. 'Catherine Hall.'

Anne and Alice sat and observed the next hour of apologies, explanations, and excuses, Anne thinking what a waste of time this all was. She was sure restorative justice was a very worthy thing in the right circumstances but these were definitely not the right circumstances. It was obvious that Catherine Hall's recollections of Harry Ellis's murder didn't even approach the reality. She was still insisting that Amelia Goddard was her daughter Elizabeth and that Harry had been attacking her. She admitted to Gerald that she had killed his brother but also that he'd deserved it for violating his own little girl. Gerald had to be restrained physically by Daniel Sheppard at one point, before storming out of the room. Alice's physique noticeably relaxed as the door closed behind him.

Eventually Selina Lewis drew the agonising event to a close and the screen went blank.

'Any questions I can help you with?' asked Margaret Barker.

'Yes,' said Linda Ellis. 'What was the point of that?'

Margaret Barker looked down at her notes. 'The point, Mrs Ellis, was to try and bring some sort of closure to you and your husband. I have to say that Mrs Hall maybe wasn't quite ready for this. Normally there would be a longer process before we get to this stage.'

'I feel so sorry for her,' said Edwin.

Alice could see Linda biting her lip. Harry was the child she'd borne. He'd grown inside her, been part of her body for the whole gestation period. Much as Edwin surely loved him, it was different for Linda. Unconsciously, she stoked her belly.

Margaret Barker handed some leaflets to the Ellis's, telling them they could contact her at any time if they felt they needed help, before packing up her things and standing, thereby indicating everyone should leave.

Anne and Alice spoke briefly with the Ellis's. Linda seemed ambivalent to the whole proceedings, whilst Edwin appeared relaxed and almost pleased with the outcome. He thanked the officers for their support and asked if they would like to join them for lunch – an invitation they declined, citing getting back to work in Maldon.

As they watched them leave, Anne turned to Alice.

'I suspect you might need a drink after that,' she said.

'I'd love one but…' she gently rubbed the bulge in her midriff.

Anne nodded. 'Bit of a pain being pregnant, isn't it?'

Alice grinned. 'No, it's the most wonderful thing in the world. And I'm quite happy to join you for a lime and soda if you fancy finding a pub where the Ellis's aren't.'

It looked as though the Ellis's had wandered towards the tube, presumably to eat somewhere nearer the West End, so Anne took hold of Alice's arm and led her to the nearest hostelry.

The nearest hostelry was a sprawling place that was pretending to be an old inn but was evidently modern. They even had designer sawdust strewn across the floor. The beams looked as authentic as a movie set down to the artificial cobwebs interweaving the plastic hops that encircled them. Still, the pub seemed incredibly popular with tourists, judging by the number of people from all parts of the world that were taking up most of the seating – even though it was barely midday.

Alice managed to find a table in the corner with high stools placed next to a round table – not very authentically ancient – just before someone from The United States, judging by their loud accents, attempted to grab it. They looked as though they'd escaped from some nineteen-sixties sit-com as they loudly inquired if there was anywhere to sit in this place? The management were very adept at ignoring them.

Alice thanked Anne for the soft drink, enviously eyeing her boss's wine.

'I suppose I should drink something non-alcoholic in support,' she said, sheepishly.

Alice pointed at the roof. 'Oh look, a flying pig.' Her arm followed a curve towards the door. Suddenly she stopped, her face instantly pale.

Anne turned to see Gerald Hall advancing towards them. She jumped off the stool and stood in front of him. He looked over the top of her at Alice.

'Is that mine?' he said bluntly.

Alice didn't answer.

'You're not welcome here,' said Anne, still holding her ground against the tall man.

'Is it?' he repeated.

'You're not the only person in her life.' Anne spat the words at him.

Alice was looking at the table, her eyes closed, hoping it would all go away. She couldn't take this confrontation now.

Gerald looked down at Anne. 'You'll be telling me it's yours next.' He laughed sarcastically.

'How come you're not behind bars, paedophile?'

'A case of mistaken identity, DI Edwards.' He grinned. 'It seems DNA is not all that accurate, after all.'

'Just go away.'

He took a step towards Alice but Anne kept her body between them.

'It's okay, Anne.' Alice lifted her head. 'I don't know if it's yours or not, Gerald. I haven't seen you for a long time.'

'I tried to see you. You didn't want to.'

'And I still don't. Please go now.'

'I'll demand a paternity test,' he said.

Alice almost laughed. 'They're only as accurate as DNA tests, though and you don't believe them, do you?' She stared into his eyes. 'Does it make you feel good that you got away with raping your niece simply because she died? And because her mother is too mentally disturbed to know what the hell is going on? And because, by resigning, the great Metropolitan Police Force will cover up for you? Does that make you feel good? Because it makes me feel sick, Gerald.'

He glared at her. 'If that's mine,' he said pointing at Alice's stomach. 'I will make sure I have all the rights that belong to me as the father, don't you forget it.'

'Get out!' intervened Anne. 'We are still police officers and you are harassing this young lady. I will arrest you if you don't leave immediately.'

Gerald smiled and patted Anne on the head. 'I will go but you haven't heard the last from me, Alice.' He turned and went to the bar.

'Shall we leave?' said Anne.

'No, finish your drink,' Alice replied. 'He doesn't scare me.'

Anne looked over to the bar where Gerald stood with a smug smirk on his face. He raised his glass to her and she raised her middle finger.

*

Alice was remarkably jolly on the journey home, not appearing to be at all upset by the encounter with Gerald Hall.

Anne, however, was seething. 'What are you going to do about him? I can make sure he doesn't come anywhere near you, Alice, get an injunction or something,' she said as the train passed through Ingatestone on the way back to Chelmsford.

'I don't care, Anne. He does have some rights, I suppose. You said that, remember. He is obviously the father. I haven't slept with anyone else in the last year or two. In some way I feel it's a huge relief.'

'It'll need to be managed. I'll see what I can do.'

Alice laughed. 'You're sounding like Abeer's aunts, now. I'm actually quite glad it's out in the open to be honest. He would have to know at some point, wouldn't he?'

'But he could stalk you. He's an unstable person. He's a rapist and a paedophile.'

'He's also the father of my child. My child will have some rights, Anne, you told me that and I think I'd rather it came out now than some time in the future.'

'But he's...'

'The father, Anne. Whatever else he is, he is the father of this.' She patted her abdomen.

*

'How did it go? asked Abeer as they arrived at Maldon Police Station.

'Waste of fucking time,' said Anne, sitting down at her desk.

Abeer looked at Alice, who shrugged.

'She's still saying she was protecting her daughter as Harry was attacking her,' said Anne, switching on her computer. 'Oh fuck!'

'What?' the two others gathered round her screen.

'Allan Goddard has passed away.'

'Probably a blessing,' said Alice.

'Probably someone getting rid of a problem,' replied Anne.

'Do you think June did it?' said Abeer.

Anne shrugged.

Minnie Dawson knocked and entered. 'Someone to see you at the front desk. Shall I send them through? She's a bit...upset.'

'No, I'll come out.' Anne stood up.

'Shall I come?' Asked Alice.

Anne shook her head and went out. She was expecting June Goddard but as she turned the corner she saw Amelia standing by the front desk.

'Hello, Amelia. Are you alright?'

Amelia Goddard nodded and stood there with a glazed expression.

'How can I help you?'

'You can't,' said the girl.

'Would you like to sit down?' Anne gestured to Minnie to find a chair.

Amelia ignored the proffered seat and remained standing. 'My daddy's dead,' she said.

'Yes, I heard. I'm so sorry.'

'Are you?' said Amelia seeming to awaken from her stupor.

'Yes, I am, Amelia.' Anne took a pace towards her. The girl took a pace back.

'It was my fault.'

'No, Amelia. It really wasn't.'

A tear dropped from the girl's eye. 'What do you know?'

'I know he'd had a stroke, Amelia. Sometimes people don't recover.'

The glazed look had reappeared on Amelia's face. Suddenly, as if the floor had opened up, she collapsed in a heap. Minnie got there first and started to pick her up.

'Leave her,' said Anne, kneeling next to the stricken girl as Minnie laid her down gently. 'Get an ambulance.'

Amelia's eyes were open but there was no sign of awareness.

'Amelia? Can you hear me?' asked Anne. There was no reply. Anne checked her pulse and breathing – both were okay – she appeared to be in some sort of trance.

'Ambulance could be three hours,' Minnie informed Anne.

'Can you get Alice out here please, Minnie?'

The honey monster went down the corridor as Anne gently lifted Amelia's shoulders. As soon as Alice arrived, followed by Abeer, Anne detailed each of them. Minnie picked Amelia up, tenderly for such a big woman and helped take her to Anne's car. Abeer was told to inform June Goddard that they were taking her daughter to Broomfield Hospital while Alice tended to Amelia in the back seat of the car.

Amelia groaned a couple of times on the journey but was pretty unresponsive to Alice. 'Her pulse rate's quite high,' she said.

'I'm going as fast as I can, Alice. How's her temperature?'

'She's quite warm but not sweating or anything.'

Anne reached over to the glove box, withdrew her blue light, plugged it in and stuck it to the roof of her car. No doubt she'd be in trouble when Horobin got her report but getting Amelia to the hospital as quickly as possible was paramount.

Less than fifteen minutes later Anne was using her warrant card to get priority attention for the girl. Alice was allocated the task of diverting June – who Abeer had radioed to say was on her way – to reception, away from A&E. Amelia was taken away and Anne went down to the front of the hospital and lit a cigarette in front of the No Smoking sign.

June Goddard was distressed when Anne caught up with her and Alice. She was demanding to see Amelia immediately which wasn't possible. Eventually, Anne guided her towards one of the coffee franchises.

'I'm sorry to hear about Allan,' she said as Alice went to fetch them drinks.

'Are you?'

That was what Amelia had said. Was Anne missing something here? Was there some blame being directed her way? 'Yes, I am, June. It must be very hard for you at the moment.'

June actually laughed. 'Hard?' She looked at the cup Alice had placed in front of her as if she didn't know what it was. 'How come you brought Amelia here instead of an ambulance?'

'Speed, June. There was a long wait. Do you know why Amelia came to see me at the police station?'

A shocked expression came over June face. 'The police station, why?'

'That's what I'm asking.'

June didn't answer.

'She seemed to think Allan's death was her fault.'

'She's a teenager,' June replied, as if that explained everything.

'Has Amelia ever taken drugs, June?' asked Alice.

'No. Certainly not.'

'When Amelia collapsed in the station, her eyes were glassy as though she'd taken something. Are there any drugs in your house? Prescription drugs?'

'I have some sleeping pills but she wouldn't take them.'

'When she went missing, June,' Anne continued. 'We found some websites she'd been looking at that encouraged…well…suicide.'

'Why didn't you tell me?'

Anne realised she'd made a mistake not letting June know about the websites. It had been a decision she'd taken in the hope that Amelia would be found rather than increasing June's anxiety about her daughter. Now, things would be different, if Amelia had made some sort of cry for help by taking an overdose before coming to the police station.

'I assume Amelia has been going to her therapy meetings?'

June shrugged. 'I don't know. I've been too busy trying to care for my husband.'

A text came through on Anne's phone. 'Excuse me a minute,' she said, leaving Alice to stop June following her.

'She's going to be fine,' said the doctor when Anne met him further down the corridor. 'She'd taken something that didn't agree with her. Nothing serious, probably something homeopathic.'

'Like a herbal potion?'

The doctor laughed. 'Could be. Nothing very Harry Potter, though. Sometimes something as innocuous as herbal tea can upset people's balance.'

'Thanks, Doctor. Where is she?'

'She's in a corridor near A&E. We've done checks on her and she'll be able to go home soon.'

*

'Is she alright?' Abeer looked seriously worried when Alice and Anne arrived back at the office.

'Seems to be,' said Anne. 'Do we know how Allan Goddard died?'

'He had a stroke, Anne,' said Alice.

Anne nodded.

'Did Amelia know Agnes Waterhouse?'

Alice looked at Anne. 'Do you think…?'

'I'm not sure what to think, to be honest. The doctor suggested Amelia had taken something herbal. Something homeopathic. Who do we know that dealt with such things?'

'But she was in custody – and then dead. When would she have given anything to Amelia?' said Abeer.

Anne sighed. 'I don't know. Where's Allan Goddard at the moment?'

'Undertakers,' Abeer informed her.

'What, no autopsy? He was involved in our case. Who released the body to the undertakers?'

Abeer shrugged.

'Get on to them. I need Sarah to look at that body.'

*

June Goddard was not keen to let Anne see her daughter the next day but as she'd been given a clean bill of health by the doctor – rest and relaxation being the prescription – Anne had insisted she spoke to the girl first. Amelia was not concerned about it and it was her who told June to leave them alone.

'Yes, I did see the witch woman,' admitted Amelia. 'Well, she came to see me. I was sitting in the garden and I saw her peering over the hedge. She'd always scared me before but somehow I felt no fear. She was beckoning me towards her. I checked my parents were inside and went over. She was very nice. She told me how sorry she was about my ordeal and how she should have realised I was in the tunnel sooner. It was like she was blaming herself. She asked if I would meet her in the ruins. I told her my mother would never allow that and I wasn't sure I ever wanted to go there again but she asked me to try. She said she knew how to help me much better than the therapy sessions I was going to. The therapy wasn't helping me at all. I didn't like the man who was giving them but my mum insisted they were doing me good. Anyway, I told mum I needed to go out for a walk. She reminded me what happened last time and refused to let me. We had a row. I was very angry and I stormed out. Mum came after me but I hid until she went back inside. I thought she'd call the police.' She looked up at Anne. 'I didn't care. I had some sort of urge to see the witch. To see if she could help me.'

'Were you looking at those websites again?'

Amelia laughed. 'No. They were no help. I wasn't suicidal. I just wanted to feel better. Do you believe there's a supernatural world?'

'I don't know, Amelia.'

'Well, I didn't but when I met Agnes in the ruined chapel, there was a sense of…I don't know…wellbeing. I never understood what that word meant before but it was like everything that was bad was slowly vanishing, like a painting left out in the rain. I can't say I felt happy but I didn't feel as sad as I had been. Does any of this make sense?'

Anne took the girl's hand. 'Of course.' It didn't make sense to Anne but she hadn't been through the trauma that Amelia had. The girl had been looking for something to cling to that would make her feel better, something to ease her anxiety, something to help her explain what had happened to her.

'She gave me some herbs, warning me that I should be careful as to how much I used. It was strange. She gave me a hug – a real squeeze – and told me everything would work out alright. I took the herbs home, hiding them from my parents. I was spending most of my time in my room and mum was constantly asking if I wanted a cup of tea.' She laughed. 'Tea solves every problem in my mother's world. I said I just wanted a mug of hot water and I seeped the herbs in it as soon as she'd left my room.'

'And it made you feel better?'

Amelia nodded. 'A hundred per cent. I felt relaxed and sort of warm, I can't explain it very well, I'm afraid.'

'And then what happened? Why did you end up in hospital, do you think?'

Amelia sighed. 'Each time I drank the potion – I called it that – the feeling lasted for less time, you know?'

'So you took more?'

'No, well, yes, I suppose so. I'd run out, so I went back to the ruins but she wasn't there. I knew where she lived – Harry had been there – so I walked over to her house but it was empty. No-one answered the door. I went back to the leper hospital and looked at Agnes' herb garden.'

'How did you get in?'

Amelia looked sheepish. 'There's a gap in the hedge. Harry showed it to me that time we...'

'So you picked some more herbs?'

'Yes but when I took them I came over all funny. That's why I came to you. I couldn't tell my mother.'

'Did these herbs have blue flowers, Amelia?'

'Yes, why?'

'They were poisonous. Aconitum Napellus or Monkshood. Is that what Agnes gave you before?'

Amelia shook her head. 'They looked the same but they all looked the same. I thought they'd all do the same thing.'

Anne's immediate response had been the fear that Agnes was deliberately killing off anyone who'd been involved in the murders. Jed, Brad, Harry. What about Allan Goddard? 'You're sure they weren't the same herbs, Amelia?'

'The first ones didn't have flowers. Did I do right coming to you? I didn't know what else to do.'

Anne smiled. 'You did the right thing but you shouldn't have just picked any old herb in the witch's garden. You never know what she might have been growing there.'

'Do you know where she is? I'd like to get some of the right stuff.' She stared open-mouthed for a moment. 'They're not illegal, are they?'

'No, they're not illegal as such but you shouldn't pick wild plants you know nothing about.' Anne paused. 'I'm afraid Agnes has passed away.'

Amelia's eyes opened wide. 'No. She can't. I only saw her...' She stopped, the colour draining from her face. 'Was she stabbed?'

'No, Amelia. She'd taken a lot of that herb you took – the monkshood – it was a good job we got you to the hospital or you might have joined her.' Anne chose not to mention the fact that Agnes actually died from sticking some scissors in her neck.

'Will I have to go back to therapy?'

Anne shrugged. 'Talk to the doctor. Tell him how you're feeling. Tell him the herbs helped you. There may be something safer that he can prescribe.'

Amelia was pulling at the skin by her fingernails and chewing her lip. She couldn't look at Anne.

'Is there something you're not telling me, Amelia?'

'I gave some to dad.'

'The monkshood?'

'No, the other stuff. Did I kill him?'

'We won't know what killed him, Amelia, until the doctor's had a look at him. Try not to worry. He'd had a stroke, I suspect that's what it was.'

'Because I hit him?'

'When did you hit him?'

Amelia was still looking at her hands. 'Before his stroke. Mum had told him to leave but he came round. He was rowing with mum and I heard what he said.' She looked up, tears streaking her mascara. 'He said he was Harry's dad and that Harry was my brother.'

*

'So Amelia was the one who whacked Allan with the stool? Really?' Abeer was sceptical.

'That's what she seems to be saying,' said Anne as she squeezed behind her desk in the Maldon office.

'But she's just a slip of a girl,' added Alice. 'She'd have had to give him a hell of a wallop to bend the leg.'

'Is she covering for her mother?' Abeer looked concerned.

'I was wondering that. I spoke to June but she's still insisting the stool got bent when Allan threw it at her. Does Sarah have the body?'

'Yes,' answered Abeer. 'It was delivered to her this afternoon.'

'Right. I'll pay a little visit to Broomfield, I think.'

'What do you want us to do?' asked Alice.

'You can go home and rest. I need you to look after my Godchild. Abeer, are you alright running the office?'

'Of course.'

'If I'm not back by five, knock off and go home.'

*

'It's possible that the knock to the head caused some bleeding,' said Sarah, digging inside Allan's skull. 'But it was pretty superficial, to be honest.'

Anne was looking away from the body. A section of the bone had been removed showing a mass of grey swirling matter that Anne assumed was Allan's brain. It was not a sight she relished and was beginning to wish she'd just waited for Sarah's report.

'In what way superficial?' she asked.

'Not much more than a graze, really.'

'Not a heavy blow with a steel leg of a stool, then?'

'Unlikely. I would suggest a cup or a mug thrown at him, especially as I found pottery shards in his skin.'

'Why weren't they found before?'

'He wasn't dead. You can't do an autopsy on a living person. I would surmise, if asked, that excess amounts of alcohol could have contributed to the stroke. His liver was buggered.' She picked up a kidney-shaped metal dish that held something that looked like a dog's dinner.

Anne put her hand up to indicate she didn't want to see. 'So you're saying that no-one was culpable in his death?'

'It's not my job to say such things but it looks that way, unless you want to blame the manufacturers of heavy spirits.'

Anne grinned. 'Let's not talk about spirits. I've had my fill of them. Especially if they're wearing a monk's habit.'

Sarah smiled and placed the top of Allan's head back on his skull as if she was closing the lid of a jar.

'Don't suppose you're free for a drink anytime soon? Only wine. No spirits.'

Sarah laughed. 'Maybe a gin but not tonight, I'm afraid.'

Anne nodded knowingly. Looked like another lonely night in front of the TV.

CHAPTER THIRTY

Allan Goddard was cremated at Chelmsford Crematorium on a Friday morning in late June. In attendance were June, Amelia, Anne and Abeer. No-one else. It wasn't a private service, just no-one wanted to come. Anne thought she spotted Linda Ellis in the memorial garden afterwards but it turned out not to be her. Anne felt sorry for Linda. Whatever she thought of Allan, they had conceived Harry together but maybe that was something that she now found hard to comprehend, something she didn't even want to admit to herself.

Anne spoke briefly to June and Amelia after the cremation. Both appeared totally unmoved, as though they'd just been to a bad movie or something. Father Thatcher had taken the service and June left Anne to talk to him.

'How are you, Amelia?' Anne asked as the two of them stood awkwardly by the entrance.

'Yeah, I'm good, I suppose.' She was wearing sports gear very like the ones Harry had bought her. 'They're not the same ones,' she said, noticing Anne inspecting the clothes. 'Probably not right for a funeral but I don't really care.'

'I think you should be able to wear whatever you want to.'

Amelia grinned. 'I wish you were my mum.'

'You really don't, believe me.'

'The doctor gave me some pills but they weren't as good as what Agnes gave me. I found someone better to help me. She's a homeopath and she's changed my diet and everything. I feel so much better being Vegan.'

Anne kept her ideas on Veganism to herself. 'I'm glad for you, Amelia.'

June beckoned her daughter to join her with Father Thatcher.

'I'd better go,' she said. 'I think my mother's becoming obsessed with the church now, although I do think Frank's a nice bloke. He was very kind to me after…well…just after.' She started over towards her mother, turned and came back. 'I just want to thank you,' she said and threw her arms round Anne's neck and kissed her cheek before hurrying off.

'You see, people do love you,' said Abeer.

Anne held her head up. 'Of course they do,' she said. 'Pub?'

Abeer grinned. 'Too right.'

*

Alice was in the office when they returned.

'Been to the pub, I see,' she said as they walked in. 'Much as I love being pregnant, there are times when it pisses me off.'

Anne pointed to the ever-increasing bulge. 'You need to look after my Godchild.'

'Goddaughter.'

Anne's eyes opened wide.

'I've been told the gender.'

'Did you want to know?'

'Of course. I need to know whether to get pink or blue clothes for her.'

'I didn't think people did that anymore.'

'They don't. Apart from my mother, of course.'

'Are you going to paint my room pink?' asked Abeer, looking aghast.

Alice laughed. 'No, I told you, Chardonnay won't be moving in there for ages yet.'

'Chardonnay?' Anne's mouth was open wide.

'In honour of her Godmother's favourite drink.'

'Good job I don't drink Bishop's Finger, then.'

Abeer's mouth was wide now. 'What is Bishop's Finger?'

'It's an ale, Abeer. I don't drink Chardonnay, either.'

'I didn't think you were fussy as long as it was wine,' Alice grinned. 'Anyway I haven't decided on a name, yet. Did you know you can actually buy whole books of baby names?'

'No, funnily enough.'

'I do like the name Chardonnay, though.'

The rest of the afternoon was spent doing no work whatsoever. Catherine Hall's trial date had still not been fixed but she wouldn't be appearing as she had already been sent to a secure hospital. Harry Ellis's funeral had been held and attended by so many students and friends that they'd relayed the service at the crematorium through loudspeakers into the grounds outside, so those not able to get in could hear. Rueben had turned up with Fliss and had finally met Amelia, whose sights were now set on attending University in London and Rueben and Fliss had insisted they could provide her accommodation. Her GCSE results had been remarkably good considering the stress she's been under leading up to them. Anne had been surprised she could even manage to do them. Agnes Waterhouse had been posthumously convicted of the murders of Jed and Brad. Sarah's autopsy result had shown that Allan Goddard had died from an alcohol-related ischaemic stroke. Anne had never mentioned that Amelia may have given him an infusion of Monkshood.

Alice's morning sickness appeared to have abated and she was full of energy, something Anne was starting to find irritating. The conversations all seemed to revolve around babies. There were times when it almost made her feel broody. Almost but never enough to even think about venturing down that road. Besides the only man she ever met with any regularity was Derek and there was no way she was going to enter into that sort of relationship with him. Although there had been times when she was at home alone, watching boring television programs, that she'd almost reached for her phone but sense had always prevailed. She realised a long time ago that she could never compromise her lifestyle to suit a permanent relationship – let alone having children at her age – and yet…she would quickly put those thoughts out of her head and open another bottle.

'So,' she announced as the clock slowly went round to five. 'Time for the pub, I think.'

Abeer was looking a bit queasy. 'I think I may have had enough already,' she said.

'I can't drink,' said Alice.

Anne sighed. 'Oh well, let's hope Charlotte wants to talk to me, then.'

'Time for us to knock off,' said Alice, picking up her bag. 'See you on Monday?' She held the door open for Abeer. 'Are you going home, Anne?' she asked.

'No. I'll finish up here and head off to the Queen's for one. I'm getting sick of drinking completely alone.'

Alice smiled sympathetically and left with Abeer.

There were other people in the police station at Maldon but they were uniform and tended not to mix with CID. Anne supposed she could see if Minnie fancied a drink but she didn't know her socially and couldn't be bothered with all the small talk required with new people. Anyway, Minnie looked like she was barely out of college and most probably wouldn't want to go for a drink with an old woman like her. She thought back to her time in Chester, where the whole team would be out on a Friday night. Mind you, she hadn't been there since the pandemic. Maybe the pubs were quieter up there as well now. It seemed that people had got so used to drinking at home when they couldn't go out that it appeared to be the norm now. Gone were the days when you could barely get in the door of a pub on a Friday night.

There were no windows in the CID office, it was entombed within the building, so Anne had no idea what the weather was like outside. If it was still sunny and warm the pub would be busy until the sun went behind the buildings. Maybe she should wait and go down later when everyone had gone home. The problem with that was she knew once she was in her flat, she wouldn't have the inclination to go out again, meaning another evening of wine and TV alone.

She packed up her things and went outside nodding to Minnie on the way, who gave her a sly smile. The sun was shining and the temperature was warm for early evening. She threw her things into the boot of her car and wandered slowly along the High Street down towards Hythe Quay. As she expected the terrace was packed with workers and families enjoying the last of the sunshine. The good thing was that it meant the 'Member's Bar' was likely to be empty and she wandered round to the front of the pub.

As she opened the front door she saw that the door to the 'Member's' was closed. This happened sometimes if there was a funeral or birthday party going on but there was no sign on the door. Anne went into the back bar to be greeted by Charlotte.

'Private party going on through there?' She pointed to the 'Member's'.

'Yes, I think so. Don't know if it's finished or not. Have a look.' Charlotte went to serve a young father, whose children were clinging to his trousers begging for more fizzy drinks. Anne was glad, once again, that she was happy to be childless.

She went back to the 'Member's' and gently opened the door.

A great roar of greeting erupted from the assembled customers. Alice, Abeer, Derek and Sarah Clifford were all standing and cheering.

'What's going on?' said Anne.

Minnie Dawson was there as well.

'I've just left you at the station, haven't I?'

'Yep. I had to run. Good job I'm in training still.'

'I'm confused,' said Anne. 'Why are you all here? Have I forgotten my birthday or something?'

Alice came up and put her arm round Anne's shoulders. 'You've seemed a bit fed up recently,' she said. 'So, now you've cracked yet another case, I thought I would organise a few people to prove how much we all love you.'

Anne looked around the room. Five people. Not exactly filling The Albert Hall, but at least Alice had made an effort. 'I think you did more of the cracking than me, Alice.' She gave her a hug.

Alice led her towards an ice bucket, sitting proudly in the centre of the long table by the window and containing an unopened bottle of Chardonnay. 'This is a gift from your future Goddaughter.' She lifted the bottle from the bucket, unscrewed the cap and poured Anne a large glassful.'

'I don't drink Chardonnay, I told you.'

'Your Goddaughter tells me you'll get used to it.' Alice rubbed her tummy.

Much as she tried, Anne couldn't stop the grin on her face. 'Well, Chardonnay. Here's to you,' she said and downed the drink in one.

'More wine, Charlotte,' yelled Derek, coming over to hug Anne.

'Sauvignon?' checked Charlotte.

'No. Bloody Chardonnay. I'm going to have to get used it, by the looks of things.'

*

ABOUT THE AUTHOR

BARRIE JAIMESON was born in Leicester and moved to London to attend Drama School. Many years of treading the boards in theatres across the country followed, as well as TV and film roles. He met his wife whilst appearing in Woody Allen's 'Play It Again, Sam' in Keswick and before long, they had moved to the Essex countryside, both still carrying on their acting careers. They started a theatre company, 'macTheatre' when they arrived in Maldon, producing many shows including Maldon's annual 'Shakespeare in the Park' for over a decade, as well as musical shows written for Christmas and Burns' Night and a show with songs inspired by paintings called 'Songs from the Art'

Barrie has been writing fiction for some time and published his first novel, 'The Commercial' in 2014. Since then, he has published a further nine books. In 2021 he started the Anne Edwards Series about a detective based in Maldon, Essex. This is the third book in that series.

OTHER BOOKS BY BARRIE JAIMESON

The Greg Driscoll Trilogy:

The Commercial

The Play

The Denouement

The Dengie Draughtsmen's Cricket Club

The Anne Edwards Series:

Death at The Queen's Head

Murder on South House Chase

Short stories:

Philp Harlow – Private Dick & other stories

Cacotopia - & other stories about being locked down (also available on audiobook)

Ghostly Tales From Maldon

THE ANNE EDWARDS SERIES

DEATH AT THE QUEEN'S HEAD

THREE MEN IN A DESERT
TWO DEATHS IN ESSEX
ONE DETECTIVE SERGEANT HAS TO MAKE CONNECTIONS

What has a photograph of three young men to do with the horrific murder of a popular local bar manager? Is the death linked to the demise of a homeless man seven years previously?

Detective Sergeant Anne Edwards, newly returned to her home county of Essex is tasked with finding a brutal monster before he kills again but lack of help from her superiors, lack of DNA evidence and lack of any witnesses or suspects makes her assignment almost impossible.

A trail through marshes, barges, pubs and a church; codebreaking in the night; bad dreams and ex-lovers make for a story of intrigue and deception in the Essex coastal town of Maldon.

MURDER ON SOUTH HOUSE CHASE

A BODY IN A DITCH
A STRANGE HOUSE ON THE HILL
VIGILANTE GROUPS
RACISM AND MISOGYNY IN THE RANKS
A NEW MAN IN ANNE'S LIFE BUT IS HE ALL HE SEEMS?
ON TOP OF THIS COVID STRIKES!

The second book in the Anne Edwards detective series set in Maldon, Essex.

A body discovered in a ditch under a hedgerow sets Anne and her team off on a journey that reveals underhand goings-on at a local beauty spot as well as revelations about her own officers and herself after a chance meeting with a jogger on the seawall.

Her old friends at The Queen's Head pub notice suspicious activity down on the Hythe quay leading Anne to more encounters with people she would rather not.

Hooded monks; private schools; Bed and Breakfasts; Glamping; sporty cars and, of course Thames Barges all lead her to uncovering people smuggling and serious abuse.

Printed in Great Britain
by Amazon